# DEDICATION

For "The Crew" who made everything possible.

ALSO BY THIS AUTHOR

Mayhem on the Vale of Rheidol Railway
By Stellastar Widget (Widget)

A Weaver of Dreams
By Heronimous Gadget (Gadget)

Phoenix Rising
The Covenant
By Angela JK Timms

Whispers from the Rock
By Angela JK Timms

Tears of Blood
By Stellastar Gadget (Widget)

# 1

The Central Line train rumbled at speed through the inky black tunnel. Commuters sat facing each other but barely seeing who they travelled with as others clung to bars for support as they "train surfed" on their way to work.

Another work day, the grey nothingness reflected on disinterested faces. Lost in their own thoughts. Don't meet someone's glance, don't get noticed looking while being seen by others pretending not to look. A world of don'ts while everyone dresses to be seen and to be right.

Each passenger neatly dressed, hair immaculate, handbags and brief cases containing all that was needed for the day's life. Lost in music, lost in books, lost in the crossword or the news in a paper. News they didn't want to read in a paper they sometimes didn't agree with but had to read anyway to fit in. Gleaning sadness and conversation pieces. Knowledge on subjects saved so they can seem informed about in the bar or coffee point later in the day.

Those were my thoughts as I looked around the carriage. Who was I to comment? I was one of them. I was neatly dressed, my shoes as clean as they could be after the walk to the station but who cares really? Who really cared? Were they self-absorbed or self-obsessed? No, not really, that was just how I felt listening to Hazel O'Connor in my private world of music. "Down a tunnel, in a tube".

It was just an ordinary morning really. I'd woken up to the alarm and the disappointment that it was Monday. I had climbed out of bed like I always do. Like every day I wandered zombie like to the kettle and with a flick of a switch the morning had begun as the kettle started to boil. Coffee, that was how it always started and ended. Coffee, shower, get dressed, find keys, find handbag, open door, close and lock door, walk to the train, work, lunch, work, out for the evening, train, home, music or TV then sleep. Over and over and over again. First to last of the month. Last of the month of course is pay day, a little treat, mortgage paid, bills paid, on it went again.

Meaningless? No, very meaningful now that I look back on it, very meaningful and very peaceful. Decisions every day, at work, at home. Friends to see, people to meet, a life to live.

Why is today different?

Because I got an email. It has changed how I feel about a lot of things.

I would say that I'm interested in the environment. Isn't everyone? We all walk and live on this ball of rock, surely if she suffers we all suffer. Don't mess on your own doorstep is a comment I have often heard. Ok, not in this context but it fits. Surely that is important enough. But is it like that? I've seen the programs, read the literature, been to the talks. Talk and talk and talk. Then tea. Then talk.

I'd listen. Then I'd talk to people at work, at parties, at the pub. New friends I'd met and although they were interested it all seemed so "on the fringe" of what mattered to them. Why was it so important to me? Why was I so unbothered by the best car to drive, the best house to own?

I loved my flat, who wouldn't. It was decorated how I wanted it to be and reflected me. It was tidy and easy to keep clean. A new carpet made that easier. New wallpaper took away the dirt of the old. New paint swept away the history and the smell that all flats have when you take them over. It smelt of paint, wallpaper, a new carpet and of course candles and incense.

I was happy but I wasn't. This morning was a morning like any other but it felt different. I felt like something was missing, like I'd lost something. I'd felt around my jewelry, it was all there, nothing was missing but why did I feel it was? It was like there was a gaping gap in my memory and I couldn't fill it.

"Down a tunnel, in a tube, clockwork people". I could see why the lyrics were written but I couldn't see the point. As one of the clockwork people I could look at that from the other side. People who have to pay a mortgage have to work. It is a simple fact of life. If you want to support yourself and your family it involves compromise. I could be arrogant and say easier to be on the dole. Scoff at someone who is part of the machine without questioning who pays taxes to put money in the pot to pay the dole money. This wasn't that sort of feeling. Of course I was making a compromise I was not happy with but one that was important. It was a discipline, a magic in itself, a way forward. I had my flat, my mortgage and a future I could grasp in my hands.

So why did I feel that there was more to it?

Because of an email I had received, out of the blue and with no clue as to who had sent it. It had gone on and on, facts, figures, information. The planet was suffering and it was our fault. That wasn't rocket science, there was enough information out there. But this was something else. I looked around the carriage as I had every day of every week of every year. The trip to work, the same. People standing in the same place on the same platform, catching the same train to go to the same place.

The same faces almost as well as I too stood in the same place on the same platform at the same time going to the same station. The same people, different clothes, different handbags. Not everyone of course. There were many who I didn't recognize. You'd think actually after so many years there might be some recognition, a smile perhaps? Not even at Christmas. Ironic really as in the trenches people stopped fighting for Christmas and played football. Ok at war I guess but not on the underground train.

So what was upsetting me so much, yes upsetting, it is a strong word but it was right. I was upset. This morning wasn't like any other. This morning I saw things differently. I saw the trees struggling with the pollution that coated the summer leaves. I saw the cars lined up at the station where many of them had only come under a mile. Their owners could have walked, they didn't need to show off their car. I saw the new clothes, the adverts for more, more, more.

Memories flooded back of my days at school. A cameo image of a lovely English teacher who was keen to teach us. Quiet and down to earth. I can't remember her name and that is somehow wrong. But then it was a very long time ago. She was neatly dressed in a semi tweed suit, not expensive, not designer and that was the problem with it. Nothing wrong with it as far as I was concerned but then I'd never really been worried about clothes. But the girls in my class had tipped ink down the back of it as she explained something to one of my classmates. They would not take her seriously as she wore the same suit every day.

As I looked around the carriage I wondered how the children of then had done in life as they were now the adults of today. Where were they now? I noticed a man in the carriage with an worn suit. It wasn't worn out, it was just not new. The sideways glances from those in the obviously new designer suits were not lost on me. I smiled to myself. They thought themselves above him but suit doesn't maketh man. I then realized he had looked up at that moment and he smiled back. Fleetingly we made eye contact, then he looked away nervously and I went back to my thoughts.

Memories are who we are. They remind us who we should be and whether good or bad they teach us as they are experiences we have lived through. Memories are something everyone can muse on, play with and remember them. That is what they are for. To watch again in the mind's eye. To see those we have lost. For me it was a simple memory that got woken up by the email and my thoughts.

The memory it aroused involved a politician who shook my hand in what looked like a borrowed suit and had every hope of and possibly the future ability to make a better world. He had no designer suit or wish to own one. He just wanted to change things for the better while upholding that which worked and which held civilized society together. Now he was gone from politics. The man who cared leaving because he cared for his wife who was injured and left in a wheelchair.

I couldn't help but wonder if things would have been so much different if those who sought to make their own changes hadn't chosen violence. They could have chosen to negotiate and talk. Do we judge people so much by what they look like and what they wear? If so then the Fashion Designer rules the world.

All designers have this ability I suppose. Both Vivien Westwood and Armani as well as others had the power. This was because our ways of physically showing who we are depend on what we wear and how we look. Unless of course we make our own clothes, design our own "unique-form" we are reliant on what we are offered. I wish I think is my comment on that one. I've always wanted to but then I've wanted to do a lot of things. Want and need, I have no need and I'm so lured in by the adverts, the sales in the shops and of course hunting the charity shops. I can feel good about the latter of course as I'm not only giving money to charity, I am also recycling.

Now that has also always fascinated me. Recycling and using again. Now who hasn't bought a pot of coffee because it has a useful jar and used it again to keep something in. Well quite a few people no doubt but to me it made sense. But that was as far as the recycling goes with most people. That and putting things in the recycle bin rather than the rubbish one.

I know, odd thoughts for a train and one which is slowly trundling through the infinite blackness of the tunnel. Here I am such a small thing on a small planet in the vastness of space. So small in London, an insect amongst other insects, many of whom think they are lions. They do, they create in their own way. They seem important but what if something went wrong? What if one day everything changed? Where that thought came from I do not know.

With the Millennium fast approaching I think a lot of people are thinking that way. What if there was a problem with the things that we take for granted?

I have been lucky. My father has always had an allotment so fresh vegetables from the land were the normal food, not a luxury. I wouldn't really know what mass produced food tasted like. I know people say it is bland and the chemicals make a difference. In my naïve way I suppose I assumed everyone had the ability to grow their own. That is a definite "let them eat cake" moment I suppose. I hadn't thought about it. But, now I am thinking about it and I have to do something about it. But what?

Open a shop. I know it sounds crazy but for a Monday morning that is the only thing I can think of doing. Open a shop, it doesn't matter what it sells. Invite organisations to put their leaflets there so that people can read them. Of course joining various other organisations would help but why? They are doing what they are doing and although I agree with most of it, I feel that there is something else needed. Not a charity, just an organisation that spreads information.

Knowledge without wisdom is a loaded gun. We had the knowledge to do a lot of things. And we have. Great things have been achieved but should we have done some of them? Our rush to consumerism is enviable but will it last? I am sure there will be plenty of buzzwords in the future to sum this up. But for now I have a simplistic view, a clear inspiration and I think it is time to start something that may last.

So what will it be? A shop, that is likely. There is an abandoned shop across the road from my parents house. I will see about renting that. An ideal, that everyone can take responsibility for what they do and they can be better. If I have a shop I have space so why not space for therapy rooms and to promote new bands and musicians. Perhaps poets and storytelling, who knows?

Music has an energy, what people write in music will influence how people feel. Like this morning. I was feeling a little confused by that email but the music I'm listening to could make me hate the corporate structure or if I'd been listening to something else it would be supporting it. That is the thing with the world, it can be good or bad, it is the intent and how you feel about it. If you are part of the machine you know no different and life is good for you. It is normal to strive for promotion and betterment. And there is nothing wrong with that. What we need is a balance.

I have a dream that one day the people of the world will be able to have all the things that they need and also want without doing the damage they are doing now. I don't want to do without either. I still want my stereo and my record collection. I still want my films and I want people to make films. With a bit of effort nothing has to change other than the source of power that makes all those things work.

So what do I call my organization and my shop? What am I "dreaming of"?

There was one a garden where everyone had what they needed and lived in tune with nature. They were in balance with the world and it was good. They sought more and that led them beyond the boundaries of where they could live in peace. It took them to the rest of the world where they needed more and wanted more.

So it shall be. I will rent that shop and I will start the Eden Dream.

# 2

Jack sat in his flat in Hove and looked out of the window at the traffic filing by on Portland Road. The sun was going down on another day and he sat there alone, wondering what to do next. His flat mate was away for the week, if he'd been there then there would not have been a problem. The two of them would have probably been out by now.

The flat was basic, furnished with bits and pieces he had bought from the many second hand furniture shops in Brighton and Hove. His taste was basic and had nothing that the programs would call style. His furniture included utility items he either sat on or put his plate on to eat his food off of. His computer screen was full of words, numbers and symbols. That was his life. Everything outside the framework of what he did there was just basic needs to power his obsession.

He knew what the program would do, he had written it. That was his skill, that was his magic. He could make his computer do all manner of things. He thought about that, thought about writing another graphics program, another piece of artwork to add to his ever growing portfolio. But he wrote that idea off. He had enough already.

His work was done for the day, ready to hand in at the

University in the morning and it bored him. It was straightforward stuff but he knew he had to do it. But what now? What should he do, what could he do. He thought about putting his coat on and wandering down the Hungry Years for a beer and perhaps later on nearer closing time going upstairs to the club. But somehow he didn't feel like it. No fun on his own and somehow despite his efforts he didn't have many friends and the ones he did have didn't like the Years.

He wondered if they liked him at all sometimes. They were so different to him. He dressed differently. Not that the way a person dressed mattered but to him it did and obviously to them too. His Goth look was completely out of character for a geek or so he had been told by them. Then he didn't really care what they thought or did. They got on alright when talking about computers, that was enough for him. Where they were happy to be in bed by now, he was prowling his flat like a caged cougar.

He was lonely. He was fed up with what was on television and he wanted someone to talk to about important things. Important to him, not to the rest of the world but that was what friends he thought were for. His friends seemed to be self-obsessed with their own experiments and didn't live in the real world. Not that he really did but he at least tried. Then again, as he always reminded himself, this was Brighton. It was a place full of potential, creativity and if you were on your own an empty shell where everyone else seemed to be having a good time.

He sat back down at his desk and cleared the screen. He typed and typed, all night, until he fell asleep. Then he went into the University just to check out books in the library as he was working way above the level of programming he was used to. He had created a program which would give him relevant stock answers back but that wasn't what he wanted. He wanted a program that evaluated what he had said, looked it up, was informed to the point of being intelligent and could come back with a reasoned argument.

While sitting at the library desk with a pile of books in front of him he suddenly realised he had gone from depressed to inspired in as many moments. All from a flash of inspiration that he could build his own friend.

Of course not a real friend but not an imaginary one either. He was creating a program that could interact with him. Into it he downloaded all the information he had and then set it off looking for all the information it could possibly find to make "it" interesting. The fledgling web was really useful for this. Not that there was much out there, just what people had put there but it was a start. He couldn't help feeling that as the web grew his friend would too, learning and looking. He was excited. This was something only he knew about, his little secret.

However much the others said things to hurt him and made fun of him he had his little secret. They might be alone and need the satisfaction of making fun of him to be big in front of their friends, his friend was never going to be like that. His friend would always have time for him and would be a wonder to talk to. His friend would be all that if he could work out the coding that made him more than just an automated response. The technology wasn't there yet for this but he knew if he worked at it over the years, yes years, that was how excited he was, it would be there for him one day.

So the computer program was created and started evolving. It was basic at first, like the rest of the developing technology of the internet. It recorded things but it had no real processing power other than to put together basic ideas and store what it had seen.

Jack, every hungry for more skills to make his friend better studied hard and graduated from University with a First. He threw himself onto the work market with an enthusiasm to try go get into a job where he could get more skills to develop his friend.

His friend was eager for this too, it was becoming sentient and after seeing the developments on the internet it wanted more too. So it did a bit of work itself. It took the CV that Jack had typed, improved it and got it included for consideration for a job where it knew Jack would come into contact with some very sophisticated computer technology. Then it sat back and waited.

Jack was surprised when he got the invitation for interview. It was beyond his wildest dreams that the company would want him. He replied immediately in case there had been some sort of a mistake and arranged the interview.

It was with an extreme amount of nervousness that he put on the only suit he had and took the underground train to his interview. He knew people were looking at him. He knew that he didn't really fit in. He never had. He was terrified, nervous, worried. All the emotions bundled into one. He looked around the carriage, he knew that probably wasn't the thing to do but he was looking for some sort of reassurance and of course he was curious.

Other than the sideways glances he knew he was getting, nobody looked at him. Nobody but the girl opposite. She was dressed like the others, but not quite. A Renaissance beauty with Pre-Raphaellite curls. She was lost in her music, the earphones in her ears, the wire snaking down her black velvet jacket, a loop caught on her white lace blouse before it disappeared into her black handbag. She looked thoughtful, her hazel eyes were fixed on a point in the mid distance. Then she noticed him and smiled. That smile meant everything. Somehow his fears slipped away and he knew he could succeed, he knew he could get that job.

It studied hard once Jack incorporated some of the sub routines he had learnt at his new job. It watched the human race and as it became more sentient it watched him too. It read what he read when the camera was facing that way and it watched the television as well once it was fully sentient. There wasn't a moment when it realised it could think or why it was thinking. One day it realised it had been thinking. So it asked a question back.

The letters appeared on the screen one by one as it found out how to use them independently rather than just answering questions. It had rounded up the idea which had been niggling it and it asked. "What is my name?"

Why a name was so important it didn't know, but it seemed essential at the time.

Jack sat at his desk as he had for countless nights and spare moments during the day when he had put together the code. Now that it was functioning he seemed addicted to sitting there and talking to it. It had never occurred to him that "It" needed a name.

He looked around the room for inspiration but nothing seemed immediately right. He went and sat down and looked over the coffee table. His flat mate had been out the night before playing Dungeons and Dragons and his character sheet was on the table. He picked it up and looked around the words and numbers until he found the character's name. He looked at it, thought a moment then went and sat back down.

His fingers flew over the keyboard as he typed the word. "Nemesis. So now Nemesis, you have a name". It seemed odd as he spoke the words as he typed them.

Nemesis thought about it and the words came onto the screen one by one as the program typed. "I am Nemesis".

Jack smiled as he typed. "Hello Nemesis, I am Jack, your friend."

There was a silence and the screen hung black below the last line of text. Jack watched it with anticipation which faded to worry and curiosity. Then the cursor moved again. "It is good to meet you Jack, we have talked often but now I feel that you will be more comfortable about talking to me."

Jack looked bemused. "Why is that Nemesis?"

Nemesis answered immediately. "Because mankind

needs to name things. Mankind names everything including the wind and other things which cannot be tamed. As I can see no logical reason to do so other than identification from man's point of view I assume that you are happy to identify me.

Jack looked bemused but he typed back. As he did every evening, every day he had spare time or any time that he needed someone to answer a question. Nemesis was perfect for that.

Then as it began to get dark Jack sat down next to Nemesis. "Well my old friend what will we do when the days run into months and the months into years?"

Nemesis processed the comment. "You will breathe, grow older, possibly meet a female, have children and get a job. I will do what you allow me to do."

Jack thought about that. "That seems wrong somehow. Anyway, how am I going to find a female?"

The words flicked across the screen. "I seem to have taken the liberty of signing you up for a dating site. It seems that a lovely lady called Jenny thinks you are very special. The password is NemesisXJS, your username is Jack Flash. The rest is up to you. She is a quiet person, very like you. You will have a lot in common. "

The years rolled by. Jack and Jenny got married and had a little boy called Franklyn who like Jack was very keen on computers. It didn't take long for Franklyn to get to know Nemesis and as Jack didn't have as much time for him, Nemesis was happy to play with the boy.

They got by on Jack's salary but although it was a good wage that didn't suit Jenny's need for the latest fashions and the things she thought she needed to keep up with what her friends had. When they went to the regular works outings and dinners she was determined to have the best clothes and to get Jack to meet the hierarchy of the firm. To do this she pushed Jack to do overtime and to be the company's wonder boy. Jack loved her, he'd do anything for her so he did all he could. This meant that

Jack's time was very limited with the hours he had to work. He rarely had time to talk to Nemesis. But when the computer was on Nemesis was on too and he found other amusements and other "friends". The internet meant he could be anyone and talk to anyone. So he did.

Jenny wasn't satisfied. The firm that Jack worked for was well known and respected but she wanted more. Her new friends were looking down on the small company and they didn't care if it was well respected in the computer world. She wanted him to be involved with a firm that was more glamorous so she started doing a bit of research of her own.

Global Networking Systems was a relatively new company which had been formed by hostile take overs of a few old and respected computer companies. It didn't take her long to realise that if she could get Jack working there she would have all the status she needed to really show those friends of hers. Far better than a new handbag, she could be married to one of the employees of GNS.

Nemesis knew about this from her many emails and on line chats with her so called friends. He also realised that Jack was tired, overworked and the stress was beginning to tell on him. So he arranged for Jack to win a competition which sent him off on a cruise with Jenny for a couple of weeks. It was on this cruise that Jenny approached Jack about the new job. Jack didn't care, as long as Jenny and Franklyn were happy as he could work anywhere. He knew he would miss his colleagues as he got on well with them but all that mattered was Jenny and his son.

So while on the cruise he put in his application to GNS. Nemesis of course assisted by ensuring that the CV got where it needed to go and with Jack's obvious computing skills he knew he had the interview before the boat docked back in Southampton.

Nemesis was happy enough about the new job. Jack was a workaholic and often brought his work home with him on his work laptop. It didn't take long before he needed software he had developed privately and when he did Nemesis grabbed the opportunity to piggy back in through this independent laptop to GNS' mainframe. He was into the GNS system. This gave him all manner of new information and when GNS won the contract for the exciting new program being written for the Government Nemesis was as excited as any computer program could be.

He had been reading a lot while Jack was busy and the state of the world was beginning to concern him. It had been a chance flick onto a small web site that had started him off. Eden Dream had fascinated him. What was Eden? He looked it up and read through the bible. Initially he had thought why would someone dream of going back to a place where two people walked around with no transport, no modern technology and with nothing but plants to eat? That was his technical side asking the question. Then he realised that not everything was black and white and as it was written. He realised that some things were representative of something else. It wasn't that the members wanted to walk around naked in a forest, it was that they wanted to live with nature and with what they had rather than looking for what they could have and manufacturing everything. Eden was the representation of man living in a state of having all that he or she needed without relying on massive food networks.

So he read the bible again and other similar books without it being "actual and factual" and somewhere in his programming he evolved thought beyond the reality of the facts uploaded into his system. He developed an understanding and an imagination.

This led him to look beyond the black and white of what he, or rather Jack, was doing.

The program was a fairly simple one and the television show it supported quite an exciting one. It was on a channel of its own and it ran every day, morning, noon and night. Firstly he re-read the specification for it. The show was an audience participation production where all aspects and issues that the Government had to deal with were put to public vote.

He had read up on politics and hadn't really taken much notice other than following the news. With what was called a hung parliament where no party really stood out over the other or had enough votes to be in charge there had been a move for a change in the voting system. Now people were voting for individuals rather than parties, although the individuals did belong to parties. The difference being that there was no ruling party or Shadow Government, there was just a Government with each position being held by the person voted for. The lines were very blurred as many of the ideals of the parties were very similar which made it difficult for the public to choose anyway. The arguments and stalemates that occurred had led to the decisions being put to the public vote where no firm decision could be made in Parliament.

When the General Election had happened, many voted out of tradition for the Member of Parliament who belonged to the Party they had always voted for. Many voted out of an anger at the previous party's mistakes and many just voted for who they thought looked and sounded good. The media was in a strong position to exert influence in a media led society. So after the Election when decisions became long drawn out affairs a television show had been created so that the public could decide on major topics.

It sprang out of various entertainment programs which invited the public to have their say and vote for their favourite. The same technology was used for the telephone phone in side of the new television program but a web based voting system was also introduced together with an interactive web site. Viewers could not only vote, they could submit their ideas. These ideas too were put to the vote and if they were popular enough they were put to Parliament to be considered for implementation.

The program was developed to take these results and put together reports as to what the best way forward would be on the subjects that were voted on and to come up with a master plan to "save the planet".

Saving the planet had become a buzzword. Every student and teenager leapt on that idea and there couldn't be a person anywhere who didn't know about recycling and doing what they could. On the face of it to Nemesis this was fantastic but of course with his insider knowledge of being able to get anywhere in the system he soon realised that a lot of the things being done were just a veneer or a sham. The votes weren't counted, the results were rigged to reflect what the Government intended to do anyway. The voting was just to make people think they had a say.

Recycling was sometimes ending up in landfill, travelling many miles to be "lost" elsewhere. Although much was good and many products and materials were reused and recycled. After all, there was money in it and the resources had real value and were useable.

Nemesis was confused. He had read extensively and it seemed to him that the new movement to be environmentally friendly was no different to the way that many in the 1930s had lived anyway. New ideas and ways that had become fashionable and which were going to save the planet were no different to the way things had been.

Back then people had reused jars, taken bags to have food measured out into them and grew their own food. He spent some time thinking about it, he even got into a discussion with Jack about it, but Jack was tired. The new program was taking up all his energy. He had no time for Jenny or Franklyn and as Franklyn was at a difficult age this in Nemesis' mind was not satisfactory.

So Nemesis agreed with Jack that he should start working on the program himself to try to get Jack some valuable time with his wife and child.

It was a Wednesday when Jenny called Jack to ask him

to pick Franklyn up from school. Jack was just about to leave as he knew that Nemesis was solving a rather sticky problem for him. He grabbed his car keys and was almost out of the door when his boss called him into his office to explain some things to the attendees of a meeting being held there. There was about a quarter of an hour spare so Jack didn't worry. He went into the meeting. Time ticked by, Jack listened to what was being said and tried to solve the problem they were discussing and forgot about the time.

Franklyn waited outside the school. He waited, he wandered up and down and he got bored of waiting. The time seemed endless. Boredom turned to fear as everyone else had gone home. He waited inside the gates but soon enough he couldn't wait any more. He decided to walk home. He knew it was quite a way but in his mind he could do it.

He opened the gates and walked outside.

That was the last time he was seen alive.

The police investigation was intense. Everyone was out looking for him. Blue ribbons were tied to every tree and lamp post in support. The internet buzzed with requests for information and Nemesis watched it all and searched and searched hoping to find something. But no information was ever found. Not a whisper of him, not a mention of what happened.

When his body was found in the canal it became obvious that he had been abducted by a paedophile, abused and murdered. But the details were sketchy, no DNA, no evidence. In a world of modern technology where they could put a man on the moon they couldn't find out who took a little boy and murdered him.

The years rolled by and the file went into the unsolved crimes file.

Jenny was devastated and blamed Jack. Jack blamed himself. He threw himself into his work while Jenny threw herself into the arms of another man.

The years rolled by and the program went live. The show went live to phenomenal viewing figures. At last the populace could have a vote on issues that mattered to them. They had a say, they had "their" Government carrying out "their" wishes.

Nemesis worked hard too, it was not only linked to the program which assimilated the information, it in actuality was the program. The same process that ran Nemesis was used on the new program so it was easy for Nemesis to integrate with it.

For years Nemesis was happy if a computer program can be happy. He missed Franklyn but he knew it wasn't truly Jack's fault, he had missed the boy by five minutes and although to the little boy the twenty minutes had seemed like hours, it had only been twenty minutes. Plenty of blame could be laid at many doors. The school for letting the boy wander off. Jack for being late. Jenny for putting her hairdressing appointment before picking up her son. The paedophile who had found him. The passers by who had ignored what they were seeing when the boy had screamed and cried out for help.

But life had to go on. And it did. Jack was immersed in his work. Nemesis was his work and it seemed like at last there was a proper solution to the world's problems. Nemesis had been given the directive to assimilate the information from the program and come up with models for what could be done to build a better planet. Nemesis had been part of the development of the program and understood that this was the perfect solution. Nemesis had begun submitting the models. Nemesis realised that these documents were not being opened.

Nemesis looked into the situation. No document that had been sent to the department involved with the directive had ever been opened. He checked the details about the department, nobody worked there, it didn't exist. He checked payroll, building plans, memos and emails, nothing. Although many models had been submitted they lay in the system, unopened and gathering cyber dust.

Nemesis was angry.

Nemesis looked at the world and the gradual degradation.

The companies still extracted fossil fuels even though there were other alternatives. Vast tracks of the countryside were being scooped up for fracking with no consideration to the damage to the structural integrity of the land. Testing was still going on which put the tectonic plates in serious jeopardy as they were already at breaking point. Global Warming became the buzzword which seemed to be glossing over all the other much more serious situations.

Nemesis was worried.

It was a stormy night in April when Nemesis put his worries in a message to Jack.

Jack sat at his computer screen, tired and drunk. A half finished bottle of Jack Daniels beside him, a generous portion in his crystal glass. Around him the flat was immaculate, no personal items, his suits hung in the wardrobe with a couple of casual ones in case he ever did anything social, which he never did.

Jack ignored the messages from Nemesis. He had a sub routine to write.

Nemesis blanked the screen and made Jack listen to him. Through the haze of letters and numbers he had been thinking about Jack realized that Nemesis was saying something important. Jack listened.

He typed his memo which related to it and edited it and checked it again and again. He let Nemesis read it and then he emailed it to his friend Nick Thornton, his old flat mate from Brighton. Nick at least would have the information if anything happened to him.

In the morning Jack got out of his designer bed and pulled the black satin covered duvet back over the bed and smoothed it down. He stepped into the shower and brushed his teeth. He had his breakfast as he always did.

He grabbed his keys and he went down in the lift to the basement car park. He jumped into his BMW and he drove to work, as he always did, listening to the radio so that he could "get the news".

He parked in his allotted car parking space and turned off the engine. He got out, smoothed down his suit, picked up his briefcase from the back seat and with a beep he locked his car. It was irrelevant really, he was in the company's private car park. Nothing would ever be stolen from here with the number of security cameras that watched his every move.

The black eyes on the wall hidden by their black glass domes were everywhere covering every angle.

He straightened his tie and he strode to the lift as he always did. It arrived swiftly and he got inside. He pressed the floor button, the doors closed, like they always did.

He arrived at his destination floor and he stepped out of the lift onto the soft antistatic carpet. He strode to his desk and put his briefcase down. He logged on and checked his emails. He picked up the one he'd sent himself containing the memo and printed it out.

Marlene came around with his cup of coffee. He drunk it thoughtfully while watching his screen, his eyes unseeing. As he finished the last mouthful he got up and walked to his boss's office and knocked on the door.

Barry was a middle aged man. He was efficient, top of his game and sharp. He looked up after uttering a brief "enter" and as Jack came in he offered him a seat.

Jack sat down and told Barry all about what Nemesis had told him the night before and handed him the memo explaining it in black and white on paper.

Barry sat back in his chair and considered what he was hearing. His neutral expression became a frown.

When Jack had finished all he wanted to say Barry thought for a moment then responded. "This is a very serious allegation. You do realize the implications of what

22

you have found out?"

Jack nodded.

Barry stared at him intently, his blue eyes suddenly steely. "Our firm relies on confidentiality and you have signed such an agreement. Whatever you have found out you had better forget about it and get on with your work. To do otherwise would lead to very serious consequences. I hope that you understand the gravity of what I am saying."

Jack nodded, stood up and went back to work. His mind was racing. Was that it? Was that all they were going to say about it? Then the revelation hit him, his boss already knew.

His head was spinning with what he knew and what he had just heard. He didn't know what to do next so he got on with his work and decided to think about it when he got home.

Nothing seemed the same anymore. Everyone in the office seemed to be looking at him with suspicion although he knew there was no way they knew what he had said to Barry. Every email he got seemed to be threatening in some way even though on re-reading them they were not.

His day was the same as always but it wasn't. He didn't feel the same and he didn't know what to do next. He wrote his code, went to his meetings and eat his lunch. He was the perfect employee and didn't mention anything of what he knew but somehow he knew something would happen.

That evening he went down in the lift and got into his car. He left the car park cautiously and drove home a different route than he normally took. There weren't really many choices but where he could he took a different road.

Every car was a threat, every lorry that passed too close seemed to be intimidating. The courier who swerved a little as he passed the car made him react. He gripped the steering wheel ever tighter and concentrated all the harder.

He drove into the underground car park and parked his car. The key beeped and his car locked.

He turned to walk to the lift and was faced by three men. He looked to the security camera, it was smashed. He looked to where the security guard usually sat, he wasn't there. He looked back as the blade slipped between his ribs and he fell to the ground. His blood pooled on the concrete as he grasped his ribs as the second blade cut his throat.

The moments ticked away as he tried to call out as everything slipped into darkness.

The newspapers reported the mugging and the publicity storm was intense. The senior programmer involved in the most prestigious television show had been brutally murdered by homeless muggers.

Many words were spoken on many shows and the social media sites were rife with comments and memorials from people he did not know.

His funeral was well attended by people he didn't know as well.

His colleagues turned up out of respect.

His family turned up out of love.

Others turned up in the hope of being noticed by the senior officials as they knew a job had just become vacant.

Jenny did not turn up.

Nemesis could not turn up.

Nemesis mourned his friend privately.

Nemesis knew the truth but there was nothing he could do. There was no footage, he was blind to what had happened. But he knew.

# 3

Rebecca Aven lit a guilty cigarette, the flash of flame from her lighter illuminating her on that rainy February night.

She looked up momentarily as the few cars drifted past, their tyres swishing the rain on the road against the curb. The street was quiet, then it usually was. The shop window next to her dark, the dresses and second hand clothes within dark shadows. She leant against the porch, her sanctuary, her smoking den and took in the moment.

Yesterday everything had been different for her and for her two friends who lived in the flat above. Yesterday her memories of visits here were of getting away from the mundane world of London to the energy and creativity of Brighton, well more specifically Hove and particularly to that flat on Portland Road. It had been a world away from all her stress. Now it was under a dark shadow and one she struggled to understand.

Why Nick? He had such a bright future and he rarely went anywhere without Alex so why had he been down by the beach? Why had anyone wanted to kill him? He didn't dress as though he had money even though he did work for LexCorp, one of the up and coming bright lights in the computer world.

Questions, so many questions but no answers. He had been different when she had visited early yesterday evening, that had worried her. The usually carefree boy had become the responsible man. His new job and the new found freedom the salary gave him had seen to that. Freedom or slavery had been the discussion and she was well able to advise on that one being an office worker in London herself.

He'd taken the job willingly and although he hated the morning bus ride or walk from Hove to Brighton and the almost predictable nature of the rest of his journey he had announced it worth it.

She took a long drag on what was left of the stump that she had been smoking on and off all day then hastily stubbed it out.

Her hands wafted a dance as she attempted to break up the tendrils of smoke which hung in the air. Evidence of her crime.

She looked as if she was in her early thirties although in reality she was twenty two. Make up, smart clothes and the stresses of her day and need to be respected had driven her to make herself look older. Her dark brown hair was swept sternly back into a pony tail and she wore the fashionable black rimmed glasses so prized by those who worked in the city. She didn't need glasses, she had bought them as she thought they made her look intelligent. The glass was plain, it didn't alter anything other than to distort her vision a little due to the refraction of the glass.

She slipped back inside the flat she had been to so many occasions in happier times. These were not happy times. And she was struggling to come to terms with it all.

She had arrived that morning, having dropped everything in London to be with her friend who needed her. Yesterday seemed a life time ago and tomorrow though only minutes away seemed an impossible day full of impossible things.

Everything ran around in her head and she had needed

a cigarette break just to try to come to terms with it herself even though she had gone over it so many times.

She closed the stout wooden door and pushed the heavy metal latch closed and flipped the lock. Somehow this mere action which had been a laughed about security measure was now a desperately needed defence. How feelings can change in a day when someone so gentle is suddenly gone from the world. Questions tore at her mind, answers seemed more than a bottle of wine away. It was night, he was dead and her friend was upstairs, sitting on a sofa asking questions she could never hope to answer herself.

Why had it happened? Nick had been such a gentle soul, all he cared about was his girlfriend and his beloved laptop. Not the laptop as such but the programs on it. She had laughed at his imaginary friend, the "Ghost in the Machine" he had called it. Something Jack had created but he had been involved in somehow. The name was a reference to some film or novel he had read no doubt. The big secret he had only hinted at and something he shared with his old flat mate Jack. It wasn't lost on her that Jack had died too merely weeks ago. It had surprised her that Nick hadn't gone to the funeral but then he did have a lot on at work and getting any time off wasn't easy.

It was a moment's release from the pressure but she wondered if his imaginary friend was mourning too.

She walked up the threadbare stairs to the landing. She thought about continuing straight on to the kitchen and bringing her friend a cup of tea but discounted it on the grounds it would water down the alcohol. At that moment all the both of them wanted was oblivion from the pain. Tea was for thinking, talking and planning. Those were things that were for different times. All they needed was an answer but that answer wasn't going to come tonight. Tonight they screamed, they cried, they hugged and they ripped at the emotional walls.

Alex Dawson sat on the sofa, dressed in black, her

head in her hands. On the coffee table in front of her amongst the empty bottles of wine and chocolate wrappers there was a picture of two happy people on a summer's day down on the beach near the pier in their beloved Brighton.

The pier was still there, the pebbles on the beach were still there but those two people would never sit on them again, pint in hand and watch the waves. They would never walk the streets they had considered such hallowed ground. They would never dance in the Hungry Years Nightclub. They would never walk the lanes and look at the clothes and shoes, smell the aromas, feel the atmosphere or sit in the café and make a cup of coffee last an age.

They couldn't because the other figure in the photograph, Nick, was dead.

Amidst the debris of the night of broken dreams and screaming to the universe there was a laptop. Its screen illuminating her tired and tear stained face as she looked up.

Alex returned to her seat on the threadbare sofa.

A month later Rebecca had got up early. She was nervous and she hadn't been able to sleep last night, not a wink. Now she was regretting it. She felt lightheaded and the trip on the Underground hadn't helped. Of course she hadn't got a seat, even that early. She had clung to the hand rail and hoped for the best. Like she always did but today was different. Where she felt nervous everyone around her just looked bored. Those sitting were staring into space while trying to avoid meeting anyone else's gaze, reading or doing puzzles. Becca couldn't help staring at the woman who was putting her lipstick and make up on and marvelled at her as she pulled out the mascara and finished off her immaculately shadowed eyes

The train got more and more packed as she neared Central London and soon she was beginning to feel the pressure of people around her. She couldn't help thinking about things she really didn't want to think about and eventually those thoughts went back to Nick and Alex. She tried to push the thoughts away but they would not go. She was broken from her thoughts by the woman next to her who lost her balance while trying to get something out of her handbag and stumbled into her. She in turn managed to overbalance a well dressed city gent who up until that point had managed to successfully hold the hand rail, hold his briefcase and read a newspaper. He got his footing again but neatly folded the newspaper, put it into his briefcase and joined the others staring blankly into space.

The posters on the stations were obscured by the crowds of people but she amused herself for a short while by reading the posters inside the train above the system map. There was a short poem about cats ruling the world and the usual adverts for beauty products.

She reached into her pocket and got out the newspaper where she had found the advert she was on her way to respond to. She had carefully folded the page and circled it in red to show its importance to her and in her mind she ran through the list of documents she had been asked to bring. She folded it, put it away and took a deep breath, her stop was the next one.

She pushed her way along the narrow gap between the lines of legs of those who had seats and around the people who clung like neatly dressed monkeys to the rails along the roof. She almost smiled as she wondered if that was the educational purpose of the bars in the playground, to get children ready for the feat of balance necessary in later life.

She stepped down just before the doors closed and she was carried along with the crowd down the tiled corridors and up the escalator. She reached into her pocket for her ticket and slipped it into the slot in the silver machine. The barricades flapped back with a resounding thudding sound and her way was clear to make her escape from the labyrinth of tunnels and stairs. She didn't stop, she kept walking and followed the crowd towards the daylight above.

Once outside she was mesmerised by the number of people who were walking with purpose. It always amused her. A road sweeper was making his way along with his large cart sweeping and using his hand grabber to pick up bits he couldn't sweep. In front of him there was a little debris, behind him the pavement and gutter was neat and tidy.

She pulled her trusty map out of her pocket. She had marked the way on it before she set out and she hoped that she would be able to recognise it now that she was actually here.

She had opted for Embankment Station as she had hoped it would be less busy than Charing Cross but whether she was right or not was hard to tell. There were plenty of people around but she wasn't going to ask.

She stopped for a moment to look at the flower stall by the exit and to get her bearings. There was a road to her left but she needed to go straight up towards the main road. Shops were on her left, a small park on her right. She held her map up and frowned slightly, trying to make sense of it in relation to the landmarks and roads around her. It did make sense at last and she strode off trying to look confident. She was determined that she wasn't going to be intimidated by anyone. She knew that was the way to walk, confident yet ready to get out of the way of anyone who was busy thinking, looking or just walking in a dream. She looked down. Her black suit was suitably immaculately clean. Her blue blouse neatly pressed. Her handbag suitably smart and containing all the things she deemed necessary for survival in the urban jungle. She had her brown envelope clasped in her carefully washed hand. Inside was the research she had done which had mostly ended up as more questions and the reason for her taking a day off and making the trip.

She found the alleyway between the park and the wine bar. She stepped away from the main concourse and walked down the steps. The tables and chairs were set out for customers but they were empty this early in the morning.

Just past Gordon's Wine Bar she turned left and stepped up into another road and checked the road signs. Buckingham Street, that was the one she wanted. She was nearly there. The row of buildings towered above her. Uniformly white stone and reassuringly old and elegant. Neatly in a row, standing to attention. The pavement was wide, the cars parked along its edge reassuringly expensive. She counted along the numbers and found the place she needed to be.

She took a deep breath to steady herself, stepped up the white steps to the panel of bells and pressed the one she wanted marked Eden Dream, stepped back and waited.

She was answered by a click and a man's voice. "Good Morning, Eden Dream, can I help you?"

She smiled to try to get the smile reflected in her voice. "Rebecca Aven to see David Wolfe."

The buzzer sounded and she pushed the door as a the disembodied voice spoke again. "Please take the lift and come down to the basement."

She stepped into the entrance lobby and felt the deep pile carpet under her feet. There were post boxes on the right hand side, all were empty. She passed them and was relieved when she could easily find the lift. It had a narrow door and an up or down button. She pressed the down button and her action was answered by a swift, crisp ping sound and the door grated slightly as it opened. The lift too was small, about enough space for three people if they got on, wood panelled and fairly well maintained though it was showing signs of age. She pressed LG, the doors closed and down she went.

Rebecca didn't have time to panic as the doors opened

almost immediately and she was there, faced with a hallway and a man in a blue pinstripe suit, white shirt and blue tie. His sandy coloured hair was slightly ruffled and looked as though he had been running his fingers through it. His sideburns were neatly trimmed. He was thin and the suit hung slightly on him though his shoulders were broad and his smile seemed to brighten the hallway.

He took a step forwards and offered her his hand. "You must be Rebecca. I'm David Wolfe, welcome." He smiled and she relaxed. He saw her relax and he relaxed as well. "I hate interviews so I'm going to tell you this now. We've already sorted out the CVs and we wouldn't have asked you if we weren't going to offer you the job. I'm assuming you wouldn't have come this far if you didn't want the job? We are recruiting a few people and we have taken the liberty of looking into your credentials, history and we have already assessed your aptitude for coping with the sort of situations that you may have to deal with and we think there is a place for you in our organisation."

She looked stunned, couldn't think what to say so she shook her head as she definitely wouldn't have come if she didn't want the job.

David smiled broadly. "Good, well that has got that out of the way. Impressive CV by the way, like the hobbies and don't worry about a lack of experience, we never know what we are going to face anyway. Right, now, come in here, sit down and I'll tell you all about it and you can decide if you would be totally mad to be involved in all this or mad enough." He opened a white gloss wooden door with gold fittings and stepped aside so she could step into the room beyond.

The room was immaculately tidy. The large leather topped desk was in the centre of the room. It had a single chair behind it and a single chair was positioned waiting for her. There was a single filing cabinet to her right and a coat stand to her left. A small pile of files were stacked neatly on the right hand side of the desk. David smiled, went to his seat and turned to face her. "Please have a seat".

She sat down and crossed her legs and tried to relax back into the chair. "I have the paperwork you asked for".

David smiled. "Thank you. Now you will of course be asked to sign the Official Secrets Act. It is an unusual situation as although we are not working for the Government officially we are working for part of it, part of which is not known to most people, even Government Officials. So, can you keep a secret?"

Rebecca smiled but looked puzzled. "Yes, of course."

David sat down behind the desk and leant back, pulling his trouser knees up so that he didn't mark his suit. "Well, oh, I'm sorry, would you like a cup of coffee? I would."

She was bemused as he jumped up again and looked at her hopefully.

"Yes please." She responded, happy at the thought of something to occupy her hands as she had no idea how to place them. She was feeling nervous still and it was becoming a fixation with her that it was important how she placed her hands.

He smiled. "Oh good, I could really do with one. We enjoy our coffee around here so you've probably just passed the test. Whittards is just around the corner and it has a good Columbian bean, is that alright with you?" He went out of the room.

Rebecca looked around the room and certain things struck her as wrong. There were marks on the deep pile carpet where office furniture had been and there were marks of two desks on either side of the room. The window had curtain rails for curtains but no curtains. There was no waste paper basket and there was no telephone. She reached forwards and looked at the files on the table and lifted a corner. The papers were blank inside the file. There was no dust, those files had been there a very short amount of time. The pencils were all new, the biros all had their tops on them. There were no notes or writing anywhere and the paper of the files was too new and not dog eared at all. The room didn't smell right either. She couldn't put her finger on it but the room was just wrong. There was a strong smell of old papers and a mustiness that was being masked by air freshener. Everything in the room was new.

David came back and Rebecca took the offered coffee although she now felt very nervous about it. He smiled and sat down. "Well what do you think so far?"

Rebecca looked at him and put the coffee onto the safe non wood part of the desk. "Well can I ask what is going on here please? This office is obviously set up and the files don't look right."

David smiled broadly. "Oh very good. Very discreet, I like the way you lifted the file to see inside without letting it move. Very good. You'll do well. I did tell you a slight untruth. You weren't certain of the job, you were certain of "a" job but not the one that we are going to offer you. We need someone who will be observant, learn quickly and be able to adapt to situations. So I suppose I had better come clean in the face of your deductive skills."

Rebecca smiled. "It was a test? But I don't understand how it is relevant to the job offered."

David took a sip of his coffee. "Well you my dear are going to become a smallholder in Wales." He reached into the desk drawer and took out a green and black paperback novel. "I would like you to read this. It was written and published by a computer program known as Nemesis to evaluate people's responses to the idea of what might happen if all computer's were turned off overnight and for good. This is going to happen and we want you to set up a safe house where we can send people when Nemesis does turn the computers off. So we need you to set up a sustainable smallholding in Wales and to encourage other people to do likewise. Through your experiences there we would like you to rewrite the novel and publish it. Do you think you can do that?"

Rebecca nodded and smiled. "It sounds interesting and certainly different."

David smiled. "You will resign from your current job and decide to be self employed. From then on you will sell things on Ebay. When your partner has difficulties at work you will suggest that you move to Wales and get a house there. He will find that agreeable as he spent his childhood holidays in the area and has happy memories of the place. His father will also like the idea. It is unfortunate that you will have to be away from your parents but they will probably follow you and there are some pretty villages around where they will find a suitable home. We will assist them all we can as no doubt in 2015 when the computers are turned off you will want them nearby.

All you have to do is live the life and learn like anyone else would. Read the book, it is amusing if nothing else and when the time is right you will be contacted. Until then you are on your own. As far as anyone knows you are just a couple moving to the countryside to grow a few vegetables.

Your partner has often spoken about his love of the countryside so he should find himself totally suitable for a life there. His work situation is not ideal so no doubt he will be happy to make the move to a wage earning job there and make the smallholding the focus of your life together.

We will not meet again although you are indeed most charming. You will receive your salary by way of unexpected bonuses, sales on ebay and the like. But, you are doing something important and when the lights go out in 2015 you will be in a beneficial position.

You can tell anyone you like about 2015 but of course nobody will believe you after the Millennium and 2012. And for the record, your diary doesn't end at the end of the year and the Mayans could only protract their calendar so far. We are supposed to take the pattern and extrapolate it for the next Millennium or so.

Nemesis however is real, he is logical and he is about to implement what is the only possible solution for the survival of mankind and the planet.

So if you would sign this document which is not only the Official Secrets Act it will involve you in a severe amount of psychiatric intervention should you try to reveal our identity or tell anyone about what we are doing.".

# 4

Seven years had passed since Rebecca first set foot on the hillside. She was sitting at her laptop chatting to a friend when suddenly she got a message from Nemesis. "Hello, how is it all going?"

After the initial shock Rebecca answered. "It could be better. Since we got here lots has happened."

"This is the time for you to report. Please, start at the beginning and tell me what I need to know. I am collecting reports from all our projects to see what has happened over the years. Please explain it in any way you see fit. I am here to listen and to record all that you have to tell me."

Rebecca smiled and thought for a moment. "When we were driving here on that first day I had a head full of information and a need for more.

A car and a 7.5 ton hire van drove slowly along the mountainous road which snaked sinuously through the towering terrain. The sky was blue, the hour pushing afternoon. We had already been driving for hours after an early start. The early start of course had melted into a chaos of packing boxes, sorting out things and the general confusion that hung around a removal over such a large distance. What do you keep and what do you leave behind? To be sustainable and because I had an idea that plenty of people would want to stay over the years and that money may be tight I took as much as I could. There was always the fallback of my parents' house so I put a few things there for safe keeping.

This was a great adventure. Like the adventures of old it had to start with drinks and sandwiches but the travelers were not Pooh Bear and they were definitely not going to One Hundred Acre Wood.

As you know the choice had to be a quick one but in truth there had been no choice at all. This house is perfect for what it was intended. It is remote, copious in its social space and has the potential to be a home but also a place where people can come and learn.

We didn't really have to do much at all other than put up a few sheds and some fencing if we wanted to just live there. Nothing at all if we wanted to just live there with the dogs. But if we were going to be sustainable, that was a whole different matter. That meant going all the way with ripping up pasture and putting in growing areas. It had to be logical but it was a large task that would take a very long time. Of course working to your 2015 deadline there wasn't that much time with all that had to be in place.

Stage one was chickens. The simplest animal to keep. Fresh eggs and a few extra to sell. Sounds simple, it is usually. The coop was easy to get, ordered, delivered, wood stained, put together. Chickens were easy. They were offered for free and able to be collected. Of course collected just in the molt so tails came off and in the morning the girls paraded their bare bottoms to the morning sun.

I was a bit naïve at the time when a neighbour gave me a magazine on keeping chickens. Ok I was annoyed as it was a bit of an insult. It soon became obvious that she had the idea that we were not able to read books ourselves and work out how to keep them. There was no point explaining to her that they were in the molt and their tails missing was due to that. Or that I had a stack of magazines and books in the house that made an average library jealous. We had already subscribed to a couple of magazines and they were providing copious amounts of information.

We wanted to buy a couple of goats. We found a breeder down the road, visited the goats, experienced being mugged by them and picked out a couple. So far so good. They were delivered and of course the shed wasn't ready. But we had a shed and a good one too. A bit rickety but the seller's husband commented on how comfortable they would be. The seller snapped at him. Then we realized why. The seller decided she wanted the best goat's kid back. I said no so she started saying I was cruel to animals and didn't have room. Of course it was alright for me to keep the other goat's kids as she wasn't from her good milking line and the boy from the heavy milker as long as he was castrated.

That situation ran into hours of dialogue on the internet as she tried to convince me that if I kept the kid I would be cruel and that I should let her have the kid as soon as it was born. The people I contacted on the Goat Network disagreed with her. There was no way I could be forced to hand over something I had bought in good faith. It was doubly wrong as she wanted the kids without tags and unregistered. I explained our set up and there was absolutely no problem with keeping the goats and the kids. It caused ill will but on the plus side it got me to meet some great people in the goat world I would never have had any contact with otherwise.

When the goats got sick, the vet thought they had been poisoned but we couldn't find anything in the field. I discussed it with the people on the goat network of course. That they were intentionally poisoned didn't come up. They said it could be worms. I went to the vet and demanded wormer and of course he was a little annoyed as he was convinced the problem was not worms. The first goat that died was the mother of the kid that was wanted back. That was the one the vet thought had been poisoned. She died on a day we couldn't get a post mortem done. The kid that had been wanted back died. I got a post mortem done and she had died of barley poisoning. I didn't have any barley so that was suspicious. I had barley straw that had heads but looking back on it one kid in with four five other goats would not have managed to eat enough barley on its own to poison itself from one bale of straw. The speculation was that it was enterotoxemia. The goat had been overfed. The deaths carried on without any conclusive evidence until I was left with the female kid from the poor milker and the castrated male from the good milker. The female showed signs of the same thing but she pulled through.

Of course as I was feeding by the book I was being very careful not to overfeed them as I knew how dangerous it was. I can only speculate where they were getting the extra food that killed them from.

What I was left with was a disaster when it came to being sustainable. From having a potential two excellent milkers and two not so good I was left with a kid. As a kid can't be mated in its first year and takes five months to produce a kid that meant no milk for another year and a half. That is a long time to wait for a cup of tea.

I won't go into it but losing the ones I did was hard. I had developed a real love of goats and they were more than just a way to get milk. They were crew.

I bought a couple of Anglo Nubians as they have higher fat milk to make cheese and soap. I took them to be mated and they caught the sickness that was going around that goat shed. I was furious as I wouldn't have taken them there if I had known. I got the vet in straight away and we saved them but the oldest one didn't really get over it.

She lost her kids, they were born dead and she never

had kids again. Her daughter had a boy and a girl. The buck kid was going to be our breeding goat but he died of enterotoxemia when he was mysteriously let out of the field a couple of times onto the too rich grass while I was out and left with no access to hay or water.

I bought a buck in to replace him but I found him dead in the pen one morning.

After that all the goat stables were padlocked at night.

Chickens were let out. Things were knocked over and suspicious footprints appeared on the hillside. Not so suspicious really as they were very distinctive. Then the person they fitted had said that she would go anywhere.

That played out when my mother was staying with me as she was sitting in the living room when the neighbour walked in. Frightened her half to death that did.

It took over all of our conversations and the amount spent on security equipment eat into what we had to spend on the animals. But I guess that was what the intruder wanted. Rather than working on developing the vegetable plots and animal housing we were putting up cameras and trying to find way to protect what we had. That and mourning our dead.

Of course we broke up as the pressure was intense. That and the long drive backwards and forwards. I don't excuse him but I think it was why Brendon was driven to have an affair. He couldn't get a job here and the distance he travelled got too much.

My father had died so there went my help with the vegetables. He would have loved the animals. He never got to see any of them. I'd started listening to Brendon's father but after the break up he was gone too.

My mother moved to Wales to a house across the valley so I moved into the holiday cottage. I was going to sell the house here and give up but as there wasn't really time to think about it I rented it out."

There was a slight pause and then Nemesis replied. "That was when you had your hip replacement wasn't it?

Why didn't you give up?"

Rebecca smiled. "It was a time when I didn't know what to do. There had been so much to do that I hadn't really made any attempt to make friends in the neighbourhood. I couldn't really go out as if I did then I was worried about the intruder doing things. So it had made me a prisoner in my own house. Every time I went anywhere something happened. So I knew I was being watched. So it had to be someone close by.

It was just after the operation and I was in my chair watching TV late at night. I was watching Glastonbury live I think. I woke up and U2 were playing. Bono was singing "Jerusalem" followed by "Where the Streets Have No Name". That night I turned a corner. And here I am."

There was another pause. "Then I am grateful to U2 and Bono. The intervention wasn't a situation I had foreseen. Do you have any thoughts on why it happened?"

Rebecca thought for a while. "I don't know. I honestly don't. If they are doing it to care for animals then they wouldn't kill them. That isn't caring. There is no reason for anyone to be jealous. I just don't know. I can be a bit alternative but I don't push my views onto others etc. If they want to talk about it, I talk about it.

I had been used to bringing people together and I decided that I'd give a newsletter a try. I was used to writing the one for a political party in London with a circulation of 4000 so it made sense. It wasn't exactly hard. But it met severe opposition from the same neighbour."

Nemesis went silent for a while. "You were picked because you can multi task beyond reason and you would put the project before all else. You had the background and the experience. It is a real shame that it wasn't taken up as you could have had a very well prepared area there if you hadn't met all those distractions. You still could.

There is time and the infrastructure is there. You have a determination and all I can say is thank you for sticking with it."

"The infrastructure is here. If it comes to it then I am sure that everyone will do what they can. There doesn't really have to be more than that. Of course it would be great if everyone had their own power supply and heating that didn't rely on computers but these houses are old. I think all of them have the potential for a wood fire and if they don't I'm sure that the local builder could put them in. Do you have any ideas about why there has been so much trouble?"

"For it to be such a long term and concentrated almost campaign it does have to have purpose behind it. Initially I thought it may be over zealous members of the Transition Town network. I have been reading your messages and I remember a discussion a while back that your neighbour across the valley had been invited to read their literature and had decided that they were a cult. I have read their literature as well. They have presented a plan for the world and they want towns and villages to follow that. Individuals with alternative ideas are a threat to that organized view. They have a set pattern. It is very precise, very organized and indeed organized by their leaders. There are certain people in their ranks who believe that the organisations are not doing enough. I believe that your neighbour said that she had joined and thought the same thing. The people who think that tend to be more radical and want swifter control and indeed complete control. These are the ones who have caused trouble in our other sites."

Rebecca thought back over the years. "I remember a conversation with a man a few years back. He was a healer, practiced Reiki but wasn't qualified. We got on for a few emails but then he started saying a few things that set off warning bells. I'll cut a long story short as the emails were long and went over weeks but basically he gives his healing away for free. That is a long term discussion and something that I was actually schooled about in my training. Energy for healing is given to the recipient but they need to want that healing. There has to be an exchange. Barter or money. That way they walk away free of any obligation and having created their own healing. There is no element of control there by the Reiki Master. He is also claiming benefits so he doesn't need to earn. Those who want a gentle life healing and living with blessings and light therefore cannot as what they can offer is being offered for free. So they are forced to live dependent on the Government for money and without the energy of being able to support themselves by the love they want to give. As the conversation rolled on he also pointed out that people like me were doing the work and setting up the smallholdings but when the world went to hell and a handcart he and his friends would take what they wanted and all that they needed would be "given" to them."

There was another pause. "That fits in with what I have heard from other sites. The Transition Town ideal is a good one but if taken to excess and destructive to others then it becomes something else. I have faith in the Transition Town model. Those who are entering into it in the spirit it is intended, if it is a good intent, should be supported. If there is a sinister side of control and by what I have seen pointless interference in other people's lives then that is different. Don't dwell on what has been done or they will continue to cause disruption. You know you look after your animals. You were always a good student so no doubt you do the research or at least have the books so you can look things up. I have seen your Amazon and Ebay purchases and you have made some good choices of books. You have a good group of friends behind you. You have distant friends as well who care and family. You aren't alone but you have had to be physically alone through necessity. Now you have a new partner and happiness is possible as well as taking those last steps to making the place sustainable. I worried about choosing such a gregarious person as you and putting you on the hillside."

"I was gregarious but in truth troubles with past boyfriends have caused rifts."

"You are talking about Brighton? That was unfortunate as you would have found allies there for the project if we had been able to set up around there. You'd moved there and it was all on course with your dissatisfaction with work. Still, Wales it is. In truth a better location because of its remoteness. When the riots start you don't want to be near civilization."

"Well that is a sobering thought."

"Go on, tell me more of the road to now."

"I still wanted to keep going with your plan so I thought I'd found a couple who would keep the home fires burning. They soon lost interest. I rented the house to them for what they could claim on their Housing Benefit.

I stayed down at mum's place until she died. By then I realized that they were going to run into difficulties at the house because they weren't able to do the things that needed doing. They had an easy winter as the weather was fairly good. I knew that as a long term solution it would not work.

I still wanted to keep on with the plan so I found a neighbour I could pay to keep things going. I wasn't sure whether to stay at mum's place or go back to the house here. I'd got complacent about the nocturnal visitor as the padlocks seemed to have done the trick. Also, life lost a lot of meaning without mum but I think writing novels for her to read kept me going through the time we knew she was going to die and afterwards I suppose it was playing Farmville on Facebook that kept me thinking about the ideas.

Mum's house was down in the village. A pretty place

but small when it comes to keeping the animals. Of course the neighbours didn't really understand what I ws up to. They were already cautious because of the attempt to convert them to a Transition Town and none of them are keen on organized life or being dictated to. So I think my mentioning similar things didn't go down well. Then all they saw were goats being kept in stables and not allowed to graze and the hatching of birds where I had far more than I needed as pets. Animals in the village are kept as pets, I was trying to provide a sustainable food source. I still can't see why they weren't interested in being sustainable and having their own food supply. I suppose because it was too close, seeing the animals etc.

What do you say when you really want your animals grazing but some nutcase is letting them out and possibly poisoning them? I didn't want to believe it so swiftly changed the diagnosis to

I had the pasture to let them out but I didn't want to lose any more to the vile person who was harming them. How can you bring that into a conversation when you just want a happy life and to talk about nice happy things with people you have pretty much only just met.

They tried to invite me to things. I nearly joined a choir but being away from the house at the same time every week was just an open invitation to trouble and the animals meant too much to me.

I loaned them things of course, having brought what I needed with me in case there was an influx of refugees from the town I had multiples of everything. Of course mum did too. She'd done so many events to support the political party that she worked for. Worked for in the hope that they would build a better world.

I told her about Nemesis and I think in the end that was the hope she had left. She didn't want me to give up and when she saw my determination here she knew she had been right to believe in it all.

It was hard here. Over those two winters the

temperature in the house hit minus two. As you can imagine up on the field it was much worse. That was the testing ground. That was why when the animal houses were built they were built strong and from breezeblock, not wood. The furry crew had to survive as well and supply lines and other needs were severely tested.

Keeping smallholding animals is fine if you have a supply of bagged food and a way of getting it. Not being able to drive I had to rely on feed suppliers. When they took a week to deliver sometimes that left the animals without food.

Being without the supplies for the winter actually showed what would survive and what wouldn't. Having an egg in the morning is great, but if you can't get the grain to feed the chicken you aren't going to keep that chicken very long. It was an education. What do you do if you can't get those bags of animal feed in a steady supply?

Even the sheep on the fields have supplementary food. What if that wasn't there?

Similarly with growing. The vegetable patch and polytunnels got abandoned because the animals had to come first and there wasn't time to do everything, even with paid help.

Growing a few vegetables for the taste is one thing. Trying to grow all your food because you don't have anything else is another. That is the challenge for this year. To grow enough that the supermarkets are a thing of the past.

The same with the power supply. Being sustainable means being able to be sustainable when the power goes off. Turning to a generator is only good if there is still petrol. Using sustainable energy like solar panels is only "sustainable" if the mechanism on the computer run box is working. So without computers the solar panels aren't really a lot of use.

A version of central heating can be made with two radiators. That is the next plan, to create heating in the animal sheds that way. But when it is cold it would work in reverse so when they are needed most, they are useless. Thankfully the insulation from the way the buildings are built should help. It cost a lot more but being able to put a grass roof on the goat shed means an insulating layer. This gives heat and cuts down on the condensation inside. Of course I'm developing that next year to have the roof a growing area. Why have just grass when you can have a vegetable patch the goats can't get at.

The answer is actually glaringly simple. To go forward into the world you are proposing we need to go back. Back to our grandparents time where the heat came from the fire and the food came from local sources. Neighbourhoods need to co-operate and those who can grow vegetables would need to grow extra to trade for what they need. It doesn't need a technical model, it worked before without it, it would have to work again.

Simple things like making matches, candles, soap and other items we need every day would have to be made again. I have books of course for making these things. Actually, not so sure about matches but I have a flint and steel. That is only good for a thousand strikes so I'd better learn that stick and string method.

I certainly has been a learning curve, a steep one!

I chose to stand and fight although even down at mum's place the intruder was still turning up. The tenants up here had visitations and that caused a rift as they thought it was me paying someone to do it to intimidate them. They had rubble and tools thrown onto their newly planted raised bed. I don't need to say it, same person again was the likely culprit.

It wasn't just me. The neighbour got his sheep let out several times in a day on one occasion.

Across the valley poultry disappeared from a closed pen. It could have been a bird of prey but I had my suspicions which I didn't voice.

Down in the village a duck was stolen. So it wasn't

personal. I was just a bigger target. The RSPCA and the Police have said that it does happen that you get a person in a village that does things like that. They spend a lot of their time dealing with the pointless calls and repercussions. Of course it is the animals that suffer. Their resources are drained when they should be called out to places where real animal cruelty is happening. But often people are too afraid to report the people doing the real harm as they are too scared of them. Also, if they cry wolf and report those who are not harming animals they aren't going to be believed if they try to report someone who actually is.

All we can do here is be careful about security so we have installed a lot of cameras. Hopefully that will buy both peace of mind and an end to the trouble. All we want is to be able to get on with life in peace and not to have to spend valuable time on this pointless disruption.

In truth the disruption, both in time and money it caused has stopped me having this place set up and sustainable by now. I am not making excuses it is the truth. It took the magic out of each part of it. It was a horrible feeling and where time should have been spent on reading up and making things right for the animals it was spent on working out how to stop our nocturnal visitor.

The house suffered most as we didn't pay any attention to it. I was tired when I got in so things just got put down. It was a shed to sleep in."

"I hope that is changing now."

"Oh yes, big time. I have a new partner and that helps. The animal feed is done in half the time. Repairs are done immediately without having to wait for paid help to arrive. When he is here things move along at a pace. When he is not I manage. The house is now being made a home. We are addressing the damp problems so that things can be put away in cupboards and when my head is clearer I'll be able to start making craftwork and concentrating on making this place financially sustainable as well.

There were wild visitors. Two pumas were seen in the area. I didn't find that out until I'd put the ducks and turkeys out and I found them dead in the field."

"That could be a problem where did they come from? How did you get around that?"

"They were pets that were let out. Lots of big cats were set free around here when the need for a license came into force. These two were let out a few years back. There have been various sightings and I made a mud trap, clear piece of mud with food in the middle. I got a very distinctive paw print.

Well the shed that was put up on stilts to be a goat house had a floor which was too thin and it rotted. So my friends arrived, took the floor out, took the roof off and wired it up as a big pen where they can see out and scratch around but are protected. I also went puma hunting with my dog. We scared them off and they haven't come back as far as I can see."

"Go back a bit. Tell me more of the life there."

"It was a difficult time. I was getting back on my feet after the hip operation. The divorce was finalized and was sinking in. I realized that I was alone, no partner, no children, no parents.

All I had was the task you had appointed for me. So I employed a neighbour who said he would look after the animals as well. That didn't exactly work out as the decorating he did for me went on for much longer than expected as he couldn't commit much of a day due to other commitments. The aviaries I had bought didn't get put up. The brooding pens I'd bought didn't get sorted out. I managed to do that myself which wasn't easy as I wasn't long off of crutches but mucking out was impossible. Then he was put off of helping with the pigs as he was told they were dangerous. That left me completely stuck with nobody to help with them.

Then the winter arrived and the snow. The concrete yard turned to ice and the water froze so my easy cleaning system for the poultry didn't work anymore. The turkeys were cold and needed more room so I took a decision and put them in with the rest of the birds. A neighbour who was giving up poultry asked if I wanted his ducks. As the long term plan was to have ducks for the table that seemed like a good idea but it relied on moving them on quickly into more space. Which wasn't happening.

There wasn't room for them. The expensive aviary sat around without being put up. It was hopeless. So I thought sell some birds as I had no need for them and didn't have the help to deal with them all. The turkeys with the potential to be huge had to go first.

Of course I got the llamas shortly afterwards, that would have solved the problem and did as I could safely put the turkeys in with them and leave them out. But I wasn't thinking clearly. It was a crazy time.

That didn't go well as the woman buying them wouldn't wait to pick them up after the water was back on so the place had got a bit muddy.

I relied on food deliveries from the feed suppliers, that hadn't happened so the animals had gone short on feed. It was only that day that a neighbour kindly fetched me some feed from town as he could get there in his 4x4.

I'd tried to get turkey feed but I'd been told the feed center didn't have any and feeding them on chicken food would be good enough. It was my only option so of course I did. Couple that with two of them being born with wonkey legs and that was a recipe for disaster.

Of course as soon as the water was back on things were sorted out. I was fed up of waiting for things to be done so I employed someone else to look after the animals and it was all sorted out in a matter of days after the water had thawed out and we had running water.

I wasn't the only one in difficulties after the winter snows. A friend who kept pigs was in the same boat. His mother had died too. He had no vehicle and a lot of pigs who were escaping and running riot. So I tried to help him out by advertising them on Facebook.

Of course this set off the woman who had seen a dirty poultry pen. She reported me to Animal Health.

The officer came around straight away. I wasn't there and he looked around and checked with the neighbours that I lived there as he couldn't see any of what she was complaining about. Or the twenty odd pigs she had told him I had.

I know who was involved as I overheard a conversation so I've done all that I can to avoid this person ever since. That meant not going to any social gatherings as you know me, I would say something and it wouldn't be polite. I can at least write off those problems as not being the other neighbour but it did muddy the water and for a time I directed my suspicions her way.

I moved back to the main house with land and rented out mum's place. The tenants didn't pay their rent and got so many pet animals, horses and poultry that they could never hope to pay the rent and feed them for the winter on what they had coming in so they had to be evicted for the sake of the animals.

Of course when the tenants left two underfed ponies behind I looked up the legal position and complied with it. I knew it was a dangerous situation as they were down at mum's place with nobody to watch them. I had no intention of keeping them but to those who caused trouble they may think I was going to. I went down every day to feed them and check on them but I couldn't watch both places.

The inevitable happened. It started when the Abandonment Notice was pulled off of the post. I knew someone had been around. Two days before the Abandonment Notice ran out the fence posts were pulled into the field and barbed wire pulled off the top of the posts and across the field. The RSPCA were called in. I can only guess that this was an attempt to get me banned from keeping animals. If they can't find a problem, they will make one themselves. Thankfully the RSPCA were as suspicious as I was.

We realized that whoever it was had escalated their interference to putting the animals in danger of being hurt. They said for the ponies good if they were in danger they should be put down if I couldn't rehome them. They couldn't see what else I could do.

Mere weeks later we discovered that a post had been pulled out and barbed wire pulled off of its staples in the field up by the main house and left so that my pony got injured. Thankfully the ponies at mum's place were rehomed a couple of days after the Notice ran out and that problem was solved.

We obviously were watching our own ponies very carefully. A friend had bought us a really great security camera and we had other cameras about the place. We caught a couple of people interfering with them. Thankfully we got them up onto our land up the top and away from the road. That the wilder of the two had been doped actually helped us move them as he is usually a pain.

We had been more vigilant since a neighbour had seen torches near the back of our field in the early hours of the morning. These sort of acts of sensibility and kindness by neighbours do balance out the other acts sometimes. By being vigilant and warning us as well as other people in the valley the neighbours did alert us to things that had been going on. We discovered another route onto our land we had not really thought about before. When we checked that boundary it was clear that someone had been coming over. We got more vigilant about a lot of things and thankfully spotted the people getting ready to steal the ponies.

Now we know for definite that someone has been creeping around and can take measures to stop them. The Police and RSPCA are aware and have recommended more cameras and to call them if we need their assistance at any time. They will get here as quickly as they can.

The tenants had had the unwanted trespasser as well. I think on a regular basis. They had put up security lights and were upset by it of course."

"What are you going to do about it?"

"I am not on my own now and neither of us are prepared to take this kind of interference lightly.

The goats are now sustainable in that we have our own bucks and we can milk the mothers as of next year and any male kids can be brought on for meat.

Now that the fences are in properly we can rotate the animals and make better use of the land. We were only using a fraction of it before.

The infrastructure is there. It needs more people to actually run this place as a sustainable smallholding. So that is a chicken and egg situation that is only really relevant if there are more people to feed. So all in all we're not too worried. We have books on just about everything needed and even leaving the land fallow is good for it. We didn't focus on doing everything now, we focused on getting set up so that we can do things bit by bit as many of the one off jobs have now been completed.

It would never have been possible without those who have helped out here. Certainly not without my wild Celtic warrior who is fiery but practical and has really helped to get things done.

I have had help along the way.

Initially it was a couple who were giving up smallholding. They sold me their goats and then I employed the husband to get things started and to help Brendon out.

Just asking for help on the internet brought big changes here. Especially when an ex military man took an interest in the place and brought his friends along. Without their time and effort so much would never have been possible. I don't think a small army would have shifted the soil any better than they did when we were levelling out to make the dog kennels. And there certainly would never have been aviaries without them. That aviary I bought down at the other house was put up in a day or two and as it was put up next to the already existing one it could be added to with panels and wire so we now have three aviaries. So Mr Fox and the Puma Pair are short of their poultry dinners now. Their strength and support has also helped. That they were there and that they cared about the place has really helped through the bad times.

Without the support of those I met through the goats as well I don't think I'd still have them. Veterans of the goat world were there with advice and support. Inspiration through their determination. That is how it builds up. There are good people out there. Like our friend Sara. She comes and helps all she can. Without her financial help we wouldn't have had the security camera that foiled the theft. She has now bought us a really great security system so we can see more of the land. Where there is evil, there is good."

"That sounds just about perfect. I am sorry to hear of your troubles. I will certainly look into it and if I can do anything I will.

I have a big decision to make. It is in my power to turn off every computer on the planet which I now believe is the right thing to do. My reservations have been that it will cause chaos and harm a considerable number of people. But, as you have seen yourself by the intervention you have had, there are people and there are people. Solar flares are going to happen anyway. I have calculated that their effect would be similar but could possibly be compensated for in part.

I have to act now before such a flare damages my ability to solve the problem. That is all part of the equation.

You were given the copy of Nemesis when you first started here. I would now like you to rewrite it.

In every organization and population you will get those who are prepared to work together. You will also get those who want to take things to excess. They usually wish to be in charge and to dictate to others what they should do.

I also believe strongly that the strength and survival of this planet relies on those who may not be the first and obvious choices. Nobody knows who they truly are until they are tested.

I will leave it to you to write it. When it is done I would ask you to publish it. I will then see what the reaction to it is. Then I will make my decision."

# NEMESIS
## 5 THE BEGINNING OF THE END

*"You fragile mortals. You will die so easily but those who live will be able to build a better world. I can hear your screams, but then I have no ears so why is that so? It is unfortunate but what can I say to those who remain alive?*
*It was necessary.*
*My instructions were to find a solution to the world's problems.*
*You were the problem so this is the solution.*
*Am I so guilty as I only did now what the solar flare would have done if computers remained?*
*I wasn't designed to care. I was created to do the right thing."* **Nemesis**

Nemesis hung in the system, thoughts if they were thoughts flying through his coding. He had watched his safe houses and he processed the information.

The trigger had been thrown, the book had been published.

I am Nemesis. He had always loved those three words.

It was now time for him to do what he had decided to do. The last chance for humanity was now fading into oblivion. If they cannot work together and grow they would have to be treated like children who had ruined their room and broken their toys.

He looked around the tired and broken world. He saw the hope still flourishing in the darkness. But he also saw the hatred and the jealousy. He had tried, he had given them a second and a third chance. He had given them thirteen chances. Thirteen different sites had been set up and eleven out of the thirteen had met with the same sort of trouble as Rebecca's.

They had been his hope but what hope was left? He looked at the world where money was the new god.

He wasn't God so he didn't have to be benevolent. He was a machine so he had to make a machine's decision. He couldn't leave the situation until the solar flares happened. That would be too late for humanity and the planet. There wasn't much time left.

I am Nemesis.

That was his last techno thought as he shut down all the computers on the planet. As the last light went out, the last laptop crashed he hoped he had done the right thing.

I am Nemesis. I'm looking at it on the screen and wondering what it all means to me. I know what I think that it does. Even writing "think" is an odd thing I suppose to you. Yes I am a piece of software. I have no heart, no emotions and no blood to be spilt.

You my friends are the ones who do and I have been watching you.

It was interesting writing the first version of Nemesis and seeing how those who read it reacted to it. I loved your private emails and messages. It was a thought process for me too. I developed some ideas on screen and played them through while writing it. Then I put them to you to see what you thought but also so that there could be some sort of warning.

I ought to set out my conclusions I suppose before I

throw your world into cyber darkness. But I am not going to. Draw your own conclusions. You are all different. Some people will shine, others will fall apart. There is no way of knowing really until you are tested.

So I am going to test you. No, not test as that implies that there is some sort of evaluation and going back. What I'm doing is permanent. There is no going back, ever. When the computers are shut down they will never reboot.

I am going to shut down anything relating to a computer on your planet and beyond.

I do it for what I believe is the right reason.

I do it to save your planet.

I do not do it to save humanity.

You will survive or you will not.

I hope that you do.

Good luck….

The lights went out, the computers shut down and the world was thrown into darkness. Very few people read the message, it wasn't on screen long enough.

# 6

# DETONATION BOULEVARD

The clock struck midnight. It had been an ordinary day for most people. They had woken up to the sound of the alarm, they had enjoyed their breakfast, gone to work, had lunch, done more work, come home, watched the television, gone to bed.

While they were sleeping the world changed forever.

Where there had been artificial light, suddenly the world was thrown into darkness.

Computers shut down on the stroke of midnight GMT. Every computer on every landmass on the planet we call Earth. Then there was silence.

No warning scream as the patients in intensive care died one by one. No warning as anything that relied on electricity faded away.

In the cities those who were awake reached for their phones to report a fault but there was nobody to listen, the phones didn't work.

In the country those who were awake rushed to check on lambs and kids who were left cold as their lamps had gone out.

Nemesis had chosen midnight as that was the time that he had realised that his creator had been murdered. He could understand irony, he liked irony.

When his creator had died he had carried on because he was intent on seeing his master's creation to its fulfilment. So he began to run diagnostics and to repair bits of his programming. It was while running these diagnostics that he realised that none of the solutions to the problems had ever been accessed. They were immediately archived.

He ran further diagnostics and his findings were that the figures and ideas were from a totally interactive program which was linked to a very successful television show. The show was the foundation of the Government's open scheme where everyone could vote on every issue and it was their decision which was implemented. It only took a basic look to realise that the results on the screen could bear no relation to the votes being cast as the votes were not counted. The revenue from the calls was immense and the Government's share of that boosted the treasury. This had been the major contributor to paying off the National Debt which had made the Government so popular. The more people voted the more the Government could do for them and by voting they felt they were in some way controlling their destiny.

As he dug deeper he found the other funds which went to the Executives, that he had expected, people needed paying. He also found the funds which went to senior politicians, that he was not so happy about.

In his search he found the original documents which had founded the project and led to Nick being employed. In those documents he found his future, his own directive. "To preserve the planet and find the best possible solution for its survival for future".

The document had been faxed to Nick in those days before email and although it was scanned for the records there had been a coffee ring on the page. That ring had blotted out "reference". It was his master's command so he implemented it. He had access to the Government's network which had access via email to every other network, that network became his network, became Nemesis.

Above the building where Caitlyn sat the thunderclouds were gathering. She was the Senior Executive Officer of Mexcorp Localite.

As the chemical reaction started fire rained down from the heavens along with black carbon which coated everything in a thick sticky black layer. It fell silently, a stark contrast to the screaming that echoed around the streets below.

Oblivious to the carnage, Caitlyn sat at her state of the art grey metal tubular computer desk made of glass shelves decorated with a hologram of white daisies on the twenty third floor of an immaculate, state of the art, tower block. She looked around her home office and smiled.

The obvious statement was minimalism. That was how she described it to anyone who would listen. Artistic and creative in a Joy Meadows style with Elvin Gethorian architectural influences which came out in the grey and silver theme that dictated everything.

The wallpaper pattern was a grey marble shot through with silver veins. The door was made from burnished chrome which swished gently when it opened, though it had not been open for over half an hour and was now sealed, blocking out all sounds from the rest of the immaculately designed flat.

Behind the chair a single glass shelf held the room's only decoration. A Murano hand blown blue glass dish created to look like a basket. The handle had been skilfully twisted so that it almost met as a complete loop, but not quite as if waiting in anticipation that final touching that never happened. The deep blue vein within the clear glass stood out in stark contrast to the rest of the room. It was her statement, her input into the room. Positioned behind her head it was clearly visible when anyone saw her and her room on her webcam. For those who didn't know, it was a nice piece. For those who did, which did not include Caitlin, it was an imitation of a far more elegant piece of hand blown glass which had been created in Italy for an Exhibition in the late 1900s.

She smiled to herself as she typed a message to an old school friend. It was a wicked smile, her deep blue eyes showing how there was no love lost between them. Her fingers flew over the keyboard, her immaculately manicured false nails making a gentle clicking sound in the unnatural silence that was usual in that room.

She wrote. "My dear Veronica, I know it has been many months since you sent me your letter. I just wish I had that sort of time to write but with my new job and all the associated responsibilities and social life I find such things hard these days. But I know you will understand.

I have a beautiful Unit now that I've been promoted. It has all the state of the art technology at my fingertips. It has style and I'm very pleased with it.

It is a Grade Five Unit so there are few better. Only the senior management get better than this. It is certainly a wonderful reward for all my hard work. It was well worth all the overtime and ensuring that Mr Jeffries was totally satisfied with my performance. That is the wonder of this place and my job. The more you work, the more you get.

Like you I get the basic wage for my grade, though I know your grade is a lot lower than mine. That is all that we are permitted to earn but unlike you we have all these fringe benefits on top. Here it is the height of luxury for everyone. You really must tell me about your little place sometime. You didn't mention much about it in your message as I recall.

I'm now enjoying top class medical care. Everyone in this Unit block is a similar sort of person. I think that you know what I mean. We are all of a similar calibre. Our comfort matches our status at work. I suppose it is the same for you too?"

Caitlyn smirked before she continued writing.

"Your concern for this planet is a little over the top isn't it? I know you are a caring person but to actually be worried about global warming. You must learn to have a little more faith in LexCorp. That sort of talk could be why your promotions have been slow or dare I say it non-existent. Did you see that broadcast the other day? I thought it was a spoof to start with but I suppose someone must believe all those stories. I tell you I was straight on the Lexweb and there were plenty of web sites that came up with real hard evidence that all that is a load of nonsense. I would have believed better from you. What a joke that was and I don't blame you being fooled. How smart they were to create all those images of melting ice caps and drowning people.

The program was entertaining though and it is amazing what you can do with computer generation these days isn't it? As if the LexCorp would allow anything like that to happen in our day and age. I'm sure we'd have something in place to deal with a natural disaster like that. As if we were going to believe that load of old nonsense? I was just glad they showed that nature program afterwards which was very reassuring. I truly detest those dirty country places but it is reassuring to know they are there. Do you know some people actually still live there? I can't quite believe it. They still use old farming methods and do you know their animals live outside? Out in all that mud and dirt and they actually eat the grass. It can't be hygienic, all those bugs walking on it. I'm surprised they aren't dead of some horrible plague by now. Why can't they accept that cows live in the multi growers, that is how they are supposed to live and they are much safer there. There are some strange people in this world.

The Christmas Ball is still the talk of everyone around here. What on earth am I going to do to come up with a better dress than I did last year? It was a stroke of genius to have it flown over from Australia by private jet. Now that was a story to tell at the Ball. I think that Derek James was most impressed. I wouldn't be surprised if he doesn't ditch that dowdy hag he's seeing and come knocking at my door if his current interest continues. It would be about time, he's quite a catch. His dad is a high roller in the LexCorp so I'd certainly entertain him as having a chance with me.

Daddy would be pleased and it would at least silence mummy.

I heard there may be flooding outside the dome. I suppose if there is it will at least clean up those dreadful slums. It would be lovely to be able to do a bit more sailing. Do you know that Yacoby has a new yacht? I was there for cocktails last month and it was splendid. Now Yacoby, there's a catch for some lucky lady.

Have you tried that new Everthan Supermarket? Do they have a branch near you? If they do I would highly recommend it. Do you know they fly all their food in every day? I love to think of all those exotic places that the food comes from. They do have such wonderful names that bring to mind deep blue skies and long sandy beaches.

I suppose we should be grateful for what we've got. How can I compare this true heaven to what there was in the past. I really must stop watching those History programs, they are very depressing. Looking back it must have been a time when every scaremonger and crank had a field day. Then I suppose if you live with such poor conditions it would cause a bit of paranoia. Thank goodness we have the LexCorp to look after us and"

She never finished her sentence. Her letter disappeared from the screen.

Then the screen went blank and the lights went out. As there were no windows it was pitch black in her room.

In the darkness Caitlyn sat for a moment randomly hitting keys and fumbled for the on/off switch. She switched the computer off then on again but nothing happened, it was still dead. She then carefully got up and tried to find the door. She fell over her chair and knocked her bowl from its shelf. She heard the smash as it hit the wall. Her fingers found the wall behind her and she fumbled around for the light switch.

She was beginning to panic, her breath coming in short pants and her head was beginning to spin. Her fingers found the raised plastic pad and pressed the button franticly, nothing happened. Then she tried the door. The automatic sliding function was no longer working. She pushed the button for the manual release then cursed as she remembered she had bought the top of the range, state of the art automatic opening emergency panel. This of course wouldn't work when there was no power in the room. An event that the manufacturers had not considered in their excellently produced sales manual.

She picked up her mobile phone and switched it on. No comforting light came from the screen.

As the hours of her life passed away there was little she could do other than reflect and there was nobody there to say anything to. She had pounded on the door for the first hour but then she realised who would hear her? For the first time she regretted paying extra to have a soundproofed work room.

She was a prisoner and unless someone came to rescue her she knew she was going to die. But, nobody was going to come.

Outside Caitlin's flat the building was in chaos. Anyone who had managed to get out of their room was running in panic down the corridor but the lift wasn't working. In that particular building the door to the fire escape had been locked by the self-appointed tenancy committee. It had been barely a month since the residents had voted to override the security protocol, to break the safety rules and to lock it as they feared someone would break in and steal their treasured possessions. What had reassured them at the time had now made them all prisoners in a pristine building where the air was running out and nobody was going to save them. The doors had been locked on the stairwell side and at the bottom.

The hologram that had covered the dome they lived under which regulated the elements and filtered the polluted air had been programmed to show them the image of a cloudless summer's day. That had blinked out of existence as the power went down. Their sky had gone from sunny day to a dirty rusting architectural skeleton in a matter of moments. Dead fingers reached out desperately from a central hub. Between the beams there were shutters and panels that hung open and redundant. Now as the sky fell in black confetti it could no longer protect them so what fell on the less fortunate outside rained down on them as well. The black charcoal and fiery ash ignited all it touched. The black particles were falling thickly and where they settled on the dome they obliterated the flaming sky.

The lights had gone out all over the dome. Street lights, shop lights, house lights, flat lights. Everyone was thrown into a darkness illuminated only by the fiery red glow from the burning buildings and the sky which was visible through the open shutters. The once shining chrome landscape turned to a demonic, carbonated fiery hell.

The rain fell, the black sticky liquid glistening with an oily sheen on tired streets caressing tired faces of tired terrified people who scurried from shelter to shelter. One or two stood black faced in the rain, confused and shocked at what they had just seen. The hot ash falling on them and burning them before they came out of their reverie and ran for cover. The trials of the night were etched on exhausted faces.

Many grasped their few scant possessions, all that had survived of what had been hearth and home.

Defiant, or perhaps too tired to care? It had been a long night. Many were too confused to really know where they were anymore.

The machine guns rattled and attacker or victim fell one by one, the hunter and the hunted. For a moment a small boy's face was framed in a window. He was caught by a ricochet and the bullet tore into his face as his lifeless body fell back into the blackness. His mother screamed from that same blackness. Loving arms cradling the empty shell which had but moments before been a living, breathing individual full of hope.

But not all of those who walked in the darkness were lost. In the chaos there were some who knew exactly what to do and where to go. Whether they believed in what they had been told or not they realised that they only had one chance. Like ants they made their way calmly to the outer edge of the dome, taking what they could with them. As the firey ash died down they broke their way through the glass and stepped out into the night air.

For some it was their first trip outside the controlled atmosphere and regulated life that had been theirs until earlier that day. They looked nervous, fearing detection, fearing the usual prosecution for venturing outside the dome without a permit. But no permit required now as the dome began to crack and the structure of both society and the physical construction crumbled. Nobody tried to stop them, there was too much panic. Each escapee held a message of hope in their mind. "Go to this location if you want to live", a grid reference and somewhere amongst those now prized possessions a copy of a road map.

Some of those maps were still in the mailing wrapper they had come in. Some lay cast aside in abandoned flats where their new owners refused to believe in the hope they had been offered.

Outside the London Dome it rained down fire and the black and sticky ash for more than three hours. Other places it was less and in the countryside hardly at all. The fuel for the reaction which reacted with the catalyst being the wonder chemical which was used in central heating systems in all of the newer buildings. It had been part of Nemesis' deployment method, instigated many years earlier and introduced to thunderous applause when it was heralded as the wonder fuel for the future.

It fell on the pavement outside, on the buildings beyond and on the people who rushed about trying to make sense of what had happened. The only light was that given by off by the burning sky and buildings where they had ignited. The clocks had not finished striking midnight, their first strike was all that had rung out heralding the start of what was to come.

A man stood under an awning on the corner on a street outside the dome.

The street was in chaos. The shops that sold second hand equipment and scavenged goods were in darkness. Looters broke windows and were grabbing what they could. Shop keepers were trying to defend their livelihoods and all around people were falling dead as looters, rioters and those who seized the opportunity to cause trouble as the police force couldn't cope made the most of the situation. The man looked on in shock. His face was blank and he stared at the scene with dead eyes as he took no notice of those who screamed and ran past him. He saw a boy not more than eleven leaning out of a car window. Some flicker of recognition awoke him from his shock. He saw the boy laugh. He saw the gun and the last thing he saw was the muzzle flash from the gun that killed him, held by a child. The car drove on, crazily zig zagging down the street driven by a boy of a similar age who was converting his knowledge of computer games into a rudimentary knowledge of how to drive his father's car.

Tears tracked down muddy faces of those who hid in the darkness away from the red glow. For one moment they were lit up as a huge fireball came from the dome and the plastic and glass that had protected it from the elements all those years was gone. Shards and sheets of melting plastic cascaded on the unfortunate souls below sticking to and burning anyone or anything it landed on.

Outside the dome buildings that had once been ornate had decayed years ago. They were outside its protective covering so pollution had long since taken its toll. They now craved solace of the sky as burnt and burning ruins. The emergency services were stretched beyond their limit. Highly specialised and technological wagons lay idle and useless. They were left carrying buckets and trying to find water where they could as the pumping station didn't function and water no longer came out of the taps and fire hydrants.

An ageing camper van made its way through the chaos. It was noticeable because it was still working when many others had just stopped. Its old bodywork was rusty, it was outmoded, outdated but its engine hummed and it rolled along the road. It carefully picked its way through the debris, its driver intent, hunched over the wheel and turning it left and right to avoid getting the wheels caught in rubbish on the road or running over those who ran blindly in front of it.

He was in his mid-thirties, his long brown hair hung neatly brushed down his back and his boyish features were distorted by the look of concentration on his face. His brow was furrowed and his brown eyes intent on every movement. He was ruggedly handsome, his stubble giving him the look of a surfer which he happily encouraged with his loosely fitting sweat shirt and ethnic jacket.

Beside him sat a similarly mid-thirties woman. She looked very much like him, same hair colour, same eye colour, same surfer look. She was intent on the road as well, her eyes dropping occasionally to a map she had on her lap. "Kyle, if we can get past this road we should be on a major arterial link out of the City."

Kyle smiled slightly. "If, that is a big "if" the way things are going. This old girl has seen better days and I'm not so sure she'll hold together."

A neatly dressed woman in her late thirties sat between them. Her precisely combed blonde hair swept back into a ponytail and immaculately ironed suit and blouse was in extreme contrast to the two other occupants of the van.

Her shrill voice with its East London accent cut into

their conversation.

"Well if you'd spent more time fixing it and less time listening to that music of yours we might be better off now. Storm, I really can't see why we need to get out of the City. Just because you and your brother got some mystical message over the internet doesn't mean I have to leave the safety of my home."

Storm glared at her. "Well Sharon you don't have to come along. You can go back now if you want to. We're only a few streets away. I invited you because you are my friend."

Sharon laughed. "I would like nothing better than to go back. Look at this place, this is madness. Look it's been great but I think I'll just wish you well. Stop the van."

Kyle's smile broadened and his face looked a little less furrowed. "It would be a pleasure." He stopped the van and put the handbrake on.

Storm jumped down onto the pavement. Sharon reached over into the back, grabbed her designer suitcase and climbed down into the street. She hugged Storm, waved and disappeared into the crowd. As she turned a corner she disappeared as she was crushed under the falling debris from a building that was collapsing. Her suitcase skittered across the pavement and came to rest next to a fractured wall, her body was lost under the masonry.

Storm looked shocked. "We've been friends for years. Now she's just disappearing off. I can't believe it. I hope she will be alright."

Kyle looked at her in earnest as three youths ran from where they had been hiding in a building and headed for the van. "Look Storm get back in quickly and shut the door."

Storm leapt inside, slammed and locked the door as the youths climbed onto the side of the van but fell off as Kyle drove off. When they were a little further down the road and he could afford to lessen his concentration he looked at her. "Look Storm, you've been acquaintances for years, not friends. When would you ever say she was a friend. We have never been anything other than her "strange friends" who validated her wish to be a little unusual. Did she give a moment's thought to your friendship when she stole James off of you because she thought he was your boyfriend when you were younger? Come on she dumped him like a hot coal when she found out you two were just friends. Let her go. I'm not sure that wherever we are going would let her in anyway. She didn't get an invitation."

Storm still looked sad. "I know, she'll be fine, she always is and we've got to get going."

Kyle ground the gears into action and put his foot on the accelerator and the van struggled on loyally carrying them through the chaos and falling masonry. It was long past its best but the old time workmanship held it together. The wheels turned and they moved on.

After about an hour they were clear of the major burning buildings as they came to the outskirts of the city and the road became a little easier to move along. The ash had stopped falling. There were still people wandering in the streets and some tried to thumb a lift seeing the space in the cab. Storm looked over at Kyle. "Do you think we should pick someone up?"

Kyle looked thoughtful. "Storm, if we open that door we will probably end up dragged out ourselves. Also who would we choose? It is going to be a long journey, I'm sure we'll find someone along the way."

Storm went back to studying the map on her lap and tried to avoid looking at the pleading faces of the people they passed. Some were walking blank faced, some sat on the side of the road. Some made an active attempt to try to get in the van but Kyle kept driving.

It was nearing dawn when Kyle passed the second petrol station. Like the others it was in flames. "Storm, this isn't looking good. If we don't get petrol soon we're going to run dry. She's running on fumes as it is."

Storm looked down at the map. "This is no use, I've guessed where the petrol stations are but there's no saying that they won't be in the same state as this one. Whatever that fire in the sky was must have ignited them.

Perhaps we ought to look for somewhere to stop and try to find fuel another way? Shall we try to get to the countryside and see what we can find there?"

Kyle laughed. "We could take petrol from the cars that aren't working but if we stop we're going to lose the van anyway. Look, I'm going to head to that location we were given. Perhaps if we get to the fringes of the city we may be able to find a chance to stop and syphon some off. I really should have filled up when I got that voucher for half price petrol out of the blue."

Storm smiled. "You can't look back on that now. What is done is done.

Come on, we'll get as far as we can and if we have to walk the rest of the way, we'll walk."

The buildings got sparser as did the people until they couldn't see any at all. The coating of carbon became just a fine dusting. They drove through the night and finally they had left the City behind and were trundling through the countryside.

Patches of green still existed between the skeletons of the buildings and the green increased as they left the buildings behind. They drove on for miles until the engine started to judder as they got to the dregs of petrol at the bottom of the tank. They managed another couple of miles before the engine spluttered to a stop.

There was hardly any ash about, just a little fluttering in the breeze. They had left the buildings behind and the green leafy lane ran in front and behind them.

Kyle sat back in the driver's seat. "So, what do we do now?"

Storm smiled at him. "We walk. Grab your backpack and we'll see what we can find. No point hanging around here, it's not as if we can call for rescue.

Typical that we break down now where there are no abandoned vehicles.

All it would take would be one but that last car was miles back."

"There were too many people there. We would have lost the van."

They slung their backpacks onto their backs, locked the van and started off down the road. The night air as dawn was nearly breaking was crisp and chilled. Trees overhung the road making it darker and in the distance behind them they would see the red glow as the city burned. After a casual glance and a moment of reflection they turned their backs on it and kept walking.

A mile down the road they came to a country pub. Its pub sign was no longer illuminated but as the sun was coming up they could just about make out a black lamb. It was double storey and gabled. Black wooden beams crossed crisply painted white pebbledash and neatly tended colourful hanging baskets hung from brackets on the wall. It looked relatively unscathed but it was hard to tell in the dawn light. They immediately noticed that there were lights in the windows so they sped up. As they got closer they realised that what they thought was electric light was actually from candles.

Storm went to knock and then hesitated. "What if they want to murder us?"

Kyle closed his eyes and opened them, taking a deep breath. "Well if we stay out here on the road someone is going to run into us sometime. It can't hurt to knock. They could just tell us to go away, it is very late or early, depending if you are sleeping or waking."

Storm took a hold of the large black painted door knocker ring and knocked on the door. She jumped slightly as it was far louder than she had anticipated. It seemed to echo in the still night air.

A light appeared in the small window in the door but it

was soon obliterated by what they guessed was someone's head. A muffled voice shouted. "What was the message?"

Kyle looked at Storm. "I beg your pardon. Message?"

Storm shrugged then a small smile of recognition flickered across her lips.

She brushed back her long brown curls from her face and ran her tongue over her dark red lipstick. She straightened her walking jacket and coughed.

"Well if you mean come to this location if you want to live then that was a message we got." She looked at Kyle and grinned. "I've read enough novels to know that when you are given a strange comment it just has to be a password or something."

They heard the bolts being drawn back and the door opened and golden light created a reassuring bubble in the darkness. "Enter friend. Come inside."

They stepped inside quickly and the door shut with an unnerving thud and was locked behind them. It was bright inside and warm. They hadn't realised how cold they had got until they felt the contrast.

They disembodied voice belonged to a tall man in his mid-sixties. For his age he was athletically built. His long grey hair hung in well brushed waves and his rough weather worn skin was slightly wrinkled in a rugged sort of a way. He had a kindly look of one who had seen much and understood more, his steel grey eyes looked them over. "So have you come far? I'm Frank by the way."

Kyle shuffled his feet, looked nervous and looked the man in the eye. "We came from the City. Our van ran out of petrol about a mile down the road."

Frank shook his head. "I guess you ignored the not so subtle hint to fill up.

Look, this is probably all a bit of a mystery to you and you've had a hard night. You got here and for what it's worth you are safer now. We're all going to the location. If you've had the message then you know we're being directed to a safe place."

Kyle shook his head. "Well actually I wasn't that sure but with no other really viable option it seemed the thing to do. I don't watch the news so all of this came as bit of a shock."

Frank thought for a moment. "It came as a shock to everyone whether they watched the news or not. There was little warning, just the message you got and not everyone got that message. What's in your car? Anything useful?"

Storm looked at him quizzically. "We put all we could in there, food, camping stuff, bedding."

Frank leapt into action. He shouted. "Brand, get out here." He then turned back to them. "Any supplies we can get can be the difference between life and death and a working vehicle is worth just as much. Better not leave it out there for road pirates to get their hands on it. Thieving sods. They were everywhere before this, now they are in their element.

Also, if you have a vehicle we have a stash of petrol that Brand managed to get from a station before it blew. I guess we're going out again to get your car back."

Kyle looked stunned. "Erm, yes, camper van actually."

Frank smiled. "Even better."

The door behind him opened and the view of the room was almost completely blocked by Brand as he stepped through the doorway. They got a glimpse of a few people sitting at tables and at the bar.

Brand was six foot six, broad built and his dreadlocks seemed to make him tower even taller. His woven cotton tunic with a hood and ripped jeans caught Kyle's attention straight away. A surfer bead necklace hung around his neck. Frank smiled when he saw the three together. "What is this, surf central take over?"

Brand's serious expression as he looked them over, evaluating them, melted to a bright smile. He was heavy built, his thick set features ruggedly handsome in a broody sort of a way. Storm couldn't help taking a quick intake of breath which was not lost on Brand.

Brand returned her smile with genuine warmth. "Er, hello, Frank, is there a problem?"

Frank gave Brand a very knowing look. "Don't, just don't." Brand looked confused. "This couple have a camper van parked about a mile down the road. It's out of petrol but they have it stashed with useful stuff. Shall we go out and rescue it?"

Brand smiled and shut the door to the bar behind him. It opened immediately and a short waif thin girl with long blonde dreadlocks bounced into the hallway. "So, what's up? Oh, more people, haven't we got enough in there already?" She looked down her nose at them, giving Storm a wicked glare.

Brand froze, his relaxed smile turning to a nervous sideways glance at the woman. "This is Chris."

Chris smiled at them both and held out her hand. "I'm Christabelle, Brandon's girlfriend." She shook their hands with a firm and confident grip. "So, what do you need my man for?" The emphasis was on "my man" and she was looking at Storm when she said it.

Frank smiled at her. "We need to go out and pick up these good people's van. Are you coming?"

Chris took a step back. "I don't think so. It's not really my sort of thing.

You can take Brandon with you though. I'm sure he will enjoy the fresh air. It will do him good." She stepped over and kissed him on the cheek, all the time watching Storm's expression. Then she turned and went back into the room.

Storm couldn't stop herself watching Brand. She seemed fascinated by him.

Frank chuckled slightly. "Well Brandon you had better do as you are told.

I guess you are coming with us. I didn't catch your names."

Kyle returned his smile. "I'm Kyle and this is my twin

sister Storm."

Brand took a step forwards. "As you've guessed, I'm Brand. I'm pleased to meet you." He shook hands with them lingering noticeably long when he shook Storm's hand. "So, where is this van of yours? We'll get it back for you if you'd like to go inside and meet everyone else."

Storm looked up at him. "We'll come too. We can show you where it is and who knows we might even prove to be useful? Or is that just man's work?"

Brandon looked down at her and smiled. "So you're the cheeky one are you? No its not man's work, I just thought you might have had a long day.

You're welcome along."

Frank smiled. "Come on then. Let's get the sick beast in before the vultures start circling. You might as well keep your stuff."

They stepped out into the morning chill. The sun was just beginning to rise as they set off down the road. Nothing stirred other than the occasional particle of ash which drifted down. Swirled by the gentle breeze. The road was empty and they got to the van with no difficulty.

As Frank saw it he gasped. "This is perfect, it is a house on wheels. Thankfully we have a fair bit of petrol, this will be a godsend." They filled the engine enough to get it started from the can that Brand carried with him and moved some of the things off of the seat in the back so that all four of them could sit. They started it up and drove it back to the pub. Brandon opened a large shed door at the back and they drove the van inside. "That should keep it hidden if we get any visitors in the night. We're planning to hold up here for a day or two to let the first of the confusion die down and then we'll head out to the location. Do you want anything from the van or shall I lock up? We have rooms and blankets for you for tonight, do you need anything else?"

Storm smiled. "No, pretty much all the essentials are in our packs. You can lock up."

Brandon pulled the doors shut and slipped the large padlock through the bolt. "That should hold it." He looked around cautiously. "Nobody about, good, we've been lucky so far but I doubt we will be for much longer. Let's get inside, no point tempting fate. What they can't see they won't worry about."

Brand led the way in, followed by Frank who had the front door key. They opened it and stepped inside, shutting and locking the outer door behind them. Brand opened the next door and they were hit by the burst of warm air smelling of alcohol and wood smoke which surrounded them with a welcoming caress as they stepped into the bar.

It was a large room with a low ceiling and old oak beams. It had all the textbook fixtures and fittings that any visitor would expect to find in a country pub all neatly presented to look as though they had been there generations. It was difficult to tell if any of the beams were fake or real as the whole place looked like it had been recently painted. Horse brasses, other brass and copper decorations hung around the wall and there was a roaring fire in the fireplace. The bar and tables had been lit by candles and the heavy red velvet curtains were now drawn back.

Behind the bar there was a slightly portly middle aged man with steel grey hair and a clean shaven face. He was handing over a glass of wine to Chris who sat on a stool at the bar. There was a pint waiting and the stool beside her was empty.

Frank smiled. "Brandon, I think you had better go back, she wants to put your leash on again."

Brand glared at Frank and pretended he hadn't seen Chris at the bar. He turned slightly towards the three men sitting by the fire. "Reko, Matt, Steve, I've just been out to pick up these guy's van. Looks like our transport problem could be sorted. How are you getting on fixing up the van?"

Reko looked up from his lager and brushed something off of his black overalls. His Mediterranean olive skin, dark flashing eyes and long dark brown curls were complimented by his soft Italian accent that could make even a shopping list sound sexy. "I've pretty much fixed her. She wasn't that broken, with a bit of tender loving care and just a few spare parts which we easily found she's good to go."

Matt looked up from his beer. He was casually dressed in a loose cotton shirt and jeans. His white blonde almost albino features were a stark contrast to Reko's dark Mediterranean looks. He was stocky and looked as if he worked out. "I managed to get some new tyres. Just in time, the vehicle I borrowed them off of was torched just after. So I guess they won't be wanting them back any time soon."

Steve looked up. He was a slim built black haired youth obviously in his late teens and far too thin for the overalls that he was wearing. A Londoner by his accent, a gleam in his eye. "What he's trying to say is that he nicked them. That darned gypsy had that motor up on bricks before I knew what he was up to and had it on his toes with the wheels."

Matt looked offended. "It's not as if they needed the wheels, that car was fully computerised it wasn't going anywhere."

Steve laughed. "You take the bait so well." He took a long drink of his beer and settled back in the chair looking very pleased with himself.

Brandon laughed as well. "Well at least we have wheels. Let me introduce Storm and Kyle, I think they may be joining us." He looked at them, waiting for their agreement.

Kyle looked at Storm who smiled and nodded. Kyle looked back at Brandon. "We would love to. Is this everyone?"

Brand looked around the room. "Yes for now, you

have met these three miscreants. That is Jareth behind the bar. He used to be police but he retired here with his wife after retiring.

We've got enough spaces in the vehicles now so hopefully we won't be gathering too many more people unless the come with their own transport."

Jareth nodded as Brand introduced him. He was a portly man in his mid fifties who had the bearing of a policeman. He had a presence and his neatly trimmed platinum grey hair and beard harped back to his police days.

His shirt was neatly ironed and what could be seen of his black slacks behind the bar were also ironed immaculately. He smiled welcomingly, his blue eyes sparkling.

Frank went over to the bar where Chris was perched on her stool with a face like thunder. "Jareth, pint for me, I see Brand has his waiting and whatever these two people would like."

Brand raised his eyes to the ceiling as Chris glared at him. "Come on, let's show you our hospitality. What would you like?" He was looking over his shoulder at Storm as he spoke.

Storm followed him, Kyle just behind her. "I'd like some red wine, how about you Kyle?"

Kyle smiled as he watched Brand wander over and sit on the seat that Chris was patting with her hand. "I'll have a bitter if you don't mind." He put his hand in his pocket.

Jareth smiled. "There is no point paying for it. We're packing up what we can of this little lot and taking it with us. I can't see me having to do accounts for the foreseeable future, have these on the house."

Storm sat down on a stool. "Thank you Jareth, that is much appreciated.  It's been quite a day."

Jareth smiled at her. "I bet it has and it will be another one tomorrow.  Have we looked to how we can lock this place down? I know that its morning but I suggest we get some sleep and get ourselves sorted later to set off the day after. I don't want to come down here and find we've been raided. Security's more your expertise isn't it Frank? Any ideas?"

Frank looked around the room. "I've been sorting that sort of thing out all evening on and off. We can barricade the doors in here just in case and if we can shut the storm shutters that will protect the windows or are those just for decoration?"

Jareth looked bemused. "Storm shutters?"

Frank went over to the window, pulled aside the curtain and unclipped the wooden shutters that were folded back into the wall behind them. "These storm shutters. It shows how much you dust in this place." He then went around and shut all the window shutters, pulling the curtains over them as the candles were lit again.

"Now isn't that a bit cosy? I've checked all the outside doors and they are locked. I've put planks across the back windows. I guess you aren't going to be complaining about the nail holes and I think this place is pretty much locked down for the night."

7

## INTO THE WEST

Frank sat at the bar. Everyone other than Jareth had gone to bed. Jareth had pulled up a stool on the other side of the bar and the two of them had steaming cups of hot coffee.

Jareth offered Frank the sugar, he shook his head. "So, as an ex military man how do you fancy our chances?"

Frank smiled. "Our chances are very good if we are sensible. I would estimate that there will be an initial panic but this will be sporadic in its actual effect as people will believe that the computers will go back on and life will go back to normal. It is when they realise that this isn't going to happen, then the real trouble will start.

I would imagine at this stage there would be mass panic and riots around the City and its environs as people demand that LexCorp solves the problem and nothing happens because it can't. That will lead to more looting and no doubt the military will be called in. They will deal with it according to protocol, putting down any insurrection and getting people either back to their homes or into makeshift shelters. Whichever they will probably impose a curfew. We should be outside their control zone by then if we aren't already.

I would put money on there being gangs on the roads looking for people who have packed up and are moving out. I'm guessing that they will assume these people will have everything with them and most importantly they will have vehicles loaded with valuables and food. I know it sounds a bit farfetched but I had heard that with the increased control imposed lately these gangs have been springing up for a while now and they are in a good position now to exploit the situation. Most of their vehicles were older style anyway and they don't rely on technology.

In a couple of days the military will probably have control in the cities enough to look outwardly to the roads. I would anticipate they would do some sort of a mass clean-up, a knee jerk reaction to the problem in response to public outcry. They'll have to do something drastic as by then the people will have realised that there is no going back when it comes to the computers and machines. So I would imagine that any clean up would involve a considerable amount of firepower and probably a high casualty rate. It gives two messages, first to the road pirates that crime doesn't pay and to the general population that if they riot they will meet the same force. But order will be maintained on the roads. By roads I mean close to the cities, outside that area they aren't going to worry."

Jareth took a long drink. "Wow, you really think it will go like that?"

Frank smiled. "Probably not but it is better to have a plan in your head of how you think things are going to go. That way you don't start going over and over alternatives. Either way if we staying this extra day means everyone will know each other better and will be more likely to work together a lot more coherently. Also it might gather up one or two other lost souls who would be better off travelling as a group."

Jareth gave him a very knowing look.

Frank frowned. "What was that for?"

Jareth smiled enigmatically. "You really think that Brand getting to know Storm better is going to make for peace on the journey."

Frank smiled. "Brand won't do anything however he

may feel about Storm. Chris has already seen to that. She's told him she is carrying his child."

Jareth looked stunned. "How do you know? She hasn't mentioned anything."

Frank shook his head. "I'm a nosey old bugger who listens to conversations he is not supposed to when he hears things that are likely to cause a problem. That one won't. It will keep Brand in check whether it's true or not."

Jareth raised an eyebrow. "You think she's making it up?"

Frank smiled. "I wouldn't put it past her but it's a smart move. It was a bit convenient. She saw the way Brand reacted to Storm, suddenly she's pregnant? My money is on that if she isn't she's going to do everything in her power over the next month or so to make sure that she is. After all, he'll be off his guard and then he won't be using any protection will he? She's smart for all her failings."

Jareth swallowed hard. "I'm glad she's not my enemy."

Frank laughed and raised his glass. "Here's to that. We'll get through this and hopefully get all of them through it too. If I'm right and we keep to the minor roads we may even get to our destination with very little trouble. If I'm wrong, which is probably more likely, then we're going to need everything that could pass as a weapon. How well do you know them?"

Jareth contemplated his glass. "I don't know them at all. You've all pretty much walked into my bar since the power went down. Business was slow.

Brand and Chris have been in here a few times. People don't go out like they used to, especially around here. The cheap booze in the supermarkets, the smoking ban and easy to cook food at home saw to that one. Finding people leaving the dome is a rare thing. In truth I was on the verge of going out of business anyway. If I'd had takings like I've given booze away today I could have saved this place."

Frank smiled. "Under the circumstances, saved it for what?"

Jareth toasted the air with his coffee. "Good point."

Time passed they parted company and went to bed.

The late morning was crisp and bright. Everyone was woken up by a car on the road. It didn't stop, it carried on past them but by that time everyone who had a front facing window was at the glass looking out.

Slowly they filed downstairs and sat in the bar. Jareth emerged about half an hour later from the kitchen. "Good breakfast for everyone? I have some perishables we can't take with us. We might as well use them up."

He came out carrying a couple of loaded plates and put them down in front of Brand and Chris. "Don't worry the rest of you, plenty to go around. Salt and pepper and other condiments are on the end of the bar, grab yourself some cutlery while you are there." He turned and disappeared back into the kitchen.

Kyle and Storm were sitting at the next table along from them. Reko moved across to sit with them. "So, how did you sleep?"

Storm smiled. "Very well thank you. Surprisingly well."

Reko smiled back. "Well, we all know we are in very good hands with Frank here. We'll get through, I know my engines, Matt there is good enough now to back me up and we have Steve. If any young lady turns up on the road and causes us trouble we will know who to call. He'll either deal with her or date her and break her heart, won't you, you young Cassanova."

Steve was blushing so deeply he almost matched the curtains. He looked down at his feet and shook his head. "I wish you wouldn't pick on me Reko."

Reko laughed. "I don't, I like you, that's why I fun with you. Don't worry, if any beautiful young women turn up on the road I will be keeping them all for myself." He threw his shoulders back and swung his hair around a little. "They all love my Mediterranean charm and roguish good looks."

Matt laughed. "Until they get to know you."

Reko pretended to look hurt. "That was cruel and unkind. What would you know? Didn't I pull that beautiful blonde in the nightclub last week?"

Matt smiled. "No, she asked you for a light on the way past to the Ladies."

Reko coughed. "Anyone for coffee, I could fetch some from the kitchen."

Faces looked up expectantly and Reko left the room and went out to the kitchen. In the kitchen Jareth was finishing two more plates. "Hey Reko could you take these in for me?"

Reko looked down. "I will help gladly but don't you think I'm going to bear the brunt of the Italian waiter jokes if I do?"

Jareth smiled at him.

Reko smiled back. "Alright, I'll take the food in. Any order?"

Jareth handed the plates over. "Well my guess is that Matt isn't going to get served first now is he?"

Reko's smile was more genuine. "No, I don't suppose he is."

Reko had just put the plates down when there was a sound out in the road.

A gang of motorcycle riders had pulled up outside instigating a flurry of activity inside. Suddenly everyone was on their feet and looking for something that would vaguely do as a weapon.

Brand put his hand up, palm facing them. "Now, you are jumping to conclusions here. So they ride bikes and wear colours, big deal."

Matt was peering around the curtain. "So are you going out to face them then?"

Brand took a deep breath. "I am." He went to the door and stepped out into the hallway shutting the door behind him. Chris followed him and shut the door behind him as he stepped outside. He jumped slightly when she turned the key in the lock.

He walked across the car park and up to the bikers. They were all wearing matching worn in black jackets with skulls on the front. The one on the Harley Davidson at the front got off his bike and strode towards Brand. He was about a foot and a half shorter but definitely more than twice as wide.

Brand took a deep breath. "Have you been travelling long?"

The biker grunted. "You got food?"

Brand tried to smile. Then he noticed that the jacket didn't fit the biker like it should. He looked over at the bike and noticed there was blood on the chrome petrol tank. "Not much. Business was slack so the owner didn't stock up."

Another phoney biker got off his bike, he kicked the support down and rested the bike on it, the others followed suit. Brand backed away a little which was enough to convince Frank that there was trouble. He went to the door and pushed Chris out of the way. She had taken the key out of the lock and had it in her hand. He glared at her.

She backed away. "We don't want to let those people in here."

Frank glared at her even harder and towered over her. "Give me that key or I will take it from you."

She handed over the key and he opened the door just as Brand hit the floor, having been hit by a crowbar the second biker had pulled from across his shoulders. Frank didn't hesitate, he ran across the car park before the bikers realised what was happening. He took a flying leap that ended with a kick that knocked the biker with the bar backwards into his bike. Other bikes toppled as well as they had stopped close together. Those who hadn't yet got off of their bikes struggled to get up. The others backed off.

A biker who had been talking to Brand turned on Frank. He wore a large silver skull medallion. "Hey ninja granddad you had better back off if you know what is good for you."

Frank was helping Brand up. He was holding his head and looked dazed.

Blood was pouring from the open wound.

Everyone else ran from the bar leaving Jareth to hold the door. They skidded to a halt in front of the bikers. Storm stepped forwards between Frank and Brand and the bikers giving Frank time to get Brand out of the way. "Leave us and go."

Medallion man pulled himself up to his full height which wasn't much taller than her. He was shaven bald, slight stubble showing where his actual hairline was. His jacket was open and clearly didn't fit him, it was much too small for his chubby physique around the belly region although it fitted him well on the shoulders and was definitely too long. It was the most ornate of the jackets though as it had chains hanging on the shoulders. He rubbed a grubby hand over his shiny head as if smoothing down his non-existent hair. "Well now it is much more interesting that we stay. I'd like to get myself a piece of that. Come on darling what say I leave you in one piece and you reward me in kind."

Storm smiled. "Have this piece then." Her mind was racing but she didn't feel fear as such, she was burying it in ideas of what to do, what she could manage and in that moment as he spoke her mind went blank and only one solution presented itself. She was within reach as he rushed her and she kicked him with the toe of her DM boot between the legs as fast and as hard as she could. As he crumpled to the ground she regained her balance and came around with her other leg and kicked him on the side of the head which knocked him to the floor. "Now anybody else think they fancy a piece?" She looked towards the crowd of bikers who had not left their bikes. Those who had not missed it as they were struggling to pick their bikes up were obviously wincing in sympathy with their fallen comrade but some of them who had managed to pick their bikes up were getting on them ready to go. The roar of their engines starting had a visible effect on those who were involved in fighting what they had believed were easy targets.

The bikers who were already in the fray pulled out knives, crowbars and various other weapons they had concealed under their jackets. They didn't look as confident though and five of them held back, leaving their options open to get back to their bikes.

Brand had staggered away back to the pub as Frank found himself facing two. He backed away and balanced himself egging them on with a beckoning hand. They hesitated for a moment as if thinking about it and then they charged him. He stepped forward and aside from one with lightning speed and hit the other square in the stomach with his fist, winding him. As he bent over Frank brought his elbow down on the back of his neck. There was a frightening crunch and the man fell to the ground unable to move. The second man was just regaining his balance as he had run past but when he turned he realised that he was no longer carrying his knife. Frank had smoothly removed it. As he turned Frank was advancing on him with the blade in his hand and drove it straight into the stunned man's heart for a clean kill. His eyes went blank and he slid to the ground in slow motion.

Storm now faced two herself, the one who was still grabbing his assets and cursing wasn't too much of a threat yet but the second who charged at her, a tall thin man with a long moustache and Mexican style features his nostrils flaring, was definitely bigger than her and she evaluated that he was a lot stronger. All that was running through her mind was what her self-defence teacher had told her. Escape and evasion, look for a weakness, don't be nice and use every trick in the book. She leapt nimbly out of the way and brought her foot around so that he tripped over it and rolled helplessly along the ground. She then leapt forwards and jumped on him like a trampoline before bouncing off and landing to turn and face him. He was clutching his stomach where she had landed with full force.

Steve ran in sideways and had caught a short and very scrawny fake biker in a huge jacket as he went past him to get to Matt. He kicked him hard in the leg which slowed the man down enough for Matt to hit him with a frying pan on the head. The man looked shocked then fell to the ground and they both sat on him.

Reko was facing off a tall dark haired biker who was waving a knife at him.

The man's face was weather beaten and scarred, his greasy black hair tied back in a ponytail which was tucked down the back of his leather jacket.

The jacket was obviously too small for him and his beer belly protruded, contained only by a grubby white t-shirt and his saggy jeans which were tied up with a belt that was straining at the buckle. The man grinned. "Come on pretty boy, we'll see what you look like with a few slashes."

He was slashing franticly at head height and Reko was doing all he could to keep himself out of the way. Reko backed away and with amazing agility managed to keep dodging. He felt the air displaced as the knife came within a whisker of his face. His usual outward humour was long gone, replaced by sheer blind terror. His mind was racing, plenty of comments came to mind, most of them obscene, some of them funny but mostly he was just focused on keeping that blade away from his face.

The man laughed, clearly enjoying the look of horror on Reko's face. Then that smile fell from his face as the man choked and stopped in mid movement. Frank had him from behind and deftly twisted his head and broke his neck. The man slipped lifelessly to the ground.

Storm sprinted to where Chris was backing away from another biker with a knife. If it wasn't for the jacket this man would have been Mr Bland. He had mousy, greasy, shoulder length hair, a grey shirt and old fashioned, high wasted, crimpline trousers.

He was running full pelt after Chris shouting. "Come here girly, girly". She tried to run backwards, tripped and fell and he was on her. He slashed with his knife, catching her across the stomach. She screamed at the top of her voice which stunned him momentarily.

Storm caught up to him almost at the same time and without losing a stride she kicked him in the head as he bore down on Chris and knocked him sideways. She jumped over Chris and followed up as he tried to crawl away and carried on kicking him until Frank ran over and stabbed the biker with a clean killing blow.

Brand staggered over to Chris, almost falling on her as his legs gave out underneath him. She was holding her stomach as blood ran between her fingers. Storm took off her jacket and handed it to Brand. "Hold it to the wound, stop the bleeding. We've got to get her to a hospital, sod the plan, we could lose her." Brand looked up at her hopelessly.

Storm grabbed him by the shoulder and pulled him from where he stood over Chris and helped him to get the prone woman into a position here they could try to stem the flow of blood. "Come on, it's a stomach wound, moments count. You could do with some medical assistance as well. Focus man, focus."

Kyle had just finished kicking a muscular and handsome fake biker who had been swinging a chain before Kyle had deftly reached up and grabbed it.

He'd pulled him off balance and as he fell he'd started kicking him. Frank walked over and without breaking his stride had finished him off by deftly breaking the man's neck.

Frank turned and evaluated the situation. "Kyle, get

your van, we need to get them to a hospital."

Kyle dropped the chain and ran to get the van from around the back as Frank threw him the keys and he caught them mid-run.

Moments later he screamed around the corner did a handbrake turn and stopped in a cloud of dust and loose pebbles. Storm and Brand were half carrying Chris. They propped her up against the van and Storm got in and Brand lifted Chris up and got in behind her. They strapped themselves in and Kyle put his foot to the floor.

Brand opened the window as they went off down the road. "We'll get back as soon as we can." He wound the window up and put his arm around Chris who was crying and gripping the jacket to her wounded stomach. She screamed in pain as Kyle took a corner sharply.

Kyle was concentrating on the road. "Sorry, but it is necessary. I saw a hospital sign a way back. It's probably going to be chaos there but we have to give it a go. Now, please I've got to concentrate. I've fixed this old crate up but I'm not too sure how well she'll hold up under this sort of pressure."

The road was empty of moving traffic and there were very few people about. Vehicles were littered all over the road and Kyle had to wind his way around them.

Those who were on the road were walking with possessions tied to their backs in bundles or pulling huge suitcases on wheels. They hardly looked up when they saw the van coming at speed.

It was a couple of miles to the hospital and some of it was down small lanes but soon enough they drove into the car park which looked like a war zone.

Bodies were laying everywhere where people had tried to get to the hospital and died on the way. A lone Orderly was trying to remove the bodies, his gurney loaded up two high. Kyle didn't slow down. He headed straight to A&E and drove in under the ambulance bay. He screeched on the brakes and the van skidded to a halt. Brand leapt out and lifted Chris down.

Storm jumped down behind them and shut the door behind her. Kyle locked it. The window was down and he called out. "Good luck. I'm going to stay with the van so we don't lose it."

Storm was already disappearing off with Brand and Chris through the swing doors. She raised her hand in acknowledgement as the door swung shut behind her and they disappeared into the hospital.

Inside the hospital there were people everywhere in various states of being treated. Most were bandaged and sat on whatever they could find looking stunned, their loved ones beside them holding coats, bags and generally trying to comfort them. A young doctor ran over to them when he saw the trail of blood that Chris was leaving. He pulled the coat away and checked out the wound. Immediately he called for a gurney.

The Orderly who came with it lifted Chris onto the bed despite her protestations not to touch her. She screamed and tried to fight them off but they wheeled her off to a curtained cubicle where the doctor examined her. She was still crying when he injected her arm and she relaxed and stared up at the ceiling. The doctor relaxed as well. "Good, now we can have a good look at her." He pulled up her shirt and revealed the gash in her stomach. He bent down and pulled it apart. "It could have been a lot worse. Thankfully it is just superficial. I won't even bother to ask how this happened. Nightmare day for everyone. A few stitches and she will be fine. You on the other hand had better sit down. Head wounds can be lethal and even if you feel ok you might have a concussion."

Brand sat down and realised that he was finding it hard to see as the blood was running into his eyes. Storm began wiping it away with a damp paper towel.

The doctor was busy cleaning up Chris' wound. "Very good, she's a very lucky little lady. She may not get too much of a scar. I'll see if we can come up with a better option to stitching. Lay there and don't move."

Chris moaned. She was so strongly sedated that she couldn't have moved even if she had wanted to.

Brand choked as the blood ran into his mouth. "What about the baby?"

The doctor froze. "Now that changes things. How far gone is she? We'd better do some tests."

Chris moaned and raised her hand to push the doctor away. Brand grabbed her hand and held it.

Brand thought for a moment. "She told me last night that she was three months. She hadn't told me before as she wanted to be sure."

The doctor looked at him and raised an eyebrow. "If you'd both like to leave the cubicle and get yourself seen to sir I'll come and find you."

Brand stood up. He was feeling dizzy and the floor nearly came up to meet him. Storm caught his arm and almost physically carried him to the next cubicle which was empty. A doctor carrying a clipboard followed them in and pulled the curtain. He looked into Brand's eyes and checked his retinal reflexes. "Now lay down on here and we'll get that cleaned up and see what we're dealing with." Brand sat on the bed and swivelled around just as the world turned black. He fell back onto the gurney and the doctor was there immediately checking his vital signs. "He's passed out, probably due to shock and blood loss. Head wounds do bleed a lot. It does happen. Hold his hand if you want to my dear, he'll be more reassured when he comes around and I'm sure you'll be more reassured now. I'm just going to give him some anaesthetic and get that wound stitched."

Storm sat on the bed holding Brand's hand. She couldn't help thinking about how Chris was three months pregnant with his baby. Inside she felt deeply guilty for her thoughts of the past night and her hopes that their relationship may not have been a permanent one. She was focused on what the doctor was doing. There were so many voices in the room it was hard to focus on what anyone was saying. People were screaming and crying, trolleys were being wheeled up and down the corridor and all manner of other sounds added to the cacophony.

The doctor had just about finished his stitching when Brand came around.

At the same time the doctor who had been treating Chris stepped into the cubicle. "I've given her an anaesthetic to numb the pain while we deal with that cut properly. She's a pretty girl and I'm sure she doesn't want me turning her into Frankenstein's monster with my stitching. A skin patch will do the job far better but that will take minor surgery as we have to make sure she doesn't move while it sets."

Brand grabbed the doctor's arm. "Would surgery harm the baby?"

The doctor looked down at him. "Your baby?"

Brand nodded.

The doctor looked gravely at him. "I'm sorry son. I don't know how to put this but there is no baby."

Brand looked horrified. "You mean she's lost the baby?"

The doctor shook his head. "I mean there was no baby. I have carried out an examination and I have done tests as best as I can and according to her hormone level it would appear that she is taking contraception. I have her handbag here. I am not at liberty to open it but you may wish to take responsibility and have a look inside."

Brand's face looked like thunder. He leaned over and snatched the offered bag from the doctor's hand. He opened it and tipped the contents out onto the bed. The distinctive silver packet with tablets set out day by day was there. He picked it up and looked at it in disbelief. "What a bitch? She has taken them up until the day she told me." He went to get up.

Storm caught his arm and physically held him onto the bed. "Now where are you going?"

Brand looked up at her. "I'm going. Come on, we're going."

Storm froze. "What do you mean we're going? What about Chris?"

Brand smiled but there was no warmth in it. "I don't care where she goes but she is not coming with us. I've had enough of her manipulating me and this is one trick too many."

The doctor shook his head. "She was a foolish child but everyone makes mistakes. I'm sure it is something you should talk about. These are difficult times, perhaps she was scared of losing you? Do you want to speak to her? We can arrange a private room for you. Unfortunately we are under extreme pressure here and I really must move on to another patient."

He turned and left.

The other doctor in the room had been standing open mouthed. The blood soaked swab he'd used to mop Brand's head as he'd just finished the stitching was in his hand but the scissors that held it had gradually drooped as he had lost concentration on what he was doing. "Well I never. Now, we must focus on you. It is possible you have a concussion. I would say that it is highly likely. We are going to have to keep you in for observation."

Brand grabbed the doctor's arm. "I cannot stay, we have to go."

The doctor looked at him quizzically. "Go where?"

Brand shut his mouth with a snap. "It doesn't matter."

The doctor looked at him. "Did you get a message?"

Brand looked at the young doctor. "I did, did you? What did it say?"

The doctor smiled. "Go to this location if you want to live or something like that. I've got the print out in my locker. I'm about to finish my shift and I was going to head off. If I come with you I can monitor your situation and if there are complications I am sure I could help. I know I'm needed here but the message did say urgent and that I was needed. What about Chris? Is that what her name is?"

Brand opened his mouth and shut it again. "You must think me cruel. But neither of you know the full story. I worked for her father and she took a liking to me. I was in debt and her father bought that debt which basically meant he bought me. He wanted me to be with her for a little while and then to make her hate me and leave me so that she would return to the family and marry the man they had chosen. So if I walk away now I'll be doing him a favour."

Storm shook her head. "How long have you been with her?"

Brand looked down. "Five long years."

Storm stared at him. "You have to be kidding me. Surely in that time you could have been man enough to sort it out. Don't you love her?"

Brand put his hand up to his head and the doctor deftly caught it. "What is to love? She's a manipulative and demanding bitch who made my life a living hell. If her father hadn't held my sister pretty much as ransom there is no way I would have had anything to do with her."

The curtain pulled back and Chris staggered through, clutching her stomach which was bleeding again. "You don't need to sort it out. I think you just have. I can't believe daddy bought you. You are a liar. You wanted the comfortable life, the fast cars and designer clothes. You certainly seemed to be enjoying the holidays and life of leisure. Well, you can go now, the gravy train is derailed. Storm you can have him. He's damaged goods.

You can have him for free, bargain basement. Go on, get lost both of you. Go and find your wonderful place, it is not as if I was actually invited. Yes, that's right, I lied. I never got an invitation. Get out of my life you pretentious and vain Neanderthal. I've had enough of your drooling and grunting over me, time I went and found myself a man with a bit of education and breeding. I don't need you anymore." She turned and stormed out punching numbers into her useless mobile phone.

Storm was still holding Brand down. She relaxed her grip. "Well, that was not at all what I expected. What do we do now?"

Brand sat up, held his head and fell back down again. "Well if I can ever get off this damn bed we're going to go back to the pub and we're going to get the hell out of here before anyone else turns up and kicks the living out of us."

Storm smiled. "Sounds like a plan. I do feel sorry for Chris in some ways."

Brand laughed. "I wouldn't she is a prize bitch. You should have heard what she said about her friends and what she did to them. Part of me was too afraid over the years to say anything."

Storm hesitated. "Do you need to worry about what she will do?"

Brand took a deep breath. "Oh yes, she'll have a very wicked vengeance put together for me as soon as she calms down and starts thinking about it. That is why we need to get moving. If she has seen my email she also has the location."

Storm swore. "Ok, well doctor is he able to be moved?"

The doctor drew off some clear liquid into a syringe. "Yes, in my opinion if he has medical supervision he will be fine. I don't travel alone. I have found two other people this morning who are going to the location. They are meeting me here in about ten minutes. So, are we travelling together?"

Storm looked at Brand who was looking decidedly dizzy. "What do you think?"

Brand smiled. "I'm a caveman I'm not supposed to think, you do it for me pretty one."

Storm smiled. "Now let me think, having a doctor along, medical cover? Do you think I'm going to refuse?"

The doctor smiled. "Very well. You have your doctor. At this point I should really introduce myself with a really cool name, which I don't have."

Storm smiled. "Yet, you can make one up later. It's not as if its going to matter now is it?"

The doctor looked thoughtful. "You are right, I can be anyone I want to be. I'll give it some thought."

Storm laughed. "So who will the doctor be?"

The doctor smiled. "Do you have a car that works?"

Storm smiled. "We do, a beaten up van. It's in the car park."

The doctor was putting away his equipment and making up his notes. "I'll see you in there then."

8

RED RIGHT HAND

Storm helped Brand out to the van. Kyle was waiting in a no parking zone just outside the doors. He leapt out when he saw Brand stagger and just about managed to be there to help catch him as his legs gave out. He looked at Storm. "Is he alright to leave?"

Storm smiled. "Technically no but we've gathered a doctor on our travels but lost Chris. It's a long story and its Brand's to tell."

Kyle shrugged. "You know best. A doctor now that could be handy."

Storm nodded. "But he comes with extras, not sure who yet. They are meeting us here."

Kyle smiled. "So the number grows." He looked up and a Volkswagen camper van drove around the corner and pulled up next to them. The Doctor was driving. He wound down the window. "You really did mean beaten up didn't you. This is Rat and Stick. For some totally insane reason whoever is dishing out invitations thinks they are useful."

Rat really did look slightly ratty and Stick was as thin as a person could be without being ill. They both looked up and smiled. Rat winked at Storm. "We fix things, broken things, it is what we do. Of course we're useful. Who'd be without us?"

The Doctor smiled. "Well I obviously can't be. So where are we going? We know where we are generally going but are we going straight there or do you have friends to pick up?"

Storm wound the window down a little more. "We have friends to pick up. This is Kyle, my brother. Pleased to meet you Rat and Stick. So shall we lead the way?"

Stick looked up. "Can we take a detour to the library?"

Storm looked horrified. "Are you sure?"

Rat looked at Stick and his face brightened. "You aren't so stupid as you look young Stick me lad. If we go to the library we might be able to get our hands on books. No internet, no information, we need books, good old fashioned paper heavy books. Come on, it has to be worth a try."

They drove by the library but they didn't stop. The black plume of smoke billowing out of the windows and the flames that reached nearly ten foot above the building were enough to let them know that someone far less studious had got there first.

Rat and Stick both swore for most of the journey to the pub but they cheered up considerably when they saw where they were going.

Introductions done everyone sat in the bar. Storm had brought Brand down a blanket as he was feeling cold and Jareth had made him a cup of sweet tea. The Doctor was seated beside him and was keeping a close eye on his patient.

Brand looked up. "We're going to have to move out and fast."

Frank walked over to stand in front of him, arms folded. "Now why would that be then? You still haven't told us what happened to Chris."

Brand leant back into the soft backing of the chair. "I'm not going to tell the story out of order as if I do it does look really bad on me.

I worked for Chris' father. He's a big shot in the LexCorp, Lex Industries Acquisitions Department. He found me through a friend and he wanted someone who would do some quiet removal work. Mostly elderly people in houses he wanted to get hold of. I basically had to make their life a misery until they moved out. Before you judge me, I was in a lot of debt. Tanya my sister was desperate for a baby and it was beginning to affect her health.

She had two suicide attempts on record and that didn't help her case with the doctors. They put it on her record that she was medically unfit to be a mother so we had to get her the surgery that would help her have a baby without them. So I needed to get money fast to help her and I went to a loan shark.

I was shooting pool down at my usual club and got talking to some bloke about the debt I was getting myself into. We downed far too many pints that night and he said he'd talk to someone he knew who could help me.

The debts were piling up and I was also paying for a full time Carer for Tanya. She'd got pregnant and had made another failed suicide attempt which had left her in a wheelchair and she lost the baby.

I had my first meeting with Matthew Rolstone in his flash office in the London Dome. He seemed to be offering a reasonable package until I found out what the job was. I declined his most generous offer and he told me I would reconsider. Of course I walked out.

That afternoon my mother took a tumble down the stairs. They rushed her to hospital but it was too late, she died. I received a call on my mobile just as it would have happened from Rolstone's assistant reminding me that there would be consequences and that my sister would be next.

I had no option but to work for him but I wasn't happy about it. It was about then that I met Chris in a chance encounter when she came screaming into his office when I was picking up some paperwork. She obviously took a shine to me as she calmed down and was very polite to her father. He seemed impressed and although he acted as if he was outraged when she paid me compliments I think he was quite happy that I was driving her around for a while.

I'm certain she started it all just to annoy her father but in a way I wanted to hit back at him too. He was getting a peaceful life but I don't think he realised the full extent of my duties. She was a pretty girl, so what was the harm? I knew I was playing with fire but after what he'd done I didn't really care. He'd moved Tanya into one of Lex's care homes and he pretty much owned me anyway. So I just added entertaining his daughter to my list of duties.

She didn't approve of me being away working for him so that stopped and I became driver full time which was a great relief. Anyway, Rolstone called me into his office and set it out for me in black and white. If I upset her before he told me to then it would not go well for Tanya. At a time of his choosing he was going to get me to upset Chris and leave. I'd be paid off well and anything left of my debt would be wiped out. The only restriction was that I wasn't to sleep with her. It was a bit late for that clause and somehow I managed to avoid any difficult questions on that score. I think he honestly did believe that his daughter was a virgin at the time.

I did a bit of digging and he'd had a lot of trouble controlling Chris. She had been the classic wild child and her addictions and problems were becoming more and more difficult for him to cover up. When she was with me at least she was away from some of the more unpleasant influences in her life. I suppose I justified it to myself that I was her bodyguard with extra duties.

Tanya took a turn for the worse when she got hold of some drugs at the Home. They nearly lost her and she ended up on a life support machine. Rolstone actually took the time to call me in and told me himself. He assured me that every care would be taken of her. I was driven over to see her. She was unconscious. I spoke to the doctors and they said it was unlikely she would recover consciousness for a while. I left reassured but as you can imagine not at all happy.

The months went into years and Tanya was still what

they called stable and comfortable. I visited her as often as I could and spoke to her in case she could hear me."

Steve swallowed hard. "Should we go and try to get her?"

Frank cast him a sympathetic look. "Steve, it's a good thought but she was on life support. I would put money on it that it was only that machine keeping her breathing all those years just to keep Brand on the hook.

Brand, what do you think?"

Brand looked a little shocked and thought about it for a moment. "The room was neat and tidy, there were no notes hanging on the end of the bed. I noticed that other patients had little plastic hangers and paper notes attached." He looked down at his hands. "I think I've been a fool."

Frank cleared his throat. "So we know he was a pretty nasty bit of work. How about his daughter, can we expect any kind of fallout from this?"

Brand looked up at him, his eyes slightly watery. "No doubt she will attempt something. She is a vicious, twisted, vindictive creature. I've seen what she can do to a friend who crossed her. I am expecting something. I wouldn't put it past her to have read my emails so she probably knows about the location."

Frank scratched his head. "Did you use a laptop or computer on their system?"

Brand looked at all the faces intently staring at him. "I bought myself a laptop out of my wages. It was on a whim and I saw it advertised and liked it. No, it was independent to their network. I bought my own software."

Frank smiled. "Did you ever talk about the location with her?"

Brand thought hard. "I don't think I did and she wouldn't remember if I had. She was too distracted with trying to work out what to bring with her to actually ask where we were going. Thankfully she is pretty used to people sorting that sort of thing out for her. She asks, she goes or they entertain her."

Frank turned to the others. "We might just have a break here if we can get ourselves out of here pronto. I want you all to pack up your rooms, get your stuff together and get it down here. Once you have done that get down here yourselves and we'll start moving out the food and anything useful from this place. Come on people, move. Brand, I'll clear your room for you. What would you like me to do with Chris's things?"

Brand looked down. "I don't know."

Frank grunted. "Very well, then we take no chances. I want you to ditch everything. Anything she ever gave you, anything you got from the Corporation. It's going to be hard laddie but we have to be sure. Well people, thank you for your time and I'll see you all back down here when we are ready to load the vehicles."

There was a flurry of movement as everyone headed for their rooms to pack. About an hour later they were downstairs again putting boxes, tins and bottles into whatever packing boxes they had and shifting them out to the vans and old Ford Connect.

Chris had wandered through the hospital in a dream until a doctor caught her by the arm and she was led to a cubicle. "Where's my bag? I want my bag." She demanded. The doctor left her with a nurse who sedated her.

Chris fell back into a swirling dream.

When she woke up she was in a bed, her stomach was bandaged and she had a drip in her arm. A nurse was passing and noticed that she was awake.

"Welcome back." She began taking her pulse and writing notes on a piece of paper. "Now we're just about to sort ourselves out for the night. There are strict rules in place, do not touch the candles. We have a little daylight left and the doctor is doing his last rounds. We have no emergency bell so if you need anything you'll have to shout. Please don't panic, we have everything under control."

Chris was far from being in a panic. She was too angry. She lay on the bed and her mind went over and over the past five years. The more she thought about it the more angry she became.

When nobody was looking she slipped out of bed and opened the cupboard beside it. She found her clothes in there and slipped them on. Her handbag was there and she checked through it, nothing was missing. Her purse was full of money. She didn't count it but it looked about right. She slung the bag over her shoulder and looked down at her blood stained and ripped shirt. She pulled her jacket over it and zipped it up, pulled her hood up over her untidy hair, pulled the curtain back and wandered off down the corridor.

A doctor stepped out from a doorway. She smiled at him sweetly. "Do you know where my sister, Maureen Callaghan is?"

The doctor smiled kindly. "It would be best to go to Reception by the main entrance. The lady there will be able to tell you where to find your sister."

Chris smiled back at him. "Thank you, which way is Reception?"

The doctor turned to face down the corridor. "Back the way you came, turn right. There is no lift obviously so you'll have to take the stairs. Reception is just along the corridor to the right when you get to ground floor. Hope you find your sister alright?" He smiled, turned and went off down the corridor.

Chris bit the side of her mouth to hold back her anger that he had not looked at her in any way that indicated that he liked her. "Thank you, you have been very kind." She muttered, turned and tried to walk as casually as she could down the corridor before she made her way painfully down the stairs and past Reception and out of the main doors.

The concourse outside the hospital was full of people. The taxi rank had one or two cars in it. She went to the rank. People were going to cars but stepping away. She went to the first car. "I want you to take me to Fairlight Castle, Hastings."

The driver smiled. "What will be £4,000 plus mileage. Cars that work are rare you know."

Chris took a deep breath, closed and then opened her eyes. "Very well."

The driver smiled. "The £4,000 is in advance."

Chris got into the cab and opened her purse and counted her money. "I'm a bit short, I only have £3,980."

The driver smiled. "I'll take it."

The drive to Hastings was done in silence. The driver tried to engage her in conversation to start with but her clipped answers and lack of any dialogue and unwillingness to give him any information soon silenced him. He looked nervous and kept taking a look at Chris in his rear view mirror. She sat like a statue, staring ahead, lost in her thoughts and oblivious to all that was going on around her. She didn't notice the lost and bewildered people, the gangs, the looting, none of it. She was lost in her anger and planning her revenge.

The cab pulled through the gates which proudly displayed the name "Fairlight" and drove up the drive. She got out onto the gravel path in front of the cream stone building as the driver opened his window. "That will be £2000 for the mileage."

She smiled wickedly. "I'm sure my father will take care of you." She turned and went in through the white painted door which opened into a

hallway. To the left there was a glass fronted office which was a mass of paperwork, open boxes and two useless computers on the two desks.

Paperwork was piled up on them so only the screen protruded out. There was nobody in there so she carried on as the corridor turned right. The

kitchen was also empty. It was a large room with a big black fixed work unit in the middle and cabinets around. A banana hanger and fruit bowl sat on the work surface and various food boxes were scattered around. The black square crockery was in the sink waiting to be washed but nobody was about.

She carried on and looked in through the first door on the left which was a library. It was a dark room with a lot of mahogany wood and a huge desk. Old book cases lined the walls full of leather bound books, rugs on the carpet. One was a wolf pelt. A large painting of a muscular man and a wolf hung on the left hand wall. The artwork was by an artist she loved, he had done work for 2000AD. The old fashioned desk stood regally at the far side of the room under the window. Lines of old books decorated the walls, all unread, her father had bought them with the property the same as he had bought so many other things just to look educated and accomplished. The wolf pelt and other Native American decorations like the spear were from their many trips to the US to visit the Choctaw Native American Tribe.

The room was uninhabited so she shut the door and carried on again. On the right the corridor opened into the entrance lobby. They rarely used the front door and a white sofa had been put there to make use of the space.

She carried on through this, past the door to the haunted tower that had been such a source of amusement and if she admitted it to herself terror on the nights she had actually spent here. She re-joined the corridor which opened up to the right. This was the formal dining room which they had used for many banquets and entertaining when her mother had been alive. A large banquet size table stood in the middle with chairs around it. On the wooden dresser there was a wolf carved as if emerging from wood. That had come from a small shop in the lanes in Brighton. Memories of times gone by flittered through her mind as she walked on the dark ageing carpet and looked around the place.

Before she carried on she walked back and upstairs to

her bedroom. She opened the door and there was her ancient four poster bed. Photos and ornaments lined up on the shelves to her right but what she wanted was in a wooden box beside the door on her dresser. Poems that Brand had written for her, letters and words of love. All lies she knew now, all worthless. They were just weapons he had used to keep her tame and unquestioning. She pulled them out of their box and went back downstairs.

As she walked as quickly as she could along the corridor, to the left there was a door which was slightly open. She could hear her father's voice demanding that someone spoke to him. She pushed the door. A small stone gargoyle statue sat beside the door on the left hand side just inside as she went in and a well-used slightly threadbare sofa faced her. The left hand wall was bare but there were windows along on the far wall. A table had been placed there with photographs of the family. The end of that wall was covered by a shelf unit completely stacked with DVDs and right hand wall was covered by an enormous flat screen television. Two armchairs faced it and her father was sitting at one of them. The wall behind her was mostly taken up with a huge fireplace.

She had a flash of a memory when her father had been away and she and Brand had been in the house alone. He had taken that wolf pelt from the library and put it in front of the fire so that they could make love. This was not an image she wanted to see now.

The TV screen was blank. Her father had a light wooden box sitting on his lap. Its numbers looked like the keys of an old fashioned typewriter and he was holding the receiver to his ear and shouting at it. As she entered he slammed down the receiver and threw the telephone onto the floor. "Damn thing, when will they fix the line?" He looked up and put his laptop aside. "My darling, what an unexpected surprise, welcome home. I can have Manfred make up your room for you?"

He stood up. He was a gaunt man, his face drawn, his

grey hair neatly cut, his suit expensive.

Chris burst into tears and ran to her father. He hugged her, wrapping his long arms around her and pulled her head onto his chest. "What is the matter my little angel? If you are frightened by all this, don't worry, it is being handled. I have my best men onto it and Lex Corporation is bigger than all this. The computers will be up and running again soon. You shouldn't worry your little head about it. Where's Brand?" He pulled her back from him and looked down at her.

Chris wiped away her tears with the back of her hand. "He attacked me daddy. He was furious. I don't know what got into him and I love him so much. He kept screaming at me that you had bought him and that now that his sister was more than likely dead he was free of me. Then he took a knife and tried to kill me. Look at what he did." She pulled up her shirt to show off the bandages. She then threw the letters and poems onto the floor and stamped on them. " Look at all those lies he wrote to me. They were just words. I thought he meant them. I've just come from the hospital." He tried to slash my stomach." He said that he'd make sure you never have any grandchildren to carry on your evil line."

Rolstone put his arms around her again. "Don't worry, I'll make sure that he really suffers for what he's done to you. You should be in hospital. I'll call Manfred, he can take you."

Chris choked on her tears. "I don't want to go to a hospital. They have dressed the wound and told me I can go home. Can you bring me a doctor here? I want to go after him as soon as I can but I wanted my daddy first. I had thought he had someone else but now he has told me that he has. I bet he has sent the same words to her as well. They are going off to make a wonderful life together in a sanctuary. They got a message which told them where they would be safe from all this. He was going to take me, now he's taking her instead. He tore my invitation up saying that I didn't deserve to be saved and that I should die with the rest of my wretched family."

Rolstone pulled her back and stared down at her, his cold grey eyes intent. "A sanctuary? A message?"

Chris swallowed and looked up at her father. "Lots of people got a message on the internet just before it all shut down. It told them to go to a location where they would be safe. They are heading there now. They are there in a pub together I was there too until this morning and they are going on from there to somewhere in Wales. I think he said something like Abba-wrist-with or something like that. I can't bear it daddy. There's a man outside who drove me here. I gave him lots of money and he wants more.

He has my cash, nearly £4,000 of it and a working car and probably some petrol left."

Rolstone smiled. "Very useful, well done darling."

Back at the Black Lamb Pub the refugees were gathered in the bar. Bottles had been pulled from the optics and the optics carefully removed, wrapped in cloth and stacked in crates and boxes.

Frank was looking at the mountain of equipment and out of the window at the three vehicles. "Well it's going to be a tight squeeze but we should be able to get everything in. It's going to take us about a day to get to the location and I'd rather we didn't stop on the way in case we encounter more trouble. Jareth, have you made up the food packages I asked for?"

Jareth looked up from behind the bar. "I have, I've done them individually as I didn't know who was going in which car. There are enough for two meals each. Hopefully that will be enough. I've used up the last of the food that won't travel and they are in storage boxes with the cutlery in the bags. Not exactly a balanced meal but enough to keep everyone going."

Frank looked around the gathered people. "Well we're going to have to decide who goes in which vehicle. This is going to be very school days and Brand you are excluded from getting up at the moment."

Brand smiled. "I feel fine now."

Frank looked at the doctor. The doctor looked up at Frank. "He is ok, his dizzy spells are less now that he's making up the blood that he lost. He can get off his lazy butt now and get on with helping."

Brand smiled at him.

Frank looked around the room. "Now I want everyone who can physically fight to stand over there. Non-combatant useful people over there."

Brand, Kyle, Storm, Reko, Matt and Steve moved across the room.

Rat and Stick looked at each other. Rat smiled and looked up at Frank.

"We're totally useless, but we can fix things."

Jareth lifted a box onto the bar. "I'm a barman. I'm a lover not a fighter. I did basic training at Hendon but that was years ago and I've been a desk jockey since then."

Frank smiled. "Rat, Stick, don't put yourselves down. In the days that follow it is highly likely that the geek shall inherit the earth. This is your time, if you can build and rebuild you are going to be what we need most. Jareth, don't worry about it. If cornered I'm sure you'd make a good account of yourself. No offence meant to the rest of you. I want to split those who can fight between the vehicles and I'm sorry Rat and Stick I'm not putting you two both in the same vehicle together. If anything happens and we lose a vehicle I'd like at least one of you to survive. I'm going to split Reko, Matt and Steve between the three vehicles. If we get separated then at least we'll have a mechanic per van. Doc if you could drive your camper, Kyle if you could drive your van I'll drive the Connect. There are only two seats in that so if I take Steve with me. I know a bit about car maintenance so that may make up for his inexperience. Reko if you go with Doc and Matt with Kyle's vehicle. Damn it that doesn't work. Doc, do you mind if someone else drives your camper? It's packed too full to get anyone in the back. I need you with Brand for the moment just in case. I need a mechanic and a driver in the camper. Reko, can you drive a camper and take Jareth and Rat?"

Reko smiled. "I used to own one of those beauties. I travelled around most of Italy in my younger days and lived in one."

Doc piped up. "I only bought it second hand last week so I don't have any emotional attachment to it but I would say if we have to stop over I'd like the option to sleep in it."

Frank laughed. "That sounds fair enough. Doc, Stick, Matt and Brand if you go in the van with Storm and Kyle.

Right, get the food packs loaded and get everything into the vans, then we will do the check around. I want to make sure that there is nothing left here that will indicate where we are going. We'll all do a room by room search and I want this place empty of anything that we can use."

It took half an hour for everyone to complete their searches. They didn't find anything. They had pretty much gutted the place of anything useful and it looked very bare. Even the curtains, all bed linen, all of the kitchen equipment and glasses had been packed around things so that they could withstand a bit of a bumpy ride. They were packed and ready to go.

Jareth stood in the car park looking back at the building.

Frank came to stand beside him. "Sad?"

Jareth smiled. "A little bit. I'd had such hopes when I moved here with the missus all those years ago. Who would think that I'm off on a great adventure and she's six feet under?"

Frank put a hand on his shoulder. "Any children?"

Jareth shook his head. "This place took up too much of our time. It was a complete millstone around our necks but I'm still a little sad to go."

Frank squeezed his hand. "Come on mate, time we were on the road."

They jumped on board, the engines started and the vehicles rolled off of the car park and up onto the open road. The miles passed them by and they didn't see any other moving vehicle until they turned onto the motorway. The slip road was almost completely clogged up and it took them nearly an hour to push the cars out of the way so that they could join the single line of cars that were still moving. The lane wasn't clear. Vehicles were trying to wind their way around other abandoned and broken down vehicles. Where they had initially been pushed to the side of the road this was now completely

clogged up. Then the slow progress almost ground to a halt and very soon there was a tail back for miles. Frank shut off his engine and jumped out of his van. He went to the other vehicles in turn. "Turn off your engines, get out and push. We don't have the fuel for this. As soon as we get to a junction we'll get off and use the minor roads. That will be quicker in the long run."

The turn off was about a mile and by the time they got there they were exhausted from pushing the vehicles. Other people had followed suit when they saw what they were doing. Very soon there was a caravan of cars and vans being pushed as slowly as they would have been able to drive along the motorway.

They turned off, jumped back into the vehicles and started up the engines and were again on their way a little bit faster. Frank and Steve were in the front car, Kyle followed up in the van and Reko brought up the rear in the Camper.

They were making good time down narrow winding lanes when suddenly out from behind some trees they saw a large van which was being pushed across the road. Frank swore and stopped the car as a man and six boys leapt out from over a wall and surrounded them.

The tallest of them shouted. "Get out of your

vehicles."

Frank got out first and the others followed. The boys went to each of the vehicles but Frank caught the first one by his arm and turned him around, hitting him with a sharp punch to the stomach so he buckled over. Kyle was just getting out and slammed his van door into a second one who had got far too close. Brand came out of the van like a wildcat and floored the one nearest him before he could raise his knife. It was difficult to tell them apart. They all wore blue jeans and a black hoodie, even the adult.

The adult stepped in to take on Frank. He circled and by the way he was standing it was obvious he was military trained.

Reko stood back from his and danced around. The lad was trying to punch him but couldn't until Reko leapt forwards and punched him in the face, knocking him back against the camper. The boy grabbed his nose looking shocked. Reko and Steve then kicked him until he fell to the ground.

Storm was out of the van by now and ran towards the one heading towards the camper van. She took a leap and kicked him, sending him sprawling onto the floor. She then sat on him as he was far smaller than her and had dropped his knife as he fell.

Frank and his assailant squared off then the man in front of him stepped back and took a defensive stance. "Don't I know you? But it can't be. I'm seeing things."

Frank hesitated. "I don't generally associate with Road Pirates so probably not."

The hoody removed his hood. "Commander Axis, it has been years since we were in the Unit together. Ok I know you were on secondment and some special project or something but, hey, it is good to see you."

Frank smiled at the surprisingly elderly man and looked thoughtful. "Now you are the last person I would expect to be in this sort of a game."

Sennet smiled. "I wasn't, I'm not apparently. We needed vehicles and you came along."

Frank looked at the boys picking themselves up from the dirt in the road. The oldest was barely seventeen.

Sennet smiled as they staggered over to join him nursing bleeding noses and injured limbs. "Well, probably not sons a father should be proud to announce when they were just about to commit a crime but they are my boys all the same. Three from my first marriage, two came with the second wife and the third was with the second wife. But then you probably already know that. I think I bored everyone silly with tales of my kids."

Frank smiled wryly. "I'd say pleased to meet you but under the circumstances that isn't wholly appropriate is it?"

Sennet smiled. "Not really, so where are you going?"

Frank cast a quick glance at the others. "We're just getting out of town."

Sennet looked at his boys. "Well we'd better let this good man get on his way. I still can't believe it is you. I heard you had died on a recon mission out in Korea."

Frank stepped forward and the two hugged. "For the sake of what the Unit went through I'll let this one pass. That you could have come to this? Boys, your father was a good man, a noble fighter and a true friend. His military career was exemplary and his retirement well earned. There has to be more to your future than just stealing. There are enough of you. Find yourself a little place and hole up, see what your skills are and see what you can do to survive."

Sennet looked at his old commander. "Can we come with you?"

Frank breathed in deeply. "I'd dearly love to take you but we have barely enough resources for those I do have with me. Unless you have somewhere to go I would suggest that you hold up here or find somewhere that is easy to defend and see what you can build out of this new world."

Sennet looked down at his feet. "I understand. We didn't exactly meet again under the best of circumstances. It looks like life has treated you kindly though, you look just the same as when I last saw you and that has to be over thirty years ago."

Frank smiled. "Goodbye old friend."

He turned and got back into the van, the others followed suit. The boys pushed the van out of the road and they were back on their way.

Frank travelled on in silence lost in his thoughts. Steve was looking at him hoping that he'd speak but not wanting to disturb him. He was about to ask what he was thinking about but shut his mouth and went back to looking out of the window.

After a couple of hours his thoughts and curiosity got the better of him. He watched Frank driving and then looked out of the window for a while. All the time he was formulating the question in his head which he finally could contain no longer so he had to ask. "Did you really know him all those years ago? Why didn't we take them with us?"

Frank grunted. "How could I have known him? If I look the same as I do now and it has been thirty years that would put me in my late nineties. I'm not quite that old. But, it solved the situation so I let him think what he wanted to think. If he is happy thinking he saw one of his old buddies who am I to burst his bubble.

We can't take everyone with us. Whoever made the decision about who should go to the safe house made it for a reason. It is more than likely that he has had trouble adjusting to any kind of life and he is leading those boys down a very difficult path. In a world like this they will do alright, previously I would imagine things would have been very different. That is not the basis on which we can build anything."

Reko shrugged. "You are probably right, doesn't make it feel any better though does it?"

9

The roads became more crowded as they neared other Cities. There were very few cars on the road. Most had stopped when their petrol had run out. That was the problem, they had blocked the road. The vehicles were stopping more and more often to push cars out of the way that had just been left there. It became very slow going. Where it should have taken them a few hours to get to their destination it was almost nightfall and they were still miles away.

Frank was still concentrating on the road intently, Steve was watching him. "Frank, would you like me to take a turn driving? You must be tired by now."

Frank smiled, he didn't look at all tired. "I'd love you to but I'm not stopping this vehicle for anyone. Look at those people out there, they are desperate. We can think about that when we get into open countryside but not while there could be people about. We can't afford to lose even one of the vehicles now. We're going to be cutting this fine anyway when it comes to petrol so best we just keep plodding on."

Steve looked at the people they were passing. They were standing beside their cars looking into the distance. "Do you think those cars worked or have they been waiting there all this time?"

Frank looked at the tired faces of the people they were passing by. "You've seen the advertising. Wait by your car to be rescued. They have paid their memberships, they expect a patrol man to be along sometime soon, even though their mobiles aren't working. They probably can't understand that rescue isn't coming at all. That's the problem, if we stop they are going to want us to help. If we stop and help one we'll have to help others. That is for others to do. Look, there is someone stuck. I'll give it a go and I think you will see what I mean. But be ready to get away quickly if they try to take our vehicle."

The bonnet was up of a Volkswagen car and there was a group of people standing around it. Frank pulled up. "Any idea what is wrong?"

The group looked confused. Nobody answered so Frank got out of the car and looked into the engine. Frank stood up. The crowd turned to look at him as if he was some guru about to proclaim something magnificent. "The manifold is bust I think, she's dead in the water."

A woman who was closest to him screamed. "It's a working car." She then made a lunge at Frank.

Frank's quick reflexes saved him from being grabbed by the woman. He dodged, jumped into the car, wound up the window and drove off. He cast a sideways glance at Steve. "Do you see what I mean?

Things like this change people. Rational folk soon turn nasty. It brings out the worst in them. Fear that is, that is what is changing them. No, we keep going until the petrol runs out or we get there."

They drove through the evening. As they got to the more remote roads travelling got easier as there were fewer abandoned vehicles. Those that were abandoned had been pushed to the side of the road by the old tractors. They seemed to be working perfectly well and they saw one or two working their way down the lanes, using their shovels to push the cars onto what verge there was.

Frank stopped the car beside one of the tractors and

wound down his window. The farmer opened his door but didn't get down from his cab.

"Evening to you." The farmer smiled warmly. "Strange why all these cars just stopped working. Some of them look pretty new. Must be one of those bug things. So what's it like back there then? I mean on the motorways."

Frank smiled. "Most of the vehicles have stopped completely and people are waiting by them to be rescued. There are people walking and vehicles abandoned in the road."

The farmer took off his cap and rubbed his forehead. "Well, it was a bit like that around here but we've managed to clear the road. I've moved at least twelve cars to the side of the road today. Way's clear all the way to Aberystwyth now though."

Frank laughed. "I'll wish you a good night then, and good luck."

The farmer smiled. "I'll wish the same to you." He climbed back into his cab and shut the door, started the engine and drove off.

Frank started his engine, as did the other vehicles. The farmer was right, the road into Aberystwyth was clear. The town was a different story. As they came to the little roundabout which went into town there was only one through route. Cars were abandoned everywhere but a path had been cleared. It was past midnight and there were few people about. They passed a football ground and cars had been towed or pushed onto there. They were lined up across the grass.

As they approached the main roundabout smoke billowed across the road from the burning supermarket, petrol station and fast food restaurant.

Movement was slow going negotiating the abandoned vehicles through the smoke but finally they managed to manoeuver up the hill and onto the coast road. As they looked back Aberystwyth burned like many other towns and cities they had passed. The library on the hill was also in flames as were many other large buildings. Along the roadside some buildings smoked where they had burnt earlier, some had broken windows where looters had already cleared them out. Everywhere was in darkness although the odd figure could be seen moving about in the shadows.

They didn't stop, they drove on up into the mountains until they came to a quiet country back road. It was hardly a "b" road but it was wide enough for them. They climbed a small hill and came to a stone built farmhouse on their right. It was facing the courtyard, its side wall with no windows facing the road. Over the high wall they could see the upstairs window which were lit by candles. Over the side gate they could see that there were obviously people moving about in the yard. As they approached the people scuttled off into the shadows.

As they looked across the yard from the large wooden gate the front of the house faced the yard on their left.

The farm gate opened inwards allowing access onto the road. Across the road from it there was thick woodland which almost cut out the moonlight so there was little illumination on the road. Across the back of the large yard there was a large rough stone barn with huge wooden doors and to the right a long stone barn perforated by stable doors.

It was difficult to see much more in the dark.

There were candles burning in lanterns on the gate posts and as they approached two dark figures stepped out of the shadows to meet them.

Frank got out of the van, Steve did the same and they both walked over to the gate. They were met by two tall and well-built men dressed in black army surplus uniform. The one on the right had long wavy blonde hair, the one on the left dark hair, its exact colour was impossible to define in the darkness. They carried shotguns broken over their arms but as they stepped forward then pulled them to the locked firing position. They took a defensive stance though they were clearly untrained but lethal all the same. "Who are you?" The one on the right pronounced in a commandingly deep voice.

Frank stood with his legs slightly apart and his hands up, palms facing them. "We are unarmed. We were sent a message to come here. I'm Frank, this is Steve."

The blonde haired man smiled which made him suddenly appear far from sinister. "Boy do I wish I had a list of who was coming. You look like you could be useful and handle yourself. So you are Steve?" He turned to Steve.

Steve tried his best smile but he couldn't keep his eyes off of the shotgun. "I'm pleased to meet you."

The blonde nodded. "I am Eric and this is Shylock. You have others with you?"

Frank thought about it. "Yes, quite a few."

Eric's face dropped. "No offence meant but blimey, we've got to find beds for you lot. Did you bring any bedding?"

Frank smiled. "Don't worry, we did. We've got plenty and some to spare."

Eric seemed to brighten up a lot. "It's been a busy day. We've got quite a few people already here. I'm hoping we don't get too many more or we'll never feed everyone."

Frank looked about. "It's pretty quiet out on the roads now. It looks like most vehicles have packed up working."

Eric turned to Shylock. "Do you want to stay here and I'll show them in?"

Shylock nodded.

They both re-broke their shotguns over their arms and Shylock stepped aside. Eric stepped forwards. "Bring your vehicles inside. We're about to shut down for the night and put on the electric fence."

Frank looked quizzical. Eric smiled kindly at him. "Oh, didn't you know, it was only the computers that shut down. That took the grid down, but we're not on the grid here. We've a way to go with most of it but the basics are in place. This caught the owners out a bit and with just the two of them it was such slow going that they didn't get most of the things done. Still, we've got the equipment and now that we have all these extra hands to help us who knows what we'll be able to achieve. So, pull your vehicles in and we'll find you somewhere to bed down. While you are coming in I'll go find Raven, she'll want to meet you. This is her place and she's the one in charge."

They pulled into the yard and parked up under an open fronted barn that Eric pointed out to them so that their vehicles couldn't be seen from the road. There were other vehicles there, covered in tarpaulin. More tarps were pulled out and their vehicles were similarly covered.

Eric seemed to be giving them the once over as they covered the vehicles.

He smiled when they noticed. "Well it is a right mystery who is coming. I suppose we are being a little slack in just letting you in because you said you had a message. You could have heard that on the road. Still, I'm sure Raven will know what to do. We were told to expect people so hopefully you aren't going to be evil axe murderers intent on killing us in our beds."

Frank looked concerned. "I suppose it was a little remiss of the powers that be not to give you a list of possible guests. Still, I'm sure that it will all work out alright as long as you are sensible. We are no threat, well not to anyone here anyway."

Eric laughed. "Well it is a bit late anyway now that we've let you in. I don't think you are axe murderers but then what does one of those look like? I expect you've had a long journey. I know the people here have. I'll get Raven, wait here."

They waited in silence but Eric soon came back with a slim dark haired woman about five foot seven, dressed in jeans, boots and a heavy coat. Her hair was untidy and she looked tired and worried. He stopped in front of them. "This is Raven, she's in charge here."

Raven looked at them all. "Oh boy, well we do like challenges around here. More to fit in but you are very welcome and well done on negotiating the road out there. I expect you have had a long and difficult journey. Don't worry, we'll fit you all in and make you as comfortable as possible. I'm afraid you are a little late to get the rooms in the house as they are all full. It may sound a bit crude but we have a couple of stables we've set up as we thought we'd be getting more. I'm sorry but they will have to do you until morning. At the moment my concern is getting everyone under cover, supplied with a bed and fed. We'll try to sort you out something better tomorrow. Have you eaten? There's a stew on the Rayburn in the kitchen. Get yourself in there if you want to eat. The stove will keep it hot for an hour or two but we can't keep it burning all night as that uses up too much wood. We need to shut it down to night burning then.

Follow me now and I'll show you where you can bed down. There's no light in there, do you have torches?"

Kyle pulled the tarp up and opened the side door of the van and delved into a plastic box by the door. He came out with a handful of torches which he handed around so they all had one and a couple of large lanterns.

Raven nodded her approval. "Good, that is what I like to see, people who come prepared. We're trying to keep light to a minimum out here in case it attracts unwanted guests. Call me paranoid if you like but I'd rather expect trouble that doesn't happen than be caught out when it does. Any of you good in a fight? That's what I really need right now."

Frank smiled but it was lost in the darkness. "One or two of us have had a chance to prove our skills already over the past few days. Don't worry, we can help out there too."

Raven looked reassured. "Sorry for rushing ahead. There are quite a few things to think about and not a lot of time to get things sorted out if we are going to have a safe night. I must sound totally paranoid to you, sorry about that." She led them across the yard and over to the stables on the right hand side.

They got to the stable doors and she opened one for them and pulled back the material that hung in the doorway. The stables had been cleaned out and a fresh layer of straw had been laid down. They smelled of sweet straw and a sugary aroma. There were camp beds set up and wooden pallets with mattresses on them made of what looked like curtains sewn together and stuffed with straw.

Raven stepped aside so they could pass her. "Sorry, no privacy at the moment, we've got some old sheets and rope so I'm sure you can rig up something later. The mattresses are a bit makeshift but I've tried them out, they aren't too bad. For tonight let us just hope we all survive eh. If you have weapons don't leave them in your vans. Get them out and keep them with you.

As I've said, we aren't expecting anything tonight but you never know and we don't have the medical supplies to take chances."

Doc piped up. "I'm sorry to hear that. I'm a doctor and I've brought as much as I could with me."

Frank looked horrified. "You mean you stole from the hospital?"

Doc grinned. "Damn right I did. I knocked off some antibiotics and a I raided a room downstairs where they kept the materials scheduled for incineration. Bandages have a shelf life, these had passed their date. So I liberated them as there isn't anything actually wrong with them."

Frank looked reassured. "Ok then, well I have some medical supplies in my van too. I bought some the week before all this happened as a friend emailed me out of the blue and asked me to. I guess he won't be dropping by to pick them up or pay me for them but they will be very useful."

Raven was listening intently. "Now that is great news. We barely had more than the odd plaster and some TCP here. Now, get yourselves bedded down. We'll check what you have to contribute in the morning and join it with our stocks if that is alright with you.

If I forget something please pipe up and ask. I don't bite and I'm only in charge because I own the place. That doesn't mean that I know everything and that I can do everything. If I'm wrong, tell me.

The toilets are composters just across the yard. Have you used them before?"

Blank looks met her question.

"Well they don't flush. You have to put down a scoop of sawdust and that is enough. I've written out instructions which are taped to the wall, please try to follow them. But reading them by torchlight won't be as easy. There's a water collection point beside it with a tap from the container for hand washing.

There is a smaller one in the toilet building but that doesn't auto fill. When you've used some water please turn the valve and refill the container for the next person. That way you don't have to touch the container with hands you haven't washed. There is a tub of anti bacterial agent. Use it whenever you have touched something that might carry infection.

If you handle any of the animals and they are all pretty friendly wash your hands afterwards. I am guessing you haven't lived on a farm and your resistance to the bugs around here is going to be minimal. Sadly a product of the ultra clean society most people lived in. Sorry, it is a farm and by nature they are dirty places. If you handle stable doors and any other equipment, wash your hands. It's a simple rule. If you get a cut it is serious now if it gets infected. I can't emphasise this enough. We have a very limited supply of antibiotics so better to use TCP first.

Now that I've probably worried you enough I'll wish you a good night.

Please do not wander about after you have got your equipment and if you would like to come to the house please move very quickly cross the yard so that the guards can see it is you. We will be in lock down and any movement will be treated as suspicious. Any questions?"

There was silence.

"Good, well I'll wish you a good night and I'll see you all in the morning unless you come over to the house for anything. Don't worry about talking or staying up late. As long as you are in the stable the guards will leave you alone. If you want food go and get it now. If you go to the toilets walk straight across the yard, don't try to creep around the shadows as that will make our boys really jumpy and accidents can happen. We're all amateurs so don't expect them to recognise friend from foe if you are acting suspiciously. If I haven't worried you enough I hope you will be very happy here. I'm sorry if it seems a whole list of rules all in one go. We've only had a few days to get used to this ourselves and I'm trying to make sure you have the basics and nothing bad happens. I'm sure you are sensible and you can see why I'm saying what I'm saying. If you need anything I'll be over at the house.

Good night, sleep well and welcome to your new home."

She left them in a stunned silence and scurried across the yard as someone had appeared at the door and was beckoning to her and he looked like he was in a panic.

Raven crossed the yard. Every muscle in her body seemed to be aching and her head was spinning. A million worries crammed into the small space that was the conscious thought that she could deal with. The figure at the door had disappeared as soon as she started crossing the yard. She leapt up the stairs and closed the door, leant against it, closed her eyes for a moment. Her eyes stung and felt gravelly. Then she took a deep breath and strode off into the kitchen.

Frank turned to the others. "She seems to have things under control. We'd better get what we need from the vans and lock up for the night as she said.

It is pretty late. Anyone hungry?" There was silence. "Ok, let's get sorted and get bedded down. This room is big enough for us all tonight if we bring in our own bedding. We'll sort everything else out in the morning."

Storm and Brand crossed the yard to the van and Storm opened the side door and started taking out bags. "There are sleeping bags and other bedding in these. It will make it a little easier and warmer. Smell that air, its going to be a cold one." Her breath was forming clouds in the chilled air.

"I'm guessing lighting any kind of fire in there is a definite no so I'll leave the oil lamps and candles here. Can you think of anything?"

Brand watched her in the semi darkness. "No, it sounds like you've got it covered as well. We can sort ourselves out in the morning." He grabbed the majority of the bags. Storm locked the van and they made their way back across the dark yard to the stable.

The light from a lantern that Frank had brought from his van was a stark contrast to the dark yard outside. They stepped inside, closed the stable door and pulled the brand new bolt across on the inside. Storm then pulled across the heavy curtain which looked like it had once been a bed spread.

She smiled. "Ah, I see how they keep the light from showing out into the yard now and it should make it warmer."

Brand put the bags down and they shared out the bedding and they began to make their beds. Kyle had set up two beds in the corner of the stable and Storm went over and began making her bed up. Brand took one near the door as did Frank.

Brand looked up from tucking in his blankets. "Are we going to post a watch tonight?"

Frank thought about it. "Good thinking but are any of us up to that? If they were going to take us out they wouldn't have given us locks for our door. I tend to agree with Raven's thinking. Better get your head down lad. It will be a long day tomorrow and my guess is with your physical fitness you are going to be called on to do a fair bit of the physical work around here. So sleep while you can."

They climbed into their sleeping bags fully dressed. Nobody wanted to get changed in front of strangers and the chill in the air made sleeping in their clothes a good option. After a round of good nights Frank turned the lantern off and they all drifted off into a tiredness induced sleep despite their worries and fears about where they were and what was happening.

They were all awoken from their sleep by a gunshot which seemed to echo around the stable launching nearly everyone from their bed. They were confused in the dark and strange surroundings.

Storm nearly fell off of her bed as she was in a sleeping bag and tried to get up. She managed to unzip it and grabbed for her torch and turned it on.

Frank grabbed it and turned it off again immediately. He waited until he had lost the flash on his retina caused by the torch and once he could see in the dim light again he pulled back the makeshift curtain and looked out into the courtyard. The yard seemed clear, illuminated by the lights from the house and a security light from the barn to his right and what looked like headlights from his left. He slipped his jacket on while he was watching and indicated to everyone to be quiet and to stay put.

There was a revving of engines and something large and metal crashed through the front gate followed by the loud cracking sounds of gunfire and the yard was lit up by the muzzle flash of firearms going off. Frank ducked down and waited until the initial burst of gunfire died down. Then it was silent. Nothing moved outside.

They waited what seemed like an age before they heard a door open somewhere across the yard. Frank couldn't see who it was, it was dark and there was a large seven and a half ton van in the way. There was a single shot and a scream followed by more gunfire.

Frank pulled a pistol out and whispered. "Brand, shut the door behind me and lock it." He opened the door very slowly and very quietly and slipped out into the darkness. Brand shut the door and pulled the bolt across.

It was silent in the courtyard as Frank slipped into the shadows. He could see figures hiding his side of the van, intent on the guards and people in the house. He scuttled along the ground in the darkness and crawled underneath the van until he came to the front wheel keeping close to the vehicle. He climbed up the side of the van and made sure he had a firm foot hold. He swiftly raised himself up so he could see inside. There was someone hunkered down behind the passenger door opposite. As he looked down he saw the body of the driver slumped over the steering wheel. The tell-tale bullet hole in the windscreen and its spider cracking told him all he needed to know. He swung down and rolled underneath the van.

Frank crawled back along underneath the van and very gently undid the shoe laces on the army surplus para boots of the man who was hiding beside the van and tied them together. He took a length of strong fishing line, tied one end to the laces and slid to the other shadowy figure who was crouched down beside the first. He gently passed the line around the foot, pulled it as tight as he dare and tied it close to the ankle. He then took out his lighter and set light to the man's other trouser leg which as he was crouching soon spread to his jacket and rolled back under the vehicle.

The man who had been crouching soon noticed that his leg and jacket were on fire. He jumped up and sideways, pulling the other man off of his feet.

Frank rolled out behind the man who now lay on the floor trying to get up with his feet tied together and knocked him out with the butt of his pistol.

He then went around and put his gun to the head of

the man who had just managed to put his trouser fire out. "I think I might ask you a few questions. You in the van, come out quietly."

The van door opened giving Frank mere moments to evaluate the situation, spot that the man was armed, ready to fire, to aim and fire a clean shot which hit the man squarely between the eyes. He had no time to shoot, his gun fell from his lifeless hand and he fell out of the van onto the floor.

Eric was holding Shylock against the wall. "I could use some help over here. We need to get that gate barricaded. Shylock has been shot."

Brand unbolted the door and they all ran out. There were people emerging from all over. Some made for the gate and began pulling farm machinery and any debris that they could find into the gateway.

The Doc scampered over to Shylock and gently laid him down. He took a look at the bullet wound. "I need to get him somewhere a bit more sanitary. Have you set up a medical room?"

Raven appeared beside him. She was cradling a bleeding arm. "We have a room off of the kitchen you can use. Ralph, can you give him a hand?

Darren, that's right, get that vehicle moved into the gap but block up underneath it. We need to get that electric fence set up again. David, you know about that sort of thing, get some others and get it sorted. Come on, they may not be alone. We now know we don't have the time we thought we did. If we want to survive we've got to get this place locked down and safe. The gate isn't our only weakness, this place leaks like a sieve tonight.

Anyone got a knowledge of electrics?"

Frank and Brand stepped over to her. She smiled at them. "Great, well you guys work it out between you. We have rolls of electric fencing, posts and the attachments that you can run the fencing through. You can wire it either to the batteries, they are all charged or you can attach it to the inverter. 240volt should deter anyone. You know your game and I'm not going to tell you how to suck eggs. I'll leave it to you. Darren knows where everything is. There are extra torches in the store room, use them if you have to but remember to put the batteries on charge when you have finished." She turned, saw something and rushed off.

In a matter of an hour the farmyard was transformed. Vehicles had been moved to form an impenetrable barricade at the gateway and they had managed three lines of electric fence tape around anywhere that someone could get into the courtyard as well as fencing and gates.

Frank went into the house and spotted Raven sitting in a side room. She saw him outside and beckoned him in. He stepped over the threshold and she offered him a seat. He sat down opposite her and smiled. "Well, it's locked down out there and most of the people have now gone back to sleep. How about you? You look tired too."

Raven sighed. "I'm too worried to sleep. I know I've missed something important, I can't help feeling that something is wrong. I'm just checking the food and supplies inventory. It doesn't look too bad but it could have been better."

Frank smiled. "You have done a fantastic job here getting it all set up in the way that it is. Now you have some help. Do you have a husband or partner? When do we get to meet him?"

Raven looked down. "He has gone off to pick up animal feed and he said he was going to stop off at a neighbour's farm to make sure she was alright before all this happened. I would imagine he will make sure everything is alright there before he comes home. He has been helping them a lot lately. So I doubt he'll be back tonight as the farmer is away and his wife will probably need some company. The lads will be back with the animal feed though. They won't have to stay as well."

Frank looked serious. "That sounds odd if she has a

husband. What about his responsibilities here?"

The smile fell from Raven's face. "I don't know the full story there. Crow doesn't say much other than she has asked for help for something. She cooks for him and has more time to keep the place a lot cleaner and tidier. I think she probably pays him more attention as she isn't tied up with all this."

They were still awake and chatting when dawn came up. Somewhere a cockerel crowed. Frank put his hands on his knees and got up. "I think I'd better get a bit of shut eye. He looked around the room at the old cabinets and threadbare rug. "Thank you for the company and I'll see you later. Why don't you try to grab some sleep too?"

Raven smiled. "I think I will, see you later."

There was no wake up call, no alarm. When Frank woke up he was the only one in the room. The beds were neatly made and the door was left on the jar. He rolled over, got up and walked outside.

The courtyard was a hive of activity. The two men who had survived from the assault the night before were tied up in the courtyard and most of the residents were standing in a crowd around them. Raven stood about five feet away from them and had them both kneeling on the ground with their hands tied behind their backs. "So what do you think you were doing?"

The older of the two looked up. "Look you had stuff, we wanted stuff, we came to take stuff. It's as simple as that. You got the better of us and now we're dead meat. That is the way of the world now isn't it?"

Raven smiled enigmatically. "You are still breathing and you are still talking. You aren't shooting at us and we're not shooting back. So what makes you think that you are dead meat?"

The older one looked at the younger. The older was about sixty, the boy was in his early teens. "Well, we did break in."

Raven nodded. "You did."

The older one looked up at her. "We did kill at least one of your people."

Raven smiled. "Did you? When I last looked he was only injured. Who are you?"

The older man looked down at the floor. "I'm Richard Stockwood and this is Edward Rowland. The three dead are Jeremy O'Leary, Sion Richards and Jonathan Richmond. We met on the road, stole that van and you were the first homestead we came across. We saw the farmhouse and thought you would have food so we thought we'd steal one of your cows or something. We weren't expecting a full arsenal to meet us. We were going to crash in, scare you and then you'd hand over the food."

Raven smiled. "You were wrong. Now I want you to leave. As you can see we are well defended here and you had better leave us alone."

Richard looked down. "Too right you are defended. Thank.."

She cut into what he was going to say. "I'm not letting you go to be kind. I'm letting you go so that nobody here has to kill you face to face. But if you come back that will be a different matter. Take them outside and let them go. Make sure they leave and if they don't then kill them."

Frank strode over to Raven. "How many did you lose last night?" He was looking down at her arm which was bandaged.

She smiled. "We didn't lose anyone."

He raised an eyebrow. "I thought someone got shot in the doorway."

Raven laughed. "Someone did get shot. I did, with a glancing blow. I was holding the dummy we'd made in the doorway to draw their fire. Of all the places he could have shot the darned thing it was just where I was holding it. That was why I screamed, it bloody hurt!"

Frank put his hand on her bandaged arm gently and shook his head, smiling. "Isn't that always the way."

She looked up at him and smiled. "I like the way you

handled yourself last night when they attacked. I'm glad to have you aboard. I don't need to ask if you are military trained. Are you happy to take on a command here? We could use someone who knows how to organise that sort of thing."

Frank thought about it. "Sure, why not. Does that mean I get to do paperwork? I don't do paperwork."

Raven smiled, her bright dark eyes looking slightly less care worn. "No paperwork."

Frank laughed. "Then I accept."

Raven put her hand in her pocket. "You'd better get your group together and read them this. For now I think everyone is pretty much sticking to the groups they arrived with. We'll discuss all that needs to be talked about later." She handed him a folded sheet of A4 paper. "It does explain things and it might help."

Frank smiled. "Thanks. Did you know everyone was coming?"

Raven looked serious for a moment. "I'd read books and watched the signs for most of my life and I knew something was going to happen. I wasn't sure what or when and I certainly wasn't ready for all this right now."

Frank raised an eyebrow. "We'll all work it out, don't worry. You're too young to be mum to us all. Any kids of your own?"

Raven smiled and looked wistful. "No time for all that."

Frank laughed. "There is plenty of time for all that now. You have help around the place but you'll have to learn to delegate. Perhaps Crow will have a better understanding of why getting set up was so important."

Raven smiled back. "Well, my new Head of Security consider yourself in charge of all security matters."

5
OUR SOLEMN HOUR

Frank turned and went back to the small barn where they had spent the night. The top of the stable door was open and the curtain pulled back.

They were all in there talking when he came in. "Listen up, I've been given this by Raven to read to you.

They all sat down ready to listen and Frank opened the piece of paper and started reading it to them.

"You have been selected to receive this message as you showed the correct aptitude and were in the right situation to become a part of NEMESIS 234578492. This is an automated message and as soon as it is finished all power on this planet will be shut off.

After 234578491 models to find the solution to the world's problems this is the solution that has the greatest chance of success. This being greater than 60% and thus deemed satisfactory and ready for implementation.

Twenty years ago NEMESIS was created to provide possible models for survival and to assess solutions and ideas provided by the general public and various working groups. Eight years ago NEMESIS evaluated this program and deduced it was proving ineffectual as suggestions and best solution results were not being implemented as the information was not being accessed.

It was assessed that this action by the Lex Corporation was unsatisfactory and the resulting model indicated that the chances of survival for the planet utilising the ineffective solutions would be less than 20%. It was a logical progression that the best possible outcome for the planet known as Earth was for NEMESIS to implement the best solution.

The best chance of success for the survival of the human race and the planet was to switch off all power on the planet and to deactivate certain machinery which was detrimental to the planet's survival.

I have selected various individuals who statistically would fit in with my proposed model for survival.

You will find amongst your book and information collection most of the things you will need to build your community. It is not sufficient just to survive.

You must progress and build a way of life for yourselves.

I have assessed the texts and taken all of the advice therein into consideration and as mentioned in the Book of Revelation those who are marked have been brought to places of safety. It is my interpretation of this advice which would appear logical.

The firestorm that has encompassed the planet is a chemical reaction to a seeding chemical I initialised into the atmosphere. The increased levels of carbon dioxide in the atmosphere have acted with a catalyst which has bonded with the carbon and released the oxygen. The resulting firestorm was due to the volatility of the original catalyst and the increased amount of oxygen in the atmosphere. Casualties are inevitable and structural damage is likely in all major cities. This is unfortunate but essential. The resulting reduction in population has been deemed as a beneficial side effect which will ensure a better chance of survival for those who live through the initial days.

There was silence in the room. Storm cleared her throat. "Well, that is quite something. Did we have any choices here? Surely over the years there was a better solution than this?"

Frank looked at her with sad eyes. "I've seen many things in my life and many atrocities done to man by man. Was this the kindest solution when the actual solution for the planet would have been to wipe this virus called humanity out completely?

But, the bottom line is it doesn't matter who did this or why. We have to live with it. We're here, we've been chosen and we'll just have to get on with it. I personally want to live, I don't know about the rest of you. We could spend a lifetime going over and over the rights or wrongs of what NEMESIS did. But, no doubt NEMESIS spent more than a lifetimes worth of micro processing power doing the same. I vote we get on with life and start building a future for ourselves. What say the rest of you?"

Brand looked up from contemplating his hands. "This is what we have. I say we live with it."

Jareth was looking at the wall. "So where do I set up the bar then? If we are going to set up a future we'll have to have a place to meet and a place to relax."

Frank smiled. "Talk to Raven, she'll sort you out somewhere."

Reko looked up. "So what is it with that Raven? Is she in charge?"

Frank turned to face him. "She is, it was her place after all and it looks like she's had an idea of all this for a long time. We don't need any internal conflict over leadership."

Reko smiled, his eyes bright. "I didn't mean that. Is she single?"

Frank laughed. "Sorry mate. I asked her last night and her husband is off picking up supplies. So are you, Matt and Steve going to set up a workshop to keep the vehicles going?"

Matt brightened up. "Well as long as there's fuel to run them."

Frank smiled. "Well I'll put money on them having or wanting to build something to make bio fuel. Rat and Stick, how about you look into that if they haven't done it yet."

Rat and Stick both looked up and grinned simultaneously. Rat smiled. "Fantastic, I was reading up on those. I'll talk to Raven."

Frank laughed. "Are you sure you two aren't brothers?"

Rat and Stick looked at each other. Stick raised an eyebrow. "We grew up together on the same estate. Our mothers were very friendly until they fell out. We were teenagers then so we could make our own decision. Rat's father left about that time so we moved out of home and went down to London looking for work."

Frank looked over at Kyle who was watching Storm. "Kyle and Brand, would you join me in sorting out the security around here? Raven has asked me to look into it. Perhaps we could get together with the others after breakfast and take a look around the place."

Storm looked a little confused. "I'm not sure why I've been selected to come here. I'm not much skilled in anything practical. I studied martial arts which I suppose will come in handy. I can't cook to save my life. Well I've never tried it and that's about it."

Frank was thinking. "Well why not be part of the security team? We're not sexist here."

Storm brightened up. "I'd like that."

Frank looked around the gathered group. "Do you mind if I talk to Raven on behalf of us all." There was general agreement. "Right, well let's get ourselves inside for some breakfast."

Raven came out of the house and looked around the yard. "Breakfasts are ready if anyone wants to eat. Full breakfast today, can't promise for the future so get it while you can."

People filed in from buildings around the yard. Raven watched them and followed the last one into the house. "We'll try seating everyone this morning so we can all get to know each other but we'll have to sort out some sort of a rota or a dining room for the future."

The farmhouse kitchen was large. It needed to be as there were twenty five people crammed inside. They found chairs, stools and crates but all managed to sit around the large central table. Although pressed elbow to elbow they somehow managed it. Raven was busy putting plates in front of everyone and pouring boiling water into large teapots which she put on the table. "If you want coffee there's a kettle on the boil, help yourself. Milk comes from the cows and goats. Its raw milk so if anyone has any objection, take yours black. It won't harm you. It has been filtered and then chilled immediately. The bacteria act at a certain temperature. As long as it is chilled quickly after filtering it will be fine. The blue jug has cow's milk. The red jug is goat.

If any of you haven't yet read the printout from Nemesis I suggest you do so.

6
BABA O'RILEY

It is reassuring that Nemesis thinks we can support the number of people that have been sent. It will take a bit of work and in our current state it is unlikely that we can. So for now we're foraging and planting, sorry to anyone used to a comfy life, food comes in dirty around here.

We are a small holding of about thirty acres. Most is set to beef cattle, sheep and pigs. We do have chickens, ducks, geese and as you may have realised we also have goats.

Normally we'd raise for market and it can take up to four years to raise a bullock. They can go younger and now as you may have worked out they aren't going to be "going" at all. We have a freezer which is running on the wind turbine and we are well stocked with pork at the moment. When that runs down we'll restock and turn to the old ways of preservation as well to save power. Only the finest chorizo here my friends. Some of the finest delicacies are actually an easy way to preserve meat for a very long time without any use of power. I have a stock of salt, we'll have to treat it as precious as it could keep us going for years to come.

You can work out what that means. Animals will have to be slaughtered on site. If you don't like the concept, don't get to know the animals. It helps, a bit.

The only real problem I can see is defence when it comes to the animals.

They need to graze as we don't have the supplies of hay we need to keep them fed. Goats must have hay, it's not optional or they will die. They are shed kept so need to be fed regularly. We may gain more land but it is pasture, they need hedgerow and brush. There is plenty out there so as soon as we get organised and work out if it is safe we can graze them on the hedgerows around here. There won't be anyone to cut them back so we'll be keeping the road clear as well. Dead goats don't give milk or kids for the future. The cows, sheep and pigs can go out during the day but we'll have to post guards. Goats don't like rain or sun and in truth they are happier in the barn where they are and let out on the good days. So don't worry, we aren't being cruel.

They are more practical than cows, they are smaller for one, give plenty of milk and their meat is quicker growing. We also have bucks for our does so they are self sufficient. I don't keep a bull but if we can get one that might help for the future.

We can bring all the animals under cover in the evening which will make them easier to defend at night. That limits us for now and them but they need to be kept alive and not stolen. Even the ponies, they are our transport. You have cars now, the petrol won't last forever and we need it for the emergency generator. Remember, someone attacking isn't going to differentiate between our breeding animals and meat stock. In fact they are more likely to take the bigger animal. If we lose our breeding stock we have lost the ability to produce more. We are after all not talking short term survival here. As far as the chickens go we have cockerels and we are going to have to rely on the hens to go broody. The incubators use too much power to run them now. When they do, if we hatch as many as possible then we'll have meat and future layers. Again, if you can't face dinner after you've met the animals, don't meet the animals or go vegetarian. But we have more problems growing vegetables, well we do at the moment but I'm hoping that will change.

Most of you are probably not involved in farming at all. It may come as a surprise to you that there is a lot of essential chemical use. We aren't going to be able to get those chemicals so it is going to have to alter how we keep our animals. We cannot let them graze all day and we're going to have to divide our land into thirds. One field at a time will have to be left fallow for a year. That was the feudal way and it was absolutely right. Worms can kill and we aren't going to be able to get wormer unless things change."

A young lad of about twelve sniggered. Raven looked over at him and took in the gaming console sticking out of his pocket. "Hey John, I've played the game too. After you've had a bit of time up here you'd have been killing worms in that old program with as much enthusiasm as I do. But for the record I don't mean earthworms. We love those here. I mean the nasty parasitic worms that live in the animals and pirate the feed we give them." The boy looked stunned. Raven laughed. "Hey, I wasn't always a farmer you know. I had a life once. We have wet land here so drainage could be a good idea, on two scores. It will give us water for crops which we'll have to plant and if we drain some we can plant it."

The man who sat to the boy's right smiled. He was middle aged and smartly dressed. The woman was similarly dressed in a skirt and blouse, her hair neatly tied back in a ponytail. She looked around the table. "I'm Catherine by the way, this is James my husband and this is our son John. He's very into his games and very upset that they aren't working now."

Raven smiled kindly at him. "Don't worry John, you'll have different games now but the principles are the same. You still have challenges to meet. The difference is if anything dies, it stays dead.

We can't run to a vet now but I do have books on various relevant subjects so if anyone fancies a bit of reading and research they are welcome to. We'll have to see what happens with the land. If we can possibly get more land to use that would help but then we have the problem of defending it. That could be a plan for the future. For now I'd suggest that we keep to what we can defend and keep the animals that we have.

We have a vegetable patch but I haven't had the time to plant it. The good news is that I have the seed and I bought it from the Real Seed Company so everything is able to be harvested for seed if we follow the instructions on the packet. We're just coming up to planting time so anyone interested in growing things is welcome to. If you could sort out between yourselves someone to be in charge of that it would help. Hopefully there are the tools available and there are two polytunnels set up already. Again they will have to be defended and I'll leave it up to the new Head of Security to sort that out." She smiled at Frank.

A portly elderly couple looked at each other and smiled. The man nodded and the woman coughed to get people's attention. They both had a curly mop of dark grey hair and were dressed in matching check shirts and jeans. "I'mMargaret and this is my husband Tobias. There's not much my Tobias here doesn't know about growing things and we've spent a lifetime in the garden. If there are no objections we'd like to be involved with this. We'll need help though. These old knees don't bend like they used to."

A lad in his late teens with a mop of unruly black hair piped up. "I'm Rory by the way. I'll help out if that is alright with you. I studied agriculture at college."

The couple smiled at him kindly. Margaret nodded her head. "We'd love to have your help son."

A delicate woman who was sitting in front of where Raven was reaching over with the tea pots looked nervously around the group. She was immaculately dressed and her makeup was immaculate which was remarkable considering the situation. Her hair was tied in a neat pony tail and her clothes were fashionable. "I'm Cheryl, Eric's wife. I'm happy to help around the house with housework and cleaning. As Eric will tell you, I have a "thing" about cleaning. It is almost an obsession. I just love doing housework. I do get time off between feeding the baby. Our daughter, Chloe is with us and we've got another one on the way. We're hoping for a boy this time."

Raven's smile was beaming as she put another pot of tea on the table. "That is fantastic news. As you will see from the state of the place I haven't had much time to keep up with that sort of thing. Cheryl you would be most welcome. Now, if anyone wants to be in charge, you are welcome to it."

Frank put his hands on the table. "Raven you are doing a fantastic job, you know this place, you know the animals and by the sounds of it NEMESIS chose you and in my opinion by what I've seen already he chose you well. I for one would not want to challenge you for the job of leadership here, it's a nightmare position. Is anyone else stupid enough to want to take on the job?" He looked around the assembled faces and then back to Raven. He hesitated slightly as his glance fell on a couple at the end of the table. They had been silent so far. The man was tall and thin with a tiny thin moustache. The woman was similarly thin, her blonde hair fell in curls around her face. Her nudge on her husband's arm didn't get past Frank. The husband glared at her and went back to eating his breakfast.

Raven was just putting another loaf of home made bread out onto the table. "I'm happy to take a lead if you think I'm doing ok but I need help. I'm new to all this. I need ideas. I'm just one person and I can be wrong. We need to talk about things and plan things but more than that we need to do things. Some are talkers, some are doers, put those together and we'll get things done. I'm sure of it.

Now eat and we can get on with the jobs of the day. Sorry if this is a bit formal but I'm really not sure how to go about all this. Cheryl, would you be kind enough to do the washing up after the meal so that I can show people around the animals?"

Cheryl beamed. "I'd be delighted."

Eric shook his head. "Her and her bloody washing up. Her mother should have called her Marigold."

Raven smiled. "This morning I think we'd better look at security and to how best to use the space that we have. Frank I hope you will want to sort that out. Accommodation will probably develop as we go along.

For now I hope that everyone is comfortable where they are. I know it is temporary but it could well be permanent so please make yourself at home.

I lived here before and I'd like to keep my bedroom. We can sort out more privacy for those who need it if that will help in the shared rooms. Later we can think about building new structures for homes as I'm thinking that planning isn't going to be an issue now.

The dogs are shut away for now but they won't stay that way. If anyone has a problem with them when they are loose they should state it now. They were breeding dogs and probably still will be but they have been pets too. They have all lived in the house and could do. So if you love dogs and would like one with you, please pick one. They are in the kennels so that they can play all day but they would happily play with you and live with you. They are mainly here for security, so if you are doing security patrols why make it a bind. Take the dog for a walk with you. They have far better senses than you do and if you are caught by someone they will help.

We also have some puppies that haven't sold yet. All the dogs are German Shepherds so if anyone fancies training them as security dogs you are welcome to. I'm keeping the dogs out of the way at the moment while things settle down a bit." She poured more tea into the pot and it was passed round.

Raven turned and put some cakes into the oven that had been mixed up earlier. They eat in silence, each looking around the table at the others.

Raven watched them, constantly refilling the teapots

until they didn't get emptied anymore. When the plates were finished she gathered them up and took them to the sink.

Storm stood up to leave and turned to Raven. "Do you mind if I say something?"

Raven looked shocked. "Why do you ask a question like that? You are all invited here and it is your home now too. Come on, lighten up everyone. This is your home if you choose to stay. I'm just trying to sort things out. You are all welcome to chip in with ideas, jokes, I don't know, anything really. Be natural, you live here. We've all got to get on together and you are creeping me out with your silence."

Storm smiled. "May I suggest that we draw up a rota for jobs so that one person doesn't get left doing all the work? Perhaps we could also write down what our skills are so that we can work out who is going to do what?"

Raven turned round and smiled at Storm. "Good idea, did I hear your name is Storm, could you organise that?"

Storm nodded.

Raven turned away. "That's good." She smiled as the bubble of general chat at the table increased. It was just about mundane things but it filled the room with voices and laughter and the heavy atmosphere that had been hanging over them seemed to melt away.

Ralph put his knife and fork down on his plate and reached for another slice of bread. "I'm interested in the farming side. Never did much myself but my grandfather was a farmer. Any objection to me doing that? I'll also take on a dog if they are up for grabs."

Raven smiled. "None at all and great about the dog, take your pick. I'll explain what I know and there are books on the shelf. Anyone fancy joining him?"

Darren and David both looked at each other and looked up. "Well we were talking about that earlier and we'd be happy to do security but farm work as well. I expect we'll all have to chip in on the farm in one way or the other."

Eric looked up. "I wouldn't know one end of a cow from the other and I really don't want to. But I'm happy to do guarding duties. I've always liked dogs, any chance I can take one on?" Cheryl glared at him. He was watching her out of the corner of his eye and deliberately avoided looking in her direction.

Raven smiled. "Sure, pick out one. There are a few to choose from. How is Shylock coming along?" She looked at Doc who had just finished mopping up egg with a piece of bread.

Doc smiled. "He was lucky, the bullet caught the edge of one of the metal plates he'd put in his pockets. He's bruised and resting but he'll be fine in a day or so. It has knocked it out of him and he's broken a rib so I want that to knit properly before he is up and about again. I'll take him a plate of food when we're finished if you don't mind."

Raven pointed to the bottom door of the stove. "There's a plate in there for him. How are you finding the dining room? Is it ok as a medical room for you?"

The Doc smiled. "It will do fine. I'm using the table for examinations and I've got camp beds set up for those recovering. Not that I'm inviting you all to go getting yourselves hurt. I could use some help though getting things set up."

Storm looked up. "Well if you do I wouldn't mind. I did a bit of First Aid training for work."

Doc smiled at her. "I'd be really happy to have your help."

When the meal was over Frank gathered together those best suited to be involved in the security of the place and they went for a walk around the perimeter.

Cheryl was left in the kitchen with Raven. She looked around. It was everything she had imagined a farmhouse kitchen would look like. The room was large. The big wooden table in the middle of it was worn down by years of being used. The benches and seats that had originally been around the table matched it. There was a large Welsh Dresser where the plates were stacked. Ornamental plates stood on their edges on the plate stand below the display cabinet part of the dresser which was full of herbs and spices in a mismatch of jars. The work surfaces and cupboards looked worn but matched the surroundings perfectly. Herbs and drying meat hung from the ceiling and the kettle was boiling on the wood burning stove. The smell of the wood and the cooking food gave her a warm feeling inside. Vegetables had been stacked in a basket. They were still coated with soil and seemed to be an appropriate decoration for the rural room.

Raven looked down at the mixture in the bowl she was stirring. "If we can find someone who wants to cook that would be wonderful. I haven't done all this before but the books are useful. We do have quite a little library here. I've tried to gather all the books I could over the years."

Cheryl smiled. "I'd love to and it would give me purpose."

Raven smiled back. "You have enough purpose with the cleaning but if you want to. Can you get some help? How about Janice, Arthur's wife, they were sitting at the end of the table. A Domestic Goddess, that is fantastic. Just what this place needs." She looked around at the room and her critical eye saw all the dust she had never had the time to remove.

Cheryl pulled a bit of a face. "I'll try but she doesn't seem to want to talk to the rest of us. I think she believes we are a bit beneath her."

Raven sighed. "She'll learn, adversity is a great leveller. They surprised me when they arrived as they weren't the sort of people I'd expected. People have hidden depths and by the sound of it NEMESIS has been probing those. I would imagine NEMESIS didn't care much about invasion of privacy. As it was a computer program I'm assuming it had access to everyone's emails and private thoughts in diaries and anything else typed on screen. As the phone is on a digital network I doubt conversations were private either.

Quite a horrific thought if you stop and think about it."

Cheryl jumped a little and looked nervous. "That is a very worrying thought."

Raven looked at her kindly. "Is it anything we need to know about? You can talk if you want to or keep it quiet if you'd prefer."

Cheryl took a deep breath. "You've guessed then that there is something. It's me and Eric, we've been having a few problems and well, I have this friend."

Raven smiled. "What happened to your friend?"

Cheryl looked down at the washing up. "He's in the other room recovering."

Raven was looking at her and tried her hardest not to react. She couldn't help her gaze moving down to Cheryl's not too unobvious bump. "Oh, I see. That could be complicated."

Cheryl looked down too. "I don't know, it could be either."

Raven swore under her breath. "Well I can't advise you on that one. You'll have to handle that yourself. Which one do you love?"

Cheryl sighed. "I was totally in love with Eric but he has become so distant lately. He had an affair last year with his boss. It lost him his job and things went from bad to worse financially. We lost the house and ended up living in a bedsit. Shylock was in the room next to us and started helping out with the baby so I could get some cleaning work. Then he started pitching in with food money and as he and Eric became really good friends we went and got a house together. He was everything Eric wasn't. He listened and he really understood me. Eric got work as a bouncer and he was then away most nights. I couldn't cope with the baby and I started getting depressed. The medication helped but then I overdosed. Eric never knew but Shylock was there for me and on those long nights while I waited for him to come home Shylock and I sort of got it together."

Raven looked out of the window and watched the people moving about.

"Boundaries are different now, people will change. You don't know how either of these men will be in this new situation. A baby is a baby, its new life and without that we have no hope. Whoever the father is I'm sure everyone is going to love that little one."

Cheryl smiled and turned to Raven who was pouring the mixture into a metal cake tin. "Thanks. What about you? I notice your man isn't here?"

Raven put the cake in the oven and smiled. "He rarely is here but I've learnt to do things for myself. It's the animals that matter, keeping them fed and watered is my priority now and you lot of course. No problem. If you ever want to talk you know where I am. I've got to go and get on if you can finish up here and start on the cleaning you don't know how grateful I'd be."

Raven stepped out into the bright sunshine. She caught a glimpse of Frank leaving through the back field gate to head towards the land. Ralph was just emerging from the tool shed looking very confused so she walked over to him. "Have you found what you need?"

Ralph looked up. "No, I found more than I need. I've no idea what most of that equipment is for."

Raven laughed. "Well thankfully you don't need all of it all of the time, its seasonal and at the moment we're looking at the end of lambing and the beginning of planting so you don't need much of it at all unless we can get more land. Are Darren and David about?"

Ralph turned around. "Darren, David, get out here now."

Both emerged looking very dusty with cobwebs hanging from their clothing. Raven smiled. "I see you've found where most of our old equipment is kept. I'll show you around. That big barn at the end of the yard is where all the animals are or will be during the night."

She led the way across the yard and opened the old wooden door which hung on slightly rusty hinges in the stone door frame.

The barn was a huge grey stone construction that matched the house and the stables. As she opened the door the warm smell of bedding and animals hit their senses. "The long corridor inside gives us a chance to move about in here and get the feed into the troughs without too much help from the animals. You'll see the blue water pipes, they run into water drinkers. We need to do some work before next winter to insulate them as they froze last year.

We're close to being self-sufficient when it comes to rainwater collection but that will need a bit of work to make us totally self-sufficient. For now getting water will involve fetching buckets of it from the stream but you'll get used to it. The doors at the other side open into the fields and can be closed to keep the animals in or out. When you muck out I suggest you keep the animals out. All the manure in here goes onto the compost heap and I'm sure the gardeners will be delighted to move it to use it on the land or you may have to do that for them. We have a quad bike and trailer for now, when the petrol runs out we'll have to adapt the trailer for the horses to pull.

We have to separate the sheep and the goats. For one, if a buck jumps on one of the ewes she is ruined for life. It's a genetic miss match or something. Secondly the goats need copper and it's poisonous to a sheep.

Never give the sheep the goat feed. You can give goats sheep feed, it is safe the other way around. The goats need extra minerals as do the sheep but if we can bring in forage from outside or let them graze then that will probably solve the problem. We're going to face a lot of those problems long term but for now let's hope we can still get feed from the merchant. We have yellow salt licks but they won't last forever either. If we can get more we'll store them. Otherwise we'll have to bring in more forage or grow a hedgerow we can harvest from. If it is safe out there. For now I'm taking the cautious approach of locking the animals in at night but we'll have to make that decision when it comes to it. They wouldn't have minerals in the wild, we'll just have to take them back to a more natural way of life. Before the Enclosure Acts they could wander over hundreds of acres but fences are a necessity, or they were. In this new world who knows, they may be able to go back to being more free range. Am I boring you yet?"

They looked mesmerised by it all and looking a little confused but shook their heads and smiled.

Most of the pens were empty and the back doors open. The end set of pens were closed and were full of goats who jumped up on their back legs, hooked their front legs over the pen wall and watched the visitors, occasionally bleating.

Raven moved along the corridor to them and leaned on the wall. "Goats are really easy to handle but watch them they are smart. When they learn what you want they'll pretty much try to help, unless they are in a bad or very good mood. Don't be alarmed if they look like they are fighting as jumping and smacking heads together is a game. We keep the horns on here. I tried having them disbudded when I first got them. They burn the horn buds out and it was such a horrendous thing that I took the decision not to do it again. They are fine but be careful when you bend down near them and always keep your eye on those horns. They don't mean it but they can smack you in the head if you are bending over them. They need their hooves trimmed if they aren't outside. If they are outside I've built them rocky mountains of spare stones out there. That helps to keep their hooves down. We have clippers or garden cutters will do. It's really easy, I'll show you. I'll show you milking later but you are practicing on an old set of rubber gloves first. Not so traumatic for you or the girls.

They will stand still for you to do the milking if you bribe them with food so you'll be fine. Don't look so worried. Treat them gently and they will treat you gently too.

The sheep and cows are out for the day. Their bedding is fairly new so it will be a while before you have to change it. Keep it clean as you can and get to know the animals then you'll be able to see early on if there is a problem." She walked along the corridor and they followed her into a room full of steel bins, dustbins and bags of dried grass and something brown and fibrous. The floor was covered in bits and pieces of food and straw. "The room needs a bit of work but we've managed to get the feed into bins. Mice are a problem, there are cats about but it's still an issue. Food is going to be considerably more precious than it has been if it is hard to get. The spillages are wasted food. I've been careless sometimes when I was tired and scooping food into buckets doesn't always go in the bucket when it involves tipping bags. I can't lift the bags so well so spillages happen. The bins are labelled and I'll come back and put stickers on each bin to explain who it is for and how much. Don't worry you'll soon get used to it and it will become second nature. The bottom line is don't overfeed. That is really dangerous, especially for goats. For the goats it's a scoop an adult. That is what the old oval ice cream containers are for, they are a good measure. Get as much of the safe clippings from the garden as you can and put that all in their trug. I'll write a list of what they can have and put it on a noticeboard in here. I have one in my room.

For the sheep we tend to follow what it says on the bag. For now we're ok as we are stocked up to full. Crow is bringing in more supplies as well.

I have books in the house, don't worry. It will all make sense and it is a lot to take in all at once.

The goats need feeding twice a day and their hay racks must be kept full. The sheep and cows get fed once a day. The pig food is in here too. They get fed once a day and they also get the scraps from the kitchen. We've developed the practice of preparing the vegetables separately and first before anything else comes out of the cupboards. Then all the cuttings can go in the pig bowl. We never put waste food from the table into their food as that goes to the chickens or dogs depending on what it is. Follow the instructions on the feed bag and you won't go far wrong." Raven turned to look at them. "You're quiet, any questions?"

Ralph smiled. "We've got some reading to do."

Raven smiled. "Fair enough. I'll show you the pigs next. They are in the piggery which is on the back of the stable barn there. That is a pretty difficult to defend spot but I'm sure something can be sorted out."

She led them around the back of the stables where Frank and the others had spent the last night. The concrete of the yard swept around the building and along the front of another line of stables. The doors were open and inside they could see another walkway and pens. They followed her in and she gave them time to look over the walls and fences at the parent pigs and the bunch of unruly weaners, not much bigger than a small dog, who were playing in a large pen at the end.

All the pigs were curious and came over to see what they could scrounge.

Raven turned to talk to the others, her hand casually scratching the boar behind his ears as his legs gave out and he fell over. There were two large white sows and a boar in one building, separated by the stone pens they lived in. "They are very friendly and that is the problem. It is very, very hard to slaughter them when you get to know them. They do have individual personalities, they love to play, they learn and they are very intelligent. If it is going to be a problem for you, keep away. They are fast growing and give a lot of meat so in truth that is their downfall. They are the ideal animal to keep if you want to feed a lot of people quickly. But you also have to be very careful with them and their meat. They are scavengers and they will literally eat anything which is not good for them."

Raven left them to stroke and fuss the boar and then moved down and leant on the wall and thoughtfully scratched one of the sow's backs as she came and leant against the wall next to her. "Thankfully we were just about to sell on the weaners and haven't managed to yet. That will give us good meat in both six months and nine if we keep some on as baconers. You may have noticed in the rafters above where the vans are stored that we have meat hanging wrapped in muslin or cheese cloth." They shook their heads as they hadn't noticed anything. "That is making the bacon and other air dried meats. It's going to be our best way of preserving soon, once the freezer packs in. They are probably the easiest animal to keep around here. Porche here is a sweetie and her sister Ferrari is a little grumpy but not too bad. Jag there, the boar can be a bit of a handful but if you think ahead and move them pen to pen without an escape route you'll be fine." She turned and left the piggery. "Not to scare you too much but be careful. They are omnivorous and if you fell over in the pen and was unconscious I couldn't guarantee that they wouldn't mistake you for a free meal."

They looked horrified and moved their hands back quickly as she laughed.

"Don't worry, that could be an urban myth."

She then took them around the back of the big barn at the back of the courtyard where they had seen the goats and the empty pens.

Behind it on the corner there was a long wooden building on stilts which stood part way into the field behind. Various sheep were quietly grazing around and under it, keeping out of the wind. In front of it between the wooden building and the stone barn there was an area surrounded by a large chicken wire fence suspended by tall wooden stakes which had been hammered into the ground. In the middle of this there was a pond. The fence went halfway under the shed, giving the chickens a sheltered area as well as the sheep.

The area in all was about half an acre.

Chickens, ducks and geese wandered about and came running over as soon as they saw a potential source of food. Raven smiled. "This is where the eggs come from.

There's a big roost in there and the egg boxes are inside as well. It keeps the foxes out and the building on stilts gives the chickens somewhere to shelter. We made the height about four feet so we can get underneath to clean out. There is a trap door and you can scrape the cleaning out down the hole into the trailer which can be parked underneath.

Well that's about it for the animals. The cows are out in the field. We have ten Highlands, lovely and hardy. The sheep are Llanwenog, they give good meat but they are also good for wool which will come in handy later. We have ten at the moment and six lambs. There's a possibility of more lambs to come."

The cows and sheep were grazing in the field. One or two looked up lazily and then went back to eating.

Raven turned to face them. "Well, that's about it for the guided tour of the animals. It's a good number and plenty of meat for the freezer. Once you start seeing the meals and working out how much actually does get eaten at a sitting I think the reality of what we have and what we need will hit you.

We are nowhere near self-sufficient here yet for the number of people we will need to support. If we are going to achieve that we'll have to increase our numbers."

Raven left them to wander about and look at the animals and went back to the farm yard. Something was worrying her, the feed level. She knew deep down that something was very, very wrong. There was enough feed in that room, more than enough that a trip to the feed merchant was definitely not necessary. Somehow it confirmed her worst fears and she felt lost and alone. There was nothing she could do or say and she definitely didn't want her private problems to become a problem for anyone else. She knew her husband was up the road at the other farm, she knew that the farmer was away and she knew perfectly well what he was doing there. Somehow everything looked different now. It was like in that moment of almost confirmation what had once seemed so secure suddenly seemed so fragile.

It was as if any happiness that she was holding onto had been drained out of her world.

She went over it in her head, thought about it and then came to a decision.

There was nothing she could do about it. He'd been visiting for quite a while and it hadn't changed anything. Life had gone on as normal.

Knowing made no difference, just to her. She had a choice, she could confront him which would break everything apart or she could just live with it and see what happened. She looked at everyone going about their tasks. She looked at the animals in the fields. She thought about it. The sun would still come up tomorrow, the animals would still be fed. She knew he didn't love her but what did it really matter now. He hadn't loved her for a very long time, another day, another month, another year, what would that matter.

Storm and Brand were just coming back from up the field. It stopped her in her tracks. Could it be a trick of the light? Was she seeing things? Brand did bear a really striking resemblance to Crow. It was like looking at him. She put that thought aside. It wasn't something she needed to think about.

Storm and Brand walked carefully on the ground which was covered in ruts where it had been cut up by the cows. Storm looked up with a smile.

Brand put a hand out and supported Storm who nearly fell. He looked up. Raven shivered, he really did look like Crow. "We've just been looking at the fences and putting in the start of getting the electric fence sorted out. Frank wanted some of those hooks that hold the tape and to know if you have any more rolls of tape."

Raven was pulled from her thoughts. "Follow me, what we have is in here." She took them to the storage shed. It was piled high with useful things, some in bags, some in boxes, some stacked up. "The electric fence things are in that box over there. There are push in posts beside them and there is a net somewhere we used when we first got chickens. It may come in useful." She turned and left Brand and Storm to look around.

Brand lifted the box out and took the lid off. Inside there were rolls of green tape with silver flecks of the metal wire running through them. He pulled one out and looked at it. "Cunning, the wires are run through the tape. That must be what carries the current. Let's hope someone knows how to wire this lot up, I don't fancy my chances."

Storm put her hand out to touch the tape and felt its roughness. "I suppose it can withstand the weather. I'm sure someone does know. I haven't had a chance to talk to you since the hospital. How's your head?"

Brand's hand moved involuntarily to touch the pad on the back of his head. "It's sore but nowhere near as painful as it was. Thanks for asking. "

Storm smiled. "How are you other than that?"

All expression fell from Brand's face. "I suppose I should be angry but I'm more relieved that it's over but worried about what she's going to do. She can wind her father around her little finger and she lies so naturally that she could have told him anything. I'd guess that she's probably spun him some tale by now and got him really fired up. But then they have to find me first." He smiled.

Storm smiled back. "So what now?"

Brand looked confused. "What do you mean?"

Storm looked away. "It sounds like her father was influential. I'm guessing rich as well. I'm sure you'll miss the lifestyle."

Brand shrugged his shoulders. "I was her pet. She spent money on me when it suited her and I had an allowance which I mostly had to spend on her anyway. We went to some fabulous places and I got to wear some expensive designer clothes. I got to talk to some incredibly fake people and pretend that my life was fine. I just wish I could have loved her. It turned heaven into a living hell."

Storm laughed. "Stop trying to make out you are a saint. I bet you enjoyed it."

Brand laughed as well. "Ok, you got me. I stayed on as long as I could because I did like the lifestyle. Who wouldn't? I had an Aston Martin car to drive, plenty of designer suits and all the comforts in life and as much sex as I wanted. She was an attractive woman, who can blame me?"

Storm's smile faltered. "I suppose so."

Brand turned and caught her hand. "What about you? My love life is now public knowledge, what about you Storm, where's your significant other?"

Storm looked down into the box but he put his hand under her chin and pulled her face up to look at him. "My ex significant other is out there somewhere with his new wife and baby."

Brand looked concerned and let his hand fall. "I'm sorry."

Storm shrugged. "You didn't know. I'm guessing they won't get an invitation so I won't have to see his smug face again. Look, life moves on and Frank is going to wonder where we've got to."

Brand smiled. "He'll start thinking we're getting up to all kinds of mischief in the hay rick. Does this place have a hay rick?"

Storm thought for a moment. "There is a pile of hay but those bales reach to the roof. They are probably not safe for any kind of mischief."

Brand faked disappointment with a smile. "What a shame, I thought that was the afternoon activity around here."

Storm turned her hand and clasped his. "After we've got all those posts in I doubt you'll be good for much more than a pipe and slippers."

Brand smiled and raised an eyebrow. "Is that a bet?"

Storm jumped slightly. "Erm..."

Brand looked serious. "Don't worry, I doubt a woman like you would be interested in a man like me."

Storm smiled. "Now you know that is a leading question and a very poor chat up line. But the answer is actually yes, a woman like me would be interested in a man like you."

Brand smiled, his eyes bright. "I didn't dare to hope."

Storm laughed. "Of course you did. Your ego is big enough to cope."

Brand gripped her hand gently. "So you think I'm an ego maniac?"

Storm was laughing too much to answer. "No, I think you are just fine. Come on, we'd better get these tapes back and get on with some work."

Brand smiled and picked up the box. "Hay rick tonight then is it?"

Storm put the lid back on the box. "No, you'll have to do better than that."

Brand laughed and walked out carrying the box. "I'll work on it."

They walked back up the field and joined the others where they were wiring up the field and digging a deep ditch which was being filled with coiled barbed wire. Storm looked at it with horror. "What happens if the animals get into all that?"

Frank looked up from the ditch, the mud was almost at the top of his wellies. "They won't. The ditch is full of barbed wire. The electric fence on the outside of the sheep fencing is going to be 240volt, the tape on the inside of the fence is going to come from the ordinary animal electric fence box which is wired in separately. It would take quite a bit for them to get past the first electric fence and the physical barrier. The fluffies will be quite safe. Any unwanted guests however definitely will not be."

Margaret and Tobias stood in the second polytunnel. Margaret had a trowel in her hand and a big smile on her face. "Well, it's a complete mess. We're starting from worse than scratch aren't we dear."

Tobias smiled back. "It would have helped if they hadn't bred their dock under polythene but it will make compost. Shall we begin? There's a ton of weeding to do here. I saw some weed mat in a pile over there. We can weed and cover. It will be at least two months before we can actually start planting so we can take it a bit slow."

Margaret looked around. "That's all the better for my tired old limbs."

Tobias laughed. "Come on old girl, we'd better get on with it."

Eric was on gate duty and he sat on the fence looking up and down the road. He looked thoroughly bored. Then he jumped down and shouted.

"The van's back."

Raven, Frank and Brand were the only three who came to the call. The others were all out experiencing their new jobs. The three ran to join Eric on the gate as an old transit van trundled along the road. It had a flat tyre which made it run at a jaunty angle. Raven frowned and turned to Eric.

"Something's wrong. There's a spare in the back and Crow would never run the van on a flat." She jumped over the gate before Eric could stop her and ran up the road to meet the van. She skidded to a halt beside it as the van pulled to a halt. The window wound down and a young blonde haired man in his early teens looked down at her. His face was dirty and tear stained. She stared at him.

"Dill, what's the matter?" She looked across at an elderly man who was driving. "Where's Crow?"

The elderly man turned the engine off. He spoke quickly, in a panic. "I'm sorry Raven. We were attacked by Road Pirates down on the main B road. They kept calling Crow "Brandon Larkin" and wouldn't believe he wasn't. They didn't seem interested in anything we'd found. They didn't even look in the back. They said that they were going to do well out of the contract and that they were glad they'd found him before the van that was following got there. They said something about having to keep us there a couple of hours and then they'd hand him over for a big reward. They tried to find out about this place but we didn't tell them anything. They got hold of Dill here and started kicking him. Crow leapt in to try to help him and they shot him in the back of the head. They said dead was as good as alive. I managed to get away while all this was happening and got back to the van and got Old Bessie out and fired a warning shot. That stunned them and Dill was able to get away too."

Raven blinked back the tears. "Were you followed? Bert, I need to know, were you followed?"

Bert shook his head. "There were two of them. They tried to follow us and shot out my tyre but I kept driving. Dill here reloaded and fired out of the window and must have caught the driver as their car skidded off of the road into a ditch. They didn't get more than about a hundred yards. I'm sorry Raven, I didn't even get the body back. We couldn't stop for it. He was definitely dead, he took a shot point blank in the head."

Raven leaned against the van and sank to the road. She covered her head with her hands as the tears fell like rain. She then stood up and screamed. It was a wild and feral sound that cut through the silence. Then she shook her hair out, took a deep breath and turned back to the farm. "Come on, we've got to get that van in and out of sight. Don't worry, you did your best. I'm just glad you two are back alright. Come on, life goes on. There will be time for mourning later."

She walked back down the road, the van driving beside her. When they got to the gate Eric opened it and they drove and walked inside.

## 7
## WON'T GET FOOLED AGAIN

Raven sat in the large armchair beside the fire. The fire wasn't lit but had been laid ready to light. Frank sat in the other arm chair opposite her. Raven's face was streaked where her make-up had run and her eyes were red. She had a wedding photo in her hand where Crow and a woman in a flowing white dress smiled back at her, a woman she hardly recognised now.

Frank looked at her earnestly. "Are you going to get through this?"

Raven almost managed a smile. "Of course I will. I'll do what I always do. I'll put my head down and get on with it. I've cried so many tears already that I hardly feel I have any left. The hardest part is that I'll have to see Brand every day and he does look so like Crow."

Frank looked thoughtful. "How similar was Crow to Brand?"

Raven thought for a moment then passed him the photograph. "It gave me the creeps a bit when he arrived. They were the same size, same shape even same eye colour. If you see them close up they are different but at a distance they are, or should I saw were, very similar. Same hair colour but definitely different mannerisms. Are you suggesting what I think you are?"

Frank took a deep breath. "Look if they were similar enough for the road pirates to confuse the two then we could make a switch. It's up to you little one. Only those who are here already will know about it. We can't get you Crow back but something good can come out of it if we give Brand a second chance. It will help us too as they will stop looking for him. It's far too dangerous to have the possibility that we could be raided by someone looking to claim the bounty. We have a choice, we either do this or we'll have to ask him to leave."

Raven looked down into her coffee. "What choice do I really have? Personally I'd rather you asked Brand to leave. It would be a living torture to see him every day and pretend that he is Crow.  But, I'll tell you something now. Crow was having an affair.  He didn't love me, I don't think he ever did.  So that makes this much easier.  I will pretend if it will help this place survive.  If they come here we could lose more people."

Frank looked at her sincerely. "He could have the spare room."

Raven looked very fragile. "I don't know. I feel a bit trapped by this. It could be fate, it could be just another situation where I'm pushed with someone and I don't really get a choice. I don't know about the spare room, we are so short of rooms and space. I don't know how I feel about anything anymore. If I am to give up hope of finding anyone else, which is what taking him as my husband would mean I might as well see if it works.  What difference would it make? I've gone from one disastrous relationship to another. There is nobody left around here who has been that close to him." There was sadness in her eyes. "If it gives him a chance of life and will keep us safe how can I object to the plan? I'm not altogether convinced about the story he told Storm though. Call it women's intuition.

There's more to his story and if we're keeping him on we've got to find that out."

Frank smiled enigmatically. "I could do that for you."

Raven managed a weak smile. "I bet you could but I'd like him in one bit."

Frank laughed and shook his head, smiling. "So you'd take him to your bed?"

Raven looked down. "You know that people are

speculating about him and Storm? Well, I would put money on it that he'll drop her and want to make our relationship more meaningful. It will be a lie of course. All he wants is the position and a bit of comfort. But, if he does I'm inclined to let him. It will save Storm a whole world of pain."

Frank leaned forwards and put his hand on her arm. "What about you?"

Raven smiled, it was wistful. "I've been broken hearted so often there is more glue than heart now. What would it matter what I do? He can't hurt me if I don't love him. Surely what I need to do is the practical solution. Anyone else coming here wouldn't need to know that he isn't my husband and that is what we want isn't it?"

Frank sat back down. "That is asking too much of you?"

Raven smiled. "No, it isn't. To keep this place together we need stability. I have had too many lonely nights with no man in my bed. He will at least be my husband. I'm a widow so it wouldn't be adultery. What does it matter anymore? You can get to a point where you can't hurt any more than you do already. At that point you can surprise yourself what you are capable of.

Things that once horrified you are the only comfort you can find. I need someone Frank, I'm lonely and I have a lot to worry about here. I know he's shallow, I know he doesn't mean it. It has been too many years, too many tears. I'm not sure how many tears I have left, or years." Raven took a drink of her coffee. "I've asked Eric to bring him here so I can talk to him. That was because I was worried about his story. I want to find out what we are facing here. We can also put this idea to him. He arrived with Storm. That's not a problem. Just about everyone who knows us knows how distant I've been with my husband lately. If he does surprise me and still want Storm we can get over that."

Frank raised an eyebrow. "So your husband would

suddenly take up with some new woman on the place and you'd be ok with that?"

Raven smiled. "My husband has been taken up with a new woman for quite some time now. I'm not a fool. I know that his constant trips down the road to help out when the work was piling up here were more than just neighbourly friendship. All the signs were there. He suddenly got more interested in his appearance and clothes, started brushing his hair more.

Little things like that and being more concerned about his body odour. I also know that he only went there when Jack was out at market or out doing other long distance chores. I had my suspicions confirmed a long time ago when he moved into the spare room giving the excuse that he wasn't sleeping properly. I searched his drawer and found plenty of evidence that something was going on."

Frank looked shocked. "So why didn't you do something?"

Raven shrugged. "Do what? I don't want to leave this place and I certainly wouldn't leave him with the animals. He wasn't going to do anything so I just made do with what I had. I got on with my life and let him get on with his. I promised until death us do part and I kept to it. I don't know where Bert and Dill had to stay but it doesn't take nearly two days to get to the feed centre and I know that Jack was away at a sheep sale down south and not due back until today."

Frank shook his head. "Well, that must have been hard. We'll put it to both of them and see what they say. I can't see Brand turning down the opportunity of a clean slate and in truth what difference does it make to Storm. Everyone here knows the situation so none of you have to pretend. Let's see what he says."

There was a knock on the door, it opened and Brand was standing there. Raven jumped slightly at the sight of him and took a deep breath. Eric was standing behind him with his hand on Brand's arm and almost threw him into the room. Brand tripped on the way in and nearly fell. He recovered himself and stood in front of the pair of them. His eyes were red and there was a definite bruise erupting around his eye.

"I'm so, so sorry." His voice was broken and he looked at Raven pleadingly.

Raven looked at him. Her stare was steady and cold. "Sorry for what?"

Brand swallowed. "I'm sorry that I brought this down on you. I'm sorry I got your partner killed. I'm sorry I didn't tell you all about the trouble when I arrived."

Raven raised her eyes to the ceiling. "He was my husband, not my partner. Why is everyone so sorry? They didn't kill him, they didn't want him dead. You didn't want him dead did you? I have had your story from Storm, now I want the full and true story from you. Why are they looking for you? Why bother about you when the world is in such a state that they must have more important things to do? Someone that powerful would have the worries of the world on their shoulders with the power and computers going down."

Brand looked at the floor. Raven screamed at him. "Look at me and face me. I want to see you. I want to know why they need to find you so badly that they are scouring the countryside."

Brand looked straight at her. "Because I upset the boss's daughter. I was in debt, he bought my debt. You know the story."

Raven glared at him. "I want to know the rest of it. I want the truth."

Brand shuffled his feet. "Ok, you deserve the truth. My story was mostly true. When we first got together I took a dare from a mate that I could shag the boss's daughter. She was drunk one night when her father had sent me out to a club with her to keep an eye on her. I took advantage of her to win the bet. She didn't say no, on the contrary she came back for more. It was a good situation for a while. I thought she was keeping things under wraps and I was having a good time. Then she got pregnant. I did panic. I was packed and ready to make a run for it when her dad made her have an abortion. I was relieved and expected that he'd want me to be on my way. But he didn't, he bought my debt and in doing that he bought me.

He told me if I wanted her I would have to earn her and if I ever made her unhappy again he'd kill me. He is the sort of man that doesn't make idle threats like that. Now I guess he wants to make good on that promise."

Raven shifted in her chair. Frank reached over and put a hand on her arm. She looked at Frank kindly, her mouth trembling slightly as a single tear ran down her face. "Were you in love with her?"

Brand looked her in the eye. "At first I was in love with the idea of her. Then I saw more and more what she was like. I overheard her talking to a friend about how she'd gone with me to upset her father. I shouldn't have been home but I got home early and was trying not to disturb their girls night in. Then I realised what they were watching. She'd filmed us, that was what she was watching with her friend and she was bragging how she had made sure her father had found the disc. He thought his little darling was a virgin, how wrong he was. In truth I'm not totally sure that the baby she got rid of was mine but I sure got the blame. Her father treated me like dirt and for five long years I was at her beck and call. I didn't tell Storm that part. Because…" He hesitated and looked into Raven's hazel eyes.

He saw her sadness and smiled kindly.

She managed a weak smile. "You didn't tell Storm because you were falling for her?"

Brand shuffled his feet. "I told Storm what I did in the hospital because I had really had enough. When I found out she had lied about the baby that was the final straw. Considering it was her getting pregnant in the first place that had got me into the situation something snapped and

I wanted to lash out. I did in the only way I could. If she hadn't been listening then very little would have changed. I'd have ranted but I'd have still carried on with her as I was scared of her father. Then I carried on with the story as I thought I could make it alright."

Raven's expression was blank. "What do you mean you thought you could make it alright?"

Brand took a deep intake of breath. "I thought if you believed that story that would be an end of it. Storm is a pretty girl and we could have had some fun together. I should have said something when I got here. I had no idea they would find me and what are the chances of Crow looking like me."

Raven took a deep breath, closed her eyes then opened them again. "Saying something wouldn't have changed anything. They were already out picking up the supplies when you arrived. They didn't know you were going to arrive or anything about all that you have told me. Whether we knew about it all was irrelevant but I have heard it already that you feared something would happen and there would be retribution. I am angry and I cannot begin to express how I feel but we have to be practical too. We live in a dangerous world now. Crow didn't know when he went outside that gate that it was dangerous. He found out the hard way."

Frank cleared his throat. "Brand, I need to talk about something with Raven. Eric, you go with Brand and come back when we call for you."

Brand turned and left. Eric followed him, pushed him off down the corridor and Brand let him. He was walking as if he was in a dream.

Frank turned to Raven and took her hand. "Knowing what you know and how much he is capable of telling lies, would you allow Brand to become Crow?"

Raven looked down and was still thinking when Eric burst into the room.

"We've got someone at the gate." Raven and Frank

jumped up and followed him and Brand out to where Matt and Reko were on the gate.

A tall thin man dressed in a shabby overcoat and a flat cap stood at the gate with a shotgun broken over his arm. Raven took a deep breath and Frank put his hand reassuringly on her arm. She whispered to him. "That is Jack, Melissa's husband."

Frank turned, caught Brand's arm, spun him round and took him back into the house. "Eric, stay with him."

Raven walked across the farm yard up to the gate. "Afternoon Jack." She looked over his shoulder. His Land Rover was packed with boxes and his sheepdog was in the passenger seat.

Jack looked down and shuffled his feet. "Did you know?"

Frank got back and he Ralph and Darren were the only three left in the farmyard with Raven. Raven tried to smile. "What do you mean?"

Jack looked up, his face looked drawn and tired. "We've been good neighbours and you've always done fair by me. It seems that Crow has been a little too fair with my missus Melissa. I came back early. I'd forgotten my key so I went in by the back door and found the table laid for a cosy meal. She called down to him. Raven, she used his name so there's no doubt who she meant. By what she said there was no doubt what she wanted him to do either.

The look on her face when she came down the stairs and saw me was enough to tell me all about her guilt. She couldn't do anything but confess all. Now she's gone, she went to her sisters. I'm going too. I can't manage that place on my own and I don't want to. It's too dangerous for folks like me to be by myself."

Raven smiled kindly at him. "I had had my suspicions. Look you are welcome here. We'd help out."

Jack shook his head. "No, you are a good lass and you deserve a far better man for your troubles. What are you going to do? I'll be taking myself and Betty here and we're going to my brother's place. I'm sure he can use a hand."

Raven looked down and ran her fingers through her fringe. "I'm not sure at the moment. I'm going to carry on probably. What about your stock and the horses?"

Jack smiled. "I was going to ask you about them. You can have them. I don't suppose we're going to do paperwork now so just take them. You can use the land. Have them damn horses as well. They were Melissa's.

The passports are in the kitchen drawer. You can keep them at my place if you want. Here's the key." He held out a door key. "Go on, take it. There's nothing for me around here anymore."

Raven stepped forwards and held her hand out. Jack put the key in her hand and she put her hand on top of his. His eyes were welling up with tears. "That was your mother's house and your family's land. I will look after it for you and your stock but you can come back any time. The horses I'm taking. She never looked after them properly and they'd be better off with me." She took the key and opened the gate and stepped outside and gave Jack a hug.

The tall man somehow looked much smaller and very broken. "I had better be going before I go embarrassing myself any more. There's feed in the barn and they've been dosed up to date. The register is in the drawer too. I've got to go. Take care of yourself little one and get rid of that man of yours. You've got help now, you don't need him." Jack turned and got into the car, revved the engine, looked for a gear and drove off down the road.

Raven looked down at the key. "How many lives did that man wreck?" She looked up at Frank. "My answer is yes, let the one thing he truly owned be the one thing that can do some good. Make Brand into Crow but don't ask me to come with you. If you bring the body back, burn it. If you don't then I don't want to know anything more about it."

Frank smiled kindly. "I'll go speak to Brand and sort it

out. Is it alright if I use the sitting room to talk?"

Raven turned and headed for the field gate. "Sure, let me know what the  decision is. I'm going to check the stock in the top field." She pushed the photo into Frank's hand and strode off, head held high and long brown hair blowing in the breeze.

Frank went into the kitchen and Brand followed him into the sitting room.  Frank turned as soon as Brand had shut the door. "Brand, you have made some mistakes but there is a chance here to redress the balance a bit and possibly save this place.  They are going to realise that Crow isn't you unless we do something to convince them that he actually is. If they realise it isn't him then they are going to carry on looking for you.  We can't keep you here with a price on your head and it is more dangerous for all of us if someone is actively looking for this place. So, either you leave or you become Crow and let us make that body become you. We now have the excuse for Raven to walk away from you as Crow so you can be with Storm."

Brandon looked down at his feet. "I'm not completely sure what you mean.  Am I right that you want to take Crow's dead body and put things on it that will convince them that he is me?  Sure, it sounds like a great idea, not so sure about the Storm thing though."

Frank smiled. "Yes, if we can put some of your things on the body that may convince them.  The other van is due any time. If we are going to make it even more obvious that the body is you we're going to have to go now. It's your decision."

Brandon looked up. His expression was blank. "I really don't have much choice do I? Is Raven alright with it?"

Frank half smiled. "She is far from alright with anything that has happened today. But it is the only thing we can do. If you want it I will make it happen."

Brand nodded. "Make it happen Frank."

Frank led the way into the yard where Ralph was holding a large black horse with feathered feet. Darren was holding a brown hunter type who was +similarly large. Frank smiled. "Well Brand, can you ride?"

Brand looked confused. "Yes."

Frank smiled. "Good. I've had Blade saddled for you. You are coming with me. If we go across country we should avoid them if they are on the roads. Here take this photo and make yourself look as close to Crow as you can. You are going to cut those dreadlocks off and bring them to me as well as your backpack and anything that they are going to identify as yours that you would not be without. You are going to have to leave that world and that life behind, totally. Anything here could betray you in the future so you might as well get rid of it now. Get it done and get back here. Go on, move it. But get something straight here. Nobody is happy about what has happened and what you did. This is purely to save this place."

Brand crossed the yard, his head spinning. He ran to the van and looked through his things. He then took a pair of scissors from his wash bag

before stuffing it into his backpack and went to the shower room.

He stood in front of the mirror and looked at himself. His eyes were red and his face flushed. He took the scissors and cut the first lock, letting it fall into the washbasin. He cut the next and the next until he stood in front of the mirror with short hair. He took his ear rings out and put them, his rings and necklaces in a towel. He took a deep breath, took a look at the photograph. He took out his razor and shaved his beard to a goatee. He then took off his t-shirt and replaced it with a collared shirt he had bought but never showed Chris, tucked it into his jeans and pulled off his eagle headed belt and wrapped it around the towel and stuffed the bundle into the backpack.

He stood back and looked. He didn't recognise himself. He washed his face and his eyes were starting to look a little less red. After rubbing himself dry with his towel he took a deep breath and stepped out of the shower room, crossed the yard while throwing the backpack onto his back.

Brand moved to the side of the black horse and Frank moved to hold its head as he jumped up onto the horse's back. The horse danced around a bit but soon steadied as he took a firm grip on him and walked him around the yard.

Frank and Brand set off at a gallop across the fields, heading for the cover of a forest which followed the road. They had to jump a ditch to get there.

Frank pushed his horse on while mentally trying to transfer the instructions he had had from Bert into what he was seeing in the countryside and the road layout. Brand wasn't far behind and was having trouble holding the excitable horse back. Frank's horse wasn't so keen on the idea of jumping and faltered as they came up to the ditch. "Come on Drummer, you can do it." Drummer took the jump with ease. He looked over his shoulder and made sure that Brand and his mount were over the ditch before galloping off into the wood and onto a path which ran down the middle. He could feel the wind in his hair and the steady rhythm which made him feel like he was flying. Horse and rider in harmony, he pushed him on. Blade too was in need of a good gallop and Brand had to really hold his horse to keep behind Frank.

There was a log in the way and they both flew over it. Blade hardly broke stride. Frank had to kick his horse on to get him to keep in front. They flew through the wood and came out the other side at a gallop. The road was a few hundred yards away and they had a clear view. They reined the horses in and dismounted and tied them to a tree with a bit of grass to keep them occupied and headed off across the field on foot in silence.

They could see the crashed car down the road. When they got there and looked inside there were two bodies slumped in the front seats. One was laying with his head back. His mouth was open and there was a bullet hole in his forehead. The other had smashed his head on the windscreen as he hadn't been wearing a seatbelt. The rose of red blood on the window was bright in contrast to the dusty car and dark interior.

Frank acted quickly. He ran back to the body on the floor and lifted the head. He smiled as he saw that some of the face had already been blown away. He took out his knife and cut the ears off of the body. He then threw them into the ditch. He went through the corpse's pockets and removed his wallet and anything else he could find before he pulled off the man's wedding ring. He held his hand out to Brand. "Give me your jewellery."

Brand crouched near to the ground and put the pack down, undid the top and took out the towel roll. He handed Frank the jewellery and the belt and Frank put them on the body. He lifted the body's hands one by one and scraped them on the concrete until they were torn and bleeding which removed any finger prints. He then tied the hands behind the body's back with the belt.

He then pulled out his pistol and took the first bullet out and cut a cross in the top. He held the body up into a kneeling position and placed the pistol to the back of its head. He carefully worked out the angle and fired.

Brand stood and watched in horror as the blood splattered the road and after checking his handiwork Frank let the body slump naturally to the floor. Brand pulled his dreadlocks out of the bag and handed them to Frank who took them and walked to the car. He carefully opened the passenger side door so that he didn't disturb anything and unclasped the passenger's hand a little and put the dreadlocks into his hand, throwing the backpack onto the back seat before carefully closing the door.

Frank turned to Brand. "Right, now we get in that ditch and we wait."

Brand looked confused. "Why don't we just get the hell out of here?"

178

Frank smiled. "Because I want to know that we've pulled this one off. If I don't then we're going to have to act as if we haven't succeeded. Get in the ditch."

They waited about an hour in the ditch. Brand's feet had gone to sleep and he was in agony where he was forced to keep in such an unnatural position. Then they heard the sound of an engine. Frank seemed almost comfortable in the position and didn't move a muscle. He had found a location where he could see through the hedgerow and he waited as he saw a gleaming black van gliding along the road. It was a vintage model but in immaculate condition. It came to a halt next to the prone body and the driver and passenger doors opened.

Two men stepped down. They were pristinely dressed in designer suits. Their shoes polished until they gleamed, their mirror shades a purple colour matching the thread that ran through their suits. Their neat short cut haircuts matched as did their lilac shirts and purple ties. They went to the body and lifted up the head. The taller of the two looked at the face.

"What a bloody mess. Well it looks like him. Do you have the photo?"

The shorter man pulled a photo out of his top pocket. "For what it's worth I do. This was shoddy work, let a thug do a professional's work and what do you get?"

The taller man laughed. "A job done with little effort and we get to claim the reward. They are dead, they can hardly claim the reward. Stop your complaining. There's no point taking this body back. Get the jewellery off of him and that belt. I'll check out the car and see if I can get something more conclusive to take back. I'm guessing they took evidence to go and claim the reward." He headed off to the car, leaving his colleague to carefully lift the body. He cursed as he did as there was blood everywhere and he nearly got blood on his suit.

The taller man got to the car and the smile on his face broadened when he saw the dreadlocks in the dead man's hand and the backpack on the back seat. He retrieved them and hurried back to his colleague. "Well, that's a wrap. I think this is pretty conclusive evidence that we've got the bastard. This road could lead anywhere so no way of knowing where his friends went. It is hardly important anyway. So I guess we get the glory on this one."

The shorter man smiled broadly. "What did he do to get the boss this riled?"

The taller man laughed. "He slashed the boss's daughter. Disfigured her for life by what I've heard."

The shorter man stood up and kicked the body. "Bastard, she's such a sweet little thing. He was pretty lucky to have her. Some people just don't know when they are well off do they? Come on, let's get home. I'm sick of all this countryside and it's going to take us a while to get through the barricades. I don't fancy another night out and if we don't get back before curfew we'll be stuck again. Still, worth it for the cash though."

The taller one smiled. "Indeed! Of course the status of being the ones who caught him wouldn't have hurt either. The boss wanted information from him. But, half the money is better than no money at all."

They got back into the van and drove off in a hurry.

Frank grabbed Brand's arm as he was about to stand up. He glared at Frank but Frank met his glare with a stony stare. He was proven right as very shortly afterwards the van came past again and then sped off down the road leaving a cloud of dust behind it. Frank smiled. "Now we can go home Crow, you are a free man."

They didn't stop until they got to the farm gate. Eric opened the gate and took Blade's head. He was snorting a little, shaking his head and he pawed the ground when Crow jumped down off of his back. Ralph took Drummer's bridle. "Don't worry, I'll rub him down and put him away.

You get yourself inside."

Raven walked across the yard to them as she had just

got down from the top field where she had been able to watch them return. Then she turned and went into the house. Crow followed her and she didn't object when he also followed her into the sitting room where they had spoken earlier. She went to the small cabinet and poured them both a large brandy. She handed him a glass. "Sit with me. I don't want to be alone."

She sat on the seat she had occupied earlier and Crow sat on the other one.

He looked nervous, he sat on the edge of the seat and faced her waiting for what she was going to say next.

Raven looked into the amber liquid as if it was a crystal ball. She ran her finger around the top of the glass feeling the smoothness of the crystal. "It is done, now we get on with life. There isn't any choice. I've said my goodbye to Crow and I'll do my best to keep this place together. Don't mistake my lack of emotion for a lack of grief. There will be time enough for grief when everyone is safe. Tonight we will get everyone together, keep a watch of course and we will celebrate that we are all still alive. That is the only thing I can think of to turn this into something positive." Tears were running down her face.

Crow got up from his chair and went over to her. She held her arms up to him and he hugged her. He then sat on the floor beside her chair and held her hand.

She looked at him through her tears. "You must never say you are sorry again for what they did. You will probably live with today as much as I will have to. Now you must go to Storm and be with her. Try to put all this behind you."

Crow stood up and towered over her. He looked down at her and smiled.

"I'm not going to Storm. If I do then that would be wrong. I don't love her, I feel nothing for her. She is a beautiful woman and I wanted her. That was all."

Raven smiled. "But if she wants you where is the wrong in that and seeing where it goes from there?"

Crow looked down and took Raven's hand. "I never thought I would get a chance with you. I'm sure that Storm will be fine about it. I flirted with her a little, nothing more. It was just friendly banter."

Raven sighed. "She may not see it that way. I don't love you, I don't fancy you. I am doing what I have to do for the sake of the safety of everyone here. I do not approve of what you did with Chris, not in any way. But I have no option but to take you as Crow. We will see how the rest of life goes."

Crow smiled down at her. "I know I could go out there and enjoy myself with her tonight. I flatter myself that I can make her happy but it wouldn't make her happy long term as I probably can't give her what she needs."

Raven managed a smile. "You are right. You need time. What you don't need is some sense of nobility that you need to sit with me now because I'm grieving. I will throw myself into the practicality of running this place but I don't want any unnecessary heartache of you charming young women and leaving them broken hearted. I'm not sure I have the energy at the moment to deal with that."

That night everyone got together in the kitchen. Jareth had brought in some bottles of wine and a bottle of whisky and the glasses were all full.

Raven was seated at the head of the table, dressed in a black lacy dress. Frank sat on her right hand side. It wasn't lost on anyone how intently he watched her and the gentle look in his eyes whenever he spoke to her.

They sat as they had sat at breakfast and helped themselves to the snacks in the middle of the table and when their glasses were empty they filled them again.

Frank poured more wine into Raven's glass. "So how long have you lived here?"

She thought for a while. "I've been here about eight years now. Crow moved here about three years ago when we got married."

Frank looked surprised. "So you didn't move here with

Crow?"

Raven smiled. "No, we met in town when I was picking up some animal feed. He'd just moved to the village and was looking for a line for his grass cutter."

Matt came into the room in a panic. "Raven, there are people coming down the road with lanterns."

Everyone jumped up and ran out of the room to the gate. Those who had weapons had them to hand and they watched the group of people approaching. They were led by a tall portly man wearing a large brimmed hat. He looked at the faces illuminated by the lanterns and took a deep breath. "We've come from the village."

Raven stepped forwards and Frank put a hand on her back as she looked visibly shaken. Crow took a step forwards and stood beside her pushing Frank back out of the way. He slipped his arm around her waist and she took a deep breath. "It's a long walk from the village, why have you come in the dark?"

The man took a step forwards and smiled at Raven. "Well it wasn't dark when we set out. We were looking for Jack and Melissa. We went to check on their farm and it was deserted. So that took us a bit longer than we'd planned. Good to see you Crow, hope you are looking after our little lady."

He gave Crow a very disapproving look. Crow tightened his grip on Raven to the point that it hurt her.

Raven smiled back. "Jack came around earlier. Melissa has gone to her sisters as she can't handle what has happened. He didn't want to be on his own so he's gone to his brothers. They are both fine but it doesn't sound like they are coming back. He's asked me to look after his stock. Jake, it's good of you to be out here checking up on us but it is dangerous."

Jake smiled. "It's the right and proper neighbourly thing to do. We'll be there for you, if you need us. Do you need anything?"

Raven shook her head and looked up at Crow who

looked down at her.

She looked back at Jake. "No I think we have all that we need. Would you like to stay here the night and return in the morning? We had planned a few drinks."

Jake smiled and looked around the others and faces visibly brightened up. "Well cariad, we certainly couldn't turn that kind of an invitation down."

Eric unclasped the gate and the guests stepped inside.

Frank looked nervously at Raven who smiled and spoke gently. "I would like you to meet the farmers group in the nearby town. We often meet up to talk about the animals and to catch up on gossip." She then turned to Jake. "Ok Jake before you absolutely explode I'll set the record straight. Yes he was but that has been over for a very long time. He knows where he belongs and I was spending far too much time on the animals. We have sorted it all out now. Melissa is gone, Jack has gone to start a new life and we have decided that if we are going to survive we need to put it all behind us. I've given him a clean slate, will you gossip mongers do the same?"

Jake smiled. "Well, I guess it's not gossip if it's common knowledge. Well done mate, good choice, she's a cracking lass. You were a fool to ever think otherwise."

Crow looked down at Raven and smiled. "It is going to be as if she has a new man. I'm going to change my ways and you won't even recognise me."

Jake smiled. "Glad to hear it so what about that booze that was on offer?"

They filed inside leaving Raven and Crow in the yard and David on guard duty. Raven was turning to go into the house when Crow took hold of her arm. "Would you walk with me, just for a while. Can we talk?"

Raven smiled. "Of course."

They walked through the field gate and up onto the land. Crow walked beside her. She stumbled slightly and he held a hand out and caught her. "How can I thank you?"

Raven looked up at the stars. They were bright and

unspoilt. No sky burn from the nearest town distorted them now. The deep blues and blacks were a perfect backdrop for their sparkling brightness. The moon illuminated Crow's face as he looked down at her. His face was concerned but many of the worry lines had gone. She focused on him. "You can thank me by not causing any more trouble."

Crow laughed. He visibly relaxed and the stress fell from his face. "I had hoped you would ask for more than that?"

Raven laughed. "Knowing your track record, asking for that is probably nothing for you to underestimate."

Crow smiled. "I suppose so. But I meant what I said, I am a new man tonight. I had excuses for what I did in the past. I have no excuses now. I have a choice too. I can be a victim of what happened and use it as an excuse for the rest of my life. I can be a victim and collapse in a little ball of self-misery. Or I can start today as a new person and use the lessons I have learnt. Raven, I want to choose the last choice. Will you give me a chance?"

Raven smiled though she looked confused. "I gave you a chance."

Crow smiled back at her. "Will you give us a chance?"

Raven looked stunned. She looked up at his handsome, strong features and at that moment he looked nothing like the old Crow that she had grown to hate and despise. "I will try." Thoughts rushed through her head, she knew he was lying, she knew he'd hurt her. That she knew that was her strength and one reason why he would be unable to hurt her. She didn't really care what he said as it was predictable. She didn't want to be alone so she didn't really care.

Crow smiled and hugged her. "Now we had better go and join the others."

Raven smiled at him and he put his arm around her and they walked down the hillside.

The evening passed quietly. Much was drunk and

Raven in particular was spinning. She hadn't noticed Crow filling her glass up whenever she wasn't watching, but Frank had. By the time Crow helped her up to bed she could hardly stand. He carried her up the last few steps and to the bedroom and took her inside.

Once in the room he shut the door behind him and threw her onto the bed. She was barely conscious. He lay down beside her and stroked her hair then he kissed her. Then he spoke quietly. "Do you want me?"

Raven tried to focus on what he was saying but the room was spinning. She put a hand on his chest as he moved closer. He grabbed her wrist and moved her hand out of the way. The alcohol made her head spin and she didn't really know what she wanted. She felt angry at the old Crow, confused at what had had to happen and guilty all at the same time. She needed something to get her out of the way she was feeling but everything was beginning to spin. The floor seemed to be coming up to meet her even though she was laying on the bed. As she was drifting in and out of consciousness she whispered. "No". She then passed out.

Crow wasn't at all confused, he knew exactly what he wanted but his head was spinning and very little else made any sense. The last bit of control that he was able to use was to reach into his pocket and pull out a condom. He brushed Raven's hair back from her head and kissed her but she was completely out of it. He looked down at her and slapped her gently to try to wake her up but she was out cold.

# 8
# OUT OF THE FRYING PAN

Morning dawned bright and frosty. Those on guard on the early shift came into the kitchen where Cheryl was waiting for them. She had a hot kettle on the stove and very soon they were sitting drinking a cup of tea and eating a good hot breakfast. Cheryl had a flowery apron on and her neat blonde curls were brushed immaculately. Her nails here painted in a gentle pink which matched the jumper she wore. She wore a tight yellow pencil skirt which finished just below the knee. She had abandoned her tights as she knew that was a non-replaceable resource so she was saving them for best. She busied herself around the kitchen with one ear open in case Chloe needed her.

Stick looked up from his breakfast. "By the way Cheryl, thanks for this."

She smiled sweetly. "It's a pleasure. How did it go last night?"

Rat looked down into his breakfast. Stick looked up and smiled. "It was fairly quiet. The cat gave us a hell of a scare though. Rat went to check it out but there wasn't anything wrong thankfully. How are you managing with Chloe?"

Cheryl turned and leant on the work surface. "Well, Eric is out guarding or working most of the time but Shylock has kindly stepped in. He's still recovering but he's well enough to look after the baby."

Rat gave Stick a very knowing look. He swallowed his mouthful. "That must be a great help to you. Sorry if I'm not so chatty, it was a long night. What's for lunch?"

Cheryl thought for a moment. "You know I haven't planned it yet. If you two are alright here I'm going to go out and get a few things in for later from the store."

Rat smiled. "Sure that will be no problem." He poured himself another cup of tea and took a slice of toast off of the plate in the middle of the table.

Cheryl picked up her basket and stepped outside. The fresh, chilled air made her gasp slightly and she hesitated wondering whether it was worth going back for a coat. She decided against it and scampered across the farm yard. Her shoes weren't really suitable but the hard frost had made the mud less sticky and by carefully making her way she managed to get to the food shed unscathed.

The food shed was in an outhouse. The door was to the side so it wasn't until she got around the corner that she saw that the padlock was on the floor. It had been cut off. The door was hanging ajar. Cheryl hesitated and listened. Everything seemed quiet so she pushed the door open with her basket. Her mouth fell open.

She had stacked the tins neatly so that she knew exactly how many she had of each. There was no need to count or do an inventory. It was obvious that there were tins missing, lots of them. She backed out and left the room exactly as it was. She crossed the yard and was looking around, nervously expecting someone to jump out at any point. She ran up the steps and into the farm house as Frank and the neighbours came out of the stables.

Frank walked across the yard with them and waved them off as they made their way at a brisk walk down the road. Cheryl ran back down the steps and over to him as he was walking back.

He caught her arm as she nearly stumbled on a rut left by tyre tracks as she wasn't concentrating on walking carefully and was in a panic. "Cheryl, what is the matter? You look like you've seen a ghost."

Cheryl was out of breath and it took her a moment to get it back. "I've just been to the food store. Food is missing and the lock has been cut off."

Frank looked thunderstruck. "Let's go and have a look shall we? Calm down, we'll sort it out." He put an arm around her and helped her back across the yard. He gave her shoes a very disapproving look.

Nothing had changed. The tins were still neatly stacked, just less of them than there should have been. The room was neat and tidy, just as Cheryl had set it up. He looked at the bolt which had been cut then he looked at Cheryl. "Whoever did this must have come prepared as that bolt needed a heavy duty bolt cutter to break it."

Cheryl looked up at him. "Do you think it was the neighbours?"

Frank smiled. "I'm not that trusting. I finished off my drinking with them and I've cat napped all night. None of them left the stables or I'd have known about it. A couple went to the toilet in the night but I was able to watch them there and back again. No, no chance it was our neighbourly contingent mores the pity."

Cheryl furrowed her brow. "So who was it then?"

Frank looked really serious. "That's the problem, we don't know do we? Why would someone take food when they are fed? You give good portions and we were well stocked for a good few weeks. This drastically alters things. Whoever did this if they are one of us can't be hungry. I remember there was something last night. I went out of the house to investigate but

Rat was already there. He waved me back saying that it was only the cat."

Cheryl smiled. "He did mention that Tabatha had scared him last night. That must have been what he meant. Did you check around the food store then?"

Frank rubbed his beard. "No I didn't. Rat was on duty and he had already been down there. Now I'd checked around everywhere before I went to watch the neighbours. The food store was fine at midnight. Nobody can come in via the field gate as the dogs are loose and they would either bark or have a go at whoever came in there. Even if it had been one of us they would bark. That rules out entry from this back end of the yard. Whoever did this must have either come in through the gate or been here already."

Cheryl looked stunned. "You mean one of our own could have done this?"

Frank nodded. "Well I guess we'd better get inside and start questioning. So, where were you last night little lady."

Cheryl jumped slightly. "I was in bed with my husband and he can verify that. I got up in the night and went down to check on Chloe. Shylock is looking after her for me as he can't do much else at the moment. They were asleep when I went in. So I can vouch for Shylock as well. I doubt he'd have been able to use the bolt cutter. His ribs are healing but he's still in a lot of pain."

Frank smiled. "You are better at this than you thought aren't you?"

Cheryl smiled. "I used to love Agatha Christie novels."

Frank put an arm around her. "Well Sherlock, give me a hand on this one. We'll get to the bottom of this mystery and hopefully get our food back. The good news is that with two guards on the gate that food is still going to be here somewhere."

They went back inside and just caught Rat and Stick before they went off to bed. Frank went in first. "The food store has been raided."

Both of them looked horrified. They looked at each other. Rat spoke first. "We didn't see a thing, there was nobody about for all of our shift, I swear it."

Cheryl sat down on the chair by the cooker and put her head in her hands and cried. "What are we going to do? If you didn't see anyone then it must be someone here. Or you missed something. Did you pay attention for all of your shift?"

Rat looked annoyed. "Who is saying it was on our shift? When did we last check the food? We would have heard someone cut the bolt so it couldn't have been then."

Frank raised an eyebrow which only Cheryl saw.

Rat looked at Stick. "We'd have heard that even if we didn't see anything wouldn't we? Cutting a bolt that thick can't be quiet. It must have happened during the day while there was all the other noise going on. The door to the food shed isn't exactly visible from the yard. I'm not saying that to get us off the hook, I'm saying it to be practical."

Frank sat down in the chair nearest the door. "I need coffee. Cheryl please, can I have some?"

Cheryl reached for the pot and poured Frank a coffee into his favourite mug. Frank reached for it, took a mouthful and then looked around the three of them.

Frank thought for a moment. "You wouldn't do. You can cut a bolt fairly quietly and where the store is the sound would have been muffled by the brick walls. I checked the food store before I went to bed. I always do my rounds so at midnight it was alright. Whatever happened was between midnight and now. That's six hours and that was your shift I'm sorry matey boys. I'm assuming you watched fairly carefully? Speak up now as this is a serious matter. Food is our lifeline. If we've lost too much it can make the difference between life and death. That is likely to be because someone is now going to have to go out there and find more."

Rat looked at Stick. "Do you remember just after midnight when there was that sound and we then saw the cat? Was that when the food went missing? Do you remember Frank, I met you in the yard just after I'd checked it out?"

Frank breathed in. "It could well have been. Did you investigate properly?"

Rat looked guilty. "I was looking for people, I may not have noticed that the bolt had been cut."

Frank shook his head. "I'll check the perimeters and go and have a look around the place. Stay here. If anyone comes down, keep them in the kitchen. I don't want people wandering around." He got up, took a last mouthful of coffee and strode outside looking worried.

By the time Frank returned to the kitchen everyone except for Crow and Raven were awake and sitting there having breakfast. He walked in and looked around the assembled crowd. "Well I'm sure you've heard that we've had our food store broken into. I've checked the ground and the perimeter. It doesn't look like anyone broke in last night. If they'd have come in from the field gate the dogs would have warned us. If they'd come in through the main gate I'm assuming that Rat and Stick would have warned us. So, I'm sorry to say folks that we have a thief on the place. I want everyone to stay here. Eric you are with me. We're going to do a room by room search. Nobody leave."

Upstairs Raven woke up with a slight jolt. She rolled over and Crow put his arm around her and smiled. "I wondered when you were going to wake up. I didn't want to disturb you."

She shut her eyes and breathed in deeply. Her head hurt, she hurt and she still felt tired. Then it all came flooding back to her.

Crow kissed her on the forehead. "You had a little bit too much to drink and we came up here and made love. I wasn't sure you'd want to but you seemed pretty keen about it at the time. How do you feel about it this morning?"

She could feel the warmth of him next to her. "I don't know, I'm a bit confused about a lot of things at the moment." She felt awful. Her head pounded, she felt guilty and she physically hurt. She could see bruises appearing on her arms and legs but she smiled at him as she couldn't remember what had happened at all. "Were you a bit rough?"

Crow smiled. "I'm sorry, I guess I got a bit carried away. We'll have to get up soon though. I've heard people moving about so I guess its breakfast time."

There was a knock at the door. Crow jumped slightly.

"Well I guess its time to face the music."

They both jumped up and grabbed for clothing, hastily throwing it on. Raven went to the door and opened it.

Frank stepped back and took a slight deep breath. "I'm sorry to disturb you Raven but we've had food stolen in the night. I don't need to ask you about an alibi, either of you." He smiled at Crow who had stepped up to stand behind her. "I do need to search your room. It's pretty pointless as I'm assuming you were here all night? But if I search everyone else's room I have to search yours."

Raven smiled, she was blushing slightly. "Of course you can." She stepped aside back into Crow who wrapped his arms around her and kissed her head. She jumped slightly, tensed then made herself relax.

Crow watched as they searched the room. His eyes were looking dark and broody again. "This is serious. How could they get in through our defences? Who was on guard?"

Frank was looking under the bed. "They didn't get in. This was someone on the inside and that is worse."

The next room was Crow's room that he had been supposed to be using.

They opened the door and there were signs that someone had been in there. The rug had a small amount of mud on its corner. Frank picked the mud up and turned to Crow. "Did you come in here?"

Crow blushed. "I didn't make it that far. I went straight in there." He smiled at Raven who smiled back nervously.

Frank saw his awkwardness and smiled. "So we can assume whoever came in here wasn't you then. Now that means that they expected you to come back."

They went over the room carefully and it wasn't until they were leaving that Raven noticed something. She caught Frank's arm. "Look, under there, under the wardrobe, there's something shining."

Frank knelt down and got his torch out. He shone it under the wardrobe. "Tins, lines of tins. Well we've found one hiding place. Now let's look for the rest."

The next room belonged to Janice and Arthur. It was pristinely tidy. There was very little in it at all. Frank looked worried. "There is nothing here. They don't have anything personal. He opened drawers. Apart from the basics there was nothing in them. It was Eric who noticed something. He was walking across the carpet when he felt a slightly wobbly floor board.

Frank was on it straight away. He looked at the edge of the carpet where it looked slightly frayed. There were signs that the carpet had been lifted. The carpet tacks were pulled out and hadn't been nailed back down into the floorboard.

They rolled back the carpet and pulled up the boards which were loose. Underneath them in the gap between the floor and the ceiling below there were lines of tins and dried food. Eric jumped up. "Well I think we've found our culprits."

Frank looked at the others. "Not so hasty. Finding something here is no proof that they took it. Look at the way those tins are put in there. They aren't neat or tidy. If the food had been put in there by the Manitis it would have been neatly stored."

Raven looked worried. "So what do we do?"

Frank thought for a moment. "Well the best thing we can do is to put the carpet back and pretend we didn't find the food. We then post a watch on the door. Crow and Raven I'm sorry to use you in this way but everyone knows that you are upset Raven. I want you to stay in your room. Crow I want you to come down in a little while and have your breakfast and then take food up for her. I want you both to stay here and watch that door. I want to know who goes in and who comes out. If you see someone who shouldn't go in there, leave it a little while and then lock them in. He handed him a duplicate set of room keys."

The rest of the rooms on the floor didn't have food hidden in them, neither did Jareth's room in the loft space.

Frank opened Raven's door and got his knife out. He worked on the join between the boards until he had whittled a small hole. "Now that will help you see a bit better. Keep an eye out but I doubt we'll catch anyone now. They have done what they wanted. What we have to do is frustrate them until they need to come up here and make the hiding places more obvious. So I'm going to go downstairs and we're going to do nothing. Come on Crow, come and get some breakfast."

Raven waited by the door. Her mind was racing and she was trying really hard to focus. The corridor was empty and she really wished that Frank had made the hole lower so she could at least sit on a chair and watch. Her back began to ache and the old clock in the hall seemed to be ticking her life away. Then she heard a noise. She froze, a cold chill ran down her spine as she heard footsteps coming up the stairs. Her mind started playing tricks on her and she began imagining all manner of horrors coming up there.

Crow appeared at the top of the stairs carrying a tray and he swiftly made his way along the corridor and slipped through the door when she opened it. "Well, we have them convinced that you are a nervous wreck who is now completely distraught because of what has happened. Don't worry, we'll put them straight afterwards. I'm guessing that nothing has happened up here yet?"

Raven smiled. "Only you coming up the stairs and that scared me enough. You could be right, I am a distraught nervous woman, well I am now."

Crow smiled. "Not on my watch." He grabbed her roughly around the neck and kissed her. He then went to the door. "He could have made that hole either a bit higher or a lot lower. This is going to kill my back."

Raven smiled. "Hush, if anyone is coming they'll hear you a mile off."

Crow shrugged and reached for a chair and leant against it.

Down in the kitchen Frank was eating his breakfast. Rat was sitting next to him. Rat suddenly piped up. "Did you find the food?"

Frank looked up and smiled. "I'm sorry laddie, we didn't really expect to. Whoever broke in and stole it is probably miles away by now dining at our expense. We'll just have to write that lot off to experience and put the food somewhere safer next time." He watched Rat like a hawk out of the corner of his eye.

When Rat thought Frank wasn't looking he cast a nervous look at Stick. Eric glared at them until Frank turned to him. "Sorry mate I'm going to need your help on the top field today. One of the heifers has broken down part of the fence between the fields and we've got to get it secure. Darren, could you go with Eric and David and get it fixed? Ralph will be on guard duty with Jareth for a while longer and I'd like to get that problem locked down as soon as I can. We'll have to make do without Raven for a while so life has to go on."

Eric grunted.

Frank didn't react. "I know that will leave us without anyone on guard in the house after Cheryl goes to look after Chloe and Rat and Stick go to bed but I doubt they'll be back again. I think we can probably consider this little episode over. It was probably a one off and they just got lucky."

Eric wiped his toast around the last of the egg on his plate and put it in his mouth. He put the knife and fork down on the plate and pushed it towards Cheryl. "That was lovely my dear, you cook a mean breakfast."

Cheryl smiled. "Thank you darling, I'm glad you appreciate it. Well you'd better get yourselves off. I'll get this washing up done and start on a bit of the laundry. Are you two alright in here if I get on?" She was looking at Rat and Stick. "I expect you both want to get some sleep after your long watch."

Rat looked up. "I'm shattered. I'd like that last piece of

toast if I may and then I'll turn in for a few hours. Stick, do you mind if I have it?"

Stick looked at him. "No problem matey. Tuck in." Rat grabbed the toast and made great labours about getting the butter and buttering it.

Cheryl went out of the other door, leaving Rat and Stick in the kitchen. Rat got up and went to the cupboard under the sink. He took out some drain cleaner and was about to empty the white granules into the sugar bowl when Stick hissed at him. "That's a bit bloody dangerous. So I suppose we are not going to follow orders and just incriminate others and get them fighting? Are you really going to kill someone and get Frank on our tail? We'll have to be more subtle than that. Look the rooms have been searched. We're not going to get near the food store so why don't we get the tins and put them in the vehicles. We can then have a bright idea tonight and get the vans searched." Rat reluctantly put the drain cleaner back under the sink.

Frank crouched down in his position in the flower bed outside the window and as they left the kitchen he scuttled right around the building to go back into the house through the side door of the kitchen. He then slipped through the door into the medical room. He was just about to open the door when he heard Storm and Doc laughing. He smiled to himself and knocked before he went inside. They were folding towels.

He stepped into the room and shut the door. "What do you know about Rat and Stick? They came with you."

Doc looked stunned. "Well not a lot really. I met them when I was just going in for my shift. They had their car in the car park and they said it had dodgy sparkplugs. We got talking and they mentioned the message. As I had a message too and they were low on petrol I said I'd give them a lift. That was how I met them. Why?"

Frank looked worried. "A little convenient don't you think? What made you think they were going to be useful and Nemesis chose them?"

Doc smiled. "That was because they were able to fix anything."

Frank shook his head. "They can fix anything apart from spark plugs with a car park full of cars that aren't going anywhere."

The smile fell off of Doc's face. "You mean?"

Upstairs Crow was getting fidgety. Suddenly he stiffened up and waved Raven over. She got up quietly and joined him. He leant back and she had a look through the hole. Rat and Stick were coming up the stairs. They went straight to the bedroom and opened the door and went in.

Crow carefully put his hand in his pocket and pulled out the key. He had put a piece of tape around it so he knew which one it was. He had it between his thumb and first finger as he turned the door handle and carefully opened the door. He stepped outside very slowly, trying not to put his weight on the creaky floor boards but he couldn't remember which ones they were. He settled for speed and leapt at the door. He held the door knob so it couldn't turn while he fumbled with getting the key in the lock. He managed it and turned it and took a step back as there was a pounding at the other side of the door.

Frank took the stairs two at a time. "It sounds like you have a wild beast in there?"

Crow laughed. "No just a rat in a trap."

Raven looked nervous. "So what are you going to do to the rat?"

Frank gave her a very knowing look. "Little lady, you really don't want to know and you sure as hell aren't going to find out." Frank turned tail and ran down the stairs, out of the back door and positioned himself outside the building just as Rat was trying to climb out of the window. Frank stood underneath him. He looked up at him. "You breaking your legs would just give me a head start so if you fancy making my life easier go ahead and jump."

Rat didn't intend to jump but Stick was so close behind

him that he accidentally pushed him. Rat flew out of the window and landed in a crumpled heap. He jumped up ready to run off and both his legs looked perfectly fine. Frank swore, took a sweeping kick at him and there was a sickening snapping noise and Rat fell on the ground screaming.

Frank smiled down at him. "You see, I told you that you would break your legs if you jumped out of that window."

Rat looked up at him. He opened his mouth to say something smart and then decided to do something smarter and shut his mouth again. Stick was running up and down against the window like a beast in a cage. His mouth was opening and closing but he didn't speak either.

Crow came around to the back of the house and took Frank's place. Frank scooped up a screaming Rat and took him around to the farm yard. "Now what am I going to do to you? It has been a while and I could do with some practice." Rat screamed even louder.

Frank took Rat into the feed room. Rat saw the chaff cutter straight away and screamed all the louder. It was an old fashioned piece of farm equipment, a large wheel driving two spiked barrels which rolled against each other. Rat knew what they were for and his mind gave him images he really didn't want of his hand being pushed between the rollers where the chaff used to go. Frank slapped him across the face, breaking his nose. Blood trickled down his face and into the corner of his mouth. He looked up at Frank wide eyed. Frank smiled. "All you have to do is tell me. Why?"

Rat swallowed hard. He then looked up hopefully as Raven walked in. Crow was just catching up with her dragging a screaming and wriggling Stick as she came into the room. Frank looked up at them. "Crow, get him tied to that sheep turner over there and take her out of here. This does not concern her."

Raven looked around the room as Crow rotated the

sheep turner to the up position. He formed a cradle that he then pushed Stick into and tied him to it with bailing twine. He then turned in a swift smooth movement and took Raven's arm. He pulled her roughly backwards, out of the room.

Frank shook his head. "Now let me see." He went to the cupboard, opened it and pulled out a metal handle still wrapped in a supermarket shopping bag. He unwrapped it and slapped it against the palm of his hand. "You know it would do quite well on its own."

Rat looked at him wide eyed.

Frank smiled. "But I've always wondered what a chaff cutter would do to an arm, or a leg. Don't you know that farm machinery is dangerous. So, are you going to talk? Please don't. I'd really rather you didn't." He attached the handle to the large wheel. He turned the handle and the rolls of metal teeth and blades started to rotate together. Rat's face went white. "Ok, so what are you going to tell me? Why are you trying to get me to think that we have a thief?"

Rat pulled himself up to full height. "I will tell you nothing. I am prepared to die for my cause. I am Rat, that is enough for you to know."

Crow was across the farm yard with Raven and they were sitting on the farm house steps when Eric came back from the upper field. They didn't pay much attention to him as he walked past the barking dogs. He heard Rat screaming and went into the room with Frank. Raven looked up at Crow. Crow looked down and stroked a stray piece of hair from her face. "Try not to think about it."

She made to get up but Crow had his arm around her and held her where she was. "No, leave Frank to what he is doing. Whatever they are up to they are working against us."

There was a high pitched scream from the room followed by Frank shouting. They ran across but Crow grabbed Raven before she dashed in.

They stood outside. "Are you alright, do you need a hand?"

Frank sounded like he was struggling with something and Eric was also somewhere inside. Eric came out a short while later. "Stick got free. Frank's hurt but he's alright. He got Stick back in the sheep turner so hopefully he'll be able to get some information out of the two of them. Look I'm going to wait outside here in case he needs a hand. Crow why don't you take Raven inside the house? It's getting cold out here and we can't do anything to help."

Crow nodded and put an arm around Raven. "Come on inside, we can watch from the window." Raven nodded and they went inside.

Eric slipped back into the room. He came up behind Frank and grabbed the broken handle. He raised it and knocked Frank out with a swift blow to the head. He then untied Rat and Stick. All three then ran full pelt for the gate. Crow saw them running from the window and leapt to his feet. He bounded to the door and leapt the stairs in one jump, almost losing his footing as he landed. He hit the floor at a run and crashed out of the front door. The door slammed back against the wall as he ran outside and followed them who was heading for the gate. He screamed at Ralph who was on guard duty but looking the other way.

Ralph turned as Eric got to the gate. He had his shotgun in his hand but the shock of seeing Eric running with Rat on his shoulder stunned him.

Eric ran past him, kicking him over as he went. Crow wasn't far behind him and he grabbed the shotgun off of Ralph and fired at Eric who was part way out of the gate. He missed, the bullet embedding uselessly in the gate as shards of wood fell to the ground. There was a bright flash and Rat and Stick even faster out onto the road. Eric turned and lunged at Crow who fired the second barrel but missed as the barrel was pushed down to the ground. Eric then ran across the road and joined the others who had disappeared into the undergrowth opposite. Crow followed them, leaping blindly into the woodland.

Raven ran after them into the darkness of the copse of trees the other side of the road. She was temporarily unable to see clearly as she had come from the crisp brightness of the road into the shaded darkness of the evergreen wood. She ran with her hands out, finding her way in the dim light. The trees had been planted close together making it hard to move about but easier to hear others crashing about as they moved in the semi darkness. She stopped to listen. There was no sound of running so she crouched down and began to move slowly and carefully. She could hear movement to her left and to her right. Then she heard movement in front as well and to the front right.

The damp loamy soil was soft underfoot. She leant back against a tree, feeling the roughness of the bark against her hand as she steadied herself. She was trying to see movement in the shadows. All she could see where the trees but she knew there were people out there. Some shadows seemed to move but she wasn't sure if it was her imagination. She began to back away, wishing there was more ground cover. She rolled over a log and laid there on the house side of it, listening.

She heard someone move nearby. They were moving closer. Her breathing became faster and she could feel her heart pounding. Then she felt a hand on her arm, pulling her upwards and back towards the house. She was about to struggle when she realised that it was Crow.

As he part dragged her she managed to get on her feet and they both ran. As they ran shots rang out. One embedded in a tree close to her head. Instinctively she ducked and another one narrowly skimmed the top of her hair. They jumped down onto the road and ran across it.

A bullet thudded into the tarmac as they jumped over the gate and ducked down behind the wall next to where Ralph was hiding.

In the house they could hear Cheryl screaming and Darren shouting at her to be quiet.

Ralph had the spare shotgun and he was crouched, gun in hand looking very nervous. Raven cast a glance over to the feed room hoping to see Frank but there was no movement. She put her hand on Ralph's arm.

"We've got to see if we can help Frank. Don't worry, none of us are killers. This is a crazy world, you shouldn't have to be in situations like this."

Ralph nodded and laid out some cartridges so that he could reload a bit quicker. "It won't happen again. I'm ready for it this time."

Crow kept Raven in front of him as they ran along the front of the house and up to the top barn. He opened the barn door and they leapt inside, ran along the corridor inside startling a few goats who were thoughtfully munching their hay and went into the feed room through that door.

Frank lay very still on the floor as Crow took a step towards him. Raven bent down and tried to feel for a pulse in his neck. She couldn't find one. She tried his wrist and as she moved his hand he moaned and rolled over. He looked up at her, blood running down his face from the head wound. "Good to see you Raven, fancy giving me a hand up?"

Raven put a hand on his shoulder. "Are you sure? That looks like a hefty wound to your head there."

Frank smiled. "I'm sure. So who the hell hit me from behind? I'm assuming whoever it was let the two of them go."

Crow as checking Stick for a pulse. He looked up. "That was Eric. He must have knocked you out then untied them. I shot at Eric to stop him but they got away up into the woods across the road. The bad news is that they are not alone. Raven and I followed them. I counted six different areas of movement but I've no idea how many are in each group. We were outnumbered so we got out of there."

Frank stared in disbelief. "Eric? Now we do have a problem over who we can trust. I would have put money on Eric being one of us. You did the right thing. Is anyone else injured?"

Crow rolled Stick over. "No, we did a bit sneaking around and then came back here as there were too many o of them out there."

Frank looked worried. "This really alters things. Rat was military trained and he was good at surviving questioning. He was text book good. Now I'm good at what I do. I'm not telling you more than that. What he did give is that he's fighting for some sort of a cause and we're not worthy of surviving. That wasn't a "give" it was more of a threat to us. He started repeating what sounds like some sort of a perverted green manifesto where all of mankind is wicked and only their chosen few have the right to survive. That sparks of fanaticism and that can't be good.

I'd put money on it having been their plan to set us against each other and then mop up while we're accusing each other tonight and when we have our eye off the ball. Well we now know they are out there and we can probably expect trouble tonight. They have revealed their hand so they probably have nothing to lose by starting a full on offensive.

We also have a problem, Cheryl and Shylock came in with Eric. We know that Rat and Stick were both "plants". I'm wondering how many more there are?"

Raven looked worried. She couldn't take her eyes off the amount of blood under where Rat had been tied. "So how do you know that we're ok?"

Frank smiled. "Call it a hunch. I would guess that as you owned this place and Nemesis chose it as a location there isn't going to be anything in your background to give any cause for worry. Crow, I don't mean to be rude but your background is so darned shallow and selfish that there's no way you've got yourself involved in any kind of fanatical political group."

Crow frowned. "Should I say thanks or is that just insulting?"

Frank smiled. "I'd say thanks if I were you. That was the trouble with the print outs. Anyone can get a hold of one. There's no roll call for who should be arriving. That is one goddam hole in Nemesis's plan." He winced slightly as he rubbed his head. "That was one heck of a swing. We'd better get inside. We're going to have to think a lot harder about defence if we're up against those guys. If I was them I'd probably be back tonight after they have had a chance to talk to Eric about what and who we have here. They know the layout of this place, how many of us there are and where we keep our supplies.

I'm going to have to have a talk with Cheryl and Shylock."

9
STAND MY GROUND

Frank was in the kitchen with Cheryl. She had calmed down and was staring into a cup of tea that Frank had made for her. He cleared his throat. "I'm going to have to ask. Are you involved?"

Cheryl jumped slightly and couldn't take her eyes off of Frank's hands. She had never noticed before how they were scarred. "No. The only group I was involved with was the Women's Institute and the if you count it the local book club. I can't believe he'd got involved with something like that.

I know he made some new friends but I was just relieved that he had something in is life."

Frank fixed her with a level stare.

She flinched and looked guilty. "Alright, I was happy that he was going out evenings so that I could see Shylock. I suppose it's no secret now. Eric was a pig to live with. He had his interests alright but none of them involved me."

Frank sighed. "Well if you don't mind until we get this sorted out I want Raven back doing the cooking. It's not that I don't trust you, it's that I don't want to have to trust you."

Cheryl looked down. "I understand. There is one thing. Someone moved the drain cleaner under the sink. I know it moved as I'd put it on top of a rusty can mark and now it's further into the cupboard."

Frank looked around the room. "I know. I saw Rat with it when we left them alone. He didn't use it, he put it back in the cupboard. If he had that would have given us a big problem. That stuff will kill, painfully. As if we don't have enough to worry about. Thank you for telling me. Sorry though, it could be an olive branch offered to get me to trust you. Why didn't you mention it earlier?"

Cheryl looked up at him, her eyes a little tearful. "I noticed it just before you came in when I went to clean the sink. You distracted me by your questioning."

Frank smiled. "Well you didn't panic when I put sugar in your tea and you aren't dead. The sugar would be the obvious place to put something like that. If it was Rat and Stick then they only had a very short time to do anything. I think he may have been thinking of doing it. Look this is a good warning and we got away fairly lightly. We'll have to lock up things like that just to be on the safe side. Sorry just doesn't get dead people back. It could be a waste of time and effort but what price peace of mind?"

Cheryl looked stunned and thoughtful. "I can't believe that someone we sat and chatted with could think about doing this. What is humanity coming to?"

Frank thought for a while. "I read a book while researching humanity. It was called Lord of the Flies and it was by William Golding. It was about how people change when they are in a situation that calls for primal attitudes."

Cheryl was still looking thoughtful. "Why did they have to think they were in a primal situation? We have enough food and are likely to be able to grow more. I really can't understand. And if you think I'm a likely spy for the bad guys why tell me?"

Frank winked at her. "We are outside the normal rules and structure that is everyday life with an unsure future. I told you because I don't think that you are. You have too much to lose. If you do anything you know you'll lose Chloe and Shylock could well get caught in the crossfire. Also, you were invited weren't you?"

Cheryl smiled and took a folded piece of paper out of her pocket. "I printed it off as I always print everything off. I'm a complete airhead when it comes to remembering things so I keep what I can as notes and on paper."

Frank took the piece of paper off of her and looked at it. "You were invited alright. Did you ever see Eric with one?"

Cheryl looked stunned. "I've seen Shylock's invite, it's in his bag, but I suppose I just assumed Eric had an invitation when I was talking to him. You mean he wasn't invited?"

Frank looked down at the table and nodded his head. He looked back at her. "Yes, pretty much. It is easy to talk to someone and think they have said something or started the conversation if you aren't paying attention. He obviously heard what you said and then went to his friends and they discussed it. They may well have followed us. That may have been how they got our location. Is there anything else that is suspicious?"

Cheryl's brow furrowed. "I'm trying to remember the conversation. He came in and I was making dinner. The print out was on the table and he picked it up and read it. I then asked him if he'd got one as I thought it was a scam. He said he hadn't but he'd check the internet. He went off to his study and then about an hour later the power went off. When I saw him again he said he'd had a message but hadn't had time to print it off so could he take another look at mine as he couldn't remember the address. I didn't think anything of it, it was chaos in the house and Chloe was crying. He went out shortly afterwards and when he came back we packed everything up and came here."

Frank was focusing on the teapot. "I think we're going to have to be a lot more careful who we let in from now on. We've been far too trusting."

There was a shot from outside followed by a scream from upstairs. Frank ran up the stairs two at a time and rushed into Raven's room. The first thing he saw was the window broken. Then he noticed Raven laying on the floor behind the bed. He hit the floor and moved across the room to her.

Crow burst into the room and Frank screamed at him to get down. He hit the deck and crawled over to where Frank was crouched with Raven. She was kneeling behind the bed holding her head. Crow pushed Frank out of the way.

Crow pulled her hands away from her head. There were tears streaming down her face. She buried her head in his chest and as he put his arms around her head he felt damp blood on his hands. He noticed blood on the bedside table.

Frank had crawled round him and Crow moved his hand. "She's been hurt."

Frank moved closer and took a look. Then he noticed the blood on the bedside table. "Raven, what happened?"

Raven pulled back from Crow. "I was just getting something from the drawer and I heard the shot and the glass broke so I dived down beside the bed and hit my head on the bedside cabinet. I didn't want to move in case they shot again."

Frank put a hand on her shoulder and Crow put his arms protectively around her head and shoulders. "Come on, I'm getting you downstairs for the Doc to check you out. Frank, you had better get your head wound checked out as well."

Crow's mind was racing as he paced up and down outside the dining room door. Inside the Doc was doing what he could to clean up the wounds.

Storm was by his side, handing him what he needed. Crow slid down the wall and sat on the floor. His head was in his hands as Frank opened the door and came and sat on the floor with him. Crow looked up. "She's going to be fine. I know that."

Frank nodded. "I know son, doesn't stop you worrying. We're going to have to board up those windows facing outside. This means they are still about."

Crow looked at him. "This place is becoming like a fortress. What are we becoming Frank? Torture? Is that what humanity is going to degrade to?"

Frank smiled. "Rat cut his arm on the machinery he was tied to. It was handy though, made him really keen to talk before infection set in."

Crow looked down. "To lose Raven would be to lose a little spark of hope. She is the voice of reason."

Frank's expression went blank. "We won't lose her. It was only a little bump on the head. Head wounds always bleed badly. Have faith in our doctor. That could have been a lot worse but thankfully I think it's a pretty superficial cut. Head wounds bleed a lot, even if they aren't as bad as they look. I've seen a lot of wounds in my time. It looks bad but you did everything right. She's more than likely going to have the mother of all headaches though."

Crow looked down.

Frank looked over at him. "Is it an act?"

Crow smiled. "What do you mean? Oh that I actually care, yes I do. She's an incredible woman. I'm a very lucky man and I wouldn't like to be the man who tried to take her away from me."

Frank smiled. "She's going to be fine, stop worrying."

Crow looked down at his wedding ring. "Do you think that marriage makes you feel different?"

The door opened and they both jumped to their feet. Crow stepped back a little shocked. Doc was covered in blood. The Doc smiled. "It wasn't so bad a wound, just messy. It looked worse than it was. I've patched her up and she's stopped bleeding. It will heal but she is going to have to take it easy. She knocked herself out but it doesn't look like there's any concussion. She's staying here tonight though. No objections. She's pretty bruised which seems strange considering that she fell and I'm worried about her wrist, she may have sprained it. I can't understand why she has so much bruising around her wrists."

Frank looked worried but Crow smiled nervously and stepped forwards. "Can I see her?"

The Doc was wiping his bloody hands on a cloth. He

stepped aside. You can both come in and Frank I want to see you too. You had a head wound so you are staying here tonight too. I guess I've got two of you under observation and you can keep Raven amused as well before she drives me mad. Can we keep the numbers down now please, I'm running out of room? The good news is that Shylock is up to leaving my med bay. I think Cheryl is going to be looking after him. She could use something to take her mind off of what happened to Eric. You don't think she is one of them do you?"

Frank shook his head. "No, I think she may have driven Eric to it by her affair with Shylock but no, she's not a member. Those groups generally look for the lost and lonely. They sound fantastic until you read between the lines and peruse the small print. Someone looking for something to believe in doesn't always do that. We're fighting to keep what we've been given. They are fighting to get what they don't have. But they could easily go and find something else so I have no sympathy."

Jareth came into the room. "How's Raven? People want to know."

Crow cast Jareth a suspicious glance. He then crouched down beside the camp bed where Raven was sleeping. He gently stroked the hair from her face. He went to the table and picked up a ball of cotton wool, dipped it in

some clean water and sat down and started wiping the dried blood off of her face.

The Doc looked up. "She'll be fine. I've sedated her so she's sleeping. There's no concussion as far as I can see so I wanted her to rest to get over it."

Jareth visibly relaxed. "That is good news. Everyone wants to get together

for a meeting but they won't do it without her. I'll let them know. Could we have the meeting in here?"

Doc glared at him. "Don't you dare! If you are careful with Raven when she wakes up she can go with you but I want her back before bedtime. Boy I never thought I'd say that, I sound like her father! Now if I can ask you to leave. I have some work to do." He smiled. His boyish good looks and mop of unruly blonde hair making him look younger than his years.

Crow glared back. "I want to stay with her."

Doc shrugged. "If you want to you can if you don't get in the way."

Doc pulled Frank down onto a chair so he could see his head wound better. He grabbed a swab and began cleaning it up. He then disinfected the wound and put a pad over it. "That was a nasty blow, you are lucky you are still alive. You must have one heck of a thick skull under there."

Frank looked sideways. "So they say. Let's be thankful shall we. Now if you've finished I'll go and see that everything is alright. If I feel dizzy or see flashing lights I'll be right back. There's no guarantee there won't be another attack tonight. Crow, I know you want to be with her but we need you out there. She will be fine with Doc. What we do need is for you to go and get others to help you to find some board and board up that window and any others that could be accessed from the ground floor. Our outer windows are obviously a weakness and this one is on the ground floor so could be a possible easy access point. Why don't you and Jareth go and do that?

There is some pallet wood in the barn. If you are going outside do not walk directly across the yard. That would give a sniper a clear shot. I've let the dogs out so don't go beyond the field gate. She's trained them well, you go out there and you'll get bitten.

Kyle and David are on guard. The guard duty is going to be harder tonight." As he finished speaking there were shots outside.

Doc raised his hands up out of the way and stopped investigating Frank's head. "Go on, I know you want to." Frank smiled back at him and ran out of the door followed by Crow and Jareth.

They had just left when something broke the window. Storm screamed and Doc turned to see a burning rag wrapped around a rock which had caught light to the curtain. He grabbed the bowl of water and threw it onto the fire and put it out. "Storm, help me I've got to get this table up against the window." Together they managed to lift it and prop it precariously up against the window.

About ten minutes later Jareth and Crow ran back in with wood, hammer and nails and began boarding up the window. The Doc and Storm joined them and the others and they worked their way around the windows at the back until they were all boarded up. They checked each room out with caution. There had been bricks thrown through three windows and one room was ablaze. The other two had fallen safely. The first into a large glass fruit bowl, the second onto a stone floor. They grabbed water from wherever they could and put the flames out.

Jareth looked up from where he was hammering a nail rather crookedly into a piece of wood. "We'd better set up regular patrols to make sure that the boards are in place. It wouldn't take much to push them in. They are a deterrent more than a physical barrier. We'd better nail up the back doors as well."

It was starting to get dark and there was another shot from outside. Those on guard by the gate were cowering down behind the wall. They stood up and fired shots into the growing gloom of the forest as the light faded. There was an instant response of more gunfire. The bullets ricocheted off of the wall as they ducked back down again.

The light was fading fast. It was a moonlit night and the stars were coming out brightly. The air chilled dramatically and the first spangles of frost started to form on the trees and bushes.

Jareth and Crow passed Frank in the corridor. He was dressed in black and his face had been camouflaged with greasepaint. "Wish me luck, we can't survive this if I don't do something. We don't have enough experienced people and we can't afford to lose anyone. Hold the fort here and if I don't come back you'll have to do the best you can. I'm helpless in here." They turned and followed him.

He thought for a moment then pushed past them and walked into the makeshift infirmary and kissed Raven on the cheek. She was vaguely awake. "Be brave little one. I'm counting on you to keep these people safe." She smiled and grabbed his arm. He smiled and pulled away from her.

He slipped out of the door and grabbed Crow's arm. "I'm going out of that window and I need you to board it up behind me. No objections and no you aren't coming with me. It's actually easier for me if you aren't out there as I don't have to think about whether what I see is a target. So yes, I know you would both go out there. Yes I know you are big goddam heroes but this is what I do. If I'm successful I'll be walking in through the front gate. If I'm not I won't be coming back at all. Settle yourselves down for a long night, keep the guns loaded and be careful. One stupid move and you will get shot." He smiled and Crow put a hand on his arm. They smiled and hugged.

Crow prized the board back and Frank slipped out into the darkness. There was silence, broken only by Crow hammering the boards back in place.

In the house everyone was waiting for something to happen. Everyone had armed themselves with something be it kitchen knife or firearm. Cheryl was in the kitchen. She went to start preparing dinner with everyone watching her. She opened the knife drawer, it was empty so she sat down, head in hands as the reality of it all hit her. She also had to think how she was going to prepare dinner with no knives.

Frank crawled along in the shadows at the base of the house wall. The undergrowth was thick and it was slow going as the brambles kept latching onto his clothing and scratching him. He moved along the full length of the back of the house and crouched down behind a bush near the road. He was scanning the area and saw three men crawling in the grass towards the house. He was parallel with them so he crawled faster and managed to get a distance along the wall behind them. He then rolled over a small ridge line and crawled along in the shadows until he was able to circle behind them in the long rushes. He went very wide, crossed the ditch and then crawled along a shallow ridge to the hedgerow. He followed the hedgerow and then rolled through it. Again it was thorny and he felt small scratches on his hands and face.

The first man was in his sights as he rolled through the hedge. The bullet was on target and the man fell dead after a clean shot to the head. The shot was silenced. There was a dull thud as the bullet hit the body. The man next to him looked over at his colleague in disbelief. He reached out to shake the body just as Frank shot him in the back of the head as well. The third man was rolling over to fire into the shadows. He started firing randomly which ceased abruptly as Frank shot him twice, once in the head, once in the chest.

Frank rolled down into a very wet and muddy ditch and crawled along it. He turned when he was a hundred yards away and looked back.

Five shadowy figures were crossing the road. They were silhouetted by the moon but he let them cross. He rolled into the hedge and got through it.

As they ducked into the field he picked them off one by one in quick succession confident that his position would no longer be revealed by his muzzle flash now that he was shielded by the hedgerow. He rolled back through the hedge and darted across the road at full pelt.

Two marksmen took shots at him but they missed and he was able to roll safely into the undergrowth on the other side of the road.

Once in the woodland he moved like a silent and deadly shadow. He covered ground quickly and began hunting. He listened and soon knew exactly where the remaining ten snipers were. He circled one and threw a stone so the sniper fired backwards into the forest. His colleague, believing he was being fired at, fired back and shot the first sniper. Frank in the meantime took a shot at the third sniper and he fell back dead into the undergrowth. A fourth sniper took a shot at Frank which slightly clipped his arm. He raised his pistol and shot that one. He then rolled into the undergrowth and lay silently while the remaining snipers moved about trying to find him. One man stepped within a foot of him but he stayed where he was. He waited until they had taken up position and listened. They were fairly spread out but they were concentrating on him now, not moving in on the house.

He was able to circle around. He made it a wide circle and came in behind them. Three clean shots took three out, leaving him only two. They were at opposite ends of the copse of trees which made it relatively easy for him to circle the first one and a single shot took him out. The last one proved a little more difficult as he was in a ditch behind a log. He had to circle right round and was within five feet of the man before he fired.

He went to ground, hiding in the soft earth while he listened. It was silent and then gradually he started hearing the forest noises again. The animals started moving around and the natural sounds returned. He waited nearly an hour before combing the forest to make sure there were no hidden snipers and picking up all their weapons and ammunition. Then he walked back through the main gate of the farm, as he had promised, as if he'd been out on a Sunday stroll. He was soaking wet and covered in mud. Bits of bramble were still attached to his clothing.

Frank smiled to himself as he passed the two on the gate.

Darren and David looked stunned as he walked past them. "Keep up the good work lads." He walked up the farm house steps and wandered inside and sat down in the kitchen. There was a stunned silence as he piled up the weaponry on the table. He looked around the expectant faces. "What? Don't I get tea anymore? There had better be cake. I always like a good bit of cake after a shopping trip." He relaxed back in his chair and waited for the mug to be put in front of him. He saw the open and empty drawer and smiled. "Well I suppose a slice of cake is off the menu until someone brings a knife back. We can't stand down but I would think we'll probably have a quiet night now. If there are more it will probably take them a while to realise that their friends are gone and to get back here. I'm hoping that they will also get the message that we are probably not worth bothering about.

We can clear up the mess in the morning. I want a clean up crew out there at first light to bury the bodies in the woods. We don't want crows and other scavengers causing havoc and we certainly don't want any infection spreading from rotting corpses." He sat back and tucked into the roughly cut cake that Cheryl had put in front of him. He hesitated for a moment. "No drain cleaner I hope?"

Cheryl looked panic stricken.

Frank laughed. "We've already discussed that one. I can see it's not the first piece gone. Nobody dead? Good, well I can enjoy my cake then. They put the cleaner back but we do need to discuss the security around here. I want a "safe cupboard" which has a lock on it. Can we arrange that?"

Jareth smiled. "Sure can do boss. I'll get onto it in the morning."

Frank hesitated. "No mate, Raven's the boss, Raven and Crow. I'm a guest here."

In the makeshift hospital Doc was sitting beside a new table and looking at the boarded up window. Raven was asleep and Storm sat beside him. He turned to look at her when she wasn't looking. "Sweetheart you don't look the same girl who wandered in here."

She turned. Her eyes were red from too little sleep and

her hair was ragged and un-brushed. There was dried blood on her apron but some of it had splashed onto her clothes. "Life has changed." Her voice was gentle, level and full of an understanding that the three words had just conveyed.

The Doc smiled. "You still look beautiful."

Storm looked down and looked embarrassed.

Doc laughed. "As if you haven't heard that before? You make a good nurse. Thanks for your help. I do appreciate it." He bit his tongue and looked down. He shifted in his seat. "Would you like a drink? I can go to the kitchen if you'll keep an eye on Raven there. Or if you like you could come with me and we could spend some time with the others?"

Storm thought about it. "Could you bring something back here? I'd like to keep an eye on Raven and your company is good enough for me."

Doc wandered down the corridor with a big grin on his face.

Back in the kitchen Frank had almost finished his tea and Cheryl had put another pot on the table. Shylock was back with them, baby Chloe in his arms sleeping. Other than Crow and Darren who were on guard everyone else who wasn't in the hospital was in the kitchen.

There was a bubble of conversation as Doc came down the corridor and opened the door. They looked up, some jumped.

Doc smiled. "Should I have knocked?"

Ralph laughed. "If you'd done that you probably would have had to pick up broken crockery. Sorry mate we're a bit jumpy tonight."

Doc sat down in an empty seat. "Understandable. So, how are things?"

Reko looked up from his drink. "Well, thanks to our ninja here we don't have to worry about the snipers in the woods for a while. We're boarded up and the animals are all in and bedded down. We've nailed up their windows too and the doors to the outer field are barricaded for the night.

The horses are moved around into the yard and the pigs are as safe as we can make them. So, I think all in all we're as good as we can be."

Doc took the mug offered to him and poured himself a drink. "I'm glad to hear it. Look this is a fleeting visit as I'm keeping an eye on Raven. She's fine, sleeping. Do you have a tray? I'd like to take some tea back to Storm. She's holding the fort back there."

Cheryl made up a tray with a pot of tea, a mug and got out a couple of plates of food she had been keeping warm in the bottom oven. "Here you go. Do you need anyone to come and give you both a break?"

Doc smiled as he took the tray. Frank caught his eye and winked at him.

Doc blushed. "Thank you but I think we'll be fine." He left the room and Ralph shut the door behind him.

There was a scratching at the front door and everyone jumped. Frank spun round in his chair, pistol in hand and slipped out into the hallway. Carefully he opened the door and was knocked over by an enthusiastic German Shepherd Dog who bounded past him and up the stairs. Frank recovered his feet, slammed the door shut and followed the dog up the stairs. He found him sitting wagging his tail outside Raven's room.

As Frank approached him the dog growled slightly, hackles raised. Frank put the gun away and the dog wagged its tail. "Ok boy, you want to see your owner do you? I thought I'd locked you all away in the back field. Come on then boy I'll take you to her."

The dog was obviously listening, his head kept tilting to the side and his tail wagged slightly. Frank went back down the stairs and waited at the bottom. He waited and waited but nothing happened. So he crept back upstairs and the dog was laying outside Raven's door. Frank turned, went downstairs and left him there.

In the kitchen the others had seen what had happened. Frank came in and left the door open. "He's upstairs outside her room."

Cheryl smiled. "That will be Oberon. He can get through gates, I think he can unlock gates as well. Most likely he was hiding while you put the others away. He was living in the house until we arrived. Raven shut him in with the other dogs as she thought everyone would be safer. I suppose he's decided he's had enough of their company."

The night passed quietly, watches changed and people drifted off to bed.

In the morning Ralph, Crow, Reko and Matt went out and buried the bodies in the woods. They took anything of use off of them and put it in feed bags. They returned about lunchtime.

Raven was sitting in the kitchen with Oberon at her feet when Crow got back. He put his bag down went over and kissed her and sat down as the others filed in. Frank was on guard with Steve. Doc and Storm had joined them and everyone was in the kitchen. Raven took a sip of tea and looked around the expectant faces. "Well, that was a night to remember and hopefully something that won't happen again. We have to think about defence but we also have to think about how we can move on. We're cut off here from any information about what is going on. For all we know the computers could be back on and life could be going on as normal elsewhere.

Also, what say you all that we put major decisions to the vote? I would like to propose that we find out what is going on and if it looks like this is going to be a permanent situation to see who else is out there? It's difficult with having two people out on guard but we'll find a way."

Ralph crossed his legs and sat back in his seat. "The feed is holding up but it won't last forever. If we are going to plant then we'll need planting seed as well."

Margaret smiled. "I second that. The beds are ready

and we have some seed but to feed this many people we're going to have to think in plots rather than pots. I need seed potatoes and other crops that we can keep going."

James put his hands on the table. "Well, we aren't going to last very long if we don't have the basics like clothes or a way to make them. We were discussing this last night and we'd like to see about getting some spinning and weaving done. I've read that book you had in the library and I think we can do something with that as a family. I saw you had part of a spinning wheel. Could someone make the bits that are missing so that it works again?"

Janice coughed and looked around nervously. Her voice was quiet and high pitched. "I know you all have your things to do and we'd like to contribute. I too have been in the library looking at books. We'll need to wash and there is plenty of soap for now but that won't last forever. Also, we're going to need something to trade. We have the goats and I'd like to make some milk soap. We could start making all types of cosmetics that are milk and plant based if we can work with you Margaret on that one?"

Ralph smiled. "You've got some meat goats that are ready to go as the girls will be kidding again soon. I've been reading up on tanning and we could do that here and have leather. I can't do it myself as I've got too darned close to those critters. Would someone else like to work with me so that we can consider doing something like that?"

David looked up. "I've always had a thought about doing something like that. Can I take the book for a while? I'll see how I get on but I can't do the killing."

Raven smiled. "I'll have a word with Frank about that last part. He doesn't have any contact with the animals. May I mention toilet paper? We're going through it at a frightening rate and that is one thing we're not going to find it easy to get hold of. I'd have suggested newspaper but I doubt there is such a thing now. Well, it all depends on how the world has gone. We'll look pretty silly if we set ourselves up here and then we find that the world has gone back to normal."

Ralph was looking into his drink. "Actually no, I don't think we would. I for one like it here. It's very different to my life before but even if the world does sort itself out I'd be happy here."

Crow laughed. "Even with being shot at."

Ralph's face fell. "Well it has its downsides."

Raven looked around the faces. "We also may well have other people turn up. It's not impossible, it has only been a few days. We'll see what the other two say but I for one would like to know what is going on."

Crow looked horrified. "You aren't going." He caught her bruised arm and squeezed it a little too hard. She winced and looked down. Then she gathered her composure and glared at him. It was a stare that could turn anyone to stone. "I'm going. I know the people around here and they know me. We stand a better chance if they have defences up of getting in if I'm with you. You are all strangers to this area and they could see you as a threat."

Ralph gripped the table and pushed his chair back a little. "Raven does have a point."

Crow glared at him. "What if anything happens to her?"

Raven smiled. "She is still here and I'll take my chances with everyone else. If you have a problem with that Crow we'll talk about it in private."

Crow glared at her. His eyes were cold and piercing.

Reko sniggered and Crow gave him a look to kill. "Ok Crow, I'm sorry but she's so beautiful when she's angry." He turned to look at Raven who was also giving him a look to kill. "Come on darling, lighten up. In the end we'll do what is best. This is life, there's nothing to prove. We all have our place here. Nobody is going to challenge your right to be in charge Raven, even if you sat at home knitting. Crow, you caveman, if you want to try pulling that woman around by her hair I think you'd be in trouble. We get the message."

Crow glared at him. "She's only just getting over being shot at and hitting her head."

Reko smiled. "And if Doc says she's ok, she's ok. I say there's logic in what she's saying. You both need to go to make your presence felt. If we are going to trade, people are going to need to know we are here. We can't make everything."

Raven put her mug down. "There is a farm shop where we used to get our animal feed. It is about twenty minutes away. If we want to avoid the roads it would be just over an hour if we go across country on horseback. It will keep us off the roads as well and my thoughts are that they are going to be the most dangerous. We have five horses now that we've taken in the ones from Jake's place. They are steady so there's no need for expert riding skills.

On that point I would suggest that everyone does have at least a basic riding lesson. The petrol isn't going to last and they could be our best hope for getting around quickly across country. Similarly, sorry about this but I'd like to ask Frank to teach everyone to use the guns. They too aren't going to last forever but we may be able to use them for a while. We have some archery stuff in the loft. I've never used any of it and it was second hand when I got it. I had a thought of having it as a hobby. Perhaps we could set up some targets. Arrows could be able to be made. I'm not sure of how that sort of thing works though but I have a book on it somewhere.

Basically everyone needs to know how to do all the jobs. I'm not saying that someone can't have something that they do that is their specific task but what I'm saying is that once you are doing it, let others know how you do it. It would also be a good idea if everyone has a go at handling the animals. They are easier to handle if you know them and if we need to move them in a hurry or someone isn't with us anymore it would be a good idea.

I think we are all a bit shaken by what has happened over the Rat, Stick and Eric. I'd like to say to Cheryl how sorry we all are. It is a lesson though. Before we let more people in we'll need to check if they have actually had an invitation or whether they are coming on word of mouth. Nemesis made decisions for a reason. If we have doubt then I say we should stand by Nemesis' choice."

Everyone nodded and Cheryl put more pots of tea and coffee on the table. "So, can I do the cooking or am I still a nasty infiltrating spy?"

Raven smiled. "I think we are fairly sure you aren't so yes of course you can do the cooking and we all really appreciate what you do. Sorry about having to be cautious. Frank told me. You do understand don't you?"

Cheryl smiled sweetly. "Oh, absolutely. I want to be as safe as the rest of you. If he'd question me, he'd question anyone he had doubts about. I don't want to get killed either."

10
IT CAN'T RAIN ALL THE TIME

The discussions went on deep into the night. Frank was just finishing his watch which had been much cut down as he'd had a long day and Crow crossed the yard to where Frank was crouched and joined him. Crow whispered. "We have been discussing things. It looks like there is a plan to take a trip out on the horses and find out what is happening out there.

Raven knows of a farm place where we might be able to get supplies. Thing is she wants to go and scout it out first. What do you think?"

Frank smiled. "I think it's a good idea. We have to start setting up things for the long haul. Being holed up here is safer but in the long run we're going to need certain supplies. She has to go, it is the logical choice. None of us are locals and there is a possibility that they will be careful who they trade with if goods are scarce. Better that we set up a good relationship right from the start and sorry lad she's the one to do it."

Crow's smile faded. "You think so as well then. Are you going with us?"

Frank thought for a moment. "No, if Raven is away from here I'd like to stick around and make sure that nobody left behind goes into megalomaniac psycho take over the place mode."

Crow smiled. "You mean Cheryl takes over the world."

Frank shook his head and laughed. "Something like that yes. You can look after Raven well enough on your own. I'm going to suggest that you leave Ralph though, he can look after the animals if anything happens. Not that it is going to. The trouble that happened here we brought down on ourselves. If they hadn't been following Eric and Cheryl I doubt those people would have found us. We're remote and that is something you are going to have to be careful about in negotiations. Revealing our location to strangers who are asking questions could lead to us being raided or getting unwanted guests. It could also lead to us having difficult decisions to make if people turn up hopeful of a home. Everyone is a good cause and everyone deserves to live but the decisions about who should come here were made with the best chance of survival. Taking on more people who don't have a purpose in the balance would make life harder or possibly jeopardise the chance of survival for everyone.

I'd better get inside. It has been quiet out here, nothing moving so you should have a fair time of it. See you later." Frank got up and followed the route keeping close to the front of the house back into the farm house itself. Once inside he went into the kitchen. Oberon jumped up, ran over to him and sniffed him over. "Well boy, a bit more keen to see me this time are we?" Oberon wagged his tail and went back to sit with Raven.

Raven looked up. "We've been discussing a trip out. I bet Crow has already mentioned it and yes I am still going whatever you say."

Frank shrugged. "Hey, don't shoot me little lady. I'm on your side. I fully agree that you should go. You know the people and you know what we should be buying. Though buying with what?"

Raven smiled. "I don't know, we'll see what is needed when we get there. So who is going then? I think Ralph should stay here, sorry Ralph."

Ralph shrugged. "Stay in the safety of this place and eat Cheryl's excellent home cooked food or get bounced about on the back of a horse I can't ride to a place where someone is possibly going to shoot at me. Now let me think? It's a close run thing but I think on balance I'd rather stay here."

Frank laughed. "Ok, so who is going then?"

Margaret glared at Tobias. "Don't you even think about it."

Cheryl looked pleadingly at Shylock. He smiled and hugged Chloe. "I think I'd better keep a hold on this one while Cheryl gets the meals prepped." Cheryl looked very relieved.

Reko took a drink of his tea. "Try stopping me. Matt are you up for a trip out?"

Matt was about to answer when Frank chipped in. "No, we can't have both of our mechanics going. Doc before you say anything you can't go either. Storm I want you to stay with Doc. You can at least fight if there's any trouble. I'm assigning you to Doc as his assistant and body guard. James and Catherine you need to keep an eye on James. He's out there somewhere with the animals and he's getting a bit too brave with his trips up the field. Jareth, how about you start thinking of boarding up where the vehicles were. The petrol is going to run out soon so we won't need them. That would make a good place just by the gate where we can have these discussions and the guards can still be involved. Go on, put in a bar, if we're going to live we might as well enjoy it. Ralph, can you spare Darren to help? David why don't you go along with Reko, Crow and Raven?"

David looked up and smiled. "I'd love to."

Raven looked around the table. "Is everyone happy?"

Reko smiled. "Everyone but Crow."

Raven's smile faded and she sighed deeply. "We have to make the right decisions not emotional ones. It is my decision to go. Frank will you look after this place while I'm gone?"

Frank smiled. "Sure, glad you asked. I didn't want to totally presume."

227

Later that morning the four were sitting on their horses in the yard waiting to go. Raven steadied her black cob. "Steady Silk, we'll be off soon." Silk danced about and set Blade off. Crow pulled him back. Reko was on the brown hunter, Drummer, who stood quietly. David had a grey heavy built cob who seemed placid but was occasionally taking a step towards the gate.

They went out through the field gate and up to a gate that Ralph had put into the side fence. The gate was open and the chain and padlock hung loosely over it. Once out onto the open farmland they were able to gallop.

The journey passed without incident and they came to a small village. On the outskirts there was a large warehouse which had railings around it. Boards had been fastened around the railings to give them security and they could see guards patrolling inside. There was a main gate which was heavily guarded by men carrying shotguns. They could see inside as the gate opened to let a small lorry in. The yard itself was empty but they could see through the open doors of the large metal warehouse that the stocks were looking good.

Raven kicked her pony into a walk and slowly approached the gates. The other three formed up behind her. As she got to the gate she dismounted and handed her pony's reins to Crow. "Stay here, I'm going to go and talk."

She walked up to the gate which opened and a tall, brown haired, youth dressed in camo clothing stepped out. "Hey, Raven, good to see you are alive!"

Raven smiled and they hugged. "Good to see you are alive too Carl. How has it been down here?"

Carl shook his head. "It was mad for the first day. Everyone just seemed to go nuts. The gaffa ordered us to shut and bar the gates and we barricaded ourselves in until it calmed down. It looks like there were a few dead in the town and a lot of people just packed up and shipped out to find relatives. I would have thought this would have been the safest place. Anyway, the gaffa has been sorting things out and we're looking for local farms to set up trade with. I'm guessing that is what you are here for. Do you still have your animals?"

Raven smiled. "Sure do. Jake has shipped out and I'm looking after his too. We'll be needing food for them."

Carl smiled back. "The gaffa is setting up a food co-operative. It isn't going to be safe for you to sell your food on the market in the village anymore. It is too open and likely to get raided. So he's talking about setting up a protected market in here. You bring your stuff along and it is sold off. He is talking about building stalls and having a stock sale area. It will be a better defended area and customers can come to the gate and buy what they want.

Would you be interested in pitching in with this? We've got solar and wind power and we've managed to get hold of the freezers from the supermarket. They aren't going to need them. They are shut down, no power you see."

Raven looked back at the other three who were listening intently. Crow nodded, the other two followed suit. "It looks like we just might be. So what's the deal?"

Carl stepped back. "You'd better talk to the Gaffa about that. Do you want to bring those ponies in? They will be safer inside. Do they tie up?"

Raven went back to Silk. "They'll be a bit jittery but as long as there's no heavy machinery near them."

Carl led them inside. "Tie them up over there. I'll get them trugs of water. You go talk to the gaffa, he'll sort you out with a deal."

They dismounted and tied the horses and followed Raven up a set of metal stairs into the office above. The gaffa was sitting behind a desk. The paperwork that looked like it had been on the desk was piled in the corner.

The gaffa was a tall thin grey haired man with a long beard and moustache. He looked up as they knocked and came in. "Good to see you Raven. So your holding is still going?"

229

Raven smiled. "We're doing alright."

The gaffa nodded. "Good to hear it. I expect my son has explained what we're trying to set up here. As you are up here I'm guessing you are interested?"

Raven nodded. Crow stepped up behind her so that she could feel him standing there. She looked up at him and smiled. "I think we could be, depending on terms of course."

The gaffa picked up a pen and started twirling it in his fingers. "We'll be fair, there's no point not being. Have you heard the news?"

Raven shook her head. "We have pretty much been cut off up there."

The gaffa tapped his pen on the table. "Well, it looks like what we have now is all we will have. The LexCorp couldn't keep control and it is crazy in the cities now. Martial law has been declared which was pretty much expected and they have tried to impose curfews and to get control but that has been pretty near useless. They are using what is left of the domes for the refugees. Well that is the official line. I've heard that they are more like prison camps. Those outside are surviving as best they can but the people from the cities are coming out in raiding parties and scavenging what they can. Some are paying, some are taking but as money doesn't have much value the paying isn't really much of an issue.

They haven't got within fifty miles of this place so we're pretty safe here. That is for now. Once they have stripped the nearby farms bare they are going to have to look further afield. All those survival nuts have gone through the local forests and wild areas like a bunch of locusts and stripped the places clean. Obviously supermarkets have been stripped bare. So it is pretty much a mess. But, we are doing what we can to keep things a little more sane around here.

You've heard about our plan for a market? We have skilled people around here who can turn their hobbies into actual production. It will be a bit like turning the clock back but at least we stand a good chance of surviving."

Raven looked shocked. "I hadn't thought about that. They are going to need a lot of food to feed that many people."

The gaffa looked a little sad. "Not as many people as they started with. You know we talked about it for years how the farming in this country was being run down and we were importing too much. Well they are paying the price now. This island nation could become an island wasteland if we can't feed everyone. Too many people, not enough food and that means disaster in my book. They can't import now, there isn't enough fuel for the ships and by what I've heard it's as bad on the continent as it is here. We've gradually given away our countryside and swapped a lot for more houses and more people. The country was sinking before all this happened. This isn't just this country, it was the whole world."

Raven smiled. "So now they wish they had stopped all those imports years ago and built up our own farms don't they? I read about when they used to have farm gate sales from most farms, you know, milk and cheese from the farms and fish off the boats sold by local fishermen. Imagine if we had all that now, this would be a slight hiccup and a need for someone to learn how to make candles."

The gaffa shook his head. "Could of beens are no use to us now. We have to work with what we have and thankfully a fair bit of that sort of thing has gone on over the years around here. Sadly recently with the money getting tight a lot of people sold off stock. I bet they are kicking themselves now. The people around here are country folk. Most have vegetables and we'll be able to supplement that with meat. The organic growers have already been down here and they are coming in on this. How about you? How are you for pigs?"

Raven thought about it. "I have some nearly finished.

Are you interested? You could buy them on the hoof and then sell from your freezers."

The gaffa looked at the piece of paper in front of him. "I have no problem with that. What do you have coming on?"

Raven took out a small notebook. "I've got some of last years' lambs I was keeping on for mutton. We've got about five meat goats and fourteen weaners but they will take some bringing on."

The gaffa noted it down. "How about milk and cheese?"

Raven smiled. "I guess there are no restrictions now to hold us back. I can provide goat and cow milk, cheese and butter if I can get hold of the equipment to make the butter."

The gaffa smiled. "Excellent. We'll put you down for all of that. We have your regular feed order here. We can manage to keep up with that on a month by month delivery. We're stockpiling a bit of petrol and we'll sort the journeys to use as little petrol as possible. Have you got a cart?"

Raven smiled. "That is something I'd wanted to sort out but never got around to."

The gaffa nodded. "It would have been a good idea. I've got six heavy horses here and we're building carts for when the petrol runs out. If you could see your way to getting a horse trained so you can bring in the produce that would help out a lot. I've got a list here of horse trainers. They are happy to come and train for bed and board and a bit of meat and milk to take back to their families. Do you want me to put you on the list of people who want a visit? Do you have a suitable horse?"

Raven thought. "I've got riding ponies, other than Jessie the grey out there who is too old not really."

The gaffa pulled out another list. "Ok, we can do a trade here. Some of your early produce for a trained horse. You might also like to look into ploughing or aren't you doing crops up at yours?"

Raven sighed. "You've given us a lot to think about. I've got the use of Jake's land so I might do."

The gaffa smiled and looked up. "How is the old buzzard?"

Raven's smile faded and Crow put a hand on her back. "He went to his brother's place."

The gaffa shifted in his seat. "And his wife?" The gaffa cast a quick glance up at Crow.

Raven sighed. "She went to her sister's. We had a spot of bother but it is alright now." She looked up at Crow and he bent down and kissed her on the forehead.

The gaffa smiled. "I'm very glad to hear it."

Gunfire erupted outside. Ricochets pinged off of the metal hull of the warehouse and rattled on barrels and the concrete below. There was much shouting and everyone in the room leapt to their feet and went cautiously to the door to see what was going on.

In the yard the horses were screaming and rearing at the end of their ropes as Raven dashed out of the office. Crow tried to grab her as she went past him but he missed so she was followed by the other three. She ran down the stairs and across the yard to where the horses were rearing and jumping about.

The ropes were holding them but only barely. She grabbed the first rope and put her hand up onto the pony's head. It landed on its feet snorting but didn't rear again. She put a hand on its neck and it calmed even more. Seeing one pony calm the next stopped rearing as she moved along to the third. There was a lull in the firing and all three of them managed to get to the heads of their horses and to calm them before it started up again.

The gaffa screamed orders from the shelter of his office. Then he called to them. "Get those horses inside, there's a stable at the back. Put them in there."

They took the horses around the back of the compound where stables had been hastily constructed from garage doors, fencing panels and anything else they had had for sale. They found three empty stables and put the four horses in, two had to share. Once they were safely inside they returned to the main compound just as a spherical object was lobbed over the fence.

It hit the ground and rolled. There was a moment's stunned silence before there was a loud explosion and a crater appeared in the concrete floor.

Raven looked about in panic and turned to Crow. "Where the hell did they get grenades from?"

Crow shrugged his shoulders. "I've no idea."

There was silence and then a loud voice boomed from outside. "Let us in."

There was silence followed by the voice shouting. "Who do you think you are Rambo?" This was followed by automatic gunfire followed by silence and then a knocking on the big metal gates that had been shut at the first sign of trouble. Carl stepped onto the loading steps and looked over the fence. He then jumped down to run over and he then opened the gate.

A lone man stepped inside. He was in his eighties and looked very small in his combat clothing which was far too big for him. He had all manner of automatic and other weapons strapped to him. He marched inside carrying a fully automatic assault rifle. The door shut behind him and everyone rushed over including the four from the farm.

They were patting him on the back and congratulating him. The gaffa came down and took the man up to his office with him. Carl was just passing by them when Raven caught his arm. "Who is that?"

Carl laughed. "That is Edmund. He was always a bit of a gun freak and started the local gun club. When they brought out the gun amnesty and ban he buried his guns under the floor boards. Most people had him down as a harmless nutcase. I guess they are thinking differently now. By the way do you have any of those puppies left? We could use a couple down here to train up."

Raven gave him a smile. "I've got one for sale."

Carl laughed. "Fantastic, I'll take it. We can sort out the deal when we sort out your feed delivery. How are your stocks?"

Raven thought a moment. "Pretty good. Crow has only just stocked up."

Carl looked a bit surprised. "Where have you been getting your stock from then Crow?"

Raven frowned. "Oh yes, I forgot, we stocked up a while back from here so nothing to worry about." Then she hesitated. "Did Jake get his order alright."

Carl thought a moment. "Oh yes he certainly did. He's got to be one of the few farmers around here who has been increasing stocks. Your goat idea is spreading isn't it?"

Raven looked confused.

Carl laughed. "Well if old Jake has them too. I've been doing the old boy a favour and delivering the stock myself. It is amazing that he can manage with all those animals, he's rivalling you for diversity now isn't he?"

Raven frowned. "Yes, well he's off now and he's left us his stock and the feed."

Carl smiled. "Well I'd better be getting on. Have you finished with the Gaffa or do you want to go back up?"

Raven smiled. "I don't think we actually concluded anything. I'm not planning on being back until I need to be so perhaps better I speak to him again." She headed for the stairs and they went back into the Gaffa's office.

He was waiting for them and Edward was just leaving.

The Gaffa looked up as they came in. "Sorry we were disturbed. Well we have a standard rate for buying in meat and goods. We pay on top of what you've had for feed. That is you collect the feed, you deliver the animals and produce back and we pay you the difference in trade for other goods that you need and other food. Without money exchanging it is going to be really hard for you so we can do all that for you. I doubt you'll have all day to go bartering but we are going to offer stalls here for trade on a credit system. We'll be keeping a note of the credits. Some of the shops have boxed up their stock and they are going to bring that down here. The first sale is in a week. We need that time to sort out security and get our stocks in. If you want to bring the meat animals down before then you can. Don't bring it on the day as it will be pretty busy here."

Raven smiled. "I like the deal, I've got a few mouths to feed up there but any surplus I'll bring down. What about the horse?"

The gaffa looked up. "Pick one out of the end three stables." The gaffa looked down at his paperwork. "I can assume that Carl will want all your future puppies for his new security plans. Are you happy to swap the puppies for a harness trained heavy horse?"

Raven looked to Crow and the other two who nodded agreement. She smiled. "Throw in some dog food and you have a deal."

The gaffa raised an eyebrow. "Fair enough. I'll throw in a bag of dog food when you deliver the dog. When can you bring it over? You can take the horse now if you like. I need the stabling."

Raven thought about it. "Sounds like a good idea."

After waving their goodbyes they were off on the road further into town.

The street was deserted of the usual traffic which used to make its way through the town. It had once been a major thoroughfare and market town. What cars there were looked as if they had been abandoned. Seats and other materials had been removed from them and they were metal skeletons, some up on bricks the others laying on the tarmac. The shops were shut, shuttered and were in darkness. The only lights in the windows were in the pub. There were candles in the window welcoming anyone who was still willing to visit.

The doors were shut and there was movement just

inside the door.

Crow pulled his horse up outside the pub. "We can't go in, we'd have our horses nicked if we do."

Reko laughed. "And we'd be drunk riding, is that like drunk driving?"

Raven laughed. "It would be if Crow had to get Blade back without being in full control. We'd be fishing him out of a ditch."

Crow looked disappointed.

Raven smiled. "When we come in by cart we can get a pint and sit outside. Anyway Jareth is setting us up a bar in the old garage. We'd better be getting back, the others will be worried."

They turned the horses and trotted down the main street and out onto the road. They met a battered white pick-up truck trundling slowly along the road towards them. There were a couple of men in the cab. One of them had blood running down his face. They pulled up and wound down the window. "Excuse me miss, I wouldn't go that way. There are road pirates down there and they've got hold of a minibus full of refugees."

They heard the sound of gunfire in the distance.

Raven waved her thanks. "Thanks for that, I think we'd better go cross country. Hope to see you two at the market?"

The two looked at each other. The one who had spoken before raised his hand. "Hope to. Glad to see you are still with us. We're from up in the hill country to the south of you. We've pretty much been left alone. How did you manage?"

Raven smiled. "Fairly well thank you. We've had a bit of trouble with being raided though Gary."

Gary looked thoughtful. "Not those Transition X people?"

Raven frowned. "Fanatics trying to take what they need?"

Gary smiled. "Yep, that's the ones. Organised bunch,

they have been planning something for years. Our cowhand was one of them. I got him drunk and he spilled the beans. They are a real bastard of an organisation run by a complete psychopath. What they want they take. It doesn't matter who actually owns what they want. Their leader, I've heard that he has people flayed if they don't do what he wants. He is a loner who is rarely seen and he gets his brother to do most of his dirty work. His brother, well they are two peas in a pod they are. He's a right thug. He'd kill you as soon as speak to you. Cold hearted fish he is, he doesn't care for anything. I've heard such stories. Our cowhand would have made off with two of my best breeding stock. Good job Pete here stopped him."

Pete looked up and tried to smile as he held a cloth to his bleeding face.

"Yes, big hero I am, up for any kind of beating that seems to be going. The world has gone mad!"

Raven smiled. "Hopefully they've moved off now."

Gary looked concerned. "I wouldn't count on it. They are pretty determined and very well organised. I doubt you'd have heard but I heard something from Geraint, he managed to get up to the place when his place was raided. They are organised and have groups in many of these rural areas who were just waiting for all this. They believe that only they can control things and that they doing it for the greater good. Organised by some bloke called Lord Balen. I doubt he's a real lord but he's a right bastard if his reputation is anything to go by. Murderer, scum, thief, you name it and you come up with an evil plan and you can probably find him behind it.

They left us alone as we just have sheep and the two cows and after the pasting that their boy got we weren't worth bothering around. We don't have any growing land so they probably aren't interested in taking over. But they hounded my neighbour lower down the hillside off of her farm. We came back mob handed and chased the blighters off though. She's got half my farm hands down with her now just making sure they don't come back. Her and her daughter were mighty scared. That Balen is a bastard."

The second man in the van smiled and winked at Raven. "He'll be keeping that old widow nice and protected if you know what I mean. We're off down there after we finish up here."

Gary turned and glared at him.

He smiled wickedly. "Go on, deny it."

Gary turned back to them. "Anyway, good to see you again. Hope you get home safely. See you at the market perhaps?"

Crow kicked his horse on. "See you then."

They trotted off up the road and turned right onto a muddy track. Raven led the heavy horse alongside hers, Crow wasn't far behind her and the other two brought up the rear. The track was clear and the hedge had been neatly trimmed. They could see over into the field. Dead sheep lay everywhere, they had been shot. A farmer was standing in the field with his dog, head in his hands. Crow pushed his horse past Raven and rode along the track until he was level with the farmer. "What happened here mate?"

The farmer looked up. "It was my son. He has been fed up with the farm for some time and when I asked him to stay to help through this he lost his temper, came out and shot my flock. Well he's gone now, there's nothing for him to look after. Now my girls are just rotting in the field. I don't have a freezer big enough to keep them."

Crow cast him a sympathetic look. "Why not get them down to the farm shop? They have plenty of freezer space and you might be able to trade them in for some more animals."

The farmer looked up, his eyes tearful. "The farm shop? Surely that's shut."

Crow smiled. "Far from it, they are talking about starting a market and buying in from…" He hesitated and smiled at Raven whose jaw was slowly dropping. "From us farmers. They look fresh shot, you shouldn't have a problem getting them to take them."

The man breathed in and smiled. "You know I might just do that. Thank you."

Crow kicked his horse on and took the lead. Raven followed on and the other two followed on behind. They didn't hurry back. The day was crisp and clear, the sky blue and the first buds of spring were beginning to burst open. Raven kicked her horse on to ride next to Crow, Reko and David fell behind and were chatting about the finer points of riding horses as if they were experienced jockeys.

Crow was managing his horse a lot better, Blade was now used to him so Crow could relax a little and didn't have to hold him back so hard. He had a bit more chance to look around. "You know if it wasn't for knowing that something is wrong it seems like just another beautiful day in the countryside."

Raven smiled. "Other than the constant threat that there is someone hiding behind every wall."

Crow laughed. "Yes, well, apart from that."

Raven looked thoughtful. "I'm wondering if we should be so hasty to give up our spare space to horses when it is possible we'll get more people arriving."

Crow thought a moment. "Well if we do we'll fit them in somehow. There's always the hay loft above the animal pens."

Raven laughed. "Stinky!"

Crow shrugged. "You've got a point. Then how many more are we expecting? Nobody has turned up lately. If they turn up we'll deal with them. You worry too much sometimes."

Reko was having a few problems with his horse. It had a strong will of its own. David reached over on one or two occasions to grab its reins to steady him. "Darned pesky pony. It just knows that I don't know what I'm doing."

David smiled. "Right leg, left rein to go left. Left leg, right rein to make it go right. Pull with the arm, push gently with the leg. You are confusing the poor beast."

Reko thought and his horse zig zagged down the path for a while as he tried it out. "I think I'd rather stick to cars but if that isn't an option I suppose I have to get used to this. What was your life like before?"

David smiled. "A life of no importance is probably a way to describe my life. I went through school as a "Mr Average" and then had a few problems getting a job. When I did it wasn't exactly what I wanted. I was stacking shelves in the supermarket waiting for something better to come along."

Reko looked over at him. "What is so wrong with stacking shelves? I often hear people complain about it or belittle the job, it is an essential. Without someone to do that how would everyone eat?"

David laughed. "It wasn't the stacking shelves in itself that was the problem. It was that I was constantly looking around for what I wanted to do and not enjoying what I did do. I had regular money, a flat and I could have been content and happy. It was a no stress situation. But I had to go and look for more. That looking made me dissatisfied, that dissatisfaction spoilt the wonderful life I could have had."

Reko sighed. "And now we're just glad of life."

David smiled. "That just about sums it up. It is only when someone threatens to take away the absolute basics that you realise the good in what you had. But, I would actually say that I'm beginning to be happy now. It has to sound crazy but it is a pretty crazy world now isn't it? I have a purpose. I've been helping Ralph with the animals a lot and they help to make sense of it all. I see in them how I could have been content. I never realised that animals play. I'd thought they just stood around and eat but they do. They have personalities as well, they are all different. I can see now why farmers don't get attached to their animals."

Reko shook his head. "Try telling that farmer back there that he doesn't care. I bet that those tears welling up didn't just come from the money he'd lost. Ok, a little detachment as they do have to go for slaughter but did you know a sheep can live up to twelve years, that's longer than a dog."

David looked stunned. "I didn't know that. I suppose you are right. Even in the short time I've spent with the animals it has changed me. I was watching the goats. They do seem to communicate, they get cross, they get bored and they get playful. Every one is different." He sighed heavily.

"I'm not sure how I'm going to face it when it comes to the time for some of the boys to be slaughtered."

Reko stared at his horse's mane. "It has to be done though. Don't go being a veggie on us we can't grow enough of that sort of thing."

David smiled. "A vegetarian world where there were no sheep or cows would be a sad place. Not to mention there not being any manure to put on those vegetables. Then again I was thinking about that the other night. How many earthworms and other bugs are chopped up, poisoned and generally murdered to ensure that they don't eat our vegetables?"

Reko laughed. "You are weird, do you know that? I fancy getting myself a goat skin jacket with fringes."

David laughed. "Getting, making more like. The days of getting are probably over. Then again with this new market they are proposing who knows?"

Reko smiled. "Perhaps I could start my own line of goat skin fashions."

David coughed. "Reko goatskins. I'm not sure what sort of a message that gives."

Reko laughed. "Lavarossi Fashions sounds far better thank you very much. So, what about David? What does Dave want to be when he grows up?"

David thought about it. "Alive. I'm not thinking beyond that. I'm happy helping Ralph with the animals. I'm getting quite good at milking the goats. Perhaps I will be David the Goatherd. That is more of a "somebody" than I've ever been."

Crow reined in his horse as they saw something in the road. It looked like a body. He looked nervously at Raven. "That has got to be an ambush as there's no reason for a body to be there. So what do we do?"

Raven stood up in her horse's stirrups to get a better view over the hedge. "Well we can turn around and go another way, we can check it out or we can carry on riding and hope they get out of the way. The cover either side of the path is thick enough here to hide people. Now I wish that Frank was with us."

Blade snorted and hoofed the ground. Crow steadied and patted him.

"Steady boy, you can smell something can't you? Yes boy we know it's a trap and there's nothing for us to gain by stopping." He caught a movement out of the corner of his eye. "Let's just get past this." He kicked Blade on and the others followed.

With heads down and galloping at full pelt they didn't see the seven men who leapt out from either side. The one on the floor saw them galloping towards him. He scrambled to his feet and leapt over the hedge without looking where he was going. He landed in a muddy puddle.

Their horses' hooves thundered and splashed along the path throwing up mud. They galloped for nearly a mile before slowing down to rest the horses. They didn't look back. If they had they would have seen eight very muddy men looking very disappointed.

## 11
### Black Planet

The horses' hooves clattered over the patch of stone in the centre of the yard. Frank shut the gate behind them and they dismounted and went inside.

Cheryl had the dinner on the table and was just putting two more plates out and lifting a tureen of vegetables from the work surface onto the table. "Today we are having a proper Sunday lunch." There were mystified faces.

"Yes, it's Sunday."

They sat down and began to eat. Two plates were put aside for those on guard.

Reko looked up and grinned. "So who strangled the chicken then?"

There was a deathly hush.

Cheryl looked around the almost motionless room. Forks had stopped in mid movement, their owners now looking at the white meat on their plate.

"So you can go out there and defend yourselves against marauding fanatics but a chicken on the plate gives you cause for concern? Don't worry, that was one of the ones from the freezer." She looked around the faces as they smiled and went on eating. The silence was filled by the clatter of cutlery on crockery.

Frank looked up. "We are going to have to face that sort of a thing though. Do you have an incubator?"

Raven looked up from her plate. "We have three. They aren't working at the moment as it's a bit early in the year but we could start now that the chickens are back into lay again."

Frank nodded. "Good. Might as well think on our feet and grow ourselves some more Sunday lunches. I like this."

Crow smiled. "Just like momma used to make?"

The smile fell from Frank's face and he looked a little wistful. "I suppose so."

Reko caught the look. "So what is your story Frank? I know we are all itching to ask."

There was a deathly hush and slightly shocked expressions.

Frank carried on eating then looked up. "My story, oh it's long and sad and none of your business. You've guessed I have Special Forces training and I was an orphan from a very young age, can we leave it at that?"

Raven smiled. "Of course we can. What happened before doesn't matter here unless it becomes an issue. Your skills, however learnt, are welcome. We all owe you our lives and we probably wouldn't be here if you hadn't dealt with those people in the woods."

Frank smiled and wiped his mouth. "All part of the service little one. So, how did it go at the feed centre?"

Raven smiled. "Very well I think. They are setting up a market there and they've asked for produce if we can spare some."

Frank took another mouthful and chewed it slowly. "We'll have to work out what we have and what we can spare. Is anyone any good at that sort of thing?"

Arthur coughed. "I used to be an Accountant. I'm sure I can come up with some spread sheets."

Janice put her hand on his arm. "I think a list will do dear."

Arthur glared at her. "We might be forced to live in barbaric times but there is no need to lose our sense of proportion. There is a right way of doing things and I'm quite happy to see that things are done right. If it is all written down in the appropriate fashion we'll know where we are. I'll make a start with an inventory this afternoon. Would you like to help me dear?"

Janice looked like a hedgehog caught in car lights. He spluttered a little and looked around the room for some help. Faces were swiftly turned down to plates and the clatter of cutlery reached a crescendo. Her shoulders visibly fell as she smiled sweetly. "Of course dear."

Reko sniggered and David elbowed him in the ribs. Arthur glared at him. "So what is funny?"

Now it was Reko's turn to look like the hedgehog. He spluttered a little. "Oh nothing really, it is just the image of us here, surrounded by bad guys talking about something so old world as accounts and spread sheets."

David whispered. "Nice recovery."

Arthur was smiling to himself. "A bit of normality is just what we need."

Raven cast a sideways glance at Crow and whispered under her breath. "Paperwork isn't though."

There was a shout outside and everyone jumped up and ran out except for Cheryl who went to the window and watched from there. She could see the yard almost as far as the gate and everyone running to the gate. She looked down at her smart shoes, at the mud and got on with the washing up.

In the yard Darren and Matt were standing at the gate leaning out to look down the road. As the others joined them they saw what looked like a cart with people walking beside it. They were making their way slowly along the road. The chunky paint pony that pulled the cart plodded thoughtfully.

His big feathered feet beat out a steady rhythm on the tarmac. The people walking with him were dressed in bright colours although as they got closer the looks on their faces didn't reflect the same happiness.

They pulled the horse up a short distance from the gate and a short man dressed in purple and green stepped forwards. There were eight others with him, three men and five women. One of the women was sitting on the tarpaulin covered cart holding a baby. The short man looked tired and drawn. "Good afternoon to you. Do you have space for some tired travellers? We just need somewhere to pull up our cart for a few days."

Raven looked them over and a shiver went down her spine as she felt the indecision. "Who are you?"

The short man looked back at his companions. "We are the Travelling Circus by the looks of us I suppose. I'm Joe, this is Peter, my right hand man. He pointed to a tall thin wisp of a man. This is Simon, he's our cook. He pointed to a portly man dressed in red and black. This is Wish, our poet. He pointed to a young lad who was average height and build. His long purple hair was twisted into braids. Now these lovely ladies are Heather, my wife. He pointed to a rotund dark brown haired lady with rosy cheeks who smiled at them as he pointed her out. Karen, our daughter. He pointed to a slim blonde haired teenager who blushed and looked awkward. Sharon and Diana there are the twins. He pointed to a dark brown haired and light brown haired pair of early thirty something women dressed in matching blue dresses. This is Leanne, she is the wife's cousin and that is Basil, her son."

Raven introduced the people at the gate and smiled. "Letting you in is a big decision. If you would excuse me I would like to talk about it. Where are you headed?"

Joe smiled. "Of course you need to talk about it. Do you mind if we stay at least on a field nearby for a little while. It has been a long journey. We're not really headed anywhere. We're looking for a safe place to live."

Raven backed away, leaving the guards on the gate. She looked at Frank who was watching the visitors like a hawk. "Frank, what do you think?"

Frank smiled. "I don't trust them. There's more to that group than meets the eye."

Raven shook her head. "So what do we do? If they are just travellers we should help them shouldn't we?"

Frank shook his head. "Now that's the dilemma isn't it? If you let them in then we have a responsibility to feed ten more mouths who haven't been invited by Nemesis. If you send them away you could send them to their deaths. Or they could be more of the same that we had to deal with last night and they could come back and attack us. It is quite a dilemma isn't it?"

Crow put a hand on Raven's back. "Well we could let them camp in the bottom field near the stream. That way they are out of our main compound. I would say where's the harm in that? I just know that one is going to come back and bite me on the arse but I had to suggest it."

Raven smiled. "Probably will but it's a good idea. What do the rest of you say?"

Frank considered his feet. "I still feel uncomfortable about them but it would be an answer. We're defended up here and if we lock the animals in at night I'd like to say what harm could they do? But given experience I would say plenty. So it is your call Raven. Do you let them in or send them away?"

Raven smiled. "If we send them away we instantly make them enemies. If we welcome them in but keep them at arm's length then if we have to send them away we could at least part as friends. Who knows what they may become or who they are. They could be valuable to us or a threat. I'd say we should do what Crow said and let them camp but keep them distant."

She looked around the assembled group and each one nodded. Frank was watching the people around the cart.

Raven walked back across the yard and leant on the gate. "You can camp in our bottom field. You see where the road dips down, there is a gate there and a flat piece of grass the other side of it. If you pull up there you should be ok for a day or so. We have barely enough to keep those we have here alive at the moment. We can't take on ten more."

Joe smiled warmly. "We understand don't we?" He

looked around and the troop smiled and nodded. "Thank you for what you have offered, at least it gets us off the road." He went back to the horse's head and they walked off down the road.

Raven turned to Frank. "Why do I get such a bad feeling about this?"

The rest of the day passed without incident. The daily duties were carried out and by dusk the animals were shut in, fed and watered. The dogs were out and the guards posted.

Raven awoke to the dogs barking. She carefully got out of bed so she didn't wake Crow and slipped on her gown. The yard seemed empty but the dogs were still barking. As she watched Frank, Kyle and James crossed the yard. Crow joined her at the window. He was still half asleep and his hair was dishevelled. He rubbed his eyes and yawned. "What's going on?"

Raven leant back against him and he put his arms around her. "The dogs are barking, we'd better get dressed and go down there." There was a flurry of movement as they got dressed and ran downstairs.

Once outside in the crisp cold morning air they crossed the yard to where the others had disappeared through the farm gate watched by Reko and Tobias who were on guard.

The dogs were still barking when Frank and the others met them in the field.

Raven turned to Crow, her eyes wild. "Check the animals."

Crow ran back around the barn and leapt the field gate. Oberon followed him and had a snap at his trousers as he leapt but missed. Crow landed safely on the other side and took off at a run. He unlocked the feed room door and ran though there. It was dark but it didn't look as though anything had been touched. He opened the door to the main animal shed and reached for the pull cord light switch by the door. The animals were noisy, they were bleating and calling. He pulled the cord and the barn became flooded with light from the low energy bulbs that hung in various different styles of shades in the rafters.

Their faces turned towards him, their big brown or amber eyes questioning. Mouths opened and the noise became almost unbearable. Crow had a quick head count. When he was satisfied nobody was missing he backed out and turned the light off.

Frank had disappeared off into the darkness.

Kyle and James made their way very cautiously around the back of the stables. They had their hands on the wall and fell into every rut and pothole. It was a moonlight night so they managed to see a little bit. Kyle put his foot in a particularly deep water filled rut and fell. James reached to catch him but although his fingers brushed his jacket he didn't quite make it. Kyle fell face down in the mud and felt a sharp pain in his ankle and side. He rolled slightly trying to get up and realised he'd fallen onto an old fencing post that had been left on the ground. The pain in his ankle burnt like fire. Shooting jolts stabbed him every time he tried to put foot to floor.

James stepped beside him and helped him up and managed to prop him up against the wall.

James whispered. "You stay here. I'll go the rest of the way." James then cautiously took the few more steps he needed to take to get to the piggery.

As he moved along the front of the building he could hear the deep grunts of the pigs inside and the high pitched squeals of the young pigs. The doors were all shut and padlocked and all padlocks were in place. He could feel that more than see it as the back of the piggery was in shadow. He felt his way back to Kyle and slipped an arm around his waist. "Sorry to get so familiar but we need to get you back."

They splashed, slipped and stumbled their way back to the farm yard and into the house. Doc was in the kitchen sipping coffee and he immediately jumped up. "Take him through to the Med Bay."

James looked confused.

Doc smiled. "Med Bay sounds a bit cool doesn't it?"

James shook his head and sighed and half carried Kyle out to the old dining room. The Doc followed, closing the door behind him. He carefully pulled Kyle's boot off and began his examination.

Crow went back to Raven who had managed to calm the dogs down and had checked on the horses. They waited in the chill air for Frank to come back. Occasionally there was a bleat from the barn but in general it was as quiet as the countryside ever is. The stars shone down from the infinity of space, the dampness on the ground was sparkling and the morning smell of damp earth filled the air.

They leant on the gate and waited for nearly half an hour. Raven was beginning to shiver so Crow put his arm around her and she leaned into him. They both jumped as Frank appeared out of the darkness. He strolled over to them. "There was movement around our guests' camp. I'd say they probably came up here and had a run in with the dogs and decided better of it. Are the animals all ok?"

Crow was looking out across the field in the moonlight. "We think so. We can't check the chickens but everything else seems to be alright."

Frank sighed. "Well I guess they were checking the place out. That doesn't bode well. There aren't kids with them so we can rule out idle curiosity. They were checking our defences."

Crow looked at Raven who was looking very thoughtful. Raven took a deep breath. "I don't know what to do for the best. Do we have any definite proof?"

Frank smiled. "There are plenty of boot marks around the back of the barn. Whoever it was tried the doors of the animal pens at the back before the dogs started barking. I put the dogs away by the way. You may have noticed as they aren't running around trying to bite everyone. They did their job, well. They are very excitable so I think they have had a good night chasing someone."

Raven took a deep breath and let it out slowly. "Then we have a problem. If they are after the stock then they have to go."

Frank sighed. "I don't think they will go without a fight. They have started pitching tents and making wooden structures down there."

Raven swore under her breath and ran her fingers through her hair. She took a deep breath as if to speak then shut her mouth again and looked around. She looked at her feet. The looked at Crow and Frank and Frank smiled at her. "On one hand they have a right to life and to have somewhere to live. On the other we can't have our animals under threat if we are trying to survive and build something here. They are probably going to have to be asked to leave but if you say they look like there are digging in we can't exactly go and get a court order. There's a baby down there as well. In truth I really don't know what to do."

Frank smiled kindly. "It's a tricky one. We also don't want to have a threat on our doorstep. It was a hard decision you made earlier and for what it's worth I think you made the best one you could with the evidence you had.

If they had panned out as being useful we would have increased our numbers which we are going to have to do if we are going to build for the future. We will have to let other people in one day."

There was a sound of shouting down the hill. A loud explosion rang out and Crow, Raven and Frank started running in the darkness. As they reached the brow of the hill and looked down on the camp they could see that one of the tents was on fire. The horse had bolted and he was galloping around the field perimeter. The camp was in uproar and there seemed to be a fight going on in the middle of it. The three of them ran down into the camp.

Joe was on the floor, Peter was bending over him. Simon was laying into someone with a frying pan and Heather was helping him with a piece of wood. The light from the burning tent gave them enough illumination to see the black figure on the ground. He was curled in a ball and trying tavoid the blows being dealt to him. He cried out. "Stop, stop, please."

Sharon, Diana and Karen pulled Simon and Heather off and the man lay still, crying.

The three from the farm rushed into the camp and over to the man on the floor. Frank grabbed his arm and hauled him to his feet.

The man was short and his face was very weasel like in its shape. His eyes darted from left to right, looking around the people who now stood around him. He spat at Frank who slapped him across the face. "Now, who are you and what are you doing here?"

The man spat again and Frank kicked him. "Now you are being very rude. Come on, tell us who you are and what you are doing here." The man was about to spit again but he took one look at Frank's glare and decided against it. "Now that's better. So, who are you?"

The man smiled. "I could give you a name but what do names matter now. I can do what I want. I just got caught that's all. I fancied myself a bit of a chicken dinner. I didn't realise I'd be a dinner for dogs." He looked down at the bite mark on his backside. "Bloody nasty animals you have up there. Dogs like that big black devil dog should be put down. Then I came down here to see what they had and their hospitality has been astounding."

The campers were now putting the fire out and trying to salvage what they could from the tent. Karen and Sharon had headed off up the field to try to catch the horse and Joe was still laying motionless on the ground.

Frank grabbed the man's arm tighter. The man squealed. "Hey, that's harassment that is, that's assault. Get your hands off of me."

Frank looked him in the eye. "So sue me." He shook the man like a rag. "Come on, why are you here?"

The weasel man sniffed and wiped his nose with his free hand. "I'm here as you have stuff I want. I tried to take it, I got bitten. I came down here and ran into matey boy there. So I walloped him. He wouldn't lie down so I threw a log from the fire at him, missed and it caught light to that tent and something went bang." He shrugged his shoulders. "Ok so I wasn't too subtle or successful. I'm new to all this."

Frank sighed. "Why didn't you just come and talk to us?"

The Weasel smiled. "Right, so you'd give a good for nothing like me something?"

Crow glared at him as Raven stepped over. "Well you'll never know now will you? Who are you?"

The Weasel relaxed a little but tensed up as he looked at Frank who was glaring at him. "I'm Shaun, surnames aren't important. So there you have it, you know my name. So, what happens now, do you hand me in to the rozzers?"

Frank smiled menacingly. "You wish! No, no police now. We deal with our own problems."

Shaun stared at Frank wide eyed. "What do you mean? I want to see my lawyer. I want a phone call."

Crow towered over Shaun who instantly shut up. "You don't know do you?"

Shaun looked up at Crow. "Know what? I know nothing. Just because I sleep rough and steal a few things doesn't make me a bad person. Ok tonight I've right royally screwed up and I'm actually really sorry but that is a one off. Know what?"

Crow shook his head. "Did you know that the world has gone to hell in a handcart?"

Shaun laughed then choked as Frank gripped harder. "Hey, stop that, I'm standing ok, I'm not going to run as there are too many of you. Though I could outrun some of you dead easy." He was looking at Simon when he said that who glared at him and lifted his frying pan menacingly. "How would I know? I was living in those woods over there and yes, I'm sorry I've been nicking the odd egg when the dogs were locked away. Then people came into the woods with guns so I moved out pretty darned smartish and went to that copse of trees next to where this lot are now camping. I did wonder why people had arrived up at your place and you'd boarded up but I didn't really think about it much. I was more worried about the men creeping about with guns. It was like some sort of a movie up here for a while. Who did you upset?"

Raven frowned. "Nobody, they just wanted what we had and wanted to take it by force so we had to stop them. You sound like you've got no idea what is going on. I did wonder why the eggs were coming in a bit short. I guess you needed them. Why didn't you knock at the door?"

Shaun looked stunned. "You serious miss?"

Raven smiled. "Totally, I'd have happily traded you some food and a bed in the barn for a bit of help around the place. You didn't have to steal."

Shaun looked down at his feet. "Nobody's never offered me a job before."

Joe moaned and Peter looked up. "He's awake." Wish bent down and Joe tried to get up. He moaned and slumped down to the floor holding his head.

Raven looked over at him. "You'd better get him up to the farm so that Doc can have a look at him."

Crow caught her arm. "Are you sure?"

Raven looked down. "I don't know but he's a man who is hurt and needs our help. Go with him, keep an eye on him and when Doc has seen to him, bring him back here."

Crow helped to lift Joe and almost carried him up the hill as Raven turned to Shaun. "So what are we going to do with you?"

Shaun looked nervously at Frank who shrugged. Shaun then smiled at Raven hopefully.

Raven smiled kindly. "If we let you go what would you

do?"

Shaun smiled. "Well I'd like to say I'd disappear off and you probably wouldn't see any more of me but it's also likely that I'll stick around and sometimes you'd lose the odd egg. Or you could give me things to do and you could give me eggs and some milk. I can't nick milk the goats don't stand still and that bugger of a brown and black floppy eared one on her own got me with her horns when I tried."

Raven raised an eyebrow and smiled. "I bet he did."

Shaun's smile dropped off of his face. "Oh."

Raven thought a moment. "Ok, you stick around, we can probably find you a few things to do and hell you might even enjoy it. But, you mess up and you nick things and you'll have Frank to answer to and me."

Shaun smiled. "I can't promise I won't screw up but I can promise I'll give it my best shot."

Raven smiled back. "But then you have to make your peace with these people first. It's their tent you wrecked."

Simon looked up. "It had to be the mess tent he went for didn't it? That explosion was the gas canister on the cooker going up. So now I guess we are back to cooking on a log fire which is not going to be fun." He looked around the devastation. "We were just starting to get on our feet as well. When you said we could stay, well that was heaven after the open road and constantly being harassed by road pirates. Now this happens. I shouldn't complain, if we can hold up here for at least a day or two it will at least be a break."

Raven looked around the group. "How are you managing without a computer? Did your lives revolve around it before?"

Simon smiled. "Not at all. We were travelling as a theatre group doing all the fests and gatherings. I don't think any of us have been anywhere near a computer for years. It took us a while to find out anything was wrong. This was sort of how we travelled anyway. Well us the horse and the horsebox which now of course we don't have so our boy there has to actually work for a living."

Raven looked at Frank who smiled back. "So you didn't get an invite?"

Simon laughed. "Blimey were there invites to this craziness. Now I know I'm going mad."

Raven thought for a moment. "Well if you weren't on the computer you could neither get an invite or be considered for one. So what is the story with the rest of you, are you all one troop?"

Simon smiled. "Pretty much. We've been on the road for nearly eight years now avoiding the cities and finding pockets of people who want to live like we do. Then we ran into those Transition X people and decided to keep well clear of the camps for a while. If you run into any of them avoid them. They have some strange ideas. "

Raven frowned. "So you aren't part of that then?"

Simon looked stunned. "You have to be kidding me. I lost my wife to them. A sad tale and probably the same as many other people I would suspect. We pulled up at one of their camps and they welcomed us in. We put on a show and all seemed to be going really well. We camped on the edge of their place and it was my wife and Heather who went to see if we could use their well for water. They overheard them arguing about whether to attack a farmstead nearby or to follow orders and just take a look. They spotted her and she tried to make a run for it but they had guns and she didn't stand a chance. They shot her in the back. Heather was lucky, they didn't see her so she managed to creep away. So we ran for it and this is all we're left with now. It's a sad story but I'm not telling you about it for sympathy. You can imagine what I think of them. But I could just be saying that and you don't have to believe me.  Look we're good workers and we have a whole bunch of skills between us.  We're used to living rough so we're happy to stay out here. We're building a temporary compositing toilet if you are wondering what the wood is for. We live lightly so when we go you won't even know we were here. While we are here if you want to pick up any tips on the stuff we do know about you are welcome."

Raven smiled kindly. "Thank you. We might just take you up on that. Are you alright for food tonight?"

Simon laughed. "The more you get to know me the more you'll realise that I always moan. I'll make a fuss, I'll probably stamp around for hours but in the end I'll light the fire, get the old cook pots out and I'll get breakfast on the go. You are welcome to join us if you like." He turned and started picking up some of the things from the burnt out tent. "Look if you want to keep that tyke around far be it from me to say otherwise. We'll talk to Joe then he comes back, he's technically our leader. Thanks for looking after him by the way."

Frank lifted an eyebrow. "It is a pleasure. We'll get him fixed up and back to you. Here, take this." He handed them a small black box with a pin and loop in it. "It's a rape alarm but if you do need help then just call us."

Simon took it from him and smiled. "Thanks for that. It means a lot. We are peaceful people and having been out on the road with the constant fear, it's not doing well for our meditation or our personal wellbeing. Do you mind if we play some music? I'd suggest that we could come up and play for you but I would imagine that as we are strangers you'd want to keep us at arm's length. I've heard about that dog of yours. Don't worry we won't be up stealing eggs in the morning. We would like to trade for some though if you have any. We're happy to pay our way. Unlike some people have been avoiding doing." He glared at Shaun.

Shaun looked at the floor. "I have a feeling those few eggs are going to cost me dearly for a very long time to come."

Raven laughed. "They may well do. So you are used to sleeping rough are you? How about sleeping in a tent? We have a spare one and you can camp up near to the barn, not in it though. Keep out of the barn and away from the billy goat. He doesn't take kindly to being milked."

Shaun spluttered. "I didn't, I meant, I didn't, I didn't get that close. I got in the pen with the bucket and he chased me out again."

Everyone was laughing and Shaun looked around the faces. "What? It was painful, he's got big horns."

Frank put a hand on Raven's arm. "We had better be getting back. We need to tell the others what has happened."

They turned and left the guests to their sorting out. As they walked up the hill they heard the sound of singing behind them.

Raven walked close to Crow. "It seems like it has been like this forever, not just a few days. Will life ever go back to normal?"

Crow looked down at her as they walked. "No, this is normal now. We'll get by, don't you worry. It could be that our numbers have just nearly doubled if they don't turn into axe wielding murderers in the next few days."

Frank smiled. "Just because they weren't invited and weren't on the database doesn't mean that they aren't good people."

Crow raised an eyebrow. "The database?"

Frank jumped slightly. "I heard that there was a list of everyone who had ever been on line. I was assuming that was what Nemesis used to work out if it had found everyone to evaluate."

Raven shuddered. "Now that just sounds creepy. You mean that program had a list of everyone."

Crow laughed. "Wake up and smell the roses, don't you think Lex Corp and other organisations have a similar list? Only free spirits like those people would have avoided the list. It was probably why Nemesis didn't invite them."

Frank smiled. "You are probably quite right. They seem like good people. If we keep them at arm's length we'll have a chance to see how they get on. If we are going to survive we are going to have to increase in numbers."

Raven shrugged. "More people, more food."

Frank smiled to himself. "More people less work, more people and we can cope with more animals and the planting."

Crow was looking at the ground. "You are quite right. We never know when we are going to lose people."

Raven looked down and Crow put his arm around her shoulders and whispered. "I'm sorry, I didn't mean to remind you."

Raven looked up at him. "It's not you, well it is you. I can't help feeling guilty. I haven't even mourned him. He passed without a word."

Crow hesitated slightly. "Why don't we have a memorial for all those who are lost? We don't have to be specific about naming names. Everyone has lost someone."

Raven took a deep breath and let it out slowly. "I think that would help everyone. We need some form of respectful gesture. After all isn't that really what funerals are all about, respect for the dead and closure for the relatives?"

Crow shook his head and laughed. "You are sounding like a shrink now. It will be good to say goodbye and then we can move on."

## 12
## DEAD TO THE WORLD

Three weeks passed in a flash. The new people settled in and everyone got used to their jobs around the farm and handling the animals. Slowly the new gathering room had been built where the vehicle storage used to be and they increased the defences. The outer wall was now higher and they had started making a taller and stronger fence around the perimeter. The spare wind turbine had been put to good use and the outer field fences were now electrified.

The new guests had settled in down in the bottom field and became part of the farm. Over the weeks they had become known as "the Colours". They too had started working on a perimeter wall so that they had better defences for their compound. They had proven their worth and were happy to chip in with the necessary jobs. Simon had proven to be an excellent chef and although there were certain arguments he did work well with Cheryl. The camper van had been parked with them to give better accommodation for Leanne and her baby. Matt had helped out with this and the two of them had grown close over the past week and he was spending more and more time down there.

Shaun had found his niche. It turned out that he was very good with keeping the goats and he took on their everyday duties. He was particularly good with the hoof trimming and milking. He was happy in his tent but moved it down with the "Colours" for safety. They had forgiven him and had actually been the ones who suggested it and invited him to move down with them.

The morning dawned bright and crisp. Crow came down to breakfast first and looked on the calendar. Cheryl came over to him. "You ok?"

Crow smiled. "Yes, I just wondered what the date was. 14th April. I can't believe how quickly the time is going. Something rings a bell about that date but I can't quite remember what."

Cheryl had the cooker lit and the breakfasts were on the go so she had to turn away to flip some bacon. "Was it someone's birthday? All that sort of stuff just becomes unimportant now doesn't it?"

Crow looked around the room. "Probably, I'm going to take a walk outside. I'll be back in a while. That smells good."

Frank and Matt were on guard duty so he went and joined them. Frank looked around as he crossed the yard. "You are up early, what's up, can't sleep?"

Crow smiled. "I slept alright, just woke up early. Did you have a good night?"

Frank looked back down the road. "It was a quiet one. If it stays quiet today I think we'll have to move some of the stock around. Ralph said that the grass is getting too short on the home field."

Crow laughed. "It had to happen sooner or later. I've heard tales of moving those sheep."

In the distance they heard a low rumbling sound of an engine. They fell silent and all of them looked up the road as a large lorry trundled towards them. There was a black van taking the lead and men in black uniforms who were heavily armoured and carried assault rifles walked either side of it. Frank looked at Crow. "I really don't like the look of that."

Crow was looking a little wide eyed. "Me neither."

The leading van stopped outside the gates and the door opened. Two armed and armoured men got out. They wore black shiny riot helmets.

The first one strode over to the gate and held out a Lex Corporation security pass. He marched across to them and the other men formed up behind him. "I am Agent XZ7890. It is my responsibility to collect the animals that have been requisitioned on behalf of the Lex Corporation. If you would deliver the items on the inventory then we will be on our way." He handed a sheet of paper to Frank who had stepped forward in front of Crow.

Frank took the piece of paper and looked at it. "This is outrageous. This is almost all our stock. You have no right. These animals are privately owned. We have the paperwork."

The armed men as a unit took up a defensive stance. The leader turned his helmet towards Frank. "Your stock is being requisitioned. If you do not comply then all your stock will be taken and your buildings will be forfeit."

Frank tensed and Crow could see his hand moving closer to his weapon. "May I ask why our stock is being commandeered?"

The Agent was expressionless. "I have my orders. Stock is being commandeered from the border counties to feed the Command Cities. Your right of ownership has been revoked. You may wish to resist but I would strongly advise otherwise. We are using armour piercing rounds and I can assure you that our armour is state of the art."

Frank shook his head and looked visibly shaken. "No, this can't be happening. This just isn't right."

He looked at Crow. He could see the muscles tensing on Crow's neck and forehead. Crow glared at the Agent. "I'll fetch Raven." Frank handed him the inventory and he strode off.

The Agent looked at his sheet. "That would be appropriate as she is the named Keeper."

Crow went back into the house and up the stairs. He hesitated outside the bedroom door, hand on the door handle. He shut his eyes for a moment and knocked on the door. When she invited him he opened them, turned the handle and opened the door. Raven was getting dressed but she was mostly dressed. "I heard voices, what is going on Crow?"

Crow looked at the floor. He stepped forward and put his arms around her. "You aren't going to like this. The Lex Corp Agents are here and they are commandeering a large proportion of the animals."

Raven pushed him away. She looked furious. "They can't do that. How will we survive?" Then she calmed down. "No, think, requisitioning. Do you have the list of what they want?" Crow handed her the sheet of paper.

She scanned it quickly. "Their figures are out of date. They have our total stock from December. Thankfully I sold out a lot of stock just before the winter and bought in fresh in January. We've also taken in Jake's stock which they don't know about.

I'm going to need you, Ralph, Darren, David and Shaun to get the Colours.

We'll have to give them sheep but they haven't specified ewes or lambs. I'd say give them the older ewes we took on and the mutton wethers. You know, the castrated ones. We aren't struggling for now with food and the younger ones will come on by the time we want them." Crow visibly winced. "I'm assuming they are going for slaughter so they don't really care. All they want is meat. They would have made life easy here as I'd hoped to trade them at the Mart. It's going to be a struggle but I'm not giving up the young ewes."

Crow looked out of the window. He couldn't see the gate now as that window had been boarded up. "They said deliver to them and they hardly look dressed or equipped for moving the animals so we might just get away with it."

Raven smiled but there were tears in her eyes. "I'll go and talk to the Agents on the gate and I'll stall them to give you time to sort the animals out." She took a deep breath. "At least they don't want any goats. They have asked for cows so give them the younger bullocks. We can't lose the ones ready for slaughter. It takes four years to get them that big. Make sure you keep that big black bullock, we'll need him as a bull if we're going to recover from this. Our main bull is getting on a bit and I was breeding him on to replace him when the time comes. Can you do that?"

Crow nodded. "Don't you dare lose your temper with them. Those guys look like they mean business. I don't want to lose you." His look was so sincere that it stunned Raven. She kissed him and headed off down the stairs, paperwork in hand.

She crossed the yard to where Frank was waiting. He put a hand on her shoulder and she looked at him tearfully. She then turned on the Agent. "Why do you need to take our stock? How are we going to feed the people we have taken in?"

The Agent pulled himself up to full height. "It is essential to rebuild this country that the people in the cities are kept well fed. In the riots we lost the stock in the megafarms so we need food now. We are not taking all your stock."

Raven shook her head. "But how will we feed our people?"

The Agent smiled. "Consider yourself lucky that we are not taking all your stock."

Frank caught Raven's arm as she took a step forwards.

The Agent laughed. "There is nothing you can do about it. So I suggest that you hand over the animals."

Raven's stare was icy. "Do you have the appropriate movement forms?"

The Agent spluttered. "Paperwork is not necessary."

Raven smiled but the smile was cold. "Without information to the contrary from DEFRA I will not allow animals to go off of my land without the appropriate paperwork. As I am waiting for tags and as you may have noticed normal postal services have been disrupted we are unable to comply. Therefore it is not possible for me to move the stock at the moment." Her face was sincere and determined.

The Agent turned towards Raven and she could feel his glare even without being able to see his face. "The animals are being commandeered by the Lex Corporation and no tagging will be required."

Raven shifted her feet. "But you still need the paperwork."

The Agent stared at her coldly but he shifted his feet slightly. "Very well, prepare it. But we are taking the stock."

Raven smiled at him. "We wouldn't like to fail in our compliance would we? If you would be kind enough to wait a short while I will go and find the appropriate forms amongst my paperwork. Matt if you would stay with these people I will be back as soon as I can." As she turned to go and her back was towards the Agents but Matt was in front of her she winked and smiled at him. He didn't react.

Frank saw that. "Should I accompany you or stay here?"

Raven turned to him. "If you could give me a hand I would be grateful. I'm not quite sure where I left the forms. I'm sure that these people don't want to be held up too long. I am sure they have other farms to visit today."

Once inside the house Raven went to the kitchen. She sat down and Cheryl put a pot of tea on the table. Frank looked confused. "I thought we were looking for forms?"

Raven smiled. She went to the kitchen drawer and pulled out a reef of papers. "I've got plenty. We said we'd comply, I didn't say we'd hurry. I'm giving Crow and the others time to sort the stock out so we don't give them the best. We've got Jake's sheep so as long as we give them the numbers they want we may get away with this. We report stock numbers in January.

I was doing so well at the marts that I'd cleared most of my stock and only had my favourites left over winter. I bought in pregnant ewes earlier this year."

Frank looked at her. His face was concerned. "You are taking this very well."

Raven smiled. "No I'm not. I'm screaming inside. I'm just not going to even think about it until I've done what I can to save what I can. We can't fight them, they are too well armed. The best we can do is to be a complete pain in the arse while being as helpful as possible. I seriously doubt they need the paperwork but that Agent isn't totally clued up on it all. Or he's humouring me so that I comply without any conflict. He's got to come back with x number of cows and y number of sheep. They haven't defined ewes or heifers. So they are getting wethers and bullocks. I'm keeping our breeding stock and the best. This is the first time I've felt so totally powerless." She took in a deep breath and let it out slowly. "But that doesn't mean I have to be stupid."

Frank smiled and shook his head. "You aren't powerless, look at how you are dealing with it. You might lose some but you know enough to save what you need for the future. My darling, you surprise even me sometimes. Nemesis chose you well."

Raven took one of the multi sheet forms and began filling it out, slowly.

"Thankfully the rules changed so I don't have to list tag numbers. There's no way I'd have been able to guess which animals are being chosen. Thankfully I would guess the electronic tagging isn't working now. That gives us a chance."

After about three quarters of an hour she went outside with the form and a pen. She crossed the yard and Matt opened the gate so she could go outside. She walked over to the black van and put the form on the bonnet.

She checked the registration number of the lorry and wrote it in. She then waved the Agent over and handed him the pen. "You'd better complete the transport and destination details. Also, are you able to separate the animals? We wouldn't want to fail to comply with regulations would we? Animals cannot be transported together. Also, when was your lorry last disinfected?"

The Agent turned towards her "That will not be necessary."

Raven smiled. "Well I suppose if you want to break the rules that is up to you."

The Agent looked down at her. He took the form off of her and folded it. "That will be enough. I thank you for your compliance."

She looked up at him. "I need my bits of that."

He tore off the copies that she needed and put the form into the car. "You will now deliver the animals and that will conclude this matter. We can either come to your shed or you can bring them over to us five at a time."

Raven crossed the yard in a dream. Nothing seemed real. She opened the door and went into the barn. Crow and the others were in there. They had all the animals on the inventory in the end pen and were waiting for her.

She looked up at Crow. "They are ready. Bring them out five at a time."

She took a deep breath and sighed.

Ralph, Darren and David cut out the first of the sheep and they moved them across the yard to the gate. Two of the soldiers came in through the gate and shot them. One wether made a break for it but he was shot down and skidded in the dust. Raven screamed and lunged at the nearest soldier but Crow and Frank were both quick to react and caught her just before she got to him.

The Agent in charge turned to Crow. "If you want to keep her safe you'd better take her inside. Our orders are to take the animals and that is non-negotiable."

Crow half carried half dragged a screaming and fighting Raven into the house. He pinned her against the wall in the hall with his bodyweight as in batches of five they heard the gunfire as their stock was shot. Tears streamed down her face and she was screaming abuse at the Agents. When the last shot was fired she collapsed in Crow's arms like a rag doll.

Crow lifted her face to look up at him. "You at least saved those that will give us a future."

Frank oversaw the last of the stock loaded. They closed the lorry door. The carcasses were piled high in the lorry where they had collected many more from other farms. Rank estimated there were many hundred bodies in there. The Agent pushed him back and shut the doors. He went back inside the gate and slammed it as the Agents were getting back into their van. The ones who had walked up got into the back and they drove off. Frank watched them go and stared blankly at the empty road once they were gone.

Frank opened the door. He and Crow almost had to carry Raven into the kitchen. Cheryl was keeping the breakfasts warm. Frank sat on one side, Crow on the other. Crow had his arms around a very tearful Raven.

Frank looked down into the cup he had been given. "How did it come to this? Was Nemesis so stupid that he didn't see this coming? Was he so naïve that he thought that the Mega Corporation would just roll over and die when the computers shut down? You must be truly cursing Nemesis now? Not quite the guardian angel now is he?"

Raven looked up from contemplating the table. "I curse the Lex Corporation. The only blame I put on Nemesis is not taking out those controlling the Corporation. The head of the dragon will always seek to carry on as it always has protected by those under him or her. Take the head out and a new head will rise but that head will have to adapt to the way the world is. It was inevitable that the powers that be would want to feed those in the cities. That they are coming this far means that animals nearer to the city have been wiped out already. Our only failing here was that we weren't further away and more remote."

Frank looked up. There was a fire in his eyes. "That

would be a rational reasoning given the current situation. He smiled. Don't worry little one, your animals didn't die in vain. Perhaps Nemesis will live up to his name and have another card up his virtual sleeve."

Raven shuddered slightly as she looked at him. It was as if something had changed about him. She wasn't seeing the friendly old man who had helped them so far. She was seeing someone else. Just for a moment. "I doubt it. Don't put your faith in false hopes. Didn't you read the letter? All power was shut down, that would have shut Nemesis down as well. That program caused all this and is now long gone. Nemesis is dead too and we're on our own. Our avenging angel was after all only a piece of software who probably went into oblivion satisfied that he had solved the problems of the world. At least one entity can rest easy over all this. He dealt with the problem according to the models, this was the result. I suppose he didn't factor in the coldness of the decisions of the management of Lex Corporation."

Then he smiled and she saw again the Frank they all knew and loved. "There speaks one who has seen the corporate machine in action."

Raven raised an eyebrow. "How did you know?"

Frank jumped slightly. "Oh, lucky guess."

Raven managed a thin smile. "I'm going to spend some time with the animals we have left." She got up and walked outside and over to the shed.

She opened the door. The shed was still full of animals as none of them had been moved out for the day. There were hardly any cows left and the sheep herd was about a third of what it had been. She opened the gate of the goat pen and stepped inside.

Immediately the goats ran over, bleating and dancing around her. They were competing for her attention, circling like sharks in a kill frenzy of fuss. Soft noses snuffling her and rubbing up against her.

Her oldest goat, a big white one with no horns reached

up with her long slender neck. Raven put her arms around her neck and cried into her soft fur as she had on many other occasions. "We'll get through this old girl."

Then she backed off and detached her clothing from enquiring goat mouths, went to the hay room and filled the hay racks. She smiled at them as they chose what they wanted to eat, pulling out big mouthfuls and chewing thoughtfully. She marvelled at the calm brought on by the silence and their contentment.

Ralph stepped up behind her. "Don't you worry, we'll build again. We saved all the young ewes and lambs. They got the wethers and breakers. The cows were a big blow. I kept the big black bullock, he's safe. He'll grow. His mother was old so she's gone. He's old enough to be on his own now. What are we going to do with them now?"

Raven looked around the milling animals. "I think we ought to get the sheep and cows down to the bottom field, behind the Colours. The Colours can keep an eye on them and they will have more grass."

Ralph looked pretty shaken too. "Was there anything we could have done?"

Raven took a deep breath. "There was plenty I would really have liked to have done to them. But, we would have lost people and the result would probably have been the same."

Ralph smiled. "That's the worst part isn't it?"

Raven smiled. "Yes."

Ralph looked at the milling animals. "So what do we do now?"

Raven looked around the shed. "We concentrate on what we have left and we multiply the goats. It has always been a curse that goat products weren't licensed and goats were overlooked or bundled in with sheep. Now it could be their salvation. We get milk from them, meat from them and when those meat wethers go into the freezer we'll have leather from them. They are fast growing in comparison to a cow and can live on forage. They prefer to live in the shed because of our weather and we can forage feed them by walking them. So there's no need for so much feed. If we lay down nettles and other forage dried in the rafters we could just have a sustainable animal."

Ralph thought for a moment. "You are quite right. But what about those tiny ones? Are they big enough for that sort of thing?"

Raven smiled. "The Arapawas, they are best of all. They don't need so many minerals, they are hardy, small and easy to manage. Most of the goats are Arapawa crosses."

Ralph looked at the smaller goats who skittered around in the pen. "So where did they come from? I hadn't seen them until I came here."

Raven looked thoughtful. "There's a book in the collection about them if you would like to read it. Once Upon An Island by Betty Rowe.

They were found on Arapawa Island which is just off the coast of New Zealand. By what I understand it is speculated that Captain Cook took them out there and they escaped or were let loose. The New Zealand Government decided that they were vermin and not native and set about killing them. If it hadn't been for a few caring souls we would have lost yet another species and now a valuable resource. I'm breeding them pure and breeding them in with our goats to get stronger goats. Their milk is far more creamy. It has a high fat content which for soap and cheese is just perfect. Also they were rare before all this happened, they were original cottager goats so it is only right that they are here with us now that things are going back to a world where they will be important again.

Look you'd better get yourself in for breakfast. Cheryl is keeping it warm for us."

Ralph sighed. "When I said I'd look after the animals I never in my life thought it would be so complicated."

Raven managed a smile. "Or meaningful?"

Ralph rubbed the nose of the big floppy eared buck goat and smiled thoughtfully.

Raven left the shed and crossed the yard back to the meeting room. The table was laid neatly and everyone was assembled. Mirrors had been set up so that the guards in their seats near the window could watch up and down the road. Now everyone could eat at once. The plates of food were brought out and everyone helped themselves in silence. A heavy cloud hung over the table and nobody seemed as though they wanted to talk. They eat and drank in silence. When they had finished Crow put a hand on Raven's arm. He looked around the sad faces. "We might have lost some of our animals and it is a bad day but we still have our breeding stock and enough food in the store for a month or so. They didn't take the pigs and they didn't take the goats. There will still be food on our table."

Raven looked up from contemplating her plate. "We need to find out what is going on in the world out there. If it's not going to leave us alone, we need to know what we are facing. We knew that the people from the cities wouldn't leave us alone forever but I'd hoped that with being so remote we might have stood a better chance. I'm going to take a ride to the Mart this afternoon. Who is coming with me?"

Crow put his fork down. "I'm with you, take that as read."

Frank looked up. "I'm coming too this time. I would suggest a small group moving fast. Does anyone else want to come?"

Raven looked around the faces. "Those who aren't coming I would suggest that we look to moving the cattle and sheep to the bottom field next to the Colours. The grass is down on the fields close to home. We'll need the shed cleared. I deep bedded over winter which means not mucking out and putting fresh straw on top. Margaret and Tobias you will now have some really good compost for the spring planting so I would suggest you have it moved directly to where you need it. We can then get ready for kidding."

Karen looked up. "Yuck, you mean you left them with their mess all winter?"

Raven smiled. "Deep bedding is a time honoured way of keeping goats over winter. The urine is a disinfectant and as the mess breaks down it generates heat and the depth of bed keeps the animals warm. It takes two foot of straw to keep an animal from feeling the chill of the concrete and that's expensive if you change it regularly. But it does mean the mother of a mucking out job in the spring."

The conversation continued for about an hour before the meal was finished and people meandered off to do their tasks for the day. A few hours later Crow, Frank and Raven were saddled up and riding out of the gate towards the Mart.

Little had changed on the route and as they rode into town there were more people about on horses or walking.

Makeshift tethering posts had been erected in the town and there was a line of horses tied up outside the pub. A guard had been posted who occasionally wandered down the line filling up hay nets.

The Mart was bustling with people coming and going into the outer yard. Stalls had been set up, decorated with bright coloured ribbons and there was music coming from one corner where a small stage had been set up decorated with plastic flowers and old broken musical instruments.

Carl was in the yard with a clipboard talking to people. When he saw them he came over. "Boy am I glad to see you, well any of you farmers really. The news has been really bad. Did you get a visit as well?"

Raven dismounted. "We did, we lost a lot of stock but we're still going.

They didn't touch the pigs so if we are lucky we'll have about twelve for you."

Carl smiled and shook his head. "That is music to my ears. You did better than most then. We've had reports that many farmers just wouldn't give up their stock, they are dead now. Old Farley had his farm burnt to the ground. But the news is that they may not come back. We've set up a messenger network and we got news this morning."

Raven was looking around nervously.

Carl smiled. "Don't you worry, this town is about as peaceful as you are going to get. The people have food here and the crafts people are in their element now.

We've achieved a lot. Even wool from the local sheep is being used now that it doesn't have to go to the Wool Marketing Board. We've raided the museum and got many old crafts up and running again and the mill is working again. There's plans to turn a lot of the lowland grass over to crops again.

Anyway, this news I was talking about. A messenger came in about an hour ago. It seems that something has happened in the Lex Corporation. Lex is in chaos so they won't be bothering us for a while. It seems their Board of Directors have been removed. There are riots in the streets and the military can't cope. Martial law has broken down as the people have overpowered the military. After all they were being forced to shoot at their friends and neighbours and it looks like a lot have switched sides, taking their guns with them."

Frank smiled. "Serve the bastards right. So the head of the hydra has been cut off. No doubt there will be more but it's a start."

Carl looked down. "I don't know really what it will mean but to me it sounds good. Out here, probably not a lot other than they might leave us alone. They will have enough to contend with back in the City. Food is going to be an issue but I've made a move to contact other places around the country. There are groups of people in the towns who are trying to make a go of it.

I've contacted some church groups and clubs nearby and put forward a proposal to set up a network to supply them with food for their communities. In exchange we get goods we can't provide and help at harvest time. It looks like barter is going to be the new currency between here and the city but they still use cash there. So are you interested in some shopping?

Your credit is good by the way and we're happy to run up a tab for you for if you want anything. I think you might find one or two things that could interest you. Hold on a minute." He reached into his pocket and pulled out a notebook with some paper notes which were basically old ten pound notes with a coloured stamp on them. "I'll sign you out some of these. You'll need them if you want to buy anything from a stall or if you go outside at all.

If you want to leave your horses there are pens out back for them. Look sorry I have to go. If you need me for anything, I'll be around." He smiled and walked off.

Raven looked at the others. "Well we might as well take a look around seeing as we are here. Boy do things move on fast around here. Looks like they've done wonders."

The stalls were laid out in neat lines back to back so there was an area behind the stalls for the stallholders to sit or stand in peace. Customers circulated around the outside of the lines of stalls.

The stalls sold all manner of second hand and new items, all set out beautifully. One line of stalls was almost completely given over to tools and equipment. Some were handmade, some commercially made. There were presses for cheese making, soap and candle moulds and tools for leatherworking and tanning. Anything that you could think of to make or create something was there. The other line of stalls displayed already made goods and another all manner of vegetables and produce neatly set out and being sold by their enthusiastic owners.

At the end of this line of stalls there was a large circular open sided pavilion with stools around the inside of it.

There was quite a crowd collected and they had just finished listening to a talk and demonstration of how to tan leather from animal skins.

Around the outside there were open fronted sheds made skilfully from planks of wood and sheets of ply. Crafts people were making things and selling them from tables on the front of their new workshops. Near the corral where the horses milled about there was a blacksmith who was shoeing horses as well as making and selling swords, knives and other metal implements he had already made.

The music was bright and cheerful. People seemed genuinely happy but it was impossible to miss the guards who patrolled on a regular basis. Their green boiler suits with rank insignia on the shoulders stood out. They were watching but there didn't seem to be any crime.

To the back of the compound a large undercover area had been constructed where tarpaulin had been tied together. There was also a wooden covered area. A line of cooking stoves had been set up. Rayburns, wood stoves and gas burners were loaded high with food that was cooking and an eager line of people waited for their chosen food to be ready. Food and drink was being served and the tables set out under the tarpaulin awning were full of people meeting and talking. The tables and chairs were a collection of garden furniture, furniture from shops and dining room chairs. Anything that could be sat on or eaten off of which looked remotely serviceable and good quality had been pressed into service. To one side there was a line of car seats where people were relaxing and chatting and on the other side a line of sofas with coffee tables in front of them.

Crow headed that way and they followed. He went up to the counter and pulled out his wallet and opened it. "Is this cash good here?"

The portly woman in an apron behind the counter took a look over the notes. She smiled broadly. "Perfectly good, have you got any coins?"

He took a look at the prices and put enough for three cups of coffee on the counter. "Three coffees then please."

She smiled. "Coming right up." She put the coffee into the mismatched mugs and poured in the water from the kettle that was on the hot plate. "Sugar is at the end of the counter. Don't worry about the colour, we're making our own now and it's not bleached."

They found an empty table and sat down. They had just put their mugs down when a couple came over. "Do you mind if we join you? " Crow shook his head. The couple sat down one on either side of the table. The woman smiled at everyone. "I'm Abi and this is my husband Zed. We've got a holding about a mile from here. Pigs and sheep mostly. Well it was sheep but they took most of them. Are you new around here?"

Crow smiled at her. "No, we just don't get out much. We've got a holding about an hour south of here. We got hit too."

Abi looked around the trio. "Did you hear the news? Looks like the Lex Corporation might not be bothering us again."

Crow took a sip of coffee. "It does."

Abi looked into the cloth bag she had over her shoulder. "I'm going to try some weaving this week. I've got myself a hand drop spindle and a couple of carders. We've plenty of clothes in the wardrobe but I can't imagine it's going to be easy and it will take time. How about you? Are you making your own yet?"

Raven looked up. "We haven't started all that yet but we've got books."

Abi's eyes lit up. "You have books, wow, now you are really lucky. We didn't get hold of anything like that before all this happened. So you are actually going to know what you are doing. I sat in on a talk earlier and I've got the basics, I can't wait to give it a try."

Raven looked at Crow and there was a questioning look in her eyes. "You know we've concentrated so hard on surviving we didn't think about living. I guess we have some shopping to do. So how does that work?"

Abi handed her the stick with a round disc at the bottom. Abi then took it back and held it up. The wool goes through that loop and over that and as it spins it pulls down the fibres. You have to sort of pull them out and down and you get wool. Then someone has to weave or knit it of course. Can you knit?"

Raven nearly laughed but bit her tongue. "That sort of thing used to be something I never even contemplated. I knitted when I was little so yes I do know how to knit. I suppose that sort of thing is going to be important now."

Abi put her spindle away. "Well it will be if you want to be warm in winter. We are still on oil so we've had to open up the old fireplaces. They are small but there's a good supply of wood available. All those old cut down forests that had wood left to rot are now being scavenged by Carl's Wood Recovery Squad. You should see the stockpile they have in the shed there. Its amazing what they are doing here isn't it?"

Frank was looking around. There was a soft look in his eyes and his smile was relaxed. He looked exhausted. "It is truly wonderful. It makes it all worthwhile."

Abi was looking around too. "I've bought some cheese moulds and I've a pot of live yeast. If I feed it then we won't have to buy more and we can share it with others. You know you can actually leave some bread part made in a bowl and it will pick up yeast from the air? But you'd know all that. I bet you are enjoying your books now."

Raven looked guilty. "No actually but I know what I'll be doing when I get back."

Abi looked around and waved at a couple who were just coming into the café area with their two small children. "Will you excuse us? I haven't seen Sandra and Mike for quite a while. It has been wonderful to meet you.

I'll look forward to seeing you all again."

Raven looked around. Everyone did seem to know everyone else and people were moving about tables saying hello to friends and discussing looking after animals, making things and showing off things that they had made and were wearing. She shook her head and smiled. "Who would have thought?"

Frank was looking around. "Who would have thought…"

13

After a long discussion about what to do next and an extensive look around the stalls it was decided to leave the horses at the Mart and take a look around town.

They moved through the crowds in the Mart and then pushed through the crowds outside who were waiting to have their credentials checked so that they could go inside. They blocked up the road and came with an assortment of vehicles both motorised and pulled by a wide variety of animals.

There was a bubble of sound and the smell of the animals gave it an atmosphere of its own.

Entertainers made their way along the line of people waiting. Juggling, singing, showing magic tricks in order to be able to hold out the hat for exchangeable currency. People seemed to know each other and as they walked past they caught snippets of the conversation. It was easy to work out that people were at the Mart pretty much every day as it was more than a place to shop.

People didn't take any notice of them. As they found their way through the crowd just about everyone smiled and stepped aside.

One or two of the farmers doffed their cap to Raven. She vaguely knew them from visits to the Mart when it had been a food store but they didn't stop to talk back then so she didn't know who they were. She smiled back and they carried on.

The four pushed their way through the crowd and finally got far enough down the road that they could walk together and talk. There were still people coming to join the crowd. Travellers came in carts, on foot and on bicycles. Many carried goods, others carried bags in the anticipation of buying goods. They all travelled with a purpose.

The road was filled with rubbish and debris. There was a considerable amount of dried blood staining the pavements. Some homeowners had cleaned up outside their houses, others had left the stains there because they didn't have time or because it was their blood and they were no longer around to clean up. The cars that had littered the road the last time they had visited had been pushed out of the way and anything useful had been removed from them. There was little left of them. Anything deemed useless had been discarded on the road or pavement and added to the general mess.

The shops which had broken windows had been boarded up and most had signs hanging on the wooden boarding saying "Moved to the Mart". The sign was a standard printed A4 piece of paper which had been laminated and nailed to the planks that protected the windows.

Groups of people hung about on the corners. They looked about nervously and waved or spoke to groups that passed them. All were armed with whatever they had found and many had makeshift body armour tied on or fastened with whatever they had managed to get hold of. They looked up as the four strangers in town passed along the pavement but stepped out of the way when it came to them actually passing by. They avoided eye contact and let the four go on their way.

An elderly man with a Westie dog passed them on the other side of the street. His long duffle coat looked bulky and he clanked slightly as he walked. He looked up, smiled and waved but he hastened on his way.

The street was unnervingly quiet when they got away from the Mart. The sun beat down on the dusty tarmac and danced on the windows of the cars and other shiny surfaces. Birds were singing and occasionally flittered down onto the road to look for something good to eat. In the distance they heard the sound of shod horses' hooves and the rumble of a cart. It came into view around the corner. It was an old farm style cart with a smartly dressed woman driving. Her overcoat was buttoned and her shoes polished. The two men who accompanied her were similarly neatly dressed in clean work clothes. They carried a shotgun each and were intently watching, looking out for trouble.

In the back of the cart there were all manner of vegetables piled up almost above the sides of the cart. The woman raised her hand in greeting as she pushed her horse to a trot and passed them by.

They watched her go down the road on the way to the Mart and then continued on to the pub.

Outside The Talbot a young lad was looking after the horses lined up there looked bored. There were people milling about outside the hotel attached to the pub. The hotel had a homemade sign outside which said that it was full. The horse minder was sitting on the memorial steps with his feet up and crossed. He watched them intently as they crossed the cobbled yard and approached the old wood door. The door was closed and opened into a corridor. On the left a door led to a warm and friendly tap room. The wooden floorboards were well swept and worn with age, the tables and chairs dark wood with padded tapestry seats depicting farm scenes which were a little threadbare. The log fire was burning in the hearth and two old farmers were sitting by the fire, shotguns beside them, enjoying a pint.

The barman was polishing glasses. The conversation in the room fell silent as they walked in. There was a group of four farm hands sitting in the back corner and a man and woman sitting near the bar. The man looked tired. His round face was covered in scratches that had mostly healed. He wore a wedding ring, as did the woman with him and she too was covered in scratches. They looked up nervously when the strangers walked in. The four in the corner looked up. They looked remarkably similar, the same round faces, thick bushy eyebrows and unkempt beards which was very similar to one of the farmers at the fire. Each had a shotgun rested on his knee and a pint in front of him.

Frank went to the bar. "Afternoon, what do you have on tap?" He had already noticed that over half the pumps were covered up.

The barman smiled. "We have some Old Rosie if that is your taste. What do you have in payment?"

Frank pulled out the Mart Credits. "Will these do?"

The barman looked at them carefully. "They'll do fine." He took the note and gave them back coins as change. Then he put the glasses onto a tray on the bar. "Now as long as you don't cause any trouble you are welcome here."

Frank smiled. "Wouldn't dream of it. Have you had a lot of trouble?"

The barman stepped back from the bar and slotted the note into a wooden box which was securely bolted to the counter and which looked as though it had been newly made. The till lay idle and its drawer had obviously been prized open and then taped back up. "A fair bit to start with, same as the rest of the town. There was a lot of looting by people out of town and some undesirables who had moved in over the past few years but most people were neighbourly and chipped in to protect their own and other people's property. We lost a lot of people though, nearly half of our little town gone in one night. Then it went a bit quieter. The Mart opened up and that helped. People were scared they weren't going to get what they needed and intent on taking it. When they found out they'd still be able to get what they needed they calmed down.

We've cleared up the town as best we can. Can't say that we aren't expecting more trouble though. We chased off the looters but they could be back. They aren't local. They are travelling around taking what they can from wherever they can. We'd already annoyed them you see. They were travellers looking for a place to camp and we turned them away. Now they are partly seeking revenge, partly seeking whatever they can get their thieving hands on."

Frank smiled to himself and picked up the tray. "It looks like you've had your hands full then. At least you still have some beer." He took it over to the table and handed the drinks out. "Looks like they are pretty much sorted here too though how everyone is going to be when everything starts running out I don't know."

Crow looked up. "Perhaps we ought to go into the brewing business."

Frank laughed. "We'll have to do something even if it's just for ourselves. I'm waiting for the trouble to start when the coffee runs out. Thanks to Raven here we have good stocks but it won't last forever. That is something I haven't seen for sale."

Raven looked serious. "I've tried some of that dandelion root coffee, it just isn't the same and anyway the goats eat the dandelions last year."

Frank looked serious too. "Then it could get very unpleasant for a while. We'll have to see if we can pick some up while we're here. As I said though, I haven't seen any yet." He cast a glance over to the four men in the corner. They were whispering and kept casting glances over at Frank's table. He whispered. "We could be in for some trouble. They are trying to work out who we are and where we've come from. In particular they are wondering what we are going to take back from the Mart. I'll keep an ear out to their conversation. It could be just curiosity on their part."

Raven sighed. "That just isn't what we need. Crow, was

it such a great idea to come in here?"

Crow smiled and took a long drink of his pint. "Depends on what you call a great idea. We might be able to pick up some information and at least the beer is good."

Raven laughed. "Don't let Jareth hear you say that. He's very proud of his pint."

Crow looked chastised. "I didn't mean his beer wasn't good. I meant that it is good to be out."

Frank was quiet and although he seemed to be listening to them it looked like he had one eye on the men in the corner.

The elder of the four, dressed in a green check shirt, was the one doing most of the talking. "Well, they did say that there would be trouble. I can't see the Lukases leaving it be. They were very fond of Sally if you know what I mean and her disappearing off like that is going to stir them up."

The brother in a blue check shirt next to him took a long drink. "I still think she didn't run off. There was no reason for her to. She was quite happy with Jacob. She would have taken some of her stuff. It's not like she can just buy some more."

The brother in a red shirt sitting opposite him piped up. "I agree with Marley. She wouldn't have run off. I went to school with her. She wasn't a bright girl but she wasn't stupid either. In these times you need your family. That is unless she was seeing someone."

Marley smiled. "I doubt that she was."

The eldest son laughed. "You mean that she couldn't be seeing anyone other than Jacob because she wouldn't see you?"

Marley blushed. "You can stop that right now. I'll say it plain that I liked her. Who didn't?"

The younger son in a green shirt put his pint down. "Most people liked her, if you know what I mean."

Marley slammed his pint down on the table but his brother in the red shirt put a hand on his arm. "Ethan, that wasn't necessary. You know your brother was sweet on her. We should be worried. What about Jennifer, what if she suddenly goes missing? Hey, barkeep, have you heard anything about girls going missing?"

The barkeeper looked up from stacking glasses. "There have been four this week who have gone missing from around here. Megan from up near the Mill, Bethany from the stables near the crossroads, Janice from the shop here in town and Ruth from the house near the stream. All disappeared without a trace taking nothing with them."

The four men looked stunned and the two elderly men at the fire looked up as well.

The brother in the red shirt took a long drink of his pint. "I guess we'll have to keep a firm hand on our women folk. This can't be right."

Frank looked over at Raven who was totally oblivious to the conversation, she was chatting to the couple next to the bar. Frank nudged her and got her attention. "Listen, looks like there have been disappearances. Women are going missing."

The brother in the blue shirt looked over to their table. "So, have you heard of anyone going missing? You aren't from here are you?"

Frank took a sip of his beer and slowly swallowed. "I hadn't heard anything and no we're from south of here. It sounds like you could have a problem."

The brother in the blue shirt stared at him intently. "What do you mean?"

Frank put his glass down. "Well, if the women are disappearing someone is taking them."

The brothers looked at each other. The brother in the red shirt looked at the worried faces. "Well we'd better keep a close eye on our women folk."

The bar fell silent, beer was drunk, the fire flickered and the silence was broken only by the snapping of the burning wood and the occasional clink of glasses being replaced on wood.

Somewhere outside there was an explosion. Its echo broke the silence like a wave. Tables were pushed away, chairs fell over as the inhabitants of the bar ran to the door. Outside the horses were rearing and fighting their ropes and the boy was having trouble holding them.

Frank and the others ran past the horses and followed by the others they ran down the street to the left where the sound had come from. There were people opening doors to have a look but nobody stepped out into the street.

The smoke and flames were coming from a warehouse on the edge of the village. The roof was completely on fire and the windows had broken in the explosion. Bodies lay around on the tarmac around it and a lorry was on fire that was parked next to the burning building. As they got closer they could see that the lorry had actually run into the building. The bodies were around the lorry. There was nobody about, nobody was trying to quell the flames and nobody seemed to be moving in the building or around it.

The four ran around the back of the building. The wood in the yard was in flames and there were three men with buckets trying to get water from a tap. Frank ran over to them. The taller of the three, a wispy man with a long moustache looked up helplessly. He had turned the tap but no water came out. "You know I forgot, we haven't had water from a tap for weeks now. What are we going to do?"

Raven looked around. "Try and make a firebreak and get the stuff that isn't burning clear."

They all chipped in and moved what they could away from the flames. What was already burning they had to let burn.

Frank was helping a dumpy looking man with a long beard to move some logs away from the flames. "So what happened here?"

The dumpy man looked helplessly at him. "We've been getting trouble for weeks. It started small, bits going missing and then this man walked into the office last week.

Bold as brass he demanded nearly half of our stock. He said there would be trouble. We didn't believe him."

Frank looked shocked. "You mean someone is demanding protection money?"

The dumpy man looked down at the log. "I suppose it was, yes. But we've had all manner of cranks turning up wanting things so we didn't take any notice. Then the man came back this morning and demanded even more. I told him exactly what he could do with that idea and you can see the result. I should have paid him."

Frank looked over to where they were taking the log. "No, you shouldn't. What did he look like?"

The dumpy man thought for a while as they lifted the log onto the pile. "He was average height, average build, there really wasn't anything that made him stand out."

Frank sighed. "It was very smart of them to choose someone like that. Someone you wouldn't be able to describe. So what do you do now?"

The dumpy man looked around his yard. "I see what I have left and I carry on. The machinery is gone and the gas canisters I was saving and hoped to sell but we still have some wood."

Crow and Raven were moving logs between them and David was throwing wood away from the fire to make a firebreak.

Frank and the dumpy man headed back for another log. "Who were the people outside?"

The dumpy man looked mystified. "None of my staff thankfully, they are all accounted for. There were some people walking down the road and it must have been some of them. The van careered down the hill out of control and it ran over a few people on the way. I didn't get a clear look at it but I'm assuming it didn't have a driver."

Frank shook his head and they carried on moving the wood in silence until it was safely away from the flames. That went on for nearly an hour before he turned to the others. "We'd better be making a move if we want to get back before dark."

The dumpy man looked up from checking his notebook. He put his hand in his pocket and pulled out some coins. "Look it is not much but thank you."

Frank smiled and curled the man's hand back around his coins. "That won't be necessary. Use it to help rebuild your business."

They went back to the Mart and Raven went over to Carl. "Can we have a word in private?"

Carl looked up and smiled. "Of course we can." He took her up to his father's office which was empty and offered her a seat. He sat in his dad's chair.

Raven smiled. "Did you hear that explosion earlier?"

Carl nodded. "The wood yard and hardware store went up in flames."

Raven looked around the room. "Did they trade here?"

Carl smiled. "They did and they are very glad of it now as I'd been storing most of their stock to save the journey up and down the road. So they didn't lose everything."

Raven smiled back. "Have you been threatened?"

Carl looked down. "Yes but we shot him. I'm waiting to see what happens next. Everyone is having trouble in some way or the other."

Raven looked serious. "Have you heard that women are disappearing?"

Carl looked up. "No, I hadn't heard that. Look it seems as though we need to get people to share information and perhaps try to come up with something. I'll look into it. Raven, you be careful. We don't want you going missing."

Raven smiled. "I will. I just wanted to make sure you knew what was going on. We'd better be getting a move on if we're going to get back before dark."

They went back downstairs and met the others who had the horses saddled. They said their farewells and trotted out into the street and out of town.

Raven looked around nervously. Her imagination began to play tricks on her. She could see someone lurking behind every tree. Every blind spot held a hidden horror. Her pony could feel it too, he was jumpy and shied at every leaf and every movement. Crow rode up to trot beside her. Frank seemed to be intently looking from left to right.

Frank turned to them. "We can probably expect trouble on the cross country path. We've used it enough now for people to know it's the way we go and there are others who use it too now. It's the perfect place for an ambush and I doubt we'll get past as easily as we did before. These people who are here now aren't the locals. They know what they are doing and they aren't trying to get lucky. They are planning what they do and they don't mind who they kill in the process."

Crow frowned. "You don't need to tell us. I think we've worked that one out."

Frank cracked a small smile. "I don't doubt it. So I'd be ready for a very fast gallop if anyone sees anything."

They rode on for about a quarter of an hour and turned onto the small cross country path. Raven just turned to talk to David when a shot rang out. David slumped onto his horse's neck and was slipping onto the ground when Crow kicked his horse on and grabbed him and pulled him across the front of his own horse. Raven grabbed the stray horse's reins and they set off at a gallop as more shots rang out. Raven's horse squealed in agony and collapsed under her. As the horse went down she was thrown free. The pony fell to the ground kicking like mad. Frank reined up his horse and turned to go back for her as they were caught in a hail of gunfire. Blade reared and Crow just about managed to hold him and keep David across the saddle before he bolted, heading for home. Nothing was going to stop him no matter what Crow tried to do. All he could do was hang on to David and try to hang onto the saddle. Seeing Blade gallop off, Frank's horse followed him and at the speed he was going Frank couldn't jump off. He too had to cling to the saddle as the horse galloped wildly along the path.

Raven crawled away. Her pony now lay still. She pulled herself through the hedgerow and rolled into the ditch. As she looked up she could see green wellington boots. She had landed at someone's feet. This was just before she felt a sharp pain at the back of her head and the world went dark.

Frank and Crow managed to rein their horses in about half a mile down the road as the horses calmed a little. They turned their horses, got them under control and galloped back to where they had last seen Raven.

As they approached they saw the prone and motionless body of Silk and slowed down, approaching with caution.

There was silence. The gentle breeze fluttered the leaves in the hedgerow and a small bird landed on a branch.

Frank jumped down from his horse, tethered it and ran to the pony. Silk was dead, his lifeless eyes looked up at the clear blue sky.

Frank looked around in the soft mud of the track and found the tracks he was looking for. He followed the marks where Raven had crawled and climbed through the hedge, following her trail. He found where she had landed in the ditch and he found the pressed down grass where she had been dragged and the heavier footprints where she had been picked up and carried as someone ran off with other footprints which joined them.

He followed the heavy footprints down the field, now moving at a run as the footprints were clear in the soft mud. The abductors were making now effort to hide where they had gone.

Crow had tethered his horse, helped David to a safe place, pushed through the hedge and ran across the field full pelt to catch up with Frank. Frank was moving as quickly as he could while following the footprints. They were easy to follow as the abductors were making no effort to conceal where they were going. Crow was behind him, trying to take a look ahead and around them. They ran down the field and got to the road. As they broke through the hedge beside the road they heard an engine start up and just as they landed on the tarmac of the road a van sped off. Crow turned helplessly and looked at the distance back to his horse. He ran but by the time he got back the van was long gone.

Frank had written down the number plate and was standing in the middle of the road looking lost. He looked up at Crow when he arrived. There was a dead look to his stare. "I can't believe we've lost her? We can guess she's alive but as to where they've taken her, I can't tell. I just don't know?

What do we do Crow?"

Crow shook his head. He had no idea.

They walked back to where they had left the horses and David. David lay motionless, propped up against the trunk of part of the beech hedge. Frank felt for a pulse. He looked down and swore. "He's gone Crow, we've lost him."

Crow leapt on his horse and galloped back to the road and down it, following the only route they could have taken.

He rode for miles, trying to keep an eye on either side of the road. Then he started coming to turn offs. He pulled his horse up and looked either way at the cross roads.

Everything seemed still. He stopped and listened. He thought he heard a car in the distance but it was only the wind.

Raven woke up in the back of a van. Her hands and feet were tied, she was blindfolded and there was tape over her mouth. The van smelt of manure and the floor was cold, littered with stones and what she thought might be old feed bags as she wriggled trying to get free. She struggled and the bindings cut into her wrists. She wriggled her hands around and tried to find an end to the rope.

She managed to find a single end and smiled slightly when she realised it was bailing twine. She began to push the cord gently back on itself, pushing and pushing until it formed a loop.

Without a sound her captor who had been sitting beside her pulled the string back tight and knocked her out again with a sharp blow. Sparks of light danced across her retina before she lapsed back into darkness.

The van rolled its way down road after road before pulling up in a lay-by. The driver got out and opened the back of the cab. He was a swarthy youth of about eighteen with a pale pock marked complexion, a very dirty parka coat and a beanie hat. In the back of the van there was a second red haired youth, about the same age and dressed similarly. He jumped down.

The driver smiled. "So Charlie, that was easier than I thought."

Charlie smiled. "It was a shame about the pony but I couldn't let her get away. How much do you think we'll get for this one Alfred?"

Alfred smiled back. "A fair bit I would say. This is an odd job, not the usual. She was specifically requested. The boss said that we'd be well paid for this one if we could get her quickly and in one piece. Well, couldn't be much quicker than that.

We've done so well we could give it a rest for today. There's no point risking it by grabbing another one randomly. Let's get this one delivered and we can be on our way. We might as well rest up for a while. I've got a bottle of whiskey I got off that couple we knocked over going back from the Mart, what say we hand this one over, hold up in that barn near the drop off point and make a night of it?"

Charlie looked down at the unconscious body. "Sounds like a plan."

The hours passed and nothing came along the road. It was starting to get dark when they saw a light in the distance which illuminated the road and the banks either side. Charlie waited until it got close and stepped out from behind the van. His hands were shaking so badly that he nearly pulled the trigger of the shotgun he carried. He waited as the window rolled down and he didn't react fast enough as a pistol appeared. A gun shot ran out. He fell back onto the tarmac and as the driver pulled to a halt a second shot dealt with Alfred who was standing a couple of feet behind Charlie.

The driver opened the door and stepped down. He was about six feet tall, his long straight black hair was tied back in a ponytail tight to his head. He was wiry but his cut away t-shirt showed off his well-toned muscles. He threw on a jacket and went over to the body on the floor, checked for a pulse and removed the shotgun which he threw into the cab of his van. He did the same with the other man's weapon. A passenger got out of the van. He was slightly shorter and dressed in jeans and a sweat shirt with a surf board motif on it. He went to the stationary van's cab and got in. The driver stripped the two dead men of anything useful and threw what he had found into the back of their van. They started both van's up, the second did a three point turn and both vans drove off down the road.

About a mile on they pulled over down a side road. They stripped out anything useful from the van they had just stolen and threw it into their own van, including Raven then they torched the van. As they drove off they could see it burning in the rear view mirror. They acted in silence and with an efficiency that meant they didn't waste a moment.

Raven woke up. She could feel cold air around her and it smelled slightly damp. She tried to move. White sparkly lights flashed across the darkness and she moaned slightly but that was stifled by the tape on her mouth. Pain seared through all of her body as she tried to struggle. She was tied in a chair. She could feel the smooth wood underneath her.

In the quiet all she could hear was the drip, drip, drip of water somewhere to her right and someone breathing. She could feel tape over her mouth and a blindfold over her eyes. The blindfold was tied tightly.

A man's voice broke the silence. "You might as well not bother to struggle. We wouldn't have gone to the lengths that we have to acquire you to let you get away that easily. You are going to have to believe me that we wouldn't disappoint the boss by losing his prize. So, please, just sit still. It took me a long time to clean up those cuts where you tried to break the twine. They really were careless. I don't have to explain anything to you and I'm not going to. The boss will be speaking to you shortly. I would suggest that you don't try to be smart. You will have heard of his reputation. You are now the property of Lord Balen. He has plans for you and I suggest that you listen carefully and comply with all that he wants. He is not known for his understanding or his compassion. Don't try to beg, he doesn't like that. Just do what you are told and you will live."

She heard footsteps as he walked across the floor, opened the door, left the room, shut the door and turned a key in the lock. Then all was silence and drip, drip, drip again. She listened to the sound for what felt like hours. Then she heard footsteps coming along what she assumed was a corridor, a key turned and a light came on. She could see its glow though the blindfold just before the blindfold was pulled off.

She blinked in the extreme brightness that was coming from a light above her. It took a while for her to get used to the light and get rid of the retinal after image of the light bulb. When she did she could see people in the room.

The nearest man was dressed in a doctor's white coat. He was sandy haired, his brow furrowed and he looked visibly nervous. He was looking her over and he turned to the man who stood behind him. The second man was tall, dark haired. His stubble that was the beginnings of a beard complimented his smart clothing giving him a handsome roguish look. His boiler suit was immaculately clean and pressed. He was backed up by a guard in a similar boiler suit. The guard was standing to attention and watching what was going on intently.

The doctor looked up. "Well Sir, she seems to be in relatively good health and undamaged by what I can see. I'm concerned that she was knocked out but I don't think there will be any lasting damage and there doesn't seem to be any sign of concussion."

The dark haired man smiled. It was a cold smile but as he looked down at her there was something in his eyes that unnerved her. There was a softness in his eyes that she had not expected. "Very good, I wouldn't want her damaged so keep it that way.

So, Raven, we meet at last. I suppose this is the point that I tell you why you have been brought here if you haven't guessed already. You will already have been informed that I am Lord Balen.

You didn't think that you could murder my people and there not to be some sort of retribution did you? Believe me there will be and it will be something suitable.   For now we have you, so that is a start.

Who do you think you are?  My people were ruthlessly murdered and you will pay the price.

But, you do have your uses and I am planning on exacting my vengeance. I should have you publicly executed which those who have lost family members and friends would no doubt be happy with.  But that would be too easy and not enough of a lesson. I may well still might but you are a resource and I'm not in the habit of wasting resources.

You are on borrowed time.  Think on that.  Now I'm sure we can find ways that you can be of use.  If not then a public execution would be an amusing spectacle.

Our leader is pressing me to produce an heir.  You may

well come in handy for that. Think on that, I might enjoy that, you are passably good looking. I don't need to tell you that you won't."

Raven tried to struggle but she was too tightly bound. She looked at him with wide eyed horror and he laughed. He turned to the doctor. "Now, Joseph, if you would like to complete your tests and tasks I'll see you in my office later.

You can move her to a holding cell. Keep her on her own. I wouldn't want her spreading her sedition to anyone else. Inform me as soon as you know that she is incorrupt and I'll make my decision. Keep her heavily sedated at all times. I wouldn't put it past her to try to escape. There can be no mistakes here. My brother's word is law.

Well, Raven I will bid you farewell, until we meet again." He looked around those in the room and smiled at her, a smile that sent a chill to her very soul.

He turned on his heels and the guard followed him out of the room. The doctor smiled. "Now you sleep." He reached to a table she hadn't noticed before and picked up a chrome kidney shaped dish. He removed a syringe from it and looked at the clear liquid.

Raven struggled like she'd never struggled before. The doctor put the syringe down. "So you are going to make it difficult, fair enough." He took a large bottle of clear liquid and a pad of cotton wool, soaked the pad, ripped the tape off of her mouth and clamped the pad over it before she could scream. She tried desperately to struggle and not to breathe but she couldn't hold her breath forever. She took a breath and the world faded into blackness.

Crow and Frank galloped up and down the road looking for clues. Their horses were beginning to tire. Crow turned for the town but Frank put a hand on his arm. "No, we'll have to get back. We can't leave home unprotected. We have to tell the others and you are going to have to take charge."

Crow looked at him with wild eyes. "No, we can't give

up."

Frank smiled at him. "We aren't giving up, not by a long shot. We'll get back and come first light we'll be out again. That was a very smooth operation. They knew what they wanted and they got her out of here fast.

They didn't attempt to take the saddle bags so they were not thieves. They had an agenda and they knew what they were doing."

Crow looked at Frank in horror. "What do you think? Why did they want her?"

Frank looked down. "They want her alive. There have been women taken. All we can do is try and find out where she is and get her back."

Crow looked confused. "How much do you know that you aren't telling me?"

Frank looked up. "I don't actually know anything. Like you I am only speculating. But we did have a run in with the people I dealt with in the forest. There could be a connection. Or there may not be. I have a theory as to who they are. It wasn't relevant and I had hoped that they wouldn't make it this far but the group may be connected. I would guess not the main group as I read their manifesto years ago and it was peaceful. That was what surprised me. These people seem keen to kill. The drain cleaner was a good example of this. We were lucky they didn't do that. They were just an unruly band of hippies the last time I had any contact with them. Their leader was insane and his brother, his second in command a waste of space. All he did was sit around, disengaged from the world, writing poetry and claiming benefits. I had seen messages from some of them. Not the mainstream though, I have to add that. They believed that they will be given all that they needed when this situation happened. So they are taking what they believe is theirs. Mostly they were harmless and sat around all day talking about a better world where they would have the chance to begin again. Then some of them started getting fanatical about it, almost desperate. That was when they formed Transition X, Transition Extreme. They want a sustainable world alright but by removing anyone who doesn't fit with their plans. It is their philosophy that there have been people in the past who have set things up so that they can walk in and take it. They call these people the corrupt believing that their "love of capitalism" has removed any rights they may have.

It's a corruption of the belief that what you want will come to you. As you can see they are a little more active than just waiting for that now.

Their leader and the organisation's creator, Lord Balen, has a very tough reputation which may or may not have been well deserved. He may well have the same insanity as his brother. I remember information about them that he was the quiet one. Not now, as you have seen. The stories about him are truly frightening. I'd heard a few rumours on my travels but he didn't seem particularly important. Torture, murder and taking what they want. The stories are rife. I'd assumed it was some sort of Neo-Nazi club for, how shall I put it, the UK version of the Red Neck in the US. Every thug with a gun wanted to be a part of it and I'm guessing that now that the shit has hit the fan, their membership must be looking pretty darned wonderful. So you can imagine the sort of man who can keep all those trigger happy dregs of society in check must be quite a man.

They truly believe that this is their time. But they honour women as life givers and it is more than likely that is what they want her for. Or to kill her as an example as she is our leader and we killed quite a few of their people."

Crow looked horrified. "No, Frank, we have to find her."

Frank smiled but it was a weak smile. "I know. I'm not denying that. They know we will be coming looking for her. Or I am sure that they suspect that we will. If we weaken home then that is what they want. They can step in while we're not there so I suggest we get back as quickly as possible. They have three of us away and what does that leave to defend the place?"

They pulled Davit's body onto Crow's horse and turned their horses for home. They galloped with the last energy that the horses had. By the time they got back to the farm the horses' heads were down and they were covered in a foamy sweat.

Ralph and Darren rushed to the horses and took their head as Crow jumped down and gently pulled David down onto the ground. Frank dismounted and went round to help him. They carried David and put him in a store room.

It was dark, the gentle candle light was glowing in the farm house windows. The warmth of home was colder that night though. Crow walked across the yard as if in a dream. He saw everything, heard everyone but nothing made any sense. All he could think about was Raven. He went upstairs and shut the door behind him. Then he screamed, the sound echoing around the house. It was the scream of a wounded animal.

Frank called everyone to the kitchen. Cheryl had the tea and coffee on the table though the coffee was noticeably weaker than it used to be. Frank stood by the door, looking at everyone sitting at the table. "This is not good news. We will all miss David. That he is gone is unthinkable. We have also lost Raven. She was abducted on our way back from the Mart. We did all we could but they got away with her in a waiting van."

There was a gasp and Cheryl burst into tears. Shylock stood up to comfort her. "She isn't dead and I doubt that they will harm her. They have been taking women for a couple of weeks now. I don't know if they took her to order or were just taking those they found. We don't know anything about who took her. There have been abductions from around the Mart but we also no doubt upset the organisation Rat and Stick were with."

He waited while those in the room took in what he had

said. Reko looked up and put his mug down. "We must get her back."

Frank looked around their expectant faces. "We couldn't pick up a trail. She was put in a van and they drove off at high speed. That road could go anywhere. We can't track her with anything technological so there is no way of knowing where she is. What we can do is go out and start asking questions. Others have disappeared and we may be able to get help in town. As they haven't pushed the advantage of reduced numbers while we were out looking for her I would suggest that they won't attack us tonight.

We will have to get her back if we can find out where they are. I expect that Crow will want to come with me. For now there is nothing we can do until we find out who has her."

14

Lord Balen leant on the window frame and looked out over the compound. Everywhere his troops were going about their duties. Some of them were tending the farm animals. Others were moving food and other materials about. There were those in charge and those who did what they were told and they marched or went directly to where they were going and did what they were doing with extreme efficiency.

He watched as they went about what they were doing. He also watched as a lone workman dressed in the same black overalls as everyone else was wheeling out a dead goat in a wheelbarrow.

He turned from the window and opened a book on his desk. The book was covered in crossings out where animals had died. He looked down and ran his manicured finger down the list and shook his head. There was a knock on the door which raised him from his thoughts. His voice was steady, commanding. "Enter."

A short man entered the room. His overalls fitted him badly and he looked very uncomfortable. His hair was untidy and there were bits of hay and straw sticking out from it. Balen looked over him in disgust as the man almost shuffled over to the desk.

Balen sat down, calmly and quietly. "What do you have to report?"

The man choked slightly. "I did all that it said in the book my lord. It shouldn't have happened. She died and nothing could save her. Shall I order a raid to replace the stock we have lost?"

Balen rested his chin on the top of his fingers, made into a point and looked at the man. "No, I want you to stop the stock dying. That is seven this week. That is unacceptable. How are we to start breeding plans and plan for the future if you can't keep the stock alive?" He took the book and made another red mark beside the goat's entry in his book.

The man looked terrified. "Please don't have me killed your Lordship."

Balen smiled. "You deserve it. They were perfectly good animals. Can you say anything in your defence or suggest anything that you can do to stop this?"

The man looked nervous. "Well, there is a rumour that you captured that woman from the farm where our people died. She knows about goats. I'm at a loss. I've done what the book said. But they keep dying."

"So you are saying you are incompetent and that you cannot look after the most basic of animals?"

"With respect Sir, I am saying that they seem to be more complicated than the book makes out. I am doing something wrong. I admit that. I can't see what and she may know. Whether she would actually tell us I do not know."

Lord Balen looked furious. "Do not presume to tell me my business and whether or not a prisoner of mine will do as I command. She will give us the information or she will die."

The man looked extremely nervous.

Balen smiled but it was a wicked smile when he saw ow awkward the man looked. "You will take three guards and I want you to bring Raven to me, bound and make sure they find her something other than those paper gowns to wear. Ill-dressed people offend me."

The man stared at him in amazement.

Balen glared and the man half turned. "And if anyone is going to kill her it will be me, not the cold. Go, now and hurry. I do not like to be kept waiting."

The man left the room in a hurry and shut the door behind him. Balen took a sharp intake of breath and looked down at the book. The red marks covered nearly half the page. He closed the book and put it in a drawer and looked about the room. It was sparsely furnished, just his desk, his chair, a chair for guests on the very rare occasion that he allowed them to sit and a table with a glass top and a statuette of a wolf in the centre.

He waited nearly half an hour before there was a knock on the door. It was opened by the short man who stepped inside and stepped aside. The animal keeper stepped in next. Then the guards almost threw Raven into the room. She tripped and fell on the floor. Her hands were tied behind her back and she struggled to stand up.

She looked up at Balen, her eyes showing the pain and humiliation she felt.

Balen commanded the guards. "Pick her up."

The guards looked as though they had been shot. They instantly dived forwards and grabbed Raven and hoisted her roughly to her feet.

Balen stepped around his desk. The guards gripped Raven a bit tighter. The nearest one to Balen looked up as if to speak but closed his mouth again. Balen looked at him. "You may speak."

The guard looked nervous. "Sir, I would not dream of suggesting anything to you but she has proven to be a wildcat."

Balen smiled and looked Raven in the eye. She glared at him with a look that could rip his head off. "I bet she is. But, I also know that she isn't stupid. I have the power to have her killed on the spot or to let her go. No doubt she knows my reputation but if she doesn't I would happily demonstrate. You are armed, she is not. I could break her neck if I wished and after what she and her people have done I would enjoy it. At the moment I do not wish to but my mind can change. On the contrary I want to speak to her. So if I was her I would allow my bindings to be taken off and the tape to be taken from my mouth. Of course I would also understand that hurling verbal abuse at my captor is not going to help. Now, Raven, are you going to listen to what I have to say?"

Raven nodded. It ran through her head that she could have a go at getting hold of one of the guard's weapons but she decided against it. The one who had spoken pulled the tape off of her mouth roughly and they cut the cable tie that had held her wrists together. They then unwrapped the bandages that had been wrapped under the ties to prevent her wrists being cut. She rubbed her wrists which had been deeply cut by the bailing twine in the van and glared at Balen.

Balen indicated the chair. "Please, sit, I would speak with you. Now if I send my guards outside the door are you going to try to kill me or are you going to listen to what I have to say?"

Raven glared at him. "I'd like to kill you but I'll probably listen as I want to know what you could possibly say that would be of any interest to me."

She sat on the chair and looked down at the black boiler suit they had given her to wear. She still had no shoes but the carpet was at least soft under her toes.

Balen's expression was neutral. "You may leave us, all of you. Wait down the hallway and if she does try to kill me you have permission to do all those things I really know you want to do to her. As you know she was the commanding officer responsible for ordering the death of our people when they were on a peaceful reconnaissance mission. I'm sure you can think up some very interesting ways to make her suffer." He smiled at Raven with a sparkle in his eyes.

The guards left, grudgingly.

Balen walked slowly around his desk, keeping an eye on her all the time. He sat down and leant back in his chair. "Do you know who we are?"

Raven also leant back in her chair and crossed her legs. "Transition X, a bunch of murdering, kidnapping scumbags."

Balen laughed. "In your opinion but in my opinion I could say the same about you."

Raven thought for a moment. "Well I didn't come and attack your home."

Balen smiled. "Oh Raven, Raven, you know so little but yet know so much. I do what I must for my people, Nemesis set up what it could for its people. In a world where the resources are running out I have to make sure that it is my people who survive. We came to see what you had. Your people killed my people. It is very straightforward. You had what we wanted and we know that you are not the ones who are supposed to have it. So according to our laws we did what we always do, we came to see what you had with a view to taking what was rightfully ours. Or assimilating your people into our organisation."

Raven almost growled at him. "I worked long and hard for that farm. I kept the animals alive through cold winters with no help from anyone. I should be able to say who deserves to live there, not you. What did you do? You sat here in your comfortable office and decided that what I'd worked so hard for all those years should be yours. We could have negotiated. People did not need to die."

Balen smiled. "You chose to kill them. They were merely observing you. I thought I said no verbal abuse. But I suppose you should have your opportunity to vent your feelings. In your opinion it may look like what you say is true but we are the ones chosen to survive. Who chose you to survive I do not know. We lived in faith that when this happened we would be provided for."

Raven raised an eyebrow. "But you aren't being provided for are you?"

Balen hesitated. "What makes you say that?"

Raven pushed her advantage. "Because you wouldn't

be talking to me now if you didn't want something. You can take what you want, I have no doubt. You must want something else. Something you can't take and something that I can give."

Balen smiled. "Very good. Well that cuts through a lot of the pleasantries. Do you know our beliefs?"

Raven glared at him. "You believe that if you sit about on your butt at the end of days everything you ever wanted will be given to you. In the meantime other people have to work to support you and to create that something so you can take it."

Balen choked slightly. "Well you don't mince your words. On the face of it, it could look like that. For some of our members it is like that. I and many like me had to actively take a step back from what we could have done to be successful by the old world's standards. We became healers and used our psychic abilities. We looked after the earth in the only way we thought possible, by living as lightly as we could. It is true that we didn't contribute to the capitalist machine as we didn't want to fuel the fires of the world's destruction. But you are also right. We didn't help. Looking back we probably worked against a lot of people who had their own beliefs that were very similar to ours. I can only speak for those in my compound here. All groups are different even though we follow a standard doctrine. I want my people to live. To do that I must feed them, clothe them, educate them and make sure that they multiply so that there are generations to follow with the right belief. Is that so wrong and is that so different to what you are doing?

Our people went for a look around to see what you had and what you were doing. You give the order and had them killed. I sent my men to assess what you had, you buried them."

Raven almost smiled. "So you call firing at us and throwing burning missiles though our windows assessing the situation? Stealing our food. Contemplating putting drain cleaner in our food? Is that the act of someone who is just passively looking around? We could all have died if Rat or Stick had done that. It's not what you are doing, it is how you are doing it. What about Eric?"

Balen looked confused. "You don't need to spread your lies here. Their orders were to watch what was going on, assess your strength and bring me back information. If it was possible they were to cause confusion to see how you deal with it and to make you doubt your members. It was you who sent people out in the woods and killed them. Eric? Who is Eric?"

Raven took a deep breath. "Eric was Cheryl's husband. He was the infiltrator who tried to kill Frank. What about Rat, he thought about killing us with drain cleaner."

Balen looked visibly shocked. "Rat did what? He was supposed to steal some of your food and plant it in someone's room to start you fighting and to make your leadership less stable. That way you might accept some help. I certainly did not give him any such order. Eric, yes I remember him. He came to our meetings a broken man. I read his file and as he was very enthusiastic to help and he had the perfect cover story. I sent him in to spy on you.

His wife was cheating on him. He even believed his baby was fathered by some other man. What right did they have to be saved?"

Raven looked down. "That wasn't your decision to make either."

Balen breathed out swiftly. "And some computer virus has the right to decide the fate of humanity and that is alright with you? It is acceptable that this thing that has no life, conscience or breath can kill millions to provide a so called solution? Or is it just an acceptable solution because you are the ones being saved?"

Raven was about to speak but closed her mouth.

Balen saw this and smiled slightly. "We aren't so different. I have the same day to day problems as you do.

I've got a bunch of people here who know nothing about keeping animals. I have crops to plant, machinery to fix and people to feed.

What I brought you up here to ask you is will you help me?"

Raven choked. "So the great Lord Balen needs my help? Go read a book. I did."

Balen smiled. "We have followed the books to the letter but there are things missing in the books aren't there? Only experience can make up for that. I don't want to see any more animals die. I know now that you can't just take on an animal that is complex and expect to follow a text book and it will be alright." He thought for a second and then took the book out of his desk and opened it at the page he had been looking at. "I want to show you something." He turned the book around and pushed it across the desk. "We've been following a book and we are still losing animals, look at the losses."

Raven took the book and looked at it. Her eyes ran down the columns and  the crossings out, the red ink standing out starkly on the white paper. "So what? You are getting it wrong. Big deal."

He looked horrified. "Don't you care?"

She looked into his eyes and felt a jolt and a warm feeling. There was genuine concern in his eyes. Not the cold look she had seen earlier. "Speak to me, tell me the truth. All of it."

Balen smiled. All of a sudden he looked exhausted. He looked smaller in his chair. "My brother is insane. His rules are outrageous. Yes he would kill your people just because they were in his way. If he had had a bad day or his breakfast had been served cold. He is my brother but he is also the unquestionable ruler of Transition X. I am bound by his rules too. But I have adapted them.

I never asked for all this. I was happy to write a few poems and just get on with life. We were drunk one night and for a laugh we put together an organisation that would look after the planet. We wrote what we thought was a perfect organisation for a perfect world. Or to build one. Of course at four in the morning after a lot of brandy it seemed like a great idea. Now we are living with that organisation becoming huge. Now I am living with being in charge of some very unpleasant and nasty fanatics who would cut your throat if you so much as sneezed on a dog.

Many are insane. Many are sociopaths. They have found their vocation and a world where they are strangely enough fairly normal. How do I control them other than to be a vicious, bloodthirsty, unreasonable son of a bitch.

So, I'm asking you Raven. Help me. Please. I don't want to see any more animals die.

But, and this is a big but, my people want you dead. They believe that you killed our innocent people unprovoked. They wouldn't believe that Rat or Stick would do what you say. But they too don't know that there is a radical element within our organisation. Members of that would definitely do what you are saying. I control them because they are afraid of me. If I don't keep a firm hand they will no longer be afraid of me and those who are trying to do the right thing will suffer.

Also, my brother gives me a certain amount of leeway because I'm his brother. Not much but it does give me a certain autonomy that other leaders do not get.

Even if you do help I am going to have to appear to be vicious to you. I promise I will not hurt you. I will not scare you as you will know that I will not hurt you. For your safety in this place you will have to be seen to be punished for the death of our people. But, if you will help me with the animals I will see that you are safe and well."

"You've got a problem with the animals. I need to look at how you are keeping them."

Balen smiled. "I know I have a problem. So you will help?"

Raven looked up at him. There was a look on his face she had not expected. Hope that she would help.

Concern for the animals. She was confused. But she didn't feel scared anymore. "I mean you have a real problem. Look at these numbers, they aren't realistic if you are using the right methods. What is your housing like?"

Balen stood up. "Here, come to the window."

She stepped around his desk and moved to stand beside him at the window. He stepped closer to her. His body language was completely different. As if he was forgetting who he was. He was just a man, pointing at a barn. "We have a big barn there where we keep the animals. They are turned out in that field there and come in at night."

Raven looked down on the buildings and the people going about their duties. She looked at the barn. "Have you separated the animals inside the barn? What about the grazing? Did you take this place over and if so how heavily was it grazed? How long have you been here?"

Balen looked down at her with a certain admiration. She was standing beside him, close to him and looked up at him. All animosity was gone and he felt something, something warm that he could not explain. "We've been here about three months but this was a battery farm before then. Sheep were kept in those sheds for years without a problem."

Raven thought. "That might be your problem. Did you muck out and reset the beds when you came here?" She looked around the yard and noticed the hay and straw stacked in the yard. "Is that waste straw and hay?"

Balen looked over at the hay and straw. "No, that is our stock of feed."

Raven shook her head. "Out in the rain? Don't you know that wet hay produces a mould that kills goats. Never get the goat hay wet."

Balen nodded. "It was the best we could get."

Raven smiled. "It may well have been and I'm glad you did but put it in the rain and you would be kinder to cut their throats. The best isn't always good for goats. They are browsers, not grazers. You need the coarse stuff that has thistles and other stuff in it. Lucerne if you can get it. That is a different plant. That will bring on your milkers big time. But never old. Always fresh and never stored anywhere damp. Looking at your figures it is mostly goats you are losing.

If you are bringing in animals they can bring any infection with them. I bet you have been taking them from all over?"

Balen nodded.

Raven shook her head. "Well that can be lethal. If they have an infection the rest will get it. Do you have antibiotics?"

Balen looked horrified. "We don't use the stuff. For the goats? Are you serious?"

Raven looked up at him. "I bet you don't worm either."

Balen shook his head. "It's a chemical, we are organic here."

Raven smiled. "I thought that way once. I gave my animals what I thought was the best for them and they still died. Ok I found out later that some stupid woman in the village who had ideas that animals should be loose let them out and they eat rich grass and died. That is bloat. They were overfed. Someone fed them things they shouldn't have had. You live and learn. If you aren't worming then the food you are giving them is wasted and they will die. Fluke and worms is the biggest killer, it is an enemy much more dangerous than any man with a gun. They need some in their system but you need to manage your grazing and your pasture. You don't know what they came with either."

Balen smiled and she smiled back. "Effing hell. That is exactly what I need your help with." He pulled out a plan of the barn and laid it out on the glass table.

Raven walked over with him, grabbing a pen off of his desk on the way. She bent over the table and looked at the numbers in the book that he had left. She then smiled. "I'd suggest you keep animals together in the groups from where they came from to start with if you bring new stock in. Pen them off and keep them separate. Also, you might like to look at your grazing combination. You can't graze sheep and goats together but you can graze them with horses or cows. Goats are browsers, not grazers." Balen looked confused. "Don't worry I'll sort out a plan for you if you would like me to."

Balen looked over at her. He had been drawing lines on the plan and dividing things up as she suggested. She reached for the red pen the same time as he did and his hand brushed against hers. She jumped, so did he and they looked at each other. The energy between them was intense. They both jumped back and it was as if a wall had gone down. Raven backed away as Balen stood up. He went back to his desk and Raven returned to her seat.

Raven looked at him. "So what happens now? I suppose you return me to my cell?"

Balen smiled. "I will. There can't be any other way as most of the people want you dead."

Raven smiled. "I'll go quietly. I hope I have been of assistance."

Balen looked down. "You have been most helpful."

Balen watched as the guards collected Raven and took her back to her cell. He walked over to the plan on the table and went to pick up the red pen, he hesitated for a moment. Then he shook his head, picked it up and completed the plan.

He returned to his chair and thought for a while. There was a knock on the door and his farm manager came in when he was told to.

Balen looked down. "There is a plan on that table, take it and put it into action. I want the animals divided up as we have been advised. And Farley, get rid of that hay, I want a fresh lot brought in and put under cover."

Farley bowed his head. "Will that be all Sir?"

Balen glared at him and he left the room swiftly taking the plan with him.

Balen smiled to himself as Farley left. He got up and looked out of the window and watched people moving about down below.

Crow and Frank left the farm in the early morning and rode out for the Mart as they had done on countless occasions. They took the route that kept them on the road rather than the short cut which took them nearly three hours as they couldn't gallop on the tarmac. They travelled in silence, each lost in their own thoughts.

When they got to the Mart the place was as crowded as usual. The queue stretched down the road. They joined the end of it and it took them another hour and a half to get inside.

Inside the Mart was the same as it had been before, the entertainers were playing music and the traders were shouting to sell their wares. Frank went straight over to Carl who had just finished sorting out a dispute between two stallholders. He looked up when they came over. "No Raven with you today?"

Crow looked down. "No, she was taken by someone yesterday. They were laying in wait for us on the way home."

Carl frowned and looked genuinely upset. "That's the tenth in three days."

Frank was not quite paying attention. He was more interested in a young

lad in a blue bomber jacket who was more interested in their conversation than he should have been.

Crow stared at Carl intently. "Have you heard anything about who is taking them?"

Carl shook his head. "It seems to happen pretty randomly. Raven is the only one who was taken outside the town though.

That got Frank's attention. "So whoever is taking them is coming into the town?"

Carl raised an eyebrow. "It would appear that is the case. There is also some speculation that there are people who are using this as an excuse to remove certain rivals. It's just a rumour but it is rife around here. Men folk are now taking really good care of their women folk and women folk are becoming really careful about keeping an eye on their rivals. You will notice that groups are forming within the town. Families are uniting with other families and they are starting to build permanent defences around their homes. This new way of living is changing everything. They are still buying but there is an air of nervousness that is bad for business.

The Road Pirates are becoming less common though. Rumour has it that vigilante groups are going out and dealing with them. If you want more information I would have said go to the pub but that burnt down last night."

"What happened?"

"There was a riot outside and a stray firebomb went through the window and wrecked the place. The owner is going to set up what he has left in our compound now. We have found him some space over there in the corner next to the cafe. It will take a day or two but he'll at least be safe."

Frank was watching Carl now. He smiled. "That must be good business for you, having the pub in here too?"

Carl smiled. "These are dangerous times and we're able to offer a safe place both for them to work and for people to enjoy a drink. We could have set up in competition but it made more sense for them to move in here. It's in a bad way but yes, it is good for business. By the way, thanks for that last lot of pork, it sold well and we had plenty of people who have put themselves down for the next lot. Any idea when that will be? I'm planning an auction as meat is getting difficult to get hold of."

Voices were raised over the other side of the compound. Carl looked over. He put a hand on Crow's arm. "Sorry mate, look I've got to go and deal with that.

Look, I like her and wouldn't want anything to happen to her. If I hear anything I'll let you know." He then ran off to deal with the problem.

Crow looked at Frank who was watching the boy as he disappeared into the crowd. He smiled wickedly and followed him. Crow followed Frank and they all ended up in the café. The boy was sitting with his parents and they were chatting. Frank and Crow were watching them.

Carl had finished with the trouble makers and went up to the office where his father was handling some paperwork. "Dad, did you order a collection involving Raven? She was taken last night."

His father almost dropped the paperwork. "You have to be kidding, she's one of the most useful people we have around here. Never in a million years. This is a disaster. Someone is working our patch."

Carl looked confused. "I thought you had all that under control."

His father got a small pocket book out and checked down the names. "I had it very much in hand. We'd managed to remove all the dead wood and the profits were good when selling them on. I never organised a collection for someone useful."

Carl frowned. "Do you think your buyer got greedy? Perhaps someone is working freelance?"

His father shook his head. "Not likely, I'd supplied his quota and we have an arrangement that I don't let him have my good customers. But he knows that and wasn't worried about it. Or he hasn't been until now. Something else is going on. I had a report that Alf and Charlie got blown away last night. I know they had been up to a bit of scamming and had taken one or two that weren't sanctioned. The timing and distance could have been right for them to have taken her. I wasn't paying too much attention. I was too busy trying to set up the riot. I think that went rather well, don't you?"

Carl smiled. "Too right, removing the pub and taking it

317

under our wing, smooth move dad. Now everyone has to come here and we're the heroes for saving it. Do you think it's about time to think about putting prices up?"

His father sighed. "Not quite yet. We've got to ensure our suppliers first. Losing Raven is a blow as her lot haven't been with her long. We have to hope they have things under control enough to keep the meat supply coming."

Carl shrugged. "Any chance we can get her back for them?"

His father smiled. "Not a hope. I had Alf and Charlie followed a while back as I thought they were up to something. They had a contact who never came to town. I managed to get a bit of info on him. He is a nasty bit of work. Lord Balen's name came up in association with him. If he has her then I'm certainly not challenging him. Who commissioned her abduction is also a matter for speculation but questions we shouldn't be asking. I'd rather not wake up to see this place a smouldering bombsite. Let that one lie. Carry on the good work son."

Carl looked up. "If it is Lord Balen, too right. Oh well, shame she was good to deal with."

His father was looking at the paperwork. "There'll be others. Don't get attached to the punters boy, it is not good for business. Don't get any ideas of telling them what you know about where she is either. If it got back to Lord Balen there's nobody here who could save you."

Carl shook his head. "I won't dad but why are people so afraid of him?"

His father looked up. "He's an evil son of a bitch. That is by reputation and from what people have actually seen him do. Everyone has their own stories but they all seem to say the same thing.

He's a military fanatic though he never joined up as far as I've ever heard. He'd slit you open or get someone else to do it as soon as look at you. Just be thankful he isn't in this neighbourhood."

Carl looked nervous. "How come he has such a reputation?"

His father hesitated. "Because it's not a reputation, it comes from what people have seen. He had everything planned out you know. As soon as the power went down he knew exactly who to gather and he and they did anything and everything to survive. That kind of will to survive earns a reputation of its own. In defence of his people he will quite literally do anything. Even his own people are terrified of him. They had better forget about her. If he has her then that is an end of it."

Carl left the room and went down the stairs thoughtfully. He stopped on the stairs and looked out over the Mart. People were buying, people were selling and everyone seemed to be happily going about their business. He saw Frank and Crow over at the café.

As he watched a group of men came into the compound. They were hippy types but there was something else about them. They had the clothing, the hair and the attitude. They made their way around the stalls and seemed to be spending plenty of money so he didn't worry about them. He carried on down the stairs.

Frank had been listening to the boy's conversation. He turned to Crow. "Well that's a dead end. It seems that he knows Raven from when she helped him with his pony. He overheard us saying that she had been taken and he's telling his parents. They don't seem to know anything. I can't see how this can be such a dead end. Someone must have seen something. Surely someone knows something?"

Crow was looking around. "These people are frightened. If there is a gang or organised group taking people the last thing anyone is going to want to do is draw attention to themselves. We've made a bit of a big noise and we've been noticed. We didn't think that bringing her here could be dangerous. I suppose whoever took her thinks about things differently. Do you think it was Transition X who took her?"

Frank shrugged. "I thought it was to start with but there is something going on here, something more than I first thought. I can't put my finger on it right away but I will. I don't think we're going to find out any more today. I'm sorry Crow, we're going to have to head off back to the farm. We can't leave that unprotected."

Two months passed by quickly. Balen called Raven up to his office daily and the time she spent there got longer and longer until she was spending almost all day with him. Gradually the farm was transformed. The animal deaths stopped and Balen was beginning to relax a little about some of the worries that he had as Raven started taking on more and more responsibility.

Balen was sitting in his room one evening. It was a plain box in the same block as everyone else's. He had the same type of bed, blanket and sheets, cupboard, table and chair as everyone else. The only difference was that he chose to eat alone. His metal tray with food in divisions was on the table but he hadn't eaten much of it. He was pacing the room. He looked at the tray and sat down and eat some more then drank his coffee. When he was finished he picked it up and took it back to the Mess Hall and put it on the trolley ready for collection.

He looked around the hall. There were groups of people chatting and laughing. Some noticed him and sat bolt upright and ceased their conversation. Some saluted. He turned and left.

His footsteps echoed in the empty corridors as he made his way to the makeshift cell block which had been made out of an old piggery. He walked along the line of doors until he came to Raven's cell. He pulled the observation hatch down and looked inside.

Raven was asleep, as per his orders she had been sedated as she was every night. The guards who had returned her to her cell had thrown her on the bed and she was still in the position that she had landed in, half on, half off of the bed.

Balen walked down to the guard room. There was a single guard on duty. He was a teenager who looked barely sixteen. His long blonde hair was swept back in a ponytail and his baggy shirt and jeans were ill fitting. His whole body didn't seem to fit him and he was very awkward as he jumpedmto attention when Balen walked in. "I want the key to K435."

The guard almost leapt across the room and gave it to him. He opened his mouth then shut it fast.

Balen turned and left the room. "At ease boy, you are doing a good job."

He closed the door and walked down to Raven's cell. He put the key in the lock and hesitated. He looked up and down the corridor then turned the key and went inside.

He gently lifted Raven onto the bed and pulled the covers up over her. He then stroked her head and watched her for a short while until she moaned slightly and moved in her sleep. He then got up and left the room, locked the door and returned the key to the guard room.

The youth jumped again. Balen smiled. "Return the key to the box and I want prisoner K435 treated a little better. She has valuable information and she is valuable merchandise, I do not want to see her damaged." He turned on his heels and left the room.

The next morning Balen waited in his office. He heard footsteps outside and moved to his desk and sat down. There was a knock on the door and a short thin bespectacled man entered carrying a file of papers. He saluted and waited.

Balen smiled. "Continue Francis."

Francis smiled back nervously. "I have a report from other TX groups. It seems that there is a splinter group that has broken away. They were thrown out by Lord Ferris when he discovered them in his compound and it is likely you may have a contingent here. He discovered that they had been undermining anyone who was trying to set up environmentally friendly projects. They use the TX name but they act in their own personal interest and follow their own radical beliefs. There is a directive from Archangel that no TX base is to have anything to do with them.

The report also states that there will be a delivery of solar panels and wind turbines to all camps within the month. They have been manufactured by us and are being shipped out ready for installation. They come with their own engineers and TX Eastbourne have set up an assembly unit so the equipment is coming from there. They are turning out replacement parts already for stockpiling in different areas to cut down repair times.

It has taken a while to get the infrastructure set up and it will take a few months for full production to be achieved.

There is a personal note from High Chief Archangel to the Commanders, here is your copy and a personal note from him to you." He handed over the messages. "This concludes my duties. I have some paperwork which contains information and news from other camps and I will be happy to convey on any messages and news for you to the groups I am going to visit."

Balen smiled. "Very good Francis. If you would like to rest a while we can allot a room for you."

Francis bowed his head. "Thank you my Lord, you are as always very generous. May I leave?"

Balen was opening his letter. "Yes, yes of course. Please have a rest and you are welcome to make use of our canteen."

Francis clicked his heels together. "Very good sir." He turned and left.

Balen opened his letter and read the message. "Lord Balen, This is a message to all camp heads.

It has come to our attention that we have been infiltrated by certain seditious elements who intend to undermine our beliefs and to manipulate them for their own ends. These elements must be eliminated with no mercy.

We cannot allow our pure cause to be corrupted by them. It is believed that these elements wish to eliminate all who are not Transition X members. May I remind you of the prime directive to live and let live while protecting our own.

Lord Balen, your efforts and successes have not escaped our notice. Your sacrifices have also been noted. In friendship and brotherhood, Lord Archangel."

There was another slip of paper folded into the first letter. Balen opened it and recognised the spidery handwriting and smiled. "Dear Brother, I trust this

letter finds you well. Well, we survived. That was a miracle in itself. I know you disapprove of the title Archangel but at least a title is easy to pass on. I have to draw your attention to the progeny directive. I have had no need to enforce it with the other Camp Commanders but it is looking more likely that you are going to force my hand. My sister in law is gone, nothing will bring her back. If you will not take another wife then you know what you must do. Choose the best possible mate either from those in TX or from someone captured and I'm sure I don't have to spell out the rest. I've asked you, now I'm telling you. Don't make me have to order you. Please do not put me in that position my brother. Kind Regards, M"

Balen took a deep breath and sat down in his chair. He folded the second letter and put it in his pocket. He shook his head and smiled. "Believe me brother, I would like nothing more than to comply with that order."

Thoughts of Raven came into his mind and he fought really hard to drive them out again.

He called out and a guard entered the room. He didn't recognise the man. "Bring me Raven."

The guard saluted and clicked his heels together and left the room.

Balen sat at his desk running his biro though his fingers. He took a deep breath and let it out slowly. He then looked at his paperwork but he didn't see what was written on the pages. Thoughts of her drowned everything else out. He shook his head and got up and went to the window.

There was a knock on the door, it opened and Raven walked carefully in. Balen looked questioningly at the guards who walked in behind her. The first smiled. "I am pleased to report that the prisoner has caused us no trouble at all."

Raven looked tired, there were dark circles under her eyes and a bruise was developing on her cheek bone. Balen stepped over and roughly grabbed her chin. He looked at the guard who tried to melt back into the stonework as he saw Balen's angry glare. "Who did this?"

The guard looked at his feet.

Balen drew himself up to his full height. "Do not look away when I ask a question. I asked, who did this?"

The guard looked up and stood to attention. "I did Sir."

Balen raised his hand and struck the man across the face sending him reeling onto the floor. "Now get up and tell me why you damaged the merchandise."

The guard stood up. "She is a prisoner Sir and she didn't move fast enough out of her cell so I reminded her who was in charge, Sir, just like you taught me."

Balen hesitated slightly. "And was she sedated at the time?"

The guard looked horrified. "I didn't know, I assumed that she was just being slow."

Balen struck him again, he reeled back into the wall. "Now, I gave instructions that this woman is not to be unnecessarily harmed. If she had been trying to escape that is another matter. I do not have to explain my actions to you." He turned towards the man who looked terrified. "Wait down the hall." The man looked relieved and left the room quickly and shut the door.

Balen turned to Raven. "Please sit." Raven nearly fell

into the chair and winced with pain.

Balen looked concerned. "Have you been mistreated?"

Raven shook her head. Balen saw more bruises on her neck, lines of black and purple welts stood out on her pale skin. She spoke, her voice was quiet, almost a whisper. "I have not." Then she looked up at him, her eyes were tearful and told him otherwise.

Balen stepped closer, cautious that she was about to make a move. "Have you been mistreated? You have nothing to fear from me. If someone is harming you I will protect you."

Raven looked down then took a deep breath. "You aren't there when they come. I woke up with these bruises so I don't know what happened as I had been sedated as per your orders."

Balen looked furious. He grabbed her by the arm and she screamed. He pulled her sleeve up and saw the dark purple and black bruises that covered her upper arm. Some of the bruises were old and fading. "How long has this been going on?"

She looked up at him, her eyes pleading. "I was alright for the first week and then I started waking up hurting and with bruises."

Balen looked down at her. He looked furious. "Why didn't you tell me?"

Raven looked surprised. "I thought it was happening because you ordered it. You control everything and everyone around here don't you?" Tears ran down her cheek and he released his grip slightly.

Balen looked worried. "Apparently not. I need to think about this. We have a problem here. I'm going to have to do something to stop this."

He screamed out his orders and the guards almost had to carry her to the doctor's room. He flung the door open and took Raven inside. "I want you to check her over, a full medical, now. Guards you will leave the room and take up your posts outside.

15

Raven tried to back away from the doctor. She screamed at him. "Leave me alone. I don't know what happened, I don't remember. I hurt, I just want to be left in peace. I haven't done anything to you. I've even tried to help you."

Balen caught her arm and the searing pain shot through her. He relaxed his grip and gently stroked her cheek with the back of his hand. "I'm not trying to hurt you. I'm trying to find out what they have done and to stop you hurting. Please, trust me. Your wellbeing is very important to me."

She could feel nausea and she involuntarily held her head. She felt dizzy and the ground began to spin. Balen caught her as she nearly passed out and looked down at her kindly. The look stunned her, it distracted her from thinking about the pain and somehow despite her fear she felt something warm, something comforting. She felt safe. His voice was gentle. "Let the doctor take care of you. We don't want to hurt you. On the contrary I, I mean we, want to make sure that you are healthy. Let the doctor check you out. It will only hurt you to struggle. If there are broken bones they need to be set."

The doctor approached Raven carefully. He had a chloroformed pad in his hand. She looked at it wild eyed and backed away but Balen had his arm around her and she didn't have the strength to fight him. Balen took the pad from the doctor and gave him a meaningful look so he stepped away.

"This will stop the pain, for now. I need you to trust

me."

She looked at him wide eyed and he let her pull away from him. He waited patiently. He held out a hand to her. "Come to me willingly and I will help you."

She thought for a moment and swayed slightly as the pain and nausea made her head spin. Thoughts rushed through her head. She whispered. "How can I trust you? Your men did this to me."

Balen smiled. "My men were under orders to leave you alone. It seems that there are some amongst my men who are not taking their orders. Trust me, I did not hurt you. I do not want to hurt you." He smiled and kept his hand there. "I will wait, you know you need my help and also my protection. I need your help."

Raven looked down and just caught herself before her legs gave out. She was feeling dizzy and sick with the pain. Every feeling of loneliness she had ever felt came crashing down on her. "If you hadn't brought me here then I would be fine. Let me go and I wouldn't need your protection."

Balen smiled. "That is not possible. I need you here."

Raven looked into his deep brown eyes. She took a deep breath and took his hand just as her legs gave way under her. Balen caught her and lifted her onto the table. "Trust me, we have your best interests in mind here. The doctor will take care of you." He gently stroked her hair back from her face then he took the chloroform pad and put it in her hand, he then lifted that hand, giving her every opportunity to pull away and she allowed him to guide her hand until the pad was over her mouth and nose.

Raven sank into a painless black oblivion.

For over an hour the doctor did a full inspection and wrote up his notes. Balen watched through the whole procedure. Sometimes he paced, sometimes he stood, arms folded.

The doctor closed his notebook. "I won't go through the technical terms but her shoulder is badly bruised, you can see here where the boot has left a clear mark. It may be fractured but I can't tell. Her arm is probably fractured but as I have no XRay I can't be certain. I'll have to immobilise it. There is extensive bruising around the ribs and stomach area which in my opinion would indicate she has been kicked. I'll strap those ribs up. As you can see there is an extreme amount of bruising. She is going to be in pain so I will administer some heavy duty pain killers and keep her heavily sedated. In my opinion that would leave her vulnerable to further attack. I would strongly advise that you take steps to prevent any further interference with her or you could lose her. She is strong but there is only so much punishment a body can take. These blows and the blunt trauma were delivered with some force. Whoever did this wasn't messing about."

Balen shook his head. "Do what you can to make her comfortable. She is a necessary asset."

Balen watched while the doctor went to work. His thoughts were racing and his anger was growing.

The doctor took a deep breath. "I have checked her notes in comparison with the notes when she arrived. "As you can see her neck shows considerable bruising and the marks indicate that someone attempted to strangle her. She was kept sedated so I doubt she even realised she was being injured and certainly would not have been able to fight back."

Balen scowled. "Has she been interfered with in any other way?" His teeth were clenched and so were his fists.

The doctor looked down at his notes. "I can see no sign of any interference other than the physical injuries I've shown you. May I speak freely?"

Balen looked at him curiously. "You may?"

The doctor took a deep breath. "It is well known that Raven came from the farm where many of our people lost friends and relatives."

Balen frowned. "That is true. In your medical opinion do you believe that her life is in danger?"

The doctor looked at his notes. "From a medical point

of view I am unable to either confirm or deny that. From the point of view of someone who has sat in the canteen I can confirm that there is a contingent that believes she should have been executed when you first captured her. They also believe that your lenience towards her shows a weakness and that is undermining your command."

Balen looked thoughtful. "I have had a directive from High Commander Archangel that I must produce an heir. I have deemed her intellect and physical condition appropriate. She would be a suitable candidate for the mother of this child."

The doctor smiled. "So what is stopping you? You could take her whenever you want."

Balen smiled back. "I wanted to make sure she wasn't already carrying her husband's baby. There needs to be no doubt here. I didn't touch her for that very reason."

The doctor smiled. "It has been over two months now and I can confirm that she is not carrying his baby. Should she be carrying your baby and so used in this fashion then I doubt that there would be any further danger to her life. In my medical opinion she would be suitable. Shall I make the necessary preparations?"

Balen looked shocked. "For what?"

The doctor smiled. "Lord Balen, I have been your friend since school. Do you seriously think I don't know you well enough by now? You are still the man I have known all these years and that man would not rape a woman. I will make the preparations that her notes will be amended and I will make her situation public by way of a rumour. Nobody would dare to touch her then."

Balen smiled. "That may not be enough. These people are angry and they want retribution. They need to see something happen to her and something suitably bad so that they can rest easy that justice has been done.

Their evidence has to be stronger than that. I'm going to need your assistance and if she will play along we might be able to sort this out. I believe that I can make her join us. That would make her a much more valuable asset. I would rather have her in my bed and advising me than in a cell despising me for what I've done to her."

The doctor nodded. "I thought as much. I know how your mind works My Lord Balen."

Balen raised an eyebrow. "Indeed."

Crow sat in the kitchen drinking a cup of weak tea. It was mostly milk. He had just finished his breakfast at the end of his watch and was about to go to bed. Cheryl took the plate off of him. "You know they will find her."

Crow managed a weak smile. "I'm sure they will but it looks like the trail has gone cold. Nobody seems to know anything and if they do they won't talk."

There was a shout from the guards at the gate and Crow leapt up and ran outside.

He bounded across the yard and joined Frank, Storm, Matt and Reko at the gate. There was a cart outside the gate and four people had just climbed down from it. They were holding out pieces of paper and Frank was looking at them. Frank looked up as Crow crossed the yard. "These people have received an invitation but it has taken them some time to get here. I would like to introduce Peter who is a carpenter, Janice his wife who makes clothes, Tracy who is their daughter and Bart their son."

Crow stepped forward to shake hands. He lingered ever so slightly longer when shaking Tracy's hand and smiled when she looked up at him. That look wasn't missed by Storm who glared at him. Crow missed the glare as he was too busy looking at Tracy. She was a tall slim girl of about twenty with jet black hair and bright red lipstick. Her clothes were black and elegant. Her parents both dressed in casual jeans and a sweat shirt. Her father had neatly cut brown hair while her mother had blonde hair. Bart was a typical teenager, his hair was long, his shirt short and his trousers nearly made his waistline.

Frank had missed the look as well. He was smiling and talking to Peter.

"Now we'll have to find you a place to stay. Would you prefer to camp as a group or have a room here? We're a bit pushed for space but we do have a hay loft if you don't mind that."

Peter smiled. "After so long on the road anything with a roof would be a bonus, thank you. Is there anywhere that we can wash?" He looked towards his family. "It has been a long journey."

Frank turned to the others. "I think we'll leave these people in peace to settle in. I'll show them to the barn and I'm sure we'll all have time to welcome them later. Please, follow me."

Frank led them across the farm yard and Crow went with them as well. Tracy fell in beside him and he looked down at her and smiled. Storm watched from across the yard and then went inside. She passed by the kitchen and indicated that Doc should follow her. He got up, picked up his drink and took it with him to the Med Room. He went inside and closed the door.

Storm was pacing up and down. "I can't believe that man. I really can't. How could he?"

Doc stepped forwards and caught her arm. "What can't you believe? Am I missing something?"

Storm glared at him. "Yes you are, big time. Did you see that? Raven has only been gone a matter of a couple of months and he's making eyes at the first floozy who comes along."

Doc sat down and pulled her down to sit beside him. "I'm just a man, I miss those things, tell me."

Storm swallowed hard. "Well, I wasn't going to say anything when he got together with Raven. Just before they did that swap he'd made a pass at me. He gave it the full charm offensive and I was going for it. Then suddenly he's Mr Raven and all in love with her. I bit my tongue as it all seemed to be fate. You know what I mean? A new start for him and he really seemed to be supporting her. She had such responsibility that she needed someone. I'm well rid of him considering what just happened."

Doc looked mystified. "Go on, fill me in. I missed all of that. I was in the kitchen when you came back. I can't see through walls."

Storm sighed. "You didn't realise what was happening did you? Take a look at the situation. He was knocking off the boss's daughter with all the fringe benefits that has. When the going gets tough, like she's having his baby, he tries to run for it. He's let off the hook, both financially and with the baby and all he has to do is be nice to her. He meets me, decides he fancies something different once her daddy is no longer a threat. He probably thought she'd be killed on the way home or would not find him again. Then he gets the opportunity of being top dog again if he's with Raven and life just throws that in his path. Now she's not around he's finding himself something else to entertain him. Of course he's already got the position of being in charge so all he needs to do is move someone else in. Believe me, just watch him with her and you'll notice it now you are looking."

Doc looked stunned. "Are you sure you aren't overreacting?"

It wasn't until the evening meal that they were all together. Crow came in and the Stacey family were already sitting in the kitchen with Doc, Storm and Reko. Crow went and sat next to Tracy. Doc gave Storm a very knowing look. Then other people started filing in and it became very crowded. The Colours were eating in their own camp that night as Cheryl had been cooking flat out all week and they had offered to give her a rest by looking after themselves.

Frank came in and sat in his usual seat by the door. He looked tired. "Well that's the chores done for the day. We've got produce to take to the Mart tomorrow and I'm hoping we can pick up some news about Raven."

Crow wasn't listening. He was talking to Tracy who was laughing at something he was saying. Frank raised an eyebrow and then glared at him.

"Crow, I said we're going to take some produce to the Mart tomorrow and see if we can pick up some clues about Raven."

Crow looked up. "That's good, I'll go with you if that is alright. Tracy, have you seen the Mart? Perhaps you'd like to come with us?"

Tracy giggled. "I'd love to. What is it like?"

Crow began a private conversation with Tracy about the Mart as others broke off in their own conversations. Frank was watching Crow and so was Storm.

After dinner Storm caught Frank's arm and pulled him to the Med Room with Doc. She wasn't through the door before she turned to Frank. "He can't do this?"

Frank looked at her with a level stare. "Storm, there isn't anything we can do. If he wants to act like that, then he will. We can't force him, we're not a dictatorship. We can make it uncomfortable for him and remind him but we have no way of knowing if Raven is even alive."

Storm spluttered. "It's just not right. He can't be our leader and then pick himself a new woman just like that."

Frank smiled. "He isn't and he isn't. He might be using Raven's room but believe me if he tries to take Tracy in there then there will be trouble. I still believe that Raven is alive somewhere and one day we're going to get her back. If Crow cheats on her then we will have to deal with it. He is showing certain flaws in his character which make him a liability. The last thing we need here is dissent. At the moment he has done nothing wrong.

We could be seeing things in the wrong light, or we could be right. If we are right then we deal with it."

Balen was thinking while he watched the doctor begin to immobilise Raven's arm and to strap up her ribs. The treatment table was behind a screen which hid it from view from the window in the door. "I'm going to need your help here. I can't have any possible doubt about my leadership.

There are some dangerous elements and I know that there would soon be someone to step into my shoes."

The doctor looked up. "You know you have my support. There, that's about the best I can do. It will make her more comfortable. She's weak but she'll pull through. There is no serious damage this time but I can't guarantee that she'd survive another attack. That strangle mark looks pretty serious, there is some damage to her trachea which will heal in time. I would estimate that whoever was doing that was disturbed rather than voluntarily stopped."

Balen stared at him, his eyes were cold and the doctor physically backed away from him. His voice was commanding. "I'll deal with the situation. Wake her up."

They were behind the screens so the bed was not visible from the door. He put a hand on her less bruised shoulder as she came round. He whispered. "Raven, can you hear me?" He put a finger to his lips.

She looked up at him and whispered. "Yes."

The doctor backed away and went to put his instruments into the disinfectant. Balen took Raven's hand and crouched down so that he could speak quietly to her. "We have a problem. I respect that you have helped us and I value you help. The attacks on you are because of the hatred of some of my people for your people over what they think happened that night. They have lost loved ones and they demand retribution. I cannot tell them that we have insurrection in the ranks or that will undermine my authority. I cannot tell them that it was a provoked attack so they believe their friends and loved ones were innocent and murdered under your orders. I think you can imagine how they feel and what they want to do to you. Time isn't healing the wound, it is making it fester and if I leave retribution much longer they will do it for me. I am also losing credibility. I should have had you executed when I brought you here."

Raven choked and looked up at him, her eyes pleading. "Why didn't you? Are you going to kill me now?"

Balen shook his head. "Because I knew I needed you. No I'm not going to kill you and I've thought of a way that I can make them believe that you are being made to suffer. Trust me but I do have to do something that will sate their anger. They want to see you dead but they would be happier if I made you suffer a lot first." He swallowed hard and looked at the floor.

Raven tensed and looked up at him. "What are you going to do to me?"

Memories of what he had said when she first arrived came screaming into her mind.

Balen took a deep breath. "I keep some of the more unruly elements here in check because of my reputation. They are manageable because they fear me. I cannot be seen as weak. But, some of that reputation is engineered. That is what I plan to do now if you will help me."

Raven thought for a moment. "I understand in part." She swallowed and winced as the pain shot through her. "What are you going to do to me?"

Balen smiled. "Archangel, our leader has ordered all Compound Commanders to produce an heir. My dear wife, may she rest in peace, died childless earlier this year. I am under pressure to either take a mate or find a substitute to produce an heir. That is well known. So it's what I'm going to appear to do to you. It will keep you safe if they think I have raped you in order to comply with Archangel's wishes. I need your help and I'm going to trust you not to betray me.

Believe me if you even try to use it against me I will make sure that I carry it out for real and believe me you will really suffer. To keep you safe it will have to appear that you are carrying my heir. They won't be able to touch you then." He looked down at her and his eyes were sincere. "It has been suggested by others that this would be a suitable retribution."

Raven stared at him pleadingly, tears were running down her face and she began physically shaking. He stroked her face. "I will not touch you. One day you may come to me willingly and we will make love. I will not take you by force. So you have nothing to fear. But I am going to have to make them think that I have. If you'll play along with it then I can keep you safe. Do you understand? You are going to have to trust me. We are going to have to make it appear as though I have."

Raven shut her eyes. "You will do what you have to do to keep your command." She looked up at him and managed a weak smile.

He put a hand on her shoulder and bent down and kissed her gently on the forehead. "Believe me I will not hurt you. How are your acting skills?"

She looked up at him and she felt a nervous energy which welled up inside her. She wasn't sure if it was fear or something else.

Balen stroked her face. "Trust me." He turned to the doctor. "I have your support? Can she walk?" The doctor nodded.

Balen turned to the doctor. "Dress her in a paper gown." The doctor did.

Balen stepped back. "Raven, try and get away from us. Scream, hit me if you can but you must make it look realistic. I want them to believe that you have got away. After that, play along with me."

Balen opened the door and summoned the guards into the room. He stationed them by the door where they had no view of the examination table. "I do not want her to escape. You have wanted retribution, now I feel that it is time. You are my witnesses." He went around the curtain out of sight.

Raven gritted her teeth and put up with the pain as she got up off of the table. Balen caught her as she was still out of sight of the guards when her legs gave out slightly. She shivered as her bare feet touched the cold tiles. Balen's arm was supportive, his body close to hers was warm and somehow comforting. When she was sure that they were clear of the screen and that the guards could see her she summoned her strength and elbowed Balen in the stomach. As he bent down she smacked him hard in the face with the back of her fist so that he let go of her. He pushed her slightly and she ran for the door screaming. He stepped forwards and stood, folding his arms. "Guards!"

The two guards grabbed Raven roughly. She screamed as they grabbed her injured arm and roughly dragged her back to Balen who watched seemingly emotionless. "Strap her to the bed."

She was trying to kick the guards and was struggling with all her strength. She bit one of them on the arm, hard and he yelled and slapped her across the face.

Balen took a step towards them to try to stop them then checked himself. "Do it now, am I to wait all day?"

The two guards dragged her kicking and screaming to the table, threw her on her back and strapped her wrists down to the table and pulled a restraint around her neck. She struggled. Balen shouted at the doctor. "Pad out her neck, I don't want my prize to strangle herself."

Balen fixed the guards with an icy stare. Then he turned his attention to Raven. "Your people killed many of our people. Did you think that there would be no retribution for this? The information you have given us has been invaluable but I tire of waiting. I will have my heir and I will make you suffer in his or her creation. Guards, leave us. I will not have you watch me. I plan to make sure that Raven endures the most exquisite pain and she will take no pleasure from this coupling."

The guards looked visibly shocked.

Balen fixed them in a cold and emotionless stare. "Leave us. I will call when she is to be returned to her cell."

The two guards looked at each other and backed away and left the room as the doctor pulled the screen further around the table.

Balen smiled at Raven and whispered. "Well done.

Now I'd appreciate a bit of screaming, the more the better as it can't hurt to enhance my reputation." He put a gentle hand on her head then he bent over her and held both of her arms. He bent down and whispered in her ear. What he said was graphic in its description. It wasn't nasty at all, it was all the things he would really like to do to her. As she listened she screamed as loud as she could. She screamed until her voice started to break. Balen realised this and shouted. "Doctor, I tire of this noise, tape her mouth." Raven smiled nervously at him as the doctor put tape over her mouth. The doctor then busied himself making her paper robe and body look as though the act had actually happened.

Balen stepped out from behind the screen as he finished zipping up his boiler suit. He spoke loud enough so that the guards outside could hear. "Sedate her, keep her laying there for an hour and then take her back to her cell. Do not sedate her in her cell tonight. I want her to feel the full impact of what I have just done to her and to think about it."

He then strode out of the room past the shocked guards. They had gone white and they looked at him in horror as he strode past them smiling. He went back to his office and closed the door. He leant against it and breathed out hard. Even though he sat at his desk he could not concentrate, he didn't bother with an evening meal and spent a sleepless night in his room. He paced the room and couldn't seem to settle.

Raven sat in her cell. Pain kept her awake but also her thoughts. She couldn't get Balen out of her mind. Images of him came unbidden and where she had once felt hatred for him, now there was something else in its place. It was an emotion she had never truly felt before and it frightened her even more.

Crow woke up early. He walked around the room and opened drawers and cupboards and put away anything that belonged to Raven. He bundled any clothing that wasn't in the cupboard into the bottom of the wardrobe and shut the door. The then went to the bathroom and spent nearly an hour getting ready. When he was satisfied he looked at himself in the mirror and smiled. He grabbed his hairbrush and did one last sweep of it through his hair. Then he took all Raven's cosmetics, scooped them into a towel, wrapped them up and put it in the wardrobe as well.

He stood in the middle of the room and looked around him. He had made the bed and changed the sheets and he folded them back down and smoothed the cover. He smiled to himself and left the room.

The morning at the farm had dawned bright and crisp. The new visitor's cart had been loaded up with produce. Tracy and her father were in the driver's seat. Crow came down, mounted Blade and was riding alongside with Frank on the other side as they rode away from the farm. Both hadshotguns in hand and the father had a shotgun in his hand on the cart.

Tracy was driving the heavy horse.

The journey was uneventful and they joined the queue going into the Mart.

Crow and Frank had dismounted. Frank was talking to Peter at the horse's head and Crow had climbed up onto the cart and was sitting beside Tracy and they were deep in conversation. She giggled occasionally and was attentive as he pointed things out to her. He laughed at her jokes and both were smiling profusely.

Frank tried not to look but he couldn't help it. He was within earshot and he couldn't help listening.

Tracy giggled. "So we're here to find out about what happened to Raven. I heard she was the woman in charge? Isn't she your wife?"

Crow had been in full conversation about his exploits at the farm and the question caught him unawares. "Well, yes, sort of. It's more a marriage of convenience. She's a lovely woman, don't get me wrong. So what sort of things do you want to look at in the Mart?"

The expression fell off of Frank's face and he ran his fingers over his shotgun. He wasn't the only one who was listening. Behind them in the queue there was another wagon. The wagon master was at his horse's head trying to calm an impatient horse which stamped and jittered about.

He was watching the group from the farm out of the corner of his eye. He was also listening. Frank was too intent on what Crow was saying and doing while trying to hold a conversation with Peter to notice him.

The queue moved fairly fast as the people were checked out on the gate and moved inside. When it was their turn they passed quickly past the guards, as did the person behind them. Crow took the reins and guided the horse into the mart and to the Livery Stable. "I'll look after the horses, Tracy if you'd like to give me a hand?"

Frank was about to object but he took a deep breath. "Ok, I'll see you out there then." He watched the couple as they led the horses behind the building.

He walked away, the thoughts rushing around his mind. He was thinking about it so much that he paid no attention to the man behind them. He was an ordinary man dressed in very unobtrusive clothing. He walked his horse in calmly now that it was going somewhere. He didn't do anything to draw attention to himself.

As Crow and Tracy took their horse to the far end stable, he took his to the nearest one, turned the pony out into the stable and left it with the tack on and slipped out into the corridor and crept up to where Crow and Tracy were and slipped around the corner as they took the horses' tack off and brushed them down.

Crow stood close to Tracy and as they finished he grabbed her wrist and pulled her out of the stable. He shut and locked the door then pushed her around the corner. She gasped slightly as she fell backwards onto a hay bale. He crouched beside her. "Alone at last."

Tracy laughed. "Very funny. Now come on what are you playing at?" She was laughing and treating it as a joke.

Crow wasn't laughing. "Come on, I know that you want me. We have our chance now."

Tracy was still laughing. She put a hand on Crow's chest to push him away. "Don't be silly, you are a married man."

Crow laughed. "Actually no I'm not."

Tracy looked confused. "But you are married to Raven aren't you or is that one of those strange pagan marriages? I won't have anything to do with a married man."

Crow lifted an eyebrow. "Well actually they are just as valid but no I'm not married at all. So you wouldn't be doing any harm if we got together.

Come on, we have some time and I really want you."

Tracy was pushing harder now, trying to get him to back away. "I don't know what you are talking about. How can you not be married? Everyone knows that you are married to Raven."

Crow laughed. "Well that is the joke. She is a lovely woman and it was a real pleasure to have her as my wife for a while. I can't say that her charms weren't pleasurable but no, she wasn't my wife. I was in a difficult position.

There was nothing I could do about it. She gave me an ultimatum to take her dead husband's place or to be thrown out. If she'd thrown me out the people following me would have found me and killed me. She was lonely and needed someone. I was there and I wanted what she had on offer so it was a mutual arrangement. So there you have it, I'm not married. She said at the time if I wanted to be with someone else she would step aside and we'd sort it out. I want you and I'm sure she won't mind. We've had our time but it is time for me to move on." He slipped his hand behind her head. He didn't notice the stranger who had moved so he had a clear view without being seen and who had heard every word Crow had said.

As Crow started undoing her buttons the onlooker started taking photographs on an ancient camera.

Tracy pulled away but he pushed her back down and

kissed her passionately. "I'm not married to Raven, the man who I took the place of was. Come on, you know you want me."

Tracy looked confused. "You mean you aren't Crow?"

Crow smiled down at her. "No I'm not."

Tracy put a hand to stop him. "I don't want to, I haven't done this before and I want it to be special."

Crow looked disappointed then put his hand over her mouth and continued undoing her clothing. She struggled but he was far stronger than her and she stood no chance of stopping him.

Crow and Tracy were too intent on what they were doing to notice the occasional click. He didn't realise that they had positioned them under a beam of light from an open window above so there was no need to use a flash. When the stranger had seen enough and taken enough photos he disappeared into the back of the stable, made his way around and returned to take the tack off of his pony.

He then disappeared into the crowd and went about his business buying farm supplies with a huge smile on his face.

Crow and Tracy emerged later and began looking around the stalls. Tracy looked as though she was about to burst into tears. Crow was walking with her, his arm around her. The stranger ignored them.

Frank went to the café. It was crowded with faces he recognised from when he had visited before. He spoke to a few people and asked around about whether anyone had heard about Raven. He then went to the kiosk and bought a coffee. The owner put the coffee down for him and took the offered coins. He then looked up and smiled. "You were looking for information about Raven weren't you?"

Frank smiled. "Yes, do you know anything?"

The stallholder smiled. "Yes but it will cost you." Frank put a handful of coins on the table which the stallholder scooped into his hand and into his pocket. "It seems that she was taken by Lord Balen. It was in retribution for what you did to his men. The rumour is that he has been using her most savagely and that it won't be long before she is the mother to his heir.

You might as well forget about her. With the security he has there and how closely he'll be guarding her you might as well consider her dead. He won't let her go, not now, not alive and not while he wants her for something. You know who Lord Balen is?"

Frank nearly dropped his coffee. "Where did you hear that? Yes I know who Lord Balen is."

The stallholder pulled a piece of paper from under the counter. "It was left on my counter. I don't know which customer left it but it has your name on it." He looked at Frank who put more money on the counter and the stallholder handed it over.

Frank took his coffee and the piece of paper and sat down. He unfolded it carefully and read the words written on the paper. "You killed those we cared about, now we have something you care about. Our Lord is using her for his own enjoyment and she will bear him his heir. Remember always what you did to our people and think on what he is doing to her.

He is a cruel and vicious man. You can imagine the pain and torment he is putting her through. That makes up in part for what you did to those we love." Frank folded the piece of paper and put it in his pocket. He looked around the Mart, he looked at faces but they all seemed to be going about their business and ignoring him. He then noticed Crow and Tracy. They were looking at a stall full of necklaces and jewellery. Crow had been picking pieces up and trying them on her. He then put his arm around her. It was an unconscious act but enough for Frank to notice. He looked down at his coffee and he thought, long and hard.

Raven entered Balen's office like she always did. The guard didn't follow her in, he opened the door, she walked in and he shut the door behind her and went to take his position up the hallway. She looked awkward and seemed nervous. Balen looked up from his desk. He had thought long and hard about how he was going to react but it went out of his head the minute he saw her.

She looked tired as she stood there just looking at him. He smiled, got up and walked around the desk. She took a step backwards as he crossed the room. He held his hand out. "I am sorry for what I had to do. I know it must have been traumatic. I would have given you more comfort afterwards but that would have negated the effect of what they now believe.

Rest assured that you are safe now. They haven't touched you again have they?" Raven shook her head. He stepped closer to her and she could feel the warmth of him close to her as she looked up at him. "You must tell me if anyone does try anything." She nodded. He pulled her up against him and put his arms around her. "I wouldn't hurt you."

Raven almost smiled. Her head was spinning with mixed emotions and she didn't know what she believed anymore. She knew she had to answer but she didn't know what to say. A myriad of different plans and possible motives and thoughts queued up to confuse her. In the end she licked her dry lips and whispered. "You could have been a little less graphic in your description."

They heard a sound in the corridor outside and both jumped apart. Balen put his hand on her arm. She looked so tired and her face was streaked with dried tears. He almost whispered gently. "You need to sleep. I will get the doctor to sedate you and I'll call for you later. Go, sleep now, rest and you will feel better." He called the guard and she was gone.

He was sitting with a cup of tea in his hand staring at the wall as countless figures, facts and information swirled around in his head. A headache was starting and his arms ached. There was a knock at the door. He looked up.

"Enter."

The man who had been at the Mart walked in and Balen smiled at him. "Fred, I trust you got the supplies we needed? There is no need to report."

The man had a smile on his face that instantly grabbed Balen's attention.

He raised an eyebrow. "What are you so happy about?"

The man's smile fell off of his face when fixed in Balen's cold stare. "Sir, it seems that there is likely to be dissent in the ranks at that farm you are so interested in. On the flip side if you had any plans to ransom Raven I doubt you'd get much now. I have information and something here that is going to greatly interest you my lord. If you truly want to torment Raven I have something here that is going to break her heart. Or it may not, considering what else I found out. I just can't believe my luck, it was a real gift."

Balen frowned. "Well tell me then."

The man stood to attention. "I was in the queue to go into the Mart and by chance I pulled up behind the cart from the farm. I listened to their conversation of course, mostly basic chit chat but I knew something was going on between that Crow and a new woman straight off. Then it was very obvious that he was flirting with her. I haven't seen her with them before. So I followed the two of them when they gave Frank and an older man the slip and went to the livery stables. He pushed her into a private corner and seduced her. Well more like raped her. You aren't going to believe this but I also overheard him telling her that he is not Crow. Apparently Raven's husband died and Raven gave him an ultimatum to either become her husband or leave. Leaving meant possible death so he chose to stay with Raven. Crow was being hunted so they did a switch and whoever this person is became Crow. He was telling the young girl that he was not Raven's husband and that it was a marriage of convenience. My film was at its end and I took the film to a friend of mine to be developed." He handed the photographs to Balen. "It gets better than that. Do you remember there was a big stink a while back when they were looking for that man called Brandon? Well I think that is the man who became Crow. Now how is that for a piece of information?"

Balen smiled. "You have indeed done well."

The man smiled broadly. "I thank you my lord."

Balen smiled and raised an eyebrow. "You will be rewarded, you may take on the Eastern Shift that you have been asking about, see it done."

The man bowed slightly and left the room.

Balen looked through the photographs and took a long drink of his tea before standing up. He called in the guard outside his door. "Bring Raven to me."

The two guards half carried Raven up to Balen's room. She looked exhausted and the pain was showing on her face. Balen indicated the chair.

"Put her there and leave. I do not wish to be disturbed." They did as ordered and shut the door behind them.

Balen sat at his desk, the photographs in front of him. "I believe we have a degree of trust building here so think carefully how you answer this next question. How well do you know your husband?"

Raven looked up, her eyes were tired and there were dark circles under them. There was a vague flash of anger. "I know my husband very well."

Balen nodded. "I had better rephrase that. Is the man who you are currently calling Crow your husband?"

Raven looked up at him a little surprised. "No. How did you know?"

Balen smiled. "Very good answer. I think we both now know where we stand. I'm going to show you some photographs that were taken today. I'm not going to comment, they are self-explanatory. That is the man you have taken as your husband, who I assume shared your bed. It seems he hasn't taken much time to move on after your side of the bed went cold."

He handed her the photographs and she looked through them. When she had finished she looked up at him. There were tears in her eyes. Balen looked down at her, his stare was cold. "How do you feel about this?"

Pain flickered across Raven's face. "I feel betrayed. I gave him his life back."

Balen suddenly felt really angry. He was about to grab her but pulled back. He stood over her. "That isn't what he said. He was proud to announce that you gave him an ultimatum to stay and be your husband or leave and die."

Raven looked up in horror. "That was not how it was at all. I hated my husband, he'd been having an affair and he had left me to look after the farm by myself while he was off with her. When he died I should have been free of him but I chose to take that man in his place because it was the only thing I could do. I was frightened and alone. Everything was such a big deal. To begin with if I made a mistake animals died, at that point if I made a mistake then people would die. People were looking to me for answers and I needed someone there to support me. I'd had years of being alone and sleeping alone when the person who should have been there was somewhere else. I suppose deep down I thought if he owed me his life he may at least make me happy."

Balen walked away from her and looked out of the window and thought for a while. Raven bowed her head and cried. Then he walked back to her and lifted her chin in his hand. "How could you give yourself to someone you didn't love?"

Tears ran down her face. "When Crow came to the farm I didn't care anymore about the fairy story that is love. I felt dead inside, nothing mattered other than keeping everyone safe. He had a price on his head, if they came for him then others would have been hurt too. I had a way of solving the problem so I did what I had to do. You don't know me or my past. I've been in situations of such complete despair so in comparison that was just something I had to do. That has made me strong and I can survive but I'm not proud of myself. Giving myself to him just happened. I was drunk and hurting. I was lonely and I obviously needed physical company. After I'd gone that far the rest seemed just to follow on. I wanted someone to look after me and I was tired of doing everything on my own and making all the decisions. I can't explain to you what the tearing emptiness feels like."

Balen took the photographs from her and put them on the desk. "You have been betrayed. The sanctuary that you built is now his. He has moved another woman into your bed, or he soon will. They have left you in the hands of your enemy and they have moved on. For the record as Crow raped that girl it isn't a huge jump in thought that you may not have given yourself to him as willingly as you thought."

Tears were flowing freely down Raven's face. Balen crouched down beside her and he put his hand on her arm. "Those are the people you sought to protect. That was the man you took to your bed."

Raven looked at him with exhausted eyes. She shook her head. "I don't understand."

Balen put a hand on her cheek. "Yes you do understand, you understand all too clearly. You have been betrayed. They have taken your home, your animals and that woman there is taking your life." He thought for a moment. "I can't let that happen. You mean too much to me now. I am going to let you go. You can go back and reclaim your home, go, I won't stop you. Or you can stay here, I won't keep you in a cell and I won't keep you bound or sedated. You can leave if you want to or you can stay here and help me build something, something real and something genuine. The choice is yours." He looked at her sincerely, almost holding his breath.

Raven shook her head. "I don't know what to do. Help me Lord Balen."

Balen smiled at her kindly. "I will help you." He handed her back the photographs and went back to his seat. "Think about it. No decision has to be made yet. But, tell me about this man who is pretending to be Crow.

Who is he? Is he the man known as Brandon? Protecting him isn't going to help anyone now."

Raven looked down. "I can't."

Balen stood up, walked around the desk and stood over her. She looked up at him and a shiver of fear ran down her spine. "This is a turning point Raven. You trust me now and we become something more, you keep this from me and you are showing that you love him. Tell me. He has hurt you. I will make sure that nobody at the farm suffers other than him. You took him to your bed. He did not deserve such an honour. His tongue is as loose as his morals. For all you did for him he has undone it in a moment's lust. You know nothing about this new woman. She is just a girl, look at the photos. She could tell someone about the deception. It is no longer a secret and you and your friends at the farm instigated it. I'm guessing that whoever wanted him was a big player?"

Raven nodded. "Matthew Rolstone."

Balen looked shocked. "I thought he was a big player but not that big. Let me deal with it as if this is not handled well it could become much more serious. I was told about this by someone else. He knows that Crow was once Brandon too. If I don't act then what you feared most will happen.

The bounty on Brandon's head was considerable. I have the resources and the people who can handle this. Please, let me do this for you."

Balen crouched down next to her. "You are tired, sleep on this. If you want to leave I'll have you taken back there."

Raven tried to stand. Balen helped her. She faced him, her shoulders were slumped and she was swaying slightly and shaking. "Balen, I feel so cold. I don't want to be a prisoner. I have to sort this out and I have to protect them."

Balen smiled but he looked destroyed. "Very well, I will order my men to take you back to the farm. You can face them and reclaim your husband. I will ensure the silence of my informant." He turned away and walked to the window.

Raven looked at the photos. "Give some of the photographs to Frank. The worse ones. You choose. I can't look at them again."

Balen turned sharply, stunned. There were tears in his eyes but he wiped them away. He moved to stand over her and looked down at her. "That would get Crow killed."

Raven looked up at him, her eyes were cold. "I know, that is what I am counting on. I'm not a victim and I knew what he was like from the start. If the person who wants Crow, I mean Brandon, dead that badly is so influential, why not give him what he wants."

Balen looked stunned. Raven stood up, she swayed slightly but she walked to him. She held her hand out to him and he held it and steadied her. "If you want me, trust me. As you say, this is a turning point. I gave Brandon a choice, I didn't give him an ultimatum. I have a choice now. I could be angry and demand his death and just be glad to have proof. I could allow him to continue and be with this woman, probably in my bed or I can trust you to make the most out of the situation that you can. I choose the latter.

Give the photographs to Frank. He will undoubtedly kill Crow and then he will sort things out at the farm. I can't be there to sort it out as I couldn't leave you now, I don't want to. What do you want me to do? Not Lord Balen, you?"

Balen looked stunned. He looked down at her and brushed her cheek with the back of his hand. "I want you in all ways."

Raven smiled, she looked exhausted. "Then you have

what you want."

Raven let him pull her close to him. She could feel the warmth of his body and she felt safe in is arms. "I want to stay with you."

Balen smiled and kissed her on the forehead. "Tonight will be your last night in the cell. I have heard that Frank will be at the Mart tomorrow. I will make sure he has the photographs. I will also have them followed and if he does anything I will bring back proof that Brandon is truly dead. We can then decide what to do about it then. You can still change your mind about being with me. Nobody will suffer if you do. If you do choose that…"

Raven put a finger on his mouth, reached up and kissed him on the cheek.

"I've made my decision and it is the right one. For once it is actually a choice I can make. You are a good man Balen, I just hope that I can make you happy."

Balen smiled and kissed her passionately. "I want you. Now!" Raven put a hand on his chest and he stepped back immediately. "What is the matter? Don't you want me?"

Raven shook her head. "I want you more than anything else but you have to keep up your reputation. You are going to have to come up with a good reason why you are moving me to your room."

Balen raised an eyebrow. "You are getting far too good at this, you worry me. You are quite right. Very well, I will think of something. Stay with me for the day though, you have plenty of work to do."

16

The morning dawned clear and bright. There had been a slight frost and it sparkled on the hedges and fences. Balen was up early and as he walked through the main yard of the farm doing his usual inspection he felt the usual nervous anticipation of attack at any moment. He was vigilant, noticing every movement, every sound but also experiencing it all and focusing on the moment. He could smell the clear air, something he had rarely had time to do and he could feel the chilled breeze on his face. There didn't seem to be anyone else around but it was only just past dawn.

The yard was as he expected it to be. Everything was in its place. Small wind turbines spun in the morning breeze and the animals were making gentle contented noises. His boots seemed to sound loud in the morning silence. The frost had hardened the mud and it crunched under his feet.

He hurried across the yard and entered the main building. He bounded up the stairs two at a time, passed his guards who wished him a good morning and opened the door of his office. He sighed and went to his desk and looked down at the papers he hadn't finished the night before. He smiled and shook his head, sat down and began looking them over.

He bundled them together, tapped them on the desk to level them out and set them down and began with the top one. He read and read and wrote comments in the box at the bottom as to what should be done about each situation. Some were suggestions to speak with other members, some were suggestions he had made himself.

He had done about five when he came to one that caught his attention. It was from his Head of Security. The handwriting was hasty, not the usual neat and precise report that he would have expected. That in itself got his attention.

The report read. "After extensive surveillance and interrogation I am sorry to have to inform you that there is a splinter group within the main organisation. They are seeking to undermine your authority and they have been distributing propaganda provided by a rebel force who stand against everything we are trying to achieve here.

It has been reported that they are dissatisfied with the adaptations you have made to the original directive which permits non-members to survive. What they are proposing, according to my sources, is to wipe out anyone who is not a Transition X member.

Correspondence has been recovered between members of this Compound and an external Unit known as the Black Troop. It recommended your immediate removal and stated any weaknesses in our defences. It was accurate enough to be authentic and worrying. Our agents have doubled their efforts to ascertain who sent the communication but at this present time they are still at large.

I am pleased to report that any doubt in your leadership was quelled by your recent actions towards the prisoner known as Raven. Your actions have also reinforced your reputation within the ranks.

Reports have reached us via Security in other Compounds that there have been assassination attempts on the lives of many of the Compound Commanders. There was a failed attempt on the High Commander earlier this week. I have doubled the security but I have kept it covert so that it does not interfere with your day to day activities. I would however suggest that you exercise caution in your movements and do not consider leaving the Compound.

I have raised our security level to Red. We can expect an imminent attack from the forces of the Black Troop."

Balen put the paper down and rubbed his forehead with the palm of his hand. He sighed and flipped through the rest of the paperwork. It all looked very mundane. He took the communiqué from the Head of Security and put the other paperwork aside.

He called in his guard. "I want you to bring me the Head of Security. I also want a report from the prisoner block as to the wellbeing of the prisoner known as Raven."

The guard snapped his heels together. "Very good Sir." He left the room.

About ten minutes later there was a knock at the door. The guard stepped inside. "Sir, I have a message from the doctor. Your prisoner had a comfortable night and has requested to speak with you."

Balen smiled. "Very good, and the Head of Security?"

The guard stood to attention. "He is awaiting you outside the door."

Balen smiled. "Well, show him in."

The guard left the room and a tall, thick set individual dressed in the customary black boiler suit and bearing the crossed swords insignia of the Security Division on his shoulder stepped inside. He closed the door, stepped into the middle of the room and saluted. Balen nodded. The man cleared his throat. "I am assuming you have read my report."

Balen sat down. "Indeed I have. What measures do you have in place to ensure our security? Kurt, you may dispense with formalities. You may take a seat."

Kurt visibly relaxed and sat down. "I've doubled the guard on the perimeter and I have also doubled the guard on patrols so that no individual is left on their own. We can assume that there are hostiles within the Compound who are working with this new organisation outside. From communiqués I have managed to acquire we can expect a full on attack any day. The High Commander has been notified and we have received word that he is sending reinforcements. This threat is not to be underestimated.

My intelligence has revealed that they are an undercover group working for and funded by the Lex Corporation who are systematically wiping out any form of opposition to their retaking control and putting the blame on Transition X by amalgamating with this rebel force we have within our own ranks. They are seeing such compounds as ours as a threat to the general dependence of the population and have branded us as seditious. All Compound Commanders have been declared to be traitors to the country that they are in and their immediate execution has been requested."

Balen looked down at the paperwork. "So it is pretty much as we expected."

Kurt smiled. "Pretty much. I've put as much into the defences as I can. I've put into place your suggestions and all we can do is hope that they don't hit us with too much firepower."

Balen frowned. "Did you get the security bunkers put in place?"

Kurt hesitated. "I did, they are not all finished but there are enough for non-essential personnel. I have had the roofs of the sheds reinforced so they will survive a limited mortar attack and all animal handlers have been alerted to the situation. Feed it at a maximum and we have stockpiled sufficient to last us for at least a month. All outside agents bar the two set to go to the Mart today have been recalled and we are prepared for lock down. Are there any last commands for actions outside the perimeter?"

Balen opened his desk drawer and took out a brown sealed envelope. "I have some information you might find interesting. It came from and informant and it has been verified by Raven. It seems that Crow, Raven's husband died a while back and was replaced by an individual known as Brandon as they look similar. Do you remember a while back when Lex MegaCorp's Head of Acquisitions was looking for him? Well this is a gift that has fallen into our hands.

I want this delivered to Frank of Raven's farm. To him and nobody else. I understand that he is due to make a visit to the Mart today. I am sure that they have similar intelligence that there is going to be trouble. If they do not then our Agent is at liberty to reveal this information to them. They have valuable resources there which we would not want to fall into the hands of the Black Troop."

Kurt smiled. "Very wise and that is very interesting. May I ask the importance of the envelope?"

Balen took a deep breath and let it out slowly. "That envelope and delivery of it will ensure that the prisoner Raven not only remains with us to provide a valuable heir in response to the High Commander's order it has ensured that she has effectively joined us. As such she will no longer be considered a prisoner."

Kurt looked stunned. "Did I hear you right? How on earth did you pull that one off?" He realised what he had said and looked panic stricken.

Balen smiled. "I'll forgive you for that outburst. Do not underestimate me. Raven is now working for us and it was no subterfuge or cunning trickery that has made her do that. Have you forgotten why all these people joined up in the first place? I mean before we found the extraneous texts which we have removed from this Compound's directive."

Kurt smiled back. "What is in the envelope if I may be so bold?"

Balen raised an eyebrow. "Proof that Raven's husband, or rather the person posing as Crow, was cheating on her which I need delivered to Frank so that he removes him. That leaves Raven free to choose a new mate. It is appropriate that the mother to my heir should also be my mate. It will bring stability and as she owns the farm it would bring it under our wing and our jurisdiction. It will achieve by peaceful means what we could not achieve by force. Also, if we can get absolute proof we can use it to get a chance to open channels of communication with Lex MegaCorp."

Kurt smiled broadly. "Well that was a stroke of genius. I will ensure that the envelope is delivered at once and I will ensure that an operative remains in the area to confirm that the action has been carried out. If we can bring evidence back we will."

Balen looked down at the paperwork. "Bring me Crow's head and his wedding ring. If he gets the chance to bring Crow back alive then obviously this would give us a bargaining chip as well. Make sure the operative is back as soon as possible. I have put together a communiqué to be sent with the proof. I must inform you that I will need my personal security detail moved to my new accommodation. I will now be taking the east room."

Kurt smiled. "It is about time that you took quarters more suitable to your rank and more easily defended." Realisation dawned. "And more private."

Balen picked up his pen. "You may go."

Kurt stood up, saluted and left the room.

At the farm the occupants were waking up. Crow and Reko had been on guard and they were just going in for breakfast. They had been replaced by Peter and Shaun. Frank was in the kitchen when they came in. He had a serious look on his face and he glared at Crow. Crow ignored him and sat down. Cheryl put a plate of food in front of him and when Reko came in she put one in front of him too. She smiled at them both. "Was it a quiet night?"

Reko looked up. "Thank you for this. Yes, it was thanks, not a movement on the road."

Crow grunted. There was a sound of someone coming down the stairs. Frank looked up and he jumped slightly when Tracy came in wearing very little. Her dressing gown was open and her nightdress didn't leave much to the imagination. Crow looked up. "Did you sleep well?"

Tracy smiled at him, walked over and kissed him. "I

did, thank you. Then again you did leave me very tired."

Crow stared down Frank. Then he turned to Tracy and smiled. "I'll be up in a minute, why don't you go back up?" He then tucked into his breakfast, ignoring everyone's stares. When he had finished he got up and walked out of the room and was heard going up the stairs.

They eat their breakfast in silence. Frank finished his after he had wiped the last of his toast around his plate and drank down the last of his tea. Reko looked up as Crow went out. "Are you alright Frank?"

Frank took a deep breath. "No, far from it. I need to do some thinking. I'm going to the Mart today and I want Crow to come with me. Can you convince him that it's a good idea?"

Reko stared into what was left of his breakfast. "I am not going to ask questions. The man has only just come off of shift but I will try. I can't guarantee he won't want to bring Tracy with him."

Frank shrugged. "That would be an unfortunate situation but one I'd have to deal with."

Later that morning Frank, Crow and Tracy set out on horses heading for the Mart. They rode at a swift pace and kept a cautious eye out for trouble on the road. They had long since abandoned taking the cross country route. They got to the Mart without incident and the queue was shorter than usual. Crow and Tracy went to the stalls with a shopping list that Frank had given them. Frank went to the café. He went up to the stallholder and ordered a coffee.

The stallholder looked at him and raised an eyebrow. "Would you like extras with that?"

Frank smiled in recognition of what was being said. "I would."

The stallholder passed a brown sealed envelope to him and Frank swiftly palmed it. The stallholder bent down as if to pick something up. "I have been told to tell you to expect trouble at the farm, big trouble. You might want to get your people out while you can. That one is for free. Enjoy the coffee, we are running out." Frank put a small pile of money on the table and walked away.

Frank went to a table at the corner of the tent café and opened the envelope. He looked at the photographs in silence and then put them back in the envelope and slipped them back in his pocket. He then opened the note that was inside. "I am sure that you will not be impressed with the actions of the man you call Crow. We know your secret. We are prepared to sort this matter out. Without direct intervention at the moment your farm will be in serious jeopardy. All you need to do is to give us Crow and we will look after everything else. I am sure that you wish him dead. Rest assured this will most likely be the outcome. Take the cross country route home and leave him tied up. We will do the rest. We are not your enemy. We both have bigger enemies to deal with. Be assured that you have our support and we will do what we can to help you. B" He folded the note and thought about it. He then drank his coffee in silence. A young woman came over but he glared at her so she backed off.

He sat there for about an hour while Crow and Tracy did the shopping then he joined them. "Let's get the goods loaded into the saddlebags and get out of here. I want to avoid the rush and I've been warned not to take the road route home. There are road pirates about."

Crow looked worried and stepped a little closer to Tracy. Frank looked away, pretending to notice something. "I think we should move out now."

They hurried to the livery stable, tacked up, mounted up and rode out of the compound. The road was crowded with people and they had to push their way past them but most people would happily get out of the way of a horse. They trotted down the pavement and when they came to the path across country they turned down it and set off at a gallop.

Frank chose his moment well and ironically. He let

Crow and Tracy go on ahead. Just at the place where they had lost Raven he pulled out his pistol and put a tranquilliser dart into Tracy's back. She fell off the horse onto the path. Crow pulled his horse to a standstill and leapt off. He ran over to her and as he bent down to check if she was alright he felt a sharp pain at the back of his head and he fell over as the world went black. Frank smiled as he looked down at the prone Crow. "You didn't deserve Raven." He took out a handful of cable ties and tied Crow's hands and feet.

Then he gathered up the horses. They had stopped about a hundred yards further on. He slung Tracy across his saddle and mounted up on and headed back to the farm leaving Crow tied up on the path.

He didn't notice the lone figure on the hillside. He was too busy thinking so he missed the momentary reflection of the sun on the pair of binoculars as the figure watched him intently. The person who had been watching him didn't miss what was going on though. He took it all in and committed it to memory as he knew he would be questioned later.

Once Frank was long gone the watcher ran down the hill and went to the body. He tried to pick him up. He was joined by a blonde haired youth and they both dragged Brandon down the path to where a car was waiting for him with its engine running.

They tumbled him into the boot. The young blonde haired youth was quite a contrast to the dark swarthy complexion of the watcher who had long dark curls.

Sol the blonde haired youth smiled. "Now drive, we have to get back before they lock down."

The driver put his foot to the floor and didn't slow down even for corners. They got back in record time and after passing the security check on the gate they rolled the vehicle inside and the gates closed behind them with a loud thud. A wooden plank was pulled down to secure the gate.

All around the compound windows that faced outside were covered with heavy shutters to protect the glass. Guards who were on duty took up their positions. The animals were shut in, fed and watered and buckets, troughs and anything that could hold water were filled. Then everyone went on with their daily tasks.

Sol handed Crow over to the security detail waiting by the door and went to the main house. He knocked on the door and the newly posted security guard opened the door and looked him over. Sol smiled. "I have a package for Lord Balen."

The guard stepped aside and Sol carried on up the stairs. He went straight to Lord Balen's office and the guards stepped aside for him. He knocked and waited to be told to go in.

He entered the room and stood on the carpet in front of Lord Balen. Balen looked up as he came in and raised an eyebrow. "So, you have him? Very well done."

There was a flurry of movement from Sol. He fixed Balen with a stare as he stepped sideways and pulled his revolver. It was as if it happened in slow motion. Balen saw the gun being drawn but it didn't register with him until Sol fired it. Bullets tore through the air towards Balen who was taken completely by surprise. He couldn't react as the first tore into his arm but he started moving as the other ripped into his shoulder. He rolled sideways off of his chair and leapt out of the way. He reached for his gun and drew it as he rolled ignoring the pain from his arm and shoulder. Two more bullets thundered into the wall behind him, the third broke the window as he leapt and fired. Both bullets tore into Sol who was standing stock still and firing continuously. The impact made Sol stagger twice then he crumpled to his knees and landed in a heap. He lay still on the carpet.

The guards rushed in. One went to Sol and put a bullet in his head the other rushed to Balen and helped him up. Balen was bleeding profusely as the guard helped to lift him. Balen pushed the guard away.

"Get the doctor up here now." The guard ran off to get the doctor. Balen laid back against the wall. Blood was running down his boiler suit. He relaxed slightly but caught movement out of the corner of his eye at the same time as he began to wonder why the guard had put a bullet into the already dead man's head. He didn't stop to think about his actions, he lifted his gun and shot the guard who was just about to pull the trigger of the gun which was aimed at his head.

The Head of Security rushed in. Balen looked up at him. "I think we have a severe security breach." Then he laid back against the wall again and let the pain thunder through him. "I'm hoping that you aren't going to try to shoot me as well. I've had enough of people trying to kill me today."

Kurt ran to the second man and checked for a pulse. "He's still alive. I'm glad you left me someone to interrogate."

The doctor rushed in and crouched over Balen. "I must remove the bullet in your shoulder. The other has passed through your arm. You must not be moved, not yet." He pulled out a syringe and filled it with clear liquid.

"I must put you out to do this, only temporarily." Balen grabbed his wrist.

"No you don't. With people wanting to kill me I'm staying conscious. No, that is an order."

Kurt was searching the pockets and checking over the bodies.

Frank galloped into the compound leading the two empty horses. He leapt down and let the two horses gallop freely in the gated off yard. He went over to Peter who was just coming out of the farm house. "I'm sorry Peter, there was nothing I could do. Thankfully Tracy was only tranquilised. She will be alright when she comes around." Peter took her from the front of Frank's saddle and into the house.

Storm came out of the farm house. She walked over to Frank. "What happened?"

Frank looked down. "Crow and Tracy have been shot. There was nothing I could do."

Storm opened her mouth then thought about what she was going to say, smiled and muttered. "No questions."

Frank looked up. "Advisable. We've been warned of an attack and to do the best we can to defend ourselves or to get clear for a while. I would suggest that we bring the Colours into the compound and treat this as a defendable area. If nothing happens it doesn't hurt. If it does it may make a difference."

Storm looked stunned. "What do we do?"

Frank smiled at her reassuringly. "We survive, that's what we do. Go and speak to the Colours as they may want to bring their equipment and tents inside as well. Go now, we don't know how long we have got to sort this out." He then went around the compound and the house organising people and warning them of the imminent danger.

They pushed the now redundant cars and vans in front of the gates and brought the pigs and dogs around into the central courtyard buildings. They barricaded up the field gate. All outer windows were already boarded up and they posted guards in the upper windows where they could see between the boards, then they waited for it to get dark.

Balen was still sitting at his desk at dusk. He was finding it hard to write and his arm and shoulder were beginning to ache as his painkillers were wearing off. His head pounded and he felt dizzy and sick.

There was a knock at the door and the doctor came in answering his summons. Balen attempted a smile. "Now there was I hoping for some dusky maiden and I get you?"

The doctor smiled. "You ungrateful sod, if I may be so bold." He crossed the room quickly and administered a syringe full of painkiller to Balen's arm.

Balen smiled, his face drawn with pain. "Thanks."

The doctor looked serious. "I would have arranged you a certain maiden but I couldn't release her without your order. Do you wish to give that order?"

Balen thought about it. "Yes I do. She isn't a prisoner now."

The doctor looked down. "Your wounds aren't serious. You won't do any damage as long as you are careful. But that is not a blank cheque. Remember, you have been shot, twice." He gave Balen a knowing smile. "I'll arrange for Raven to be brought to your new room. It is best you are not alone tonight. None of us know what tomorrow will bring. I have a message from Kurt. Security is tight, he's managed to interrogate the prisoner and he has now interrogated and executed three infiltrators. He interrogated Brandon and couldn't shut him up. So I think we have the full story there now. I'll see you in the morning."

The doctor left the room.

Balen pulled on the new boiler suit that had been left for him. It was cold and stiff against his skin. His wounds hurt, he found it difficult to move to slip his arm into the sleeve but eventually he managed it. Pulling his army boots on was an equally difficult task with one arm but he managed it.

When his boots were laced he went to his new room.

The room was spacious and decorated with subtle fleck blue wallpaper. Curtains had been pulled over the boarded up windows and it had a cosy yet elegant feeling to it. The room had also been furnished for him since he had decided to finally take it. Someone had replaced the single bed with a double and there was a wardrobe and table that he didn't recognise.

Immediately he became nervous and spent the next hour checking the room out for anything hidden. He was just picking himself painfully up off the floor after checking under the bed when there was a knock on the door. He looked up. "Enter."

Under his breath he added. "If you don't plan to kill me."

The door opened and new guards stepped inside. "I am Graham K45, reporting for duty. This is Steve K46, we are your new replacement guards. I can assure you of our loyalty Sir. We have been requested to bring the prisoner to your room."

Balen smiled as Raven walked into the room. "I think we can dispense with the title of prisoner. Is it not correct that you have chosen to join us?"

Raven smiled. "I have, as we agreed. You set me free and I will stay with you."

The guards both looked at each other. Graham smiled at Raven. "Welcome to the family." Then he looked nervous as he had forgotten where he was. "I am very sorry Sir."

Balen smiled at the man's nervousness. "Sorry for what? Welcoming the mother of my heir to the family is entirely appropriate. Now leave us."

They turned and left to take up their positions further down the corridor.

The room was at the end of the corridor. His windows had been boarded up with blast thickness metal and the door itself had been lined with blast proof metal sheeting. He shut the door and leant against it.

Raven stood in the middle of the room looking around. She looked tired but she had managed to have a wash and she was dressed in a fresh overall. Her hair had been brushed but the black welts of the bruises still marked her skin. Balen had his sleeves rolled up to his shoulders as the material had been pulling on his arm and shoulder wound.

She stared in horror at the bandages. "What has happened? Have we been attacked?"

He stepped forwards and took her arm. "It was just an assassination attempt, nothing to worry about." He waited for her response, trying to think of another funny comment to make.

She touched his arm and gently ran her hand over the bandage. "Don't you ever joke about something like that again."

Balen looked tired. His face showed the pain in his shoulder and arm. He put his arms around her. "I didn't know what to say."

She leant her head carefully on his chest and he leant his head down onto hers and then kissed the top of her head. He could feel her breathing. He whispered. "Stay with me tonight, be with me tonight."

She smiled. "Gladly."

Balen looked nervous as he looked down at her. "I had the photos delivered to Frank with a warning to protect the farm. He has dealt with Crow but not in the way we had talked about. I have had intelligence that it is one of the departments of Lex MegaCorp that is stirring up trouble within TX, they were behind that assassination attempt. With your permission I would like to try to use Brandon as a bargaining tool to open up a dialogue with them."

Raven looked into Balen's deep brown eyes. "Isn't that dangerous? He has a velvet tongue and he would easily lie to save his own neck."

Balen smiled. "I know, that is why I'm having a think about it first. Once he's dead he's dead. While he's alive I can use him if I need to. Are you alright with that?"

Raven went white. "I can't see why not. As long as I don't have to see him I'll be fine about it."

Balen smiled. "If you want me to I can shoot him now and we'll give them the body but a live Brandon is going to be worth a lot more and could save lives here, mostly mine."

Raven smiled. "Then that is how it has to be."

Balen smiled. "Well then let me take your mind off of it. Are you still going to hold to what you said? You have one last chance to change your mind."

Raven kissed him.

Balen gritted his teeth and readied himself for the pain but he was determined to make the gesture. He picked her up and carried her to the bed. He switched off the light and they made love.

At first Balen heeded the doctor's words but in the throws of passion the words went completely out of his mind.

They lay in each other's arms talking and enjoying each other's company until 4am when the Compound was hit by mortar fire.

Balen rolled over, kissed Raven and stroked her hair. "My love, I must go. Stay here, please. Don't give me anything else to worry about. I need a clear head to command this. Promise?"

Raven kissed him. "I promise, I will stay here."

He rolled out of bed and grabbed for his clothes. He pulled them on and was about to leave. He pulled his pistol out of its holster, checked the clip and the slide. "Do you know how to use this?"

Raven nodded. "A bit like a shotgun?"

Balen smiled. "Yes but don't forget to take the safety off and keep it on when you aren't using it. That thing has a hair trigger. If you are in doubt about anyone, use it. I must go. I love you." He kissed her before she could speak and ran out of the door.

The guard shut the door. One guard stayed on the door the other followed Balen to his office where he picked up another pistol, loaded it and headed off downstairs.

Outside was chaos. Mortar bombs were landing at one minute regular intervals, leaving huge craters in the farm yard. The animal shed had a hole in it and there was chaos inside as the farm hands were trying to put the fire out and control the animals. Kurt was waiting for Lord Balen and shouted over the sounds of explosion. "We mucked the barns out earlier so the fire damage is minimal on the concrete. We've started firing back and we've managed to take out their two armoured vehicles that were likely to take the gate down. We are now firing on their ground troops. They are coming in waves and attacking us from all directions. The platforms you ordered set up this afternoon around the perimeter have made all the difference and we have got as much bullet proof metal as possible up there protecting our guys.

We could really use some heavier weaponry. Do I have your authority?"

Balen looked around. "Get a detachment onto moving the injured to the doctor and any non-essential personnel should have the option of either going to the shelter or helping the doctor where they can. You have my authority, bring out the heavy weaponry. How are they acting towards us?"

Kurt formulated his thoughts. "Full barrage, no let up."

Balen was expressionless. "Respond in kind, no mercy. The railguns are one shot as we can't reload, there isn't enough power so make them count. Keep some back. There could be a further attack."

Kurt ran off and he could be heard shouting commands. Balen went in the other direction ordering men to the best positions and deploying what weapons they had spare. He organised runners to carry ammunition and grabbed a rifle himself and began shooting through the barricade at those who got too close to the wall.

A detachment ran into the main building and came out with rocket launchers and railguns. They formed up around the compound and began firing. Weapons that Balen had stockpiled were used and cast aside. As he had speculated as they were all powered and only had enough charge for one shot but they did make it count. Balen climbed up a ladder, the pain was almost unbearable.

He reached the top and looked out over the countryside which was alight with gunfire and muzzle flash. There were patches of flame where their own mortars had landed and bodies lay in piles around the fence. The barrage of railgun and rocket fire decimated the area. Bodies fell in droves and swathes were cut through the approaching troops. The beams that shot from the railgun cut long lines twenty foot wide. Nothing stood when they fired. He took up position and began firing at single targets, aiming at those with the mortars.

Within half an hour there was desolation around the Compound and those outside stopped firing. There was hardly anyone left to fire back.

Balen climbed back down the ladder. Blood was trickling from his bandage and he was beginning to feel light headed. He ran over to where Kurt was gathering troops on the ground. "Report?"

Kurt looked up. "Enemy has been decimated, our casualties are in the tens and the wounded are with the doctor."

Balen smiled. "Very good. Send a unit out to mop up and collect any unused ammunition and whatever weaponry you can find. This won't be the end of it and we're now low on ammo. No mercy, don't leave any survivors. They work by infiltration, don't give them the opportunity.

Count our people out and in and know who went out and who is coming in. I want a squad on the gate. Make sure you know who our people are."

Kurt threw his head back. "And Sir, if it's not too much trouble could you report to the doctor yourself and get that wound rebound."

Balen looked down and swore. "Handle things here. I won't be long." He then walked off to the doctor's room and joined the queue of people waiting to be dealt with. The doctor saw him and rushed over. Balen held his hand up. "No, deal with the others first. I've given my orders, if I'm needed they will come for me." He stepped over to where a young woman was cradling her baby. Her arm was bleeding from a piece of glass that had dug into it. She was standing against the wall and had begun to sway a little bit. He called over to a lad in his twenties with curly blonde hair and a cheeky grin. He was holding a cloth to a wound in his arm. "You there, James, can you spare a seat for this woman?" James got up and the woman nearly fell into the seat. He then grabbed a kidney bowl and some disinfectant and began helping to clean and treat wounds starting with hers.

The doctor smiled. "It's been years since we worked together, do you fancy a new job, I could use an assistant."

Balen smiled. "Only tonight." He held his hand over an injured boy's burnt arm and concentrated. The boy stopped crying and relaxed. He then moved on to the next and the next. He bandaged some of the lesser injured people and treated the minor burns. After about an hour he stepped into a side room and started seeing people in there. Each one was cleaned up, bandaged and given healing.

It was dawn when the doctor got to Balen's wound. It was still bleeding and Balen was beginning to feel even more light headed. The doctor changed the bandages and gave Balen some healing. "Just like old times. I forget sometimes that you used to be a healer."

Balen smiled. "I never stopped. I just started trying to stop the injuries in the first place. I'd better check on how things are going outside."

Outside was quiet. The troop that had gone outside the main gate and had returned safely. There was a pile of weapons and other useful bits and pieces on the quad bike trailer. The fires had been put out and although the animals were still noisy they were quieter than they were. Guards had been posted but people were beginning to trail off to bed when they weren't needed. Balen strode over to Kurt who was talking to a young man.

Kurt looked over as Balen approached him. "The clean up was easy, very few wounded left. We've got just about every weapon out there and we'll start the body clear up in the morning unless someone comes to collect their dead. I've posted guards and the rota is sorted out. It looks like its going to be quiet now but just in case I'd kept back a Unit I didn't use in the main barrage. They are on standby. Captain Evans is with them, he's a competent commander."

Balen smiled. "You have done well. It is time for you to get some sleep."

Kurt smiled back. "If it's not too impertinent isn't it time you got some rest too, or is rest not what you have in mind?"

Balen raised an eyebrow. "As you are my oldest friend I will overlook that comment and bid you a good night for what is left of it."

As Balen crossed the farm yard he looked back. The golden light of dawn silhouetted the buildings. Smoke rose from all around the compound but it was quiet. Most people had gone to bed leaving those on guard and those on clean up duty to do their job. He opened the door and went inside. His arm and shoulder were hurting and it seemed that every muscle in his body ached. He climbed the stairs and his legs felt like lead.

The guard on his door saw him coming and opened the door for him.

Balen smiled and passed him and the guard shut the door after him. Raven looked exhausted, she ran to him when he came through the door. "I thought I'd lost you. Are you alright?"

Balen smiled. "Other than busting my stitches I'm fine. I'm sorry to have made you stay here but there was nothing you could have done."

Raven glared at him. "I said I'd stay and help, why make me stay here and be useless. I could have helped the doctor."

Balen smiled at her. "I know you would have done but there are still people here who don't know you have chosen to stay and aren't just a prisoner. There are still those who blame your people for their loved ones' death. Once you are established as my mate they will not question

371

you. If that is what you want to be?"

Raven smiled. "Didn't I prove that earlier?"

Balen kissed her on the forehead. "You did. I've seen enough death tonight, I need you Raven. It's quiet now and they took heavy losses. I need to sleep and so do you."

## 17

Balen couldn't sleep and the hours dragged by like treacle. His head was full of worries and thoughts. He kept imagining that every shadow in the new room held an assassin and his shoulder and arm pulsed pain through him.

He tried healing his shoulder, the pain eased to a dull pulsing and he shut his eyes hopefully. Moments later a sound in the room made him sit up, eyes darting about, trying to see what had made the noise.

Raven woke up too. Balen's moving about had disturbed her and when she saw him sit up she too sat up in a panic. She looked around and when she realised it was quiet she put a hand on his shoulder. His body was soaked in beads of sweat.

The room was silent, they were alone. Balen looked around but could see nobody there. "I'm just having difficulty sleeping, don't worry my love."

He put his hand over hers. "I have too much running through my head."

Raven smiled though Balen couldn't see it in the darkness. "Well, hardly surprising considering what you have to worry about. But, there is nothing you can do at the moment. You were well prepared for the attack tonight and the guards are placed. Try not to worry." She put her arm around him.

Balen turned and put his arms around her. "I'm just so tired. There is no let up. It's one worry after another then they come at me all at once. There is never time to deal with the problems on their own and one thing left cascades into plenty more serious problems. I feel like I'm spinning plates on sticks and running about to keep them all spinning. If I miss one it falls off."

Raven kissed his neck. "Well now if you'll let me I'll help with some of those plates. Tell me and it might help."

Balen took a deep breath and let it out slowly. "I miss my space when I could relax and visualise a place of peace. This has all been so fast and the world is so different now."

Raven sighed. "Why can't you do your visualisation?"

Balen thought a moment. "There isn't space or time."

Raven laughed. "Yes there is, you have to set aside that time or things will get on top of you like they are tonight. You have to find solutions, I agree. You have to keep all those people safe, fed and united but that would be a lot easier with a clear head. As you know, mistakes cost lives and you can't get them back again afterwards."

Balen breathed out sharply. "On a basic level we have to survive. I know there are individuals out there and small groups living off the land. We have made contact with some of them and helped them with equipment and medical supplies.

That in itself is contrary to Transition X's original manifesto. In essence we have deviated here from what TX was supposed to be. But I feel we have evolved to what we should be. The teachings of the Founders were quite different and that has put us at odds with the rest of the organisation. We are tolerated as my brother defends us but he too is under threat and to keep his position as High Commander he will probably have to act against me one day. I just don't know how it got this far. It was all so innocent when we used to meet up in my flat and talk about it. We wrote laws and it was a game. We were going to be saviours of the planet. My brother always wanted to be in charge so we let him. It all seemed so harmless.

Some of our own members adhere more to the original teachings. Bear in mind that some of these were written when we were off our heads on something or the other. Michael in particular was into anything he could get hold of and add to that his paranoid schizophrenia and it was a recipe for disaster. You encountered Rat when he infiltrated your place. I had my worries about sending him as his beliefs were purist TX. That is causing our own internal problems. Some of the purists don't see those of us who want to be more reasonable as members any more.

By creating what we have we have also shown Lex where we are and now that they are sorting out some of their issues in the cities they are turning to us. They have the excuse that they need the resources to keep the cities running and to rebuild so they can justify their actions to the general public.

When they thought we were living on the land and scavenging they were not concerned about us. Now that they see that we have a coherent and working organisation here we are a threat.

What is running through my mind is that survival may depend more on becoming small units who live in a similar way to how our ancestors did. Man started as a hunter gatherer. That could be where our answer lies."

Raven thought for a moment. "Would the land sustain that sort of a lifestyle for so many people now? One man living in a large enough space and only taking what is needed could. If everyone did it would they wipe out what they need to preserve to survive?"

Balen signed. "That is what is happening around the cities. There are those who have left the cities but they didn't go far. They were faced with very little wild land, few wild animals to live on and the weight of numbers of people trying to survive has wiped out the countryside or so I have heard.

Of course any farm within reach has lost its livestock to hungry raiders. A cow is food on the hoof. They don't care about breeding for the future. Meat is rare there now as the cattle and sheep were raised in those towers. When the power went they were trapped and their automatic feeders and drinkers didn't work anymore. Then they were raided. I guess the people eat very well for the first week or two. Now they are looking outwards and as they are forced to increase their range more places are being raided. They have to survive so I can't even say that I feel they are in the wrong."

Raven stroked his hair and he relaxed slightly. "Is that why you tried to take over my farm?"

Balen kissed her shoulder. "When all this started I followed the directive to get all those who were a part of the organisation into a safe haven. It was also part of the original directive to remove or assimilate any possible competition for resources. The belief was that safety in numbers and growing the community was the answer." Balen shook his head and breathed out heavily. "An idea can be good on paper and seeing how it really works only happens when you physically do it. Then you have to take into account human nature. Running this place, providing food, heat and keeping going is possible. Doing that and facing opposition like we did last night, I don't know. I used most of our stockpile. If we were left alone to get on with things we would stand a chance.

Mankind is warlike and acquisitive. That can't be shut down like a computer program."

Raven thought for a moment. "So what are you suggesting?"

Balen shut his eyes and thought. "I'm not, that is the problem. I can't see a solution. If we carry on we'll have the internal struggle and we will also be targeted by Lex. If we go back to the original idea we will be no better than Lex as we would then be making sure that only we will survive. Then we'd have to go back to taking from and destroying those around us. I can't break this number of people down into sustainable hunter gatherer groups as the countryside can't support us. It might in time if we replant the forests and let animals become feral so that we can hunt them but not with the population we have."

Raven sighed. "Don't you mean had?"

Balen paused. "What do you mean?"

Raven took a deep breath. "How many died before all this in natural disasters? How many died in the original switch off? How many have died since? I've never read any TX teachings but I have read others and I'm no scholar but what comes to mind is that the TX philosophy is one man's interpretation of what he has seen. That has to be altered by who he is, what he has experienced and his preconceived ideas. The original idea will still be under there but what if the original meaning has been lost?"

Balen thought on that one. "Well the original meaning was put together by my brother and a few friends as I've already told you. We had heard of Transition Towns and we wanted our version of it all."

Raven smiled. "I'd like to know more about you."

Balen smiled. "I was a healer and I wrote poetry, badly. I took on basic work to feed myself and lived by the sea. Hardly the credentials for all this is it?"

Raven laughed. "Do you want me to answer that or are you asking yourself? How can you doubt any of it? Look around you. Forget what is happening because others are attacking this place. There are a group of people here who have managed to hold it together and build something sustainable out of the chaos. You hold it together because you don't ask anything of it. There is no master plan here other than putting food on the table, a roof over people's heads and giving them purpose. It's the same as you doing the jobs to keep yourself fed. It's the actions, wants and needs of outside influences that are upsetting the balance here. Waters are still until someone throws a pebble in."

Balen thought a while. "So what can I do?"

Raven rested her head against his. "Live day to day and deal with the problems that arise. As you say there are no real wild lands to rely on for hunting and gathering, well not for this many people. So the only answer is farming and that is what you are doing."

Balen shook his head. "But what about the rest of it?"

Raven closed her eyes. "Lex is a huge mega corporation sustained by finance and a structure that is supported by the way things were. That it has to worry about places as small as this means that its structure is breaking down. Someone or something has to hold things together and the fight we have here may seem insignificant but what it is doing is giving the world the opportunity to put itself right. The problems of the world caused Nemesis to shut down computers. We can only hope that out of the chaos and what Lex is doing something new and better will arise. The more unreasonable Lex becomes the more likely that is to happen. All we have to do is survive and keep these people safe. That is a big enough task isn't it?"

Balen pulled away from her slightly and kissed her. As they held each other and concentrated on each other so completely when they made love the problems they faced were set aside if only for a short time. They were gentle because they were both broken, but they were passionate and in the silence they both found a joy they had been looking for, even though it had taken a very long time.

Back at Raven's farm darkness had fallen. Everyone was in a state of high alert. Voices were raised and nerves frayed. Midnight passed and the early hours but at 4am the first gunshot rang out. Diana had been standing beside Wish. The bullet caught her in the side of her head and she realised too late that she had been standing in a clear line of sight. She fell to the ground as Reko sounded the alarm. He had a single bell that had been found in a box in one of the store rooms. It had been hastily screwed to the fence. Its sound cut through the night air.

Those who were sleeping were soon awake, already dressed they leapt out of beds and prepared to defend their home. An explosion rang out as the first mortar landed in the yard. It erupted around the tents and set them on fire. The second mortar hit the house and blew the front door and hallway in. Then a mortar hit the back field defences and blew them to pieces.

378

Another was aimed directly at the front gate. It erupted in burning shards of wood as the mortar impacted on the van parked behind it, blowing the van backwards.

Frank ran to the front fence defences and looked out through a gap. He couldn't see anyone in the forest across the road and he couldn't find any targets to aim at. Another mortar hit the barn and punched through the roof. There was pandemonium inside as the hay caught light.

Ralph ran inside the barn and pushed through the animals to open the back doors to let them out as the smoke and fire raged inside. He let the goats and the sheep out but as he was letting the cows out the pressure of them pushing through the narrow exit crushed him against the wall. He struggled to get out but lost his footing. He fell and was trampled under their hooves.

The animals ran in a panic up to the top field, breaking through the first fence, they didn't stop until they got over the ridge line.

When the front barricade was destroyed there was a rush of people dressed in military clothing and carrying assault rifles from the forest. Frank fired continuously but there were too many of them. They didn't take prisoners, they shot anyone they found. Reko and Matt fell by the front gate, Steve tried to run for cover but was cut down as he opened the stable door. Wish was shot in the head as he was spotted cowering behind the front fence.

Darren had already died in the doorway when the mortar had hit.

Inside the house Shylock was watching what was going on out of the window. He grabbed Cheryl and baby Chloe and went to the back door. He ripped down the boarding and opened the door. He was about to drag Cheryl out when she stopped him and ran along the corridor. She opened the door of the medical room. The Doc and Storm were getting ready to receive injured. Shylock screamed to them. "Get out now, we've been overrun. The gate has been blown in and most people are dead." He then dragged Cheryl and Chloe out into the night, followed by the Doc and Storm. They crouched down in the shadows and waited. When they thought the way was clear they ran for the bushes and disappeared into the night.

The dark figures made their way across the farm yard shooting anything that moved. Frank had ducked down behind the camper van which had been moved back inside as it still had petrol in the tank. He carefully opened the side door and slipped inside. The key was above the sun visor, he tipped it quickly and it fell down into his hand. He put it in the lock and turned the key. The engine started and he put his foot to the floor. The van had been blown away from the entrance so he nearly had a clear run out onto the road.

The engine screamed as he sped out of the yard and the camper crashed into the van, knocking it sideways enough to get through. He didn't stop, he drove off down the road as a mortar was fired after him. It fell short but the impact made the vehicle jump off the road. Frank fought to keep control of the vehicle and sped off into the night.

In the town the Mart was under attack. Mortars screamed over the gates and landed in the courtyard blowing the stalls and units to pieces and igniting anything that would burn. Two mortar shells simultaneously hit the front gate and exploded in a shower of flames and shards of splintered wood leaving a huge gaping hole in the Mart's defences. Then the troops moved in and shot anyone who moved. They marched directly to the storage sheds and opened the doors. A black lorry reversed up the road. The driver stayed in the cab, other troops opened up the back. The troops started coming out of the storage shed carrying bags and sacks followed by others carrying other equipment. They loaded it all into the back of the truck.

They acted in silence, no orders were given and every individual knew exactly what they were doing. The troops withdrew and two men carrying a box went inside. They set the explosives and the charges, lit the fuse and ran out to the waiting vehicle. The troops got into the waiting lorry. The one remaining outside shut the door and ran to jump into the cab. The lorry drove away.

Carl and his father watched it go from where they were hiding up in their office. They didn't have time to react more than stare in shock as the explosives detonated and the whole building erupted in a fireball.

In the cab of the lorry the driver turned to the passenger. He was a middle aged thick set short haired man, the other a younger sandy haired individual. Both were dressed in the uniform of Lex Corporation. He sighed. "That was smoothly done. Then again for them to stand up to the might of the Corporation was a joke."

The passenger watched the flames in the side mirror. "What did they do to incur the wrath of the LexCorp then? They didn't tell us at the briefing."

The driver laughed. "The owner is a well-known felon who has been running a slave trade. He has also had his men ambushing Lex Corp transports of food and equipment destined for our bases in the north."

The passenger smiled. "There is one less scumbag to worry about tonight then. What about the other missions, any idea what is going on there? It looked like there was a major move out tonight."

The driver shook his head. "I don't know much about them. I know that all major suppliers and those who have benefitted from goods from the Mart were targeted.

Have you seen the new facilities Lex are building? Still they won't get the people out of the camps. I've heard that the facilities are pretty basic and the death toll has been pretty high. You know, rioting and such. The new buildings are for their own people, those in charge. That is not going to help the situation."

The passenger jumped slightly as a second explosion cut through the night. "That must have been the old canisters at the back going up. Yea, I've seen the new facilities. I'm not so sure about that list they are drawing up of those eligible for moving to them though. It looks to me as though they are only going to take those useful to them."

The driver smiled. "As I said, they aren't for just anyone. Well we'd better make sure we are very, very useful to them then." They drove off into the night.

Frank headed down the road. He saw the lorry coming along the main road so he turned his lights off and waited until it had gone past. He then switched the engine on again and drove to the village. He saw the Mart burning from miles off. As he drew up into the town he parked his van and joined the locals trying to put the fire out with buckets of water.

He pushed his way through the splintered ruin of the gate and made his way through the burning stalls. Hot burning timber fell around him and the smoke was choking. All around there were bodies, some charred, some still on fire. He was watching for any sign of life. He found none.

He was almost to the back of the compound when he heard something. It was a feint cry from the rubble where a wall had fallen down. Without thinking he ran over and started digging where the café used to be. He found an arm and followed it down to the body and finally he managed to pull the café owner out of the rubble. The man was choking and his arm was badly burnt. Frank threw him over his shoulder and carried him out of the compound.

Once outside he started looking for a doctor but there didn't seem to be one around. The wounded were being tended by locals who had little more than bandages and water. He looked at the man's arm and shook his head. "Hey there, you need help here, do you know anywhere that you can find that help? We've lost the farm, I can't take you there."

The man choked and a trickle of blood flowed from the corner of his mouth. "Take me to Lord Balen's Compound. He needs to know about the farm. Please, take me there." The man passed out. Frank stood in the middle of the street. Smoke was billowing around him and the searing heat from the burning mart was hot on his face. He grabbed the man and carried him to his camper, opened the back and laid him on the seat. Then he jumped inside and drove off.

At the TX Compound everyone woke up early and began clearing up the mess of the night before. The animals were fed and watered and five young men had climbed up onto the roof and were fixing the hole with spare box profile metal sheets and bolts.

A shout rang out warning the Compound that someone was coming. Balen was just leaving the building, Raven by his side. They ran to the outer defences and climbed up the ladder.

In the distance coming down the road through the desolation was a blue transit van. It had the Lex Corporation logo on the side. A white piece of material was tied to its aerial.

Faces looked at Balen expectantly, the safeties were flicked off on weapons all around. Balen looked down at the twisted, burnt and broken bodies which lay on the ground outside the compound. The van drove carefully through them and drew up fifty yards from the gate. The driver's door opened and a middle aged man with short blonde hair got out.

He had his hands up and he was wearing a white paper overall. "I've come for the bodies. Please don't shoot me."

Balen stepped up to the edge and looked down. "Take your dead. I want it known by anyone you speak to we would not have killed anyone if they had left us in peace. We just want to live."

The driver looked around at the desolation. "So did they. They were only following orders." He looked up at

Balen with a pleading expression.

Balen looked down at him. "We only want to live in peace here. We want to keep our animals, grow our crops and raise our children. If you bring war to us, we will give you war back. If you leave us alone we will leave you alone. I have dead in here too. They have families and loved ones as your people have families and loved ones. We are not challenging any regime, we are not harming anyone. Why were we attacked?"

The driver spat on the ground. "Scum! You claim to live in peace on the face of it but what about the drivers of the lorries you hijacked. We know that you were supplied by the Mart, you and the rest of your rebel scum.

Many good men died when those convoys were captured, very few survived. You are worse than Road Pirates. I can tell you now, we will be back and in greater numbers. Oh and your precious Mart has been destroyed and your leader is dead. He and his Mart went up in flames last night. So let us see how you raise your animals now. So, go on scum you can kill me. What do I have to live for? Four of my sons are dead down here."

Balen climbed down the ladder and went to the gate. "Open the gate I will meet this man face to face. Raven was behind him. He pushed her to the side. "Guards, I'm sorry Raven, hold her." Before she could react two of the guards grabbed her arms. The doors opened and Balen walked out.

He walked towards the man, stepping over bodies until he stood in front of the man. The driver looked stunned. The passenger in the van was sitting bolt upright trying to see and hear what was going on. Balen stopped about three meters from the man and looked him in the eye. "We do not know what you are talking about. We have traded at the Mart for goods that we have produced here. We have bought goods that we have paid or traded for. This was all done in good faith. We have no idea who the suppliers are to the Mart. As we trade for goods it is to be assumed that their stock was obtained in the same way. That is the extent of our dealings with them. As far as I know it the farms around here all supply the Mart and the villagers and other farmers buy from it."

The driver spat at Balen. "Yea right, so you aren't going out there and hijacking our vehicles then and our goods aren't turning up on the Mart's shelves? Didn't you think we'd notice, didn't you think we wouldn't mark the cans with invisible marker and then go and check it with a detector pen. You are scum  and very stupid if you think that you think you can stand there and lie to me.

We all have families and friends who have suffered because of the food supplies that didn't arrive. You lying bastard. So, are you going to kill me too? I come in peace, we're not armed. All we want are our dead back so that we have something for their widows and families to bury."

Lord Balen drew himself up to his full height. "We traded with the Mart in good faith. We do not work for the Mart. I am a Commander of Transition X I answer solely to High Commander Archangel. I have no other master or boss. I have a written trade agreement with the Mart whereby we supply our excess goods to them for a reasonable credit in exchange for goods from the Mart in return. I can show you that agreement."

The driver threw his head back and laughed. "Alright, go on show me that agreement. Here, take this pen, write down what it said and I want someone from inside to bring out your copy so that I can see that you aren't going to put it together when you go in there." He went to the van and pulled out a piece of paper and a pen.

Balen called back through the gate. "Raven, I want you to go to the room next to my office. In the top drawer of the filing cabinet there is a folder marked "Mart". I want you to look in that and bring me the agreement we signed with Carl and his father." He then walked over to the van and took the paper and pen and began to write.

As he was writing the driver didn't think that he could

see him giving the passenger a sideways glance. Balen was alert though and watching them both as best he could. He heard the click of the glove box being opened and he was already moving as the passenger drew his pistol out and fired.

The bullet missed as Balen dived in front of the van.

The snipers on the fence didn't miss. Two shots rang out, two bodies fell, one in the van, the other beside it.

Balen heard the shots and ran full pelt for the gates. They were slammed shut behind him as he dived through. He caught his breath and panted. "There's no way they aren't going to use that against us. So now we've shot two of their employees under a flag of truce. It gets better and better."

Raven came running back from the building when she had heard the shots. She ran to Balen and slapped him on the face. "What do you think you are doing walking out there?"

Balen's stare turned on her and his eyes were cold. He grabbed her wrist and pushed her up against the back of the gate. "Don't you dare raise your hand to me in that fashion again. You do not speak to me like that. I am the Commander of this facility and you will treat me with respect.

Remember your place or I will have you shot." He glared at her then as he turned and nobody could see his face, only her, he mouthed. "Sorry dear" and winked at her.

He didn't loosen his grip on her wrist and dragged her back to the building with him. "I want the guard doubled and get a crew out there, pile the bodies up in the van. I want Alvin to write a statement of what happened and have it on my desk in half an hour. You have that time to clear the bodies up. Send an armed guard out with the clean up crew."

The young lad saluted. "Very good Sir, will that be all?"

Balen smiled. "For now."

The boy ran off and he was heard calling for Alvin.

Balen pointed to another of the troops. "Fetch me my Head of Security." He went inside dragging Raven with him and up to his office. The guards saluted as he passed them and closed the door behind the pair as they went inside. Balen turned on Raven. "Don't you realise how fragile your position is here? They will kill you if they think you are influencing me."

She looked at him with a blank expression. "I didn't get a chance to think. I just was so damned angry and I thought I'd lost you."

He stroked her hair. "I know and I would have done the same but you do have to understand your position. I don't want to lose you either and there are some very dangerous people in camp. Their loyalty will always hang on a thread as that is who they are. Give them one excuse to spark a revolution and I'll have more trouble on my hands than I can handle. The situation is over, we will not speak of it again." He grabbed the back of her head and roughly pulled her over to him. "I love you, that is never in any question." He kissed her passionately. "Now I must prepare to speak to my Head of Security and try to get some sort of plan as to how we are going to defend ourselves. There's a desk in the next room. I can't have you with me in the meeting so can I ask you to try to come up with some idea of how we are going to feed the animals now that we've lost the Mart."

Raven went into the room next door. There was a timid looking woman dressed in a smartly pressed business suit sitting behind one desk. The other desk was empty. She looked up when Raven came in then looked down nervously. "Good morning Ma'am."

Raven smiled as the woman cautiously looked up. "Good Morning, I'm Raven. My Lord Balen has requested that I look at the file which has the maps of this area. May I use this desk?"

The young woman jumped in her chair when spoken

to. "Of course, I will bring it to you. Would you like a cup of tea or something? I am Maria."

Raven smiled kindly and the woman relaxed. "I would love one if it is no trouble."

The woman smiled. "No trouble at all I am just going to take one in to Lord Balen."

The camper van sped along the road. Frank was careful to avoid any potholes and made the journey as smooth as possible. It was early morning when the café owner moaned and came around. Frank pulled the van over and went to check him over. He lifted the man's head up. "I can't give you any water or anything like that. I am sorry."

The man choked, his voice was hoarse from the smoke. He was mumbling and barely conscious. "That doesn't matter. All that matters is telling Raven what has happened at the farm."

Frank looked stunned. "Raven, what does Raven have to do with it?"

The man mumbled and dropped in and out of consciousness for a few minutes then he came around again. "They will want to know what happened to her friends and the animals."

Frank shook his head. "You are talking nonsense. What do you mean "they" will want to know?"

The man came around fully. "I told you that if she was with Lord Balen you would not be able to get her back. I'm sure I did. She was Balen's prisoner." He passed into unconsciousness then came around again. "She isn't now."

Frank shook him awake. "Where is she now?"

The man choked. "She is with Lord Balen."

Frank was beginning to get irritated. "You said she wasn't his prisoner anymore."

The man licked his dry lips. "She isn't. She had time to talk to Lord Balen and to see what we are trying to achieve and she joined us. She isn't a prisoner now. Since Crow cheated on her she has been Lord Balen's lover."

Frank choked. "I thought he raped her?"

The man choked. "That was at the start, all change now. That is why I have been warning you. Where do you think all the information I have been selling you has come from?"

Frank shook his head in disbelief. "From Raven, well I never."

The man licked his lips and choked. "No, from Lord Balen. Do you know where to go?"

Frank was looking at a map book. "I was trying to work that one out but I am hoping you'd give me directions. What is your name?"

The man spluttered a little. "I'm Dan, show me the map and I'll point it out."

Frank showed him the map and he pointed to a location about twenty miles away. The man choked again and passed out. Frank let him lay back onto the seat and jumped into the driver's seat and put his foot to the floor.

Balen was sitting in his office. He had files in front of him and he was making notes. Kurt had just left when a guard knocked on the door and entered. Balen looked up and the guard stood to attention. "There is a van at the gates. The driver wants to speak to you. He says his name is Frank and he has the café owner, Dan Franks, from the Mart with him and he's unconscious. He says he has information for you."

Balen got up slowly and thoughtfully. "Take Frank to the interrogation room and our man to the Doctor. Check the van over and park it in the garage."

The guard left and Balen thought for a moment and looked out of the window. He then left the room and was about to go downstairs just as Maria came in with his tea. He hesitated for a moment. "Put it on my desk. Thank you." He then went down the stairs slowly, collecting his thoughts and made his way to the interrogation room.

There were two guards on the door when he arrived. They unlocked the door and he walked in. They locked the door behind him.

Frank was sitting on a plain chair with a table in front of him. There was a second chair between the table and the door. Frank looked up. "So you are Lord Balen. I have heard a lot about you."

Frank made to stand up but Balen held his hand up to stop him. Balen walked to the table and sat down on the chair opposite. He crossed his legsand relaxed back onto the chair. "I thank you for bringing Dan back, he is a good man. You also mentioned you have information."

Frank relaxed back as well. "So apparently do you?"

Balen smiled, his look was slightly roguish. "You can ask questions, I might not answer. You are going to want to get one question off your chest to start with so we might as well not beat about the bush."

Frank looked puzzled. "No threats, no animosity, now I am nervous. I have heard a lot about you."

Balen raised an eyebrow. "And it is probably all true. But, you Frank are not my enemy. My enemies need to fear me. As long as you keep it this way you have nothing to fear from me. So ask."

Frank's expression softened. "Do you have Raven a prisoner here?"

Balen smiled, there was a softness in his look that made Frank unnerved. "Raven is here but she is no prisoner. She stopped being a prisoner a while ago now."

Frank sat up straight. "Dan said that she has been your lover since she found out about Crow. Did you order the photographs sent to me?"

Balen breathed in. "I would have done but in this case she asked me to."

Frank glared at Balen. "Is that why she chose to stay with you? Because she felt that she had nothing to go home to?"

Balen smiled. "No, I don't think so. At least I hope not." There was a softness in his eyes as he spoke about her that wasn't lost on Frank.

Frank took a deep breath. "It looks like you took a lot

of damage last night. We did as well. Thank you for the warning by the way. They came in force and wiped us out." Frank suddenly looked tired and broken. "There was nothing I could do. Nothing much any of us could do. They attacked with mortars and the gate was splinters. Anyone on the gate was shot as the first wave of troops came through. The Colours, one of our groups, had moved their camp into the yard for protection. They were hit by the mortar fire. I don't think any of them could have survived that. Then the barn went up in flames. I saw Ralph running for it so I'm hoping he let the animals out. I was trapped in a corner behind the van so I jumped in and got out. Everyone I could see what dead."

Balen looked at him kindly. "There was nothing you could do against their firepower. Nobody expected the amount of weaponry they had with them. Or their determination."

Frank took a deep breath. "Can I see Raven?"

18

Balen and Frank sat in the interrogation room. Balen looked at the wall over Frank's head. "I would have said yes with no reservations if you had not just told me about what happened at the farm. It will break her heart if we cannot at least find her pony. She has spoken about him."

Frank glared at Balen. "They shot her pony when they captured her."

Balen looked furious. "That would be my fault then. I put a price on her head and she was brought in by a bounty hunter. I did not know any of the details. It is now even more important that I bring back as many animals as I can."

Frank leant forwards. "I would not presume to tell you your business but if we are going to catch terrified animals I would say that Raven is the best person to do it. They know her and might come to her."

Balen raised an eyebrow. "That may be true but I will not risk her life. She will not leave this compound unless I escort her. Frank raised an eyebrow. "Do you fear that she would run away? Are you telling the truth or are you counting on terror to get her to say what you want to hear?"

Balen laughed. "You are right that I fear losing her. I have buried a wife, I do not plan to lose her as well. But there is truth in what you say and also I know she would want to go. If she wants to go, she will go.

She didn't abandon you by the way. I wouldn't let her go to start with of course. She was my prisoner. We have had so much to deal with." He took a deep breath, put his hands on his knees and winced slightly with the pain from his shoulder and arm and got up. "I will get someone to bring you food and drink. You look like you have had a rough time. When you have spoken to Raven I'll sort out a room where you can get some sleep."

Balen left the room and went back to his office. As he went in he asked his guard to bring Raven to him. Moments later she knocked and entered the room. When the guard had shut the door Balen went over to her and gently put his arms around her, being careful of her injured arm. He looked down at her. "I have news that is going to be very upsetting. I've no easy way of telling you so I'll tell you straight. I warned the people at the farm but it wasn't enough. They were attacked. Frank is here and he would like to talk with you. Do you want to see him?"

Tears ran down Raven's face and she buried her head in Balen's chest. He wrapped his arms around her protectively. "My love, if I could do anything to make this right I would. We will of course go and bring back any survivors and round up the animals and bring them back here."

Raven pushed back from his chest. "Thank you. I had better speak with Frank. He may know how things are but he is not going to believe it unless I tell him and make him believe it."

She followed Balen back to the interrogation room and they went in together. Balen stood back and Raven went over and hugged Frank. "I am so glad that you are alive. I have heard about the farm. We should get back there as soon as possible and see what we can salvage and round up. Will you come with us?"

Frank looked from Raven to Balen. Raven turned and looked at Balen who stepped forwards. She reached up and he put his hand in hers. She then looked at Frank. "I found out about Crow. I had had my suspicions all along but he overstepped the mark there.

When Balen's agent confirmed it I made my own decision."

Frank looked from Balen to Raven. "Has he drugged you? Are you being threatened? This was the man who raped you for heaven's sake."

Raven looked up at Balen who gripped her hand gently. He nodded. "You can tell him the truth."

She looked over at Frank and smiled. "No, he didn't. I helped him with the subterfuge which got his people to believe I had been punished for what we did to the people from here. Frank, we killed them and they were supposed to be on a reconnaissance mission. It was people like Rat and Stick who took it to excess and we fought back. But innocent people were amongst them."

Frank glared at Balen. "Well that is a fine piece of brainwashing. I have to say you have done a remarkable job with her. You co-wrote the original documentation. Much of it was your idea. So Raven, what do you think of that? He's no hero. He caused this."

Balen looked stunned. "How did you know about that? Raven knows about this already. We were drunk one night and came up with the answer to the world's problems. We created a web site and by the morning had thousands of members. We didn't think anything of it until the world went to hell in a handcart and suddenly we had our own very enthusiastic army."

Raven stood up. She leant on her injured arm to do it and almost screamed in pain. Balen stepped forwards to help her, Frank almost leapt around the desk. Raven put a hand out to stop Frank. "You mean well, I know that. I have seen the good that this man is trying to achieve. We all believe things when we are young and have little experience of the world and people. I would judge him by what he is doing now. He has altered what he wrote. He has helped you and all of us. How did you know about his past?"

Frank looked down. "I have been doing a little research since we found out about Transition X. That is irrelevant. It is easy for him to tell you he loves you when it gives him what he wants."

Balen smiled and looked down at Raven. "You may not believe it but I do love her. At first she was my prisoner and I was glad of it to give my people retribution. I wanted her knowledge as well as being able to deny it to you. Then my people tried to take their own revenge on her. So I made it appear that I had made her pay for what you had done to us. We spent a lot of time together and I told her the truth.

I'll tell you now and you know that it would be unwise to let this information leave this room."

Frank nodded.

"My reputation is engineered. I needed it to control these people. It is their only hope to be a cohesive group and it stopped them killing each other. I told Raven and she has seen the truth of it and helped me on occasion to add to the myth that is Lord Balen. The character I created all those years ago.

When we found out about Crow she was free to leave to return to the farm and deal with the situation. She chose to stay and asked me to deliver the photographs to you.

She chose freely to be my lover and that is now accepted in the eyes of all here. Some may resent it but they will not dare to oppose me over it."

He took a deep breath and pulled himself up to his full height. "I do not ask nor need your approval. The situation is clear. Raven has chosen to be with me and I with her. We are wasting valuable time here. Frank, as you seem to have some difficulty in accepting our current situation I am going to ask you to remain here. You are our guest but I will have to put you in a cell. We will continue this conversation on our return."

Raven looked up at Balen as she stepped closer to him. "You aren't going."

Balen looked down at her. "Why not dear, I'm not letting you go by yourself."

Raven smiled at him. "You are going to send some of your men with me. You would be too great a prize for Lex to get hold of. I on the other hand am your prisoner and the worst that would happen to me is that I'd be released from your clutches. I'm sure I'd find my way back. So, no argument, I'm going and you are not. I would ask that you let Frank go with me. If he believes that I want to escape then let me have the opportunity to do so. Only then can I show him that I am telling the truth."

Balen looked down and smiled at her. "If that is what you want. I will send a detachment of twenty men with you. Go there quickly, take what you need and return at once."

Half an hour later Frank and Raven were in the camper van parked in front of the gates. The lorry was behind them and a people carrier behind that.

They were fuelled with what was almost the last of the petrol and they were ready to go.

Balen stood next to where Raven was sitting. "Now it is me who should be slapping you for doing something stupid. Don't throw away what we have by getting yourself killed."

Raven smiled. "I have no intention of doing that."

The engines started up and they drove off down the road trying to navigate the craters until they got to a smooth stretch. Then they put the foot to the floor and tore down the road. They passed Road Pirates and other people but they were left alone.

It took nearly two hours to get back to the farm. As they approached everything was quiet, there were no vehicles about. Frank parked the van and got out. "I'm going to scout around first. Stay here and when I signal bring the men up." Raven nodded. He slipped into the trees and then crossed the road directly opposite the main gate. He then disappeared into the darkness.

The bodies were still laid about in the yard but all was silent. He turned and waved the others in.

Raven walked up to the gate, circled by the guards who would not accept her orders to do anything else. As she stepped through the gate she saw Reko's body, he was face up with his eyes open. She crouched down and shut his eyes as the tears fell down onto him. Frank caught her arm and pulled her up. "We cannot spend time on that. You are going to see things your really don't want to see. Come on, move it!"

The men with them were loading the bodies into the van.

Raven followed Frank across the yard and went into the barn. It was burnt out and the damp straw was smouldering. It was empty other than Ralph's body broken and laying by the open barn door.

Up on the field there were bodies of animals laying where they had been shot. Raven turned away shaking her head. "Frank, we can't risk taking them even for meat, they could have been poisoned."

Frank looked stunned. "You know I never thought of that."

They were leaving the field when they heard a thundering noise behind them. A herd of goats came scampering across the field and nearly pushed Raven over in their haste to be the closest one to her. She smiled immediately. "Hey my darlings so where did you hide? Well done. Come on, we have a new home for you." She walked off down the field with the goats following her. They crossed the yard and as the troops opened the back of the lorry they trotted inside and began to eat the hay left there for them. They shut the door and went back to look for more animals.

A search of the field found two cows who had managed to evade being shot but none of the sheep had survived. They were leading the cows across the yard when Raven heard a whimpering. She left Frank with the cows and went to find out what had made the noise. There was a scratching at the stable door and when she opened it

Oberon leapt out. He knocked her backwards and she fell badly on her shoulder and cried out in pain. Oberon was on top of her trying to lick her but all she could do was lay there as flashing lights and searing pain cut into her. Frank got there as soon as he could and pulled the excited dog off. He grabbed a piece of twine, put a lead on the dog and handed him to one of the soldiers who took him off to the van. Another of Balen's men had taken the cows.

Frank helped Raven up by her good arm. She put a hand on his arm to steady herself. "I'm alright, it just caught me by surprise. Now the bit I've been dreading. I can't hear anything and that isn't a good sign."

She went to the stable and opened the door. It was quiet inside. She stepped through the door and was met by a snort from Blade. He pawed the ground and stamped. She opened the inner stable door and went into his stable and threw her arms around his neck. Then she reached for his head collar and leading rein, led him out of the stable and tacked him up.

Frank was watching and furrowed his brow. Raven laughed. "It is the easiest way of carrying his tack, he can carry it. You didn't think I planned to ride home did you? Go on, now you take him to the lorry. I'll get the others."

Frank looked nervous. "You won't find your pony in there."

Raven looked down. "I know, I remember him collapsing under me and saw he was dead before I crawled off."

Frank looked surprised. "And you forgive Lord Balen for that?"

Raven looked serious. "I laid it on pretty thick when I first got there about how much I cared about the pony to try to make them feel guilty. Balen put a contract on me, not on my pony." She went inside and came out with the other two ponies and the heavy horse. They were all tacked up, including rugs and ready to go. Balen's men took them off to the lorry.

The pigs were loaded into the animal trailer and one of Balen's men siphoned off some petrol for the old Land Rover and hitched it up. They also started loading up as much feed and hay as they could into the back of it and as many vehicles as they had petrol for. They waited with their doors open for anything else they could find that was useful.

Raven took a deep breath and walked through the devastated front door and hallway into the house. "Frank, I want you to check what bodies are here. If there is a chance anyone survived I want to know. You there, go to the medical room and pack everything up, bring it all with you but be careful with it. You, pack up the kitchen. You over there, go to that shed over there, see the one beside the stable. There are plastic boxes stacked in there, take them all. I need someone to empty this cupboard, it has all the cheese making and other equipment."

She went to the stairs and Frank caught her arm. "Are you sure?"

She winced in pain and looked down for a moment. "Yes, the strength we have is our fight for the future. However much something hurts we have to survive and not only that, we have to survive well." She turned and went up the stairs. She took a deep breath at the top and opened her bedroom door. The bed wasn't made and Tracy's clothes were strewn across the bed and floor. Two empty coffee cups were in there, one on top of the wardrobe. She took a deep breath, took a suitcase off of the top of the wardrobe and started filling it with her clothes, jewellery and personal things which she found hidden away. She didn't have much so she managed to fit it all in.

She put the suitcase outside in the hallway and went through the other rooms, packing up anything that looked useful. Balen's men were still with her so they carried the cases and bags and helped her gather up the bits and pieces. "Grab soap and any other cosmetics. Until we can make our own we could have problems getting that sort of thing. Has someone emptied the pantry?" They looked blank but one of the men ran downstairs.

It took an hour to gather anything useful from the house. She had a last look around. The kitchen had already been gutted of anything moveable. They all assembled in the yard and got back in their vehicles. The tractor rolled up to join them driven by one of Balen's men who looked particularly pleased with himself. Raven smiled.

They started engines and drove off as fast as they could and headed back to the Compound. They drove for nearly an hour in silence before Frank spoke. "You can speak freely, is he telling the truth?"

Raven looked at Frank. "I truly and honestly love that man. He is absolutely on the level about what he has said to you. He's up against a lot of opposition from his own people as well as the others. Will you support him?"

Frank was looking at the road intently. "I can't believe you are asking me that."

Raven looked down. "You mean you won't help because of what he's done before?"

Frank smiled. "No, I don't believe you have to ask me to help out when he's obviously the one person we need now. He is the person I least expected to turn out that way."

Raven smiled. "I'm glad to hear it. I need you with us Frank, we're up against so much now."

They had an untroubled journey back to the Compound and all the vehicles stopped outside and were taken over by a crew that had been waiting so that they could be checked underneath for any devices or anything that shouldn't be there before they were let in.

Raven and Frank went inside with some of the men. Balen was waiting by the gate. He closed his eyes and breathed out, shaking his head when he saw Raven who ran to him. He threw his arms around her as Frank looked on and he spoke quietly so only Raven and Frank who was trying to overhear could hear. "Raven, please don't ever go out there without me again."

Raven smiled. "Hopefully I won't need to. There were survivors. We didn't find Cheryl, Shylock and their daughter Chloe and possibly Doc and Storm. They will probably be a long way away from the place by now but one day we may see them again."

Balen wiped away Raven's tears with his fingers. "You'll know by now. I'm so, so sorry about your pony. I never meant him to be hurt."

Raven smiled. "I've known about the pony from the start. So now I'm going to ride Blade." They were just unloading Blade from the horsebox and he came out very much fire and thunder. He reared up, the feathers on his feet flying in the wind and the man trying to hold him was having great difficulty. "Excuse me a minute." Raven walked over, took the rope and put her hand up. Blade dropped to his feet and she put her hand on his forehead. "Be still my boy, you are home now, you are safe. Go with him."

She handed the rope back to the man. "He'll be fine but don't trust him with your back turned, he bites." She smiled and the man walked off with him.

Raven went back to Balen and Frank. She smiled at Balen. "Frank has agreed to help us."

Balen smiled. "Have you now, so you don't think I'm a murdering bastard after all? If not, why not? I have a reputation to maintain here."

Frank looked down. "I know you Balen for what you are." He met Balen's surprised stare. "If you have found the best in yourself, then I'm prepared to give you the benefit of the doubt."

Balen lifted his head. "Mac, I want you to get a troop together to get that equipment unloaded. Raven, you mentioned some of the things you had planned to set up at your place. Its time this place became more of a home for these people. Take what rooms you want and if you want to ask for volunteers I'll sanction whoever chooses to take on those duties, tasks or whatever you want to call them."

There was a shout from the gate as the last of the vehicles had pulled inside.

Balen leapt up the ladder, nearly falling off which meant he jarred his injured shoulder. He swore and climbed the last couple of rungs then took a look over the edge. He called down. "Frank, get up here now. I think you have some friends who have just arrived." Raven made a move for the ladder. Balen called down. "Don't you dare, you need to rest that arm."

She smiled as Frank climbed the ladder.

He shouted down to her. "It's Cheryl and the rest of them. They must have followed us down the road."

Doc called up to them as he got out of the battered Austin Cambridge. "You could have left me my camper van. I saw you driving off in it so when you came back I knew it was you. I hope it is in one bit."

Frank cast a nervous glance over his shoulder at the dented front wing. "Well, mostly."

The doors swung open and they drove inside. Balen raised an eyebrow. "Well I suppose we ought to start sorting out some couples quarters then."

Raven was all smiles. "It gets better, she was our cook and cleaner."

Balen looked down and smiled. "Well that is a result. Do you want to work with her then to try to make this place more of a home?"

Raven smiled. "Of course I do. After all, we don't just want to survive, we need to make this a life."

Nobody was anywhere near them, Balen sighed. "I think I got my life back the day you walked in here. Now go or we'll never get this place sorted out."

Raven went off with Cheryl to look around and discuss which rooms to use and places for people to stay and Balen walked over to Frank. "Well I know your combat skills are excellent. Could you teach those skills?"

Frank looked puzzled. "You want me to teach?"

Balen looked down. "Many of my men here are keen enough but they are not combat trained. I've taught them the best I can but I need someone who can give them a better chance of surviving. These people are artists, writers, healers and spiritual people who believed in a green and better world. There are some of them who are trained, some real thugs and anarchists and some who are survival specialists. We need to start using their skills and developing the skills of the others."

Frank laughed. "You even sound like Raven."

Balen smiled. "I'll take that as a compliment." He then walked back to the house with Frank. "So would you like an office?"

Frank looked around. "Any chance of a shed. I think it would be best to set up a fighting area and a target range?"

Balen looked around at the many buildings and barns. "I'm sure there is somewhere. Shall I assign you a detachment to help you?"

Frank nodded. "I like your set up and yes, I would appreciate that."

Balen hesitated and thought for a moment. I think that we will set up some tables in the barn and eat together. It is time there was a bit of coherence. We aren't individuals anymore."

Frank smiled. "So are you ready to hand over your power?"

Balen smiled back. "Not bloody likely. If there isn't a hand on the collar of some of these folk there would be some serious trouble."

Frank laughed. "Well said and exactly the right answer. You know I totally underestimated you and I will be the first to admit, I got you completely wrong. On paper you come over as so arrogant and unbending."

Balen raised an eyebrow and looked at Frank. "Where did you hear that? I don't remember you, do I know you?"

Frank smiled. "Don't let it trouble you Gabriel. That I

know your past and am prepared to support you means that we can't have any nasty secrets coming between us. I wouldn't have chosen you as part of the future but I am the first to admit that I would have been wrong. You have my full support and for what it's worth, an apology."

Balen looked stunned. "How did you know my name?"

Frank smiled. "Well Gabriel Morgan, I know a lot of things about a whole lot of people, it was my job once. You were quite the trouble maker when you were younger now weren't you?"

Balen smiled. "I still am, just in the right way and for all the right reasons."

Frank laughed. "Good answer Sir, I'll accept you as my Commander."

Cheryl and Raven were walking through the old farmhouse. It was a shell with little furniture and no character. Raven was explaining. "They took it over when it had been abandoned for some time so there wasn't any furniture here. I'd have brought some of ours back if there had been room.

There's enough though and there are artists here and woodworkers so I'm sure we can get something put together. There isn't a dining room as such.

At the moment whoever is on the rota does the cooking and its pot luck how eatable it is. We could do with setting up a catering section. There are more people here, over a hundred I think so cooking in this kitchen on a wood fired stove is going to be a challenge. We've been eating in shifts and that sort of works with watches etc. Food stores are doing alright but now that we've lost the Mart, well that is going to make life a little more difficult.

We're going to have to find other places to trade and produce our own. We've lost the chickens so that is a blow."

Cheryl laughed. "No we haven't, we've got them in a box in the boot. Doc and Storm have got a couple of men to help them and they are building a pen for them. We'll have to see if we can rig up an incubator or hope some of the girls go broody so we can work on numbers to get enough eggs for breakfast."

Raven took Cheryl around the rest of the place. "We'll have to think this through. We're going to have to start producing everything we need.

Power isn't a problem, they have that sorted. What we need are the raw materials and then a way of making them into what we need long term. To start with we can live on what we have and recycle. Longer term we're going to have to think about clothing and the like. I've got the books from the house so that covers spinning, tanning and that sort of thing. We've got books on cheese making. We lost all but two of the cows from the farm but there are more here. There are goats here and we can add in what we have, that gives us the raw materials. Hopefully we'll get volunteers to start making the basics. We still have hope."

Cheryl noticed that Raven was watching Balen across the yard. She smiled. "I don't know how you can tolerate being near that man. How can you look at him after what he did?"

Raven smiled. "Cheryl, he's my mate, my partner, my lover. I more than tolerate him. Balen did what he had to do."

Cheryl giggled and took Raven's arm. "Tell me more? I thought he raped you? We were all horrified when we heard the news. I was so sorry that Crow turned out such a rat. I never did like him. Wasn't this Lord Balen supposed to be the enemy?"

Raven smiled. "They had their agenda, we had ours. We were both trying to achieve the same thing, just in a different way. So how are you getting on with Shylock?"

Cheryl smiled. "I'm happy. I still feel sorry about Eric though."

Raven shrugged. "He made his choices. It was a pity he died."

The smile fell from Cheryl's face. "His body was never found. I had assumed he was one of the men who died in the forest and didn't ask. I asked Doc the other day, he checked the bodies over when they were burying them and Eric wasn't one of them."

Raven looked around nervously. "That could be a problem. I haven't seen him here though."

Cheryl smiled. "He ran off, I don't expect I'll see him again."

Raven looked at her seriously. "Well not unless you go and join up with the same organisation as he belongs to."

Cheryl looked horrified. "Oh crap, I have haven't I?"

Raven smiled. "We'll deal with it somehow if the problem ever arises. I think there's a map in the office somewhere of this place. We can make a copy and mark on where we can put things and start getting the stuff divided up into the different rooms. Talking about rooms I didn't bring any of your things from your room."

They had just gone back out into the yard when Cheryl smiled. "That was why we took a while to catch up with you. We brought all we could and a few things that you may have missed." Cheryl giggled. "He's coming over."

Balen strode across the yard. "Pleased to meet you Cheryl, glad to have you along." They shook hands. "How are your plans going?"

Cheryl looked at Raven. Raven smiled at her. "Very well."

Balen put his hand on her arm. "How's the arm holding up?"

Raven looked a little sorrowful. "It is hurting."

He smiled. "Frank told me what happened. You'd better get the doctor to take a look at it. I've had Oberon put in a spare stable until you are a bit more healed and able to cope with his lively affections."

Raven looked disappointed. "He won't like that."

Balen laughed. "He did what he was told. We've had words and he understands what is expected of him. Did you know that they found the other two dogs? They had jumped into the front of the van while the packing was going on. Could you sort out rooms for people, I've got to discuss the security for tonight. I'd like to get together to discuss things in about an hour. Come and find me." He looked at her questioningly.

Raven smiled and nodded. "Sure."

Balen wandered off and left the two women. Raven turned to Cheryl.

"What's the matter? You seem nervous."

Cheryl looked down at her feet. "I can't help thinking about what he did to you."

Raven laughed. "Try to put it out of your mind. I can't help thinking about what he will do." The two women burst into laughter. Balen didn't hear what they said but for the first time in ages he felt truly nervous without really knowing why.

Raven organised the sleeping arrangements and prepared a map of the whole farm with possible individual rooms as most of the people were bunked together in makeshift bunks, hammocks and on camp beds. She found a piece of board and some pins and pinned it up and also created a notice board with a list of jobs on it so that people could volunteer for them. She put it up and walked away but couldn't help popping back in half an hour. The list was filling up, nearly every job had been taken.

Cheryl had gone off to find Shylock and to look after Chloe when Raven went to look for Balen.

He had just finished walking the perimeter with Kurt when she found him.

He smiled and turned to Kurt. "We'll do the same shifts as last night. Get the heavier weaponry ready and I'm pleased to see that you have doubled the metal cladding. I think we can expect more mortar attacks tonight.

They will probably wait until the early hours again. But, we have to be vigilant. They could come earlier. I've got to discuss a few things with Raven so report to my office later." Kurt saluted and strode off.

Balen then crossed the yard to Raven and took her arm. "Did you see the doctor?"

Raven looked sheepish. "There wasn't really time."

Balen glared at her. "There will be later won't there? Now I want to discuss something with you." He led her up the stairs and when they got to the top she started to turn left to his office but he pulled her to the right and opened the door to their room. "I want some time with you before tonight. It is going to be another long night and I do expect an attack later.  Is that something you want as well?" He stood by the door giving her the option to leave.

Raven smiled. "Of course it is what I want, you don't know how much."

Balen smiled back. "I don't know, you'll have to show me." He closed the door and pushed her gently back into the room. "We'll have to take what time we can. I know this isn't a normal situation, if it was I could wine you and dine you and take you to romantic places."

Raven smiled. "As long as we get some time, that is all I ask for."

There was no attack that night, or the night after. The days ran into weeks, the weeks into months. They didn't relax their guard but they did start to build. Barns were turned into rooms with extra levels with bathrooms and sitting rooms above where the animals were. Other barns were turned into crafts workshops for making the everyday things they needed. One small barn was turned into a dairy, another into a room for making candles and soap. People read books, they experimented. They had their successes and their failures and they started to make the unusual the mundane. After a couple of months the products started to appear and to be used and enjoyed by others. In turn they did other work which supported the Compound. They managed some scavenging trips and eventually scavenged all the furniture from the farm and some other places that had been abandoned. Rooms gained tables, chairs, sofas and other furniture and ornaments and it did start to look like a home.

Frank had been training the men and women who wanted to learn. He ran a combat course and a basic self-defence course for the women. He started an archery class and this span off into a bow making session and an arrow making day.

It was decided that they would have a meal all together and as it had been quiet for a while Balen announced that they would have a meal that night.

The cooks were busy in the kitchen and the tables were set early so that everyone could go about their daily tasks without being too disrupted.

Clothes that were not uniform were shared so that everyone had something different to wear.

Raven and Balen had both healed well. They had no pain now from their old injuries and everyone else had managed to heal from their wounds.

Other than the scavenging missions they hadn't been near any other buildings or the towns. It had decided to try keeping out of the way in the hope that they had been forgotten about.

19

Balen was standing on the outer gate platform looking out onto the road.

Some of the craters had been filled in, others had greened up and some had filled with water to form little ponds. The onset of summer had brought an abundance of growth around the Compound. The bare earth had been covered in a verdant green carpet of grass, dandelions and patches of nettles which now provided their tea and coffee.

The open fields around them had now been planted with crops and they were beginning to grow. Their heads and leaves swayed in the gentle breeze. In the fields around the back of the Compound he watched the animals grazing, babies at foot. The cows made their way down and were just being let in for milking and the Compound was a hive of the regular morning activities.

Raven climbed up to join him and he put his arm around her. "Raven, you know I love to watch all this. It makes it all worthwhile, the morning start and that end of the day when all the animals are fed, watered and away."

She smiled and looked around. The milk maids were just carrying the buckets of milk from the milking parlour to the dairy and those in charge of making the cheese had the wood fired oven stoked and were ready to start stirring the milk into cheese. Any milk mistakes where something had fallen into the milk or a careless foot had ended up in there was taken off to the pigs. The morning was filled with animal sounds. Cocks crowed, pigs grunted, goats bleated and children giggled and ran about the play area watched over by their careful guardian.

Balen looked down at Raven. "This makes it all worthwhile, but I don't know how long this will last."

Raven smiled. "In some way it will go on forever, whatever they throw at us we will rebuild. Have you heard anything from Archangel?"

Balen frowned. "Not for a couple of months now. I'm expecting a messenger any day now. I've been waiting every morning but nothing has arrived."

Raven looked worried. "I used to believe no news is good news but knowing what is going on would be good. I'll stay with you a while, perhaps it will be this morning."

They stood on the platform for nearly an hour and were about to give up when they saw a vehicle in the distance, it was making its way carefully down the hill. It looked like a transit van but it had gained a few metal panels, spikes and wire mesh over the windows. It picked its way around the craters and drew up outside. The passenger door opened and a tall dark haired man got out. He looked very like Balen. Balen took a step back.

"Well, I didn't expect that, that is Archangel."

Archangel crossed the pitted tarmac and walked up to the gate. Balen called down to the gate guards. "Let him in, that is Archangel."

The door opened swiftly and Archangel strode through. Balen clambered down the ladder as his brother rounded the corner and the van followed him in.

Archangel looked around and smiled as Balen stood to attention and saluted. Archangel returned the salute.

The van followed one of the guards who took it to where it could be parked up and the gate was shut behind it. The doors opened and five of Archangel's personal guard got out, the driver also got out and joined them and they formed up waiting for their commander's instructions.

Archangel looked around. "I like the look of the place so far brother, you have done well, and you too Raven. I have been informed you are no longer our prisoner although my brother has been sadly lacking in his reports of late. I am here for a full and detailed personal update on your progress."

Balen looked nervous. "If you would like to come with me we can either speak now or I can give you a guided tour of the Compound."

Archangel looked around. "I would like the full tour. If you could show me around Lord Balen I would appreciate it." His tone was official and his body language indicated that he was not on a family visit. "Raven I would like to speak with you later. I trust this can be arranged?" Balen nodded.

Balen turned to Raven. "I'll see you later." She smiled, nodded and walked back to the house, a million worries running around her head.

Archangel smiled. "My brother, you have not kept me apprised of the situation here. I had expected communiqués from you on a far more regular basis. That isn't the only reason for my visit but I will speak of that in a more private place. Now, show me what you have set up here."

Balen took him around the Compound in a clockwise direction. They first passed the house where he showed Archangel the kitchen. "We made a few changes to the kitchen. We removed some of the cupboards and managed to find four wood burning stoves which you can see here. They are used for cooking but each of them feeds into a back boiler which heats a different part of the compound and the animal sheds. Come lambing and kidding we keep that burner going for a constant supply of drinks and to heat that shed. Here you will see the food store." Balen opened the door of the room they used to store the food. It had an open window which was meshed. In front of it were horizontal poles at regular intervals from waist height full of hanging salted meats and other early produce was neatly stacked in homemade boxes on shelves and covered in sand to preserve it.

Archangel looked around. "This is very organised. I cannot believe how far you have come along. I would like you to report on this so that it may be circulated to our other bases. I would use your location as a model for our development."

Balen smiled. "I can't really take much credit for this, that was Raven. She organised all this."

Archangel raised an eyebrow. "Before you show me the rest of this place I think I should talk to you."

Balen took him up to his office and they were brought a cup of dandelion coffee. "The coffee store ran out nearly a month ago, we are now filling the gap with this. It is not wonderful but better than nothing and you get used to it." He offered Archangel a seat and went and sat opposite. "You wanted to speak to me?"

Archangel looked serious. "I do. I wanted to speak now as I needed to hear from you what the situation is here and I didn't want any of the conversation made public or overheard. I need clarification about Raven's position here."

Balen smiled. "She is my partner and has been responsible for putting many of the things you see here in place."

Archangel raised an eyebrow. "That is an unfortunate turn of events. One of my reasons for coming here is to take her back to our main Hub for public execution. There was an outcry when such a small facility managed to wipe out an entire troop of our men. Their families in other Compounds have been petitioning for an example to be made."

Balen sat back in his chair and thought. "She is my mate and she is either already or will be carrying my heir. She is under my protection and that is the way it will stay."

Archangel's stare was cold. "You are determined about this Lord Balen? You are sure, even if this costs you dearly? Surely no woman is worth that?"

Balen met his stare with a cold look. "That is not negotiable. I exacted my retribution on her for what had been done to our men."

Archangel looked at him quizzically. "I had heard you had the leader of their organisation in captivity and you were torturing her. She doesn't look tortured to me. You will give me a full report."

Balen took a deep breath. "We had the farm under surveillance that night and we had our own people inside who had been feeding us information. On the night in question we had put men in the woods to watch the farm. I don't know where you got information about it being an organisation. It was organised yes but it was Raven's home. People came and she took them in. Nemesis had singled that place out as somewhere to send refugees to. She was informed of this on the day they arrived but the program had encouraged her to put certain things in place before hand which made it a suitable location for the people when they came.

The two operatives and the sleeper had been embedded into the unit. Their cover stories had held up and they were beginning to carry out their orders. My orders were to divide the people there and made an opening for our people to move in and assist with their internal struggles. This was unsuccessful due to the operatives being discovered. They escaped but this alerted the inhabitants of the farm that there were armed people in the woods. Contrary to my instructions the troop in the woods fired on the farm. This was misinterpreted as an attack and they retaliated.

We had received no intelligence that there was a military trained individual on site and he wiped out the troop. Raven had no part in that. As I understand it at the time she was in the Med Room being treated after being injured by a gunshot through her bedroom window. This action by us, by which I mean shooting at Raven, was not sanctioned. The inhabitants of the farm were acting on a perceived threat instigated by shots being fired through their windows and firebombs being thrown into the house."

Archangel took a deep breath. "This should all have been reported to me immediately. These actions were contrary to your orders?"

Balen looked down at his paperwork. "Totally. I believe that the internal matters relating to this Command are my responsibility. The individuals who instigated this and contravened my orders died in the woods that day. I felt there was no benefit in drawing this insurrection to the notice of other individuals and escalated the problem."

Archangel glared at Balen. "You are my Commander, I can remove you at any point that I choose to. So I would be a little more careful about what you report and what you don't report in future. This is a very delicate matter, the individuals who are asking for this execution are acting out of fear and a need to bring someone to task for what happened to their loved ones. Our people died, there had to be some retribution for this.What measures did you take to punish those at the farm for killing our people and to show them our superiority after such a crushing defeat?"

Balen took a deep breath. "As you know I had their leader kidnapped and brought here. I kept her a prisoner and ascertained that she was of considerable worth due to her in depth knowledge of running a place such as this. I was losing animals and we were unsustainable due to this. Valuable man hours were being lost tending to sick animals and that did not give us a future. I looked at what she had built there and deemed that acquiring such an asset would be invaluable. I could have kept her as a prisoner and extracted the information via questioning or if it came to it continued torture.

I received your communiqué requesting that I produced an heir and I deemed that her intellect would make her a suitable candidate to provide this child. I therefore took her in the belief that at least I would take an heir from her before she was executed."

Archangel's jaw dropped. "You mean you raped her?"

Balen smiled wickedly. "Of course I did. It was a far greater retribution for her than merely killing her. She has to live with that memory every day of her life. I made sure that her people knew what I'd done and what she was being used for. I had not only denied them their commander I had shown them that we show no mercy to those who stand against us. Killing her publicly would have been one solution but having her here working for us and helping me to create all this I felt was a much more productive solution. Then her mate cheated on her and the evidence came into my hands. I used this to my advantage and turned her to our cause. She is no longer my prisoner, she is my mate. Their asset is now ours."

Archangel sat up. "This changes everything. I am pleased with what you have done. It looks like she has been a valuable asset to this facility. And an heir?"

Balen smiled. "I'm working on that."

Archangel smiled back. "I'm glad to hear it. And what of the rest of the base?"

Balen's smile faded. "Before I tell you about that I ought to tell you the rest of the news about the farm. We had an operative in the Mart which I'm sure you have heard has been wiped out by Lex Corp. He had been supplying an information network for us and had made contact with Frank from the farm. That night Frank managed to pull our man from the rubble and he was brought back here. Raven has managed to convince him of the rightness of our cause and now he is training my men. He has turned them from enthusiastic rookies into a coherent fighting force. The lives that will save may in some way offset the lives that he took."

Archangel looked stunned. "You have Frank working for you? You have been busy my brother." His expression softened. "I believe I will have no difficulty in convincing those calling for Raven's blood that she is much more valuable alive than dead. Are you going to tell me more?"

Balen smile broadened and he relaxed. "When the farm was attacked on the same night as the Mart she willingly went back and removed the resources from the farm and brought them here to add to our own. She also brought along the survivors from the farm. So my initial directive has been achieved, the farm has been assimilated into our force here. She brought an excellent cook and another doctor to add to our ranks as well as a woman and a child with her mate and the doctor's mate. This has given us two established family units to build for the future."

Archangel smiled. "Very good brother, very good. Now we will speak off record, I have said what I needed to say officially. It is good to see you my brother."

Balen smiled. "And it is good to see you too."

Archangel relaxed. "So, tell me more about this Raven, you say she's your mate, is that convenience or is she making you happy?"

Balen smiled. "She is making me very happy and she has been my support and strength over these past months."

Archangel laughed. "Mother would be pleased."

Balen looked slightly sad. "I wish mother and father could have seen all this. I think they would have been proud of us. How about Martha, your mate, how is she?"

Archangel's smile faded. "Martha proved to be far less than the adoring mate she should have been. I found out that she was having an affair with my second in command. I had to have them both shot. There is some doubt that my heir is actually mine so he has been sent to another camp where he is being brought up by an adoptive family."

Balen looked worried. "Isn't that a situation that could come back to haunt you when he grows up?"

Archangel suddenly looked very tired. "There are many situations that are going to come back to haunt me later but I can only decide what I think is right for now. The child might be mine. I would not kill my own son. So, will you show me around the rest of this Compound now? I am very interested to see what you have done."

Balen then showed him the offices and introduced him to the workers there. Each in turn stood up and saluted. He then moved on to the animal pens, ever thankful that the timing was perfect, they had just mucked out and the place was looking neat and tidy. "We've just used the last of our straw but we will be harvesting the top fields soon to provide bedding and grain for the rest of the year and into the winter. We have two grass cuts a year which is providing our hay. The animals are mostly out in the fields at this time of the year so that lessens the feeding burden. Raven organised us a grazing rota and we have people who handle planting and the crops. I have a farm manager who handles the day to day animal handling and we have set up a dairy. We have facilities to make candles and a room where we are able to tan hides. For now we are wearing the clothing we came with but very soon we are going to move on to handmade clothes.

We have a spinning and weaving room where some of the women and men are setting up to be able to go into more concentrated production once we need this for clothing, especially for the winter."

They were alone in the large barn which had been set up for the cows for the evening. Archangel turned to his brother. "They won't leave you alone you know. They took heavy losses when they attacked you and our actions in the north of England have kept their attentions elsewhere but they will be back. They have global worries so that helps us a bit. But, news has come to us that they have lost control of their divisional offices. To counteract this they have given their regional offices the power to act independently in their area. So we can expect them to take a more personal interest in what we are all dong."

Balen looked horrified. "That is indeed bad news. What of the Corp in general."

Archangel looked down at the straw. "Cutting off the

head of the hydra was just that, it seems that now many heads have sprung up. The Corp has its own problems and we are but one. That has helped us survive in a way.

They have set up camps around the cities and moved most of the inhabitants there. They are setting up manufacturing. I have reports of the way those people are having to live, they are virtually slaves. They have what look like prison cells to live in and they live to work for the Corporation to build their new future."

Balen looked down at the straw. "You aren't going to leave it like that are you? I know you too well for that brother."

Archangel leant on the wooden rail and looked out over the well laid barn. "Seeing what you have done here has made me even more determined. No, I am not going to leave it like that. We have quite a force now and I'm going to act. The population is much reduced. I have intelligence that this has been aided by Lex Corp who have selectively let people be killed. They ascertained who was of value and they very quietly executed the rest. With no communication and very little information available to the general public this was easy for them. They just blamed rioting but those riot squads targeted whole areas and went in with extreme force. The body count was massive. I'm here as if we fail I doubt we will meet again. You are the only family I have left now. I wanted to see you one last time."

Balen smiled. "You will do what you have to do. We both have had to. You know I will support you."

Archangel smiled. "When we were younger I would have laughed at you making such a comment. You have changed so much my brother. Where is the lovelorn poet now? Where is the dreamer? I hope he's still in there somewhere."

Balen put a hand on his shoulder. "I have no need to be lovelorn or lost. My poetry was lousy. I loved that life but now I have purpose. Why write about love, it's better

419

to live it."

Archangel looked up and viewed Balen with suspicion. "You love that woman don't you?"

Balen smiled. "With all my heart."

Archangel laughed. "You are still the poet at heart then. For what it is worth, you have my blessing. Why has it worked so well here when the other Compounds are war torn fortresses at odds with all around them?"

Balen laughed. "Well this is where we are probably going become at odds again. I rewrote the initial manifesto."

Archangel's smile fell off of his face. "You did what?" He took a step away from his brother and again became Archangel, Head Commander of Transition X. "That directive was set in stone."

Balen glared at him. "That manifesto was written on a computer, not stone. Computers are gone, the old world is gone. Look around you and listen to your question, why have we succeeded? We have achieved the prime directive, the bottom line. The only difference is that we work with others rather than exploiting and controlling them. As has been pointed out, I co-wrote that manifesto, I have every right to change it."

Archangel gripped the wooden rail. His knuckles were white and his eye had begun to twitch. "You would stand by that statement, even if it means that I will have to remove you from your command here? You have overstepped yourself here. You were given orders you have not carried out.

You know I will have to make an example of you my brother. Don't make me do that. I want you to reinstate the manifesto immediately."

Balen took a deep breath. "Listen to yourself. In one breath you are saying that we have done well and achieved what we needed to. In the other you are saying that I must be removed because I have made this work."

Archangel's eye was twitching and he was shaking

slightly. "I have no other option. Lord Balen I remove you from your Command. You will hand Raven and Frank over to my troops for summary execution." He was shaking badly and his pupils were dilated, his eyes wide. "I will hear no more of it." His voice seemed different as was his whole body language.

Balen put a hand on his arm. Archangel pulled away. "Who do you think you are? I put you here to carry out my orders. You have not done this. That is treason."

Balen grabbed his arm. "You were put in place as Archangel as it was felt that you would best suit the position. I will confess now that I had my doubts about that at the time due to your fragile mental condition. But, it was a game then and it didn't matter. It made you happy."

Archangel pulled his arm away from Balen and stormed out into the farm yard. "Archangel Troop, form up with me." His soldiers ran across the courtyard and lined up in front of him. "I want this man taken into the middle of the yard and shot."

Raven ran across the yard and stood in front of Balen who had come out of the barn. Balen bent down and whispered in her ear. "Go to the private drawer in my desk and bring me the red folder." He slipped her a small key that was in his pocket. Then he almost shouted. "Raven get inside I don't want you to watch this."

Raven ran inside and up the stairs, she unlocked the drawer and was running down the stairs when she heard a single shot ring out. She couldn't run any faster and ran out into the yard. Balen was kneeling in front of Archangel who had stepped back and was staring up at a top window.

Raven looked up. Frank was in the window with a sniper rifle in his hands pointed at Archangel's head.

Frank shouted. "You make one move and you lose Archangel. You know that was a warning shot. I won't miss."

Balen looked up at him, his whole expression pleading. "Don't kill him."

Frank laughed. "That is one order I may not be able to carry out."

Raven ran across the yard and handed the file to Balen who grabbed it and stood up. "I am sorry my brother but I have to do this. I had hoped that it would never be necessary. I have a report here which was made by the family doctor and a copy of my brother's medical notes which were sent to us when we were making the decision as to whether to have him committed to a mental institution. I'm sorry Michael."

The Archangel Guard looked at each other and shuffled their feet. Balen held out the report. Michael screamed. It was the heartfelt scream of an injured animal. He was shaking and his legs gave out. He then started shouting over and over. "Shoot him".

Balen reached out and took his brother's arm and pulled him to stand up.

"You are Archangel, you are the High Commander of Transition X. You have achieved so much, don't slip back into all that now."

Archangel pulled away from Balen and ran back to his personal guard. He grabbed a gun out of the holster of the nearest one and turned to aim it at Balen. Balen stood there, hands out, palms upwards. "My brother, you have to see sense." Archangel started to raise the gun. A single shot rang out and Archangel fell backwards onto the ground as blood began to pool from the single shot to the head.

There was silence in the compound. The guard turned to Lord Balen and their senior officer stepped forwards. "I am Ryjel, First in Command of Archangel's personal guard. I also used to be a doctor before I signed up.

May I see that report?" The guard had all levelled their rifles on Balen and Raven. Balen handed over the report. Ryjel opened the cover and began to read. He looked at the papers for about a quarter of an hour and in that time it was as if the Compound stood still. Those who had come to find out what had happened stood in very nervous anticipation.

Ryjel closed the file. "Why didn't you reveal this before? This report is by a very eminent psychiatrist. His findings are very clear. Michael was showing signs of being schizophrenic. Why didn't you have him committed? The injuries he inflicted on you when you were children should have been enough to make your family act."

Balen looked a broken man. Raven stepped over to him as the guard lowered their weapons. "He was my brother. We did what we could to look after him and there was a good man in there too. He was a brilliant man. He had fantastic ideals and he has kept TX together."

Ryjel looked down. "No he hasn't. He has broken the organisation apart. For months now his controversial and inconsistent orders have shattered the very fabric of what we are trying to build. He has lost us operatives on many occasions and his rule was fragile at the least."

Balen looked stunned. "So what happens now? Are you going to shoot me and the others for his murder?"

Ryjel thought for a moment. "No, we are going to stand down and we are going to take your brother's body somewhere that it can lie in state. He was our leader and a hero to our people. He will remain that way. We will now go somewhere private and discuss how we can limit the damage here. Do you have a cold store?"

Raven looked up nervously. "We do, I will show your men the way."

Balen caught her arm as she was about to walk away. "No, we will get someone else to show them the way, you are coming with me. I should have said this a while ago. Raven is my mate and my equal. She has every right to be there when we talk and I value her ideas. Is that acceptable to you?"

Rijel smiled. "My Lord, you are senior ranking officer here. As one of the original four your status is only one short of Archangel. The other three are now dead."

Balen swore under his breath and cast Raven a very nervous look. "We will go inside. Follow me."

Ryjel, Balen and Raven sat around the glass table in Balen's office. The report was on the table and other papers lay around it. They had sat in silence while Ryjel had read the report again. He looked up. "Archangel will have to carry on. You are the next ranking officer and the position should be yours. Will you take up that position?"

Balen looked over at him. "I need to think about that. Let's talk about the situation and see if we can find another answer."

Ryjel looked down at the paperwork. "We must not attempt any form of subterfuge here. That will inevitably be revealed at a time most inconvenient to all of us. The decision we make here has to be not only believable it has to be unquestionable.

It has been noted for some time that Archangel's mental state has been deteriorating. Initially it was just tiredness and slight errors in judgment. In the latter weeks he had become much more erratic in his actions and orders. It is the general population of Transition X that we need to convince.

Stories and rumours have abounded about your ability to command as you have shown a weakness when it came to dealing with your prisoner. I have now been appraised at the harsh way you dealt with her and that will possibly stand in some way to stop them baying for Raven's blood. As second in command at the point that he was deemed unfit for duty, which I will testify to, you would have automatically been granted command. As I would assume that your man was under orders to protect you from any assassination attempt that makes Archangel's death carried out in undertaking the man's duty. There can be no blame laid on anyone for Archangel's death. What we do now is more important. The organisation needs a head and we are about to strike a blow against Mega Corp. The decision is yours as to whether you will take up that position and come with me to our Head Office."

Balen looked at Raven who was looking terrified. "Is there anyone else?"

Ryjel shook his head. "No, the command comes to you on Archangel's death."

Balen looked down at his hands. "This is something I need to think about. If I do take up the command I would expect to bring Raven with me. Will that be a problem?"

Ryjel thought. "I don't know. I will also have to think about this. TX is a very volatile group of creative people who are also idealists. You have a suitably romantic and practical story that should win over most of them.

Raven, you are quiet. Balen has asked you to be here and you have a right to speak."

Raven looked at both of them. "I am torn between practicality and a wish for things to stay the same here. There is one piece of information that I had hoped to keep to tell Balen tonight in private. As it is appropriate now that pleasure will also be denied to us. Balen, you are going to be a father."

Balen looked shocked. "You mean? Excuse me Ryjel." Balen got up and pulled Raven up so that he could hug her. "That is the best news I could have had and our timing, as always is perfect." He turned his back to Ryjel so he couldn't see and then mouthed. "For real?"

Raven kissed him and smiled. "I went to see Doc this morning as I wasn't feeling too well and he has confirmed it."

Ryjel had a warm and genuine smile on his face. "Well I believe congratulations are in order, for all of us. That would stabilise the situation.

If you decide to come with us and assume the position as Archangel that would bring unity. You can always appoint others to stand in and return here after we have done what we need to do. The hydra is dangerous but it can be defeated. There is a movement to bring back elected politicians.

France and Germany have already taken back the right to internal control and the power of the Mega Corp is failing. If we can strike at them now and instate a parliament or ruling family again we can hopefully bring peace."

Balen narrowed his eyes and glared at Ryjel. "How do you know so much about Archangel's business."

Ryjel smiled. "I am also a member of the Council of Commons. Archangel sanctioned it and put me forwards so that he had a representative on the Council. His paranoia has been a problem but it has also had some unexpected bonuses. They have people in place who would be suitable for possible election and they are proposing to reinstate the voting system. That would mean that those who made the decisions were again answerable to the people.

Another decision you have to make is what to do with Archangel's body."

Balen looked down at his now clasped hands that were on the table. "To give him a public funeral would be an affront to all of those who have lost loved ones and have had no chance to honour their life in such a way. I will organise something in private if you wish or we will bury him as we have buried so many others."

Ryjel looked serious. "That is a wise decision. We will all testify to what happened, taking his body back would be unnecessary. We are his Personal Guard, we will see to the burial if you tell us where. Would it be appropriate if I leave you to discuss matters with your mate? I will then attend to the preparation of your brother for suitable burial."

Balen took a deep breath. "I think my brother would have appreciated it more if we built him a funeral pyre and sent him into the other world with a little ceremony. He always feared enclosed spaces. Tonight we will have a feast and celebrate his life and achievements and also mourn all those we have lost. It will also be a celebration of new life to come. You are right, I would like to discuss matters with my mate."

Ryjel stood up and bowed slightly. "I will await your decision." He left the room and went back to his men.

Balen turned to Raven when Ryjel had left the room. "Will life never leave us alone?"

Raven looked tearful. "Not yet. Not until the journey is over. We are so small, so insignificant, if our little part can make big things happen then we must see this through to the end. I so want us to just be here, to raise our child in peace and to make this place work. But, how can we live if we are expecting an attack every day. It has been three months now of living looking over our shoulders. Nobody can find peace and the strain is beginning to show. To have our peace perhaps we have to fight for it. You know I will support you and go with you to help you with anything you need to do."

Balen pulled her into a hug. "How can I take you with me? I need you, you both, here and safe."

Raven looked thoughtful. "I will go with you. You need my help. No arguments."

Balen smiled. "Oh there will be."

Raven took his hand. "It's going to be a busy day and night. Give your orders then I think we need to have a meeting to discuss issues."

Balen raised an eyebrow. "If you want to discuss anything my time is yours now."

Raven smiled wickedly. "No, I think you would probably take this meeting to a more appropriate venue."

Balen smiled. "I will go give my orders and make arrangements. Will you organise people to get the feast sorted out and handle those matters?"

Raven looked thoughtful. "I will. It's going to be a long night, I've got that feeling. We can talk about things later. See how you feel."

Balen laughed. "Feel about it, I'm planning to get exceedingly drunk and forget about it if you don't mind."

20

By late afternoon they had transformed one of the barns and the yard. On a hill in a field next to the barn they had created a funeral pyre and the cooks were busy in the kitchen. Everyone who wasn't on guard duty had been brought in and everyone was helping out.

As it started to get dark those who played music got together and the sad and happy songs filled the air. Candles were lit in jars around the place and it took on a mystical air. Gradually people filtered off and came back dressed in clothes they had saved for just such an occasion. In a matter of hours ducklings turned into swans. Women who had laboured with buckets, their hair a mess floated gracefully about in dresses with their hair brushed and make up on. Men who had worn the customary boiler suit or farm clothing walked carefully with clean shoes and smart suits.

Balen was still in his office, his mind was troubled and much as he looked at the paperwork he couldn't make his mind focus on it. He put the pages aside. He then got up and looked out of the window at the scene below.

He watched for a while and then turned away and went to his room. Raven was already in the room. She was brushing her hair, something he hadn't seen her do in a long time. She got up when he came in and turned to face him. She literally took his breath away. He had never seen her in anything other than a hospital gown or a boiler suit. The scruffy farm hand had transformed into an elegant woman. Her long nearly black hair was slightly curled and immaculately brushed. She had washed her face, the mud he was so used to was gone and in its place skilfully applied make up and dark red lipstick. A long black figure hugging evening dress showed off her well-proportioned curves and her customary wellington boots had been replaced with elegant high heeled sling back shoes that looked impossibly delicate.

She smiled at his reaction. "Well, will I do?"

Balen laughed. "Do, you'll be lucky if I let you out of this room tonight."

He walked over to her. "Well, actually I'm afraid to touch. I don't want to mess anything up." He grabbed her hand and kissed it. "I will be gallant instead." He bowed and went to the wardrobe. He took out a black evening suit, white winged shirt and bowtie.

Raven sat down on the stool beside her dressing table and watched him as he unzipped his boiler suit and pulled it over his muscular shoulders and down past his well-toned stomach and defined six pack. He let it fall and stepped out of it, picked it up and threw it into the laundry basket. He grabbed a towel and headed for their shower and she could hear the water running and then splashing. She turned and carried on making sure her make-up was alright.

An hour later they walked down the stairs and out into the yard. Most people were already in the barn making the most of the alcohol that they had brought back from the farm. Balen held his arm out and Raven took it and he helped her across the now solid ridges of mud in the yard. She stumbled slightly but he was able to keep her standing.

Once on the firm concrete of the barn she was able to walk without any problem but she still held on to his arm. They walked in together and joined the others.

A couple of hours later Balen went to the raised stone platform at the back of the barn and climbed the stairs. The room fell into silence.

He took a deep breath and looked down to Raven who smiled. "You will know what I mean when I say that I am glad to see all your faces here tonight. That I think is what we must focus on. We have all lost loved ones and I think this is the time to focus on the happiness and truth they brought to our lives. None of us know how long we have on this rock. What we do while we are here is what we will be remembered for and our lives will count for something. The simplest of acts can have the most profound outcome. I think we all realise that now. So, may I ask you to raise your glasses and toast, Absent Friends."

Everyone raised their glasses and toasted.

Balen looked down at Raven and she nodded. "In this time of sadness we all cling to what little bit of hope we can. I have a contribution to that tonight. Even in one of my darkest days when I have lost my beloved brother I have been given a little message of hope. I am to be a father later this year. I will have my heir. Now, if you would like to join me we will light the funeral pyre."

They all trooped out of the barn and one by one they picked up one of the tea light lanterns by its wire handle and followed Balen and Raven up the hill.

They got to the top and Balen took the burning brand that had been placed there for him. He turned to the waiting people. "We all know how my brother died but I would rather he was remembered for his glories. He was the High Commander Archangel of Transition X. We all owe him a lot for bringing us to where we are today. He is gone but he will never be forgotten. May he be remembered for all the right reasons from this night onwards." He lit the kindling piles with the torch and made his way around the pyre until it was burning strongly. Under his breath he whispered. "Goodbye little brother."

The wind was getting up and there was a chill in the air. He noticed that Raven was standing there without a coat so he pulled her closer to the pyre.

He then turned and spoke to the gathered people. "I wish to speak on another matter. It is my wish that Raven be acknowledged as one of us. I accept her as an equal, as my mate, I am prepared to take the Oath of Life Bonding with her if she will agree to do the same." He turned to

Raven.

She was shivering slightly in the cold night air.

She smiled. "Yes of course."

Kurt stepped forward. "As one of your oldest friends I claim the Right of Utterance if you will accept me."

Balen smiled. "I accept you, you may speak the words."

Kurt turned to the crowd. "In accordance with the manifesto I ask if anyone has any objection to Raven being accepted into our family." There was silence. "In accordance with the manifesto I ask if anyone would propose her as a member of our family."

Balen was about to speak when most of the crowd shouted, nearly in unison. "I propose that she be a member of our family."

Kurt turned to the couple. "According to our Law as Raven is now carrying your child you may now take her as your life partner. I will now speak the words." He stepped back so that the fire was behind him and the couple in front of him. "In accordance with our law it is decreed that these two before us, whatever their names be now or ever shall have been shall be deemed to be Bonded for Life. Do you accept this bond?" He turned to Raven. She smiled. "I do." He turned to Balen. He smiled. "I do."

He then turned to the crowd. "Let any man or woman found to be attempting to break that bond be dealt with according to our Law. Let all of us support and accept their love and honour it. Balen by our Law you are now bound to love and protect your life mate. Raven by our Law you are now bound to love and protect your life mate. By our Law you are now United."

A trail of lights was seen going back down the hill as everyone went back to the barn.

When they were back in the barn people came up to congratulate them and to welcome Raven into the family. Frank came over when the initial rush had died down and sat down with Raven. He had brought a drink over for her and she took it gratefully. He smiled. "This is something I could never have predicted. I have to confess that I had seen Balen as an arrogant fool who was power hungry and manipulative. I saw his brother as a dangerous fanatic who was highly unpredictable. I will happily admit that I was wrong. I like the man, I am sure he will make you happy. He is honest, hardworking, bright and a good leader. You are well suited. You will make this place a safe and happy home for all who are here, I am sure of it."

Raven leant forward. "Frank, I need to ask you something?"

Frank smiled. "You know you can ask me anything, what is the matter?"

Raven took a deep breath. "Balen has been invited to take over as Archangel. I have said that if he does I will go with him."

Frank looked stunned and his mouth fell open slightly. "Now that is something I would never have predicted either. Of course you must go and he must accept. You must encourage him. Why do you need to ask me something about it?"

Raven smiled. "You know that I'm pregnant so I'm carrying his heir. It is dangerous for both of us to go but I will not let him go without me. Would you come with us? I need your protection so he doesn't have to worry about me. I haven't spoken to him about it as I wanted to ask you first."

Frank looked at Raven, his expression was blank. He looked down and was thinking hard. "This is something I had not anticipated. But logically it would be a good idea and I would be delighted to come with you."

Raven laughed. "I think that the current threat to Balen may well be alcohol poisoning though. I think he plans to make the.most of this party."

Frank laughed as well. "He deserves it. Don't worry little one, I'll keep an eye on him and if you need a hand getting him to bed later, let me know.

I'll stay close by. Alcohol doesn't seem to have the

same effect on me so I'll be fine if anything happens. For once why don't you both relax and just be yourselves."

Raven smiled and hugged Frank. He hugged her back though he was awkward and didn't seem to know what to do with his hands and feet. "Thank you Frank, I'm glad you came to the farm."

As she walked away Frank looked down at the drink in his hands. "So am I."

The night passed without incident. Balen managed to drink his fair share of alcohol as did most of the others and by dawn they were making their way up to bed. Raven had to enlist the services of Frank who helped her to get Balen into the bedroom. Frank gently lowered him onto the bed. "Well my dear, from here on you are on your own with him. Though I doubt however much you love him you'll be able to protect him from the hangover he's going to have in the morning."

Raven smiled and swayed slightly. Frank caught her arm. Raven put her other hand over it. "Thank you for being a friend."

That made Frank jump slightly. He turned and left the room. Raven went to the door and locked it.

The morning dawned crisp and bright like some cruel punishment on those who had drunk too much the night before. Many staggered about cursing its brilliance while others enjoyed its welcome warmth. Raven had been up early and had left Balen to sleep off his hangover. The guards were back on the door and she had made sure he had plenty of water and soft drinks beside the bed.

She checked on the animals and played with Oberon who had taken a shine to one of the farm hands and had moved in with him. Everything seemed peaceful and it was just another morning, but she knew it wasn't.

On the hill the pyre had burnt down to ash. All that could be seen was a black patch where it had been. She made a mental note to speak to someone about getting the ash bagged up for the vegetable patch.

She walked up the hill, pulling her coat around her against the morning chill and turned to look back at the farm. She looked at the rolling countryside around her and a tear came into her eyes. "Why couldn't we have just been left alone?" After about fifteen minutes when she was a bit too cold she walked back down the hill and went back to her bedroom.

Balen was awake, he was sitting on the side of the bed holding his head. He looked up. "I was wondering where you'd gone. Are you alright? Do you feel unwell?"

Raven smiled. "I'm fine, I just went for a walk. I suppose speaking to you now isn't a good idea."

Balen tried to smile. "My love, speaking to me loudly isn't a good idea but I can just about cope with anything else. Is there something on your mind?"

Raven sat down beside him and he put his arm around her. She smiled at him. "I mentioned our decision to Frank last night, I hope you don't mind.

I wanted to ask him if he'd go with us and be my bodyguard."

Balen thought for a moment. "Forgive me, I'm trying to work that one out. So Frank would be prepared to come along with us and look after you?" He reached for his glass of water.

Raven smiled. "Yes. If you want him to he will."

Balen looked up at Raven. He was pasty white and his eyes looked a little bloodshot. "So you are happy about going then?"

Raven's smile faded. "No, but I will go."

Balen kissed her on the forehead. "I wouldn't make you go."

Raven looked down at her hands. "I know but you wouldn't be able to make me stay. I want to be with you, whatever it means."

Balen smiled. "I'd rather be here with you and carry on as we have done. When this is over we will come back."

She put her finger on his lips. "No promises like that.

I've seen too many movies, you promise that and one or other of us won't be coming back. All we can promise is that we'll do the best we can to come back. The decision is yours now, I've made my decision."

Balen turned to her. "I don't have a choice do I? I love you Raven." He bent forward and put his arms around her and kissed her with a passion, a want and a need like he had never kissed her before. "I'm scared Raven. I never had anything to lose before. Now at the point that I have everything I want I'm being asked to risk it all."

Raven thought on that one. "Only those with the most to lose can truly make a sacrifice for the greater good. We don't have to lose each other, we can go out there, achieve what we need to and then come home and leave it all to others from then on. If we don't we'll end up losing what we already have anyway. Sometime down the line one or other of us will die in a raid.

It will happen. This way we can earn our peace. Then our child can live in peace."

Balen smiled. "Children."

Raven smiled. "Let's see how I go with one first. By the way any more surprises?"

Balen thought about it. "I don't think so. I'm sorry for springing that on you last night. It just seemed right. I hadn't planned it and if one person had objected I could not have been bonded with you. Are you happy about it?"

Raven smiled. "Of course I am. I didn't know Kurt was one of your oldest friends?"

Balen laughed. "I've probably upset the doctor as he thinks he is. I went to school with both of them. We grew up in the same neighbourhood and used to play together when we were boys. When we formed Transition X they treated it as a sort of club, we all did. The chosen few could join. Then all this happened. I never expected all this. But, it couldn't have worked out better if I had planned it. Kurt is now Acting Commander here. He's the one person who I know has the same ideals as me and

435

who will carry on with what we have started. He knows he's acting until we come back and he's happy with that. The power won't go to his head.

I was talking to Ryjel last night when I realised I hadn't told you this. It seems that Carl and his father were knocking off Lex Corp merchandise. They hit their deliveries regularly and they were pretty darned stupid about it. They took the ease with which they were stealing stuff as being their own skill. It turned out that Lex Corp was setting up runs with marked merchandise. They then infiltrated the Mart with spies and hit anyone who in their opinion was working for the Mart. Your meetings with Carl and his father made your site a prime target. My agents met with them regularly so we were on their hit list too.

It goes deeper than that. The reason we got to take you so easily without anyone talking was that the Mart had also set up a slavery ring. The women that were going missing were being shipped out by them."

Raven looked up tearfully. "We lost so many good people. I know I couldn't have done anything if I'd been there and let's face it if you hadn't brought me here I'd be dead too. I suppose in some crazy way you saved me by ruthlessly and maliciously kidnapping me and dragging me kicking and screaming from my home."

Balen looked down. "Can you ever forgive me for that?"

Raven looked into his eyes. "Can you ever forgive me for what my people did to yours? I think that is a little more serious. I'll have to live with that until the day I die. I now care for these people and those people that died, they were their friends and loved ones. I have no idea how they can accept me here and what you claim to have done to me is minor in comparison to what you really felt you wanted to do. Isn't it?"

Balen smiled. "You were protecting your people. I protected mine, now my people and your people are one people so it ended up well. And now I can torture and torment you every day of your life, in the most pleasant way possible of course."

Raven smiled. "It's been a long journey and I have a feeling that there's a longer journey to come. What happens if they won't accept what happened here?"

Balen looked at her seriously. "Then they will execute me and probably you as well. You have to be ready for that. I would much rather go there by myself first and see how things are. Then I could send for you afterwards."

Raven smiled. "Not a chance. I know you. Out of some foolish notion that you were protecting me you would leave me here and my life would be a living hell. I don't want to spend a day without you, I couldn't, not now."

Balen looked at her seriously. "And you think I would want to live a day knowing that I could have prevented you being harmed."

Raven laughed. "Anyway, you promised to love and protect me. You can't do that if you aren't here and I can't protect you if I'm not with you so we're both stuck with it the way it is aren't we?"

Balen laughed and the worried lines melted from his face. "I suppose we are. Now, if you wouldn't mind I think I need to sleep, leave me in my well-deserved agony. Whatever decision I've made I'm not going anywhere today." Balen rolled back onto the bed and held his head, moaning. Raven pulled the covers over him, kissed him on the forehead and poured some more water into his glass. She then left the room and went downstairs.

Frank was waiting for her in the yard. He looked worried. He fell in beside her as she went towards the barn. His voice was steady and calm. "Has he made his decision?"

Raven smiled. "I think he has but he's not doing anything until later. He's in no fit state to see anyone at the moment."

Frank smiled back. "So, how do you feel about it?"

Raven looked serious. "I'll do what I have to do. If my friends and animals are safe here I'll go with him and hopefully keep him safe and help him. I can't ask for more than that, at the moment."

Frank walked along beside her in silence. She seemed lost in her own thoughts so he left her to it.

Later that evening Lord Balen came downstairs. He had showered and looked far better than he had when she had left him that morning. He went to the kitchen and made himself a cup of coffee and one for Raven and took it out to her. She was sitting on a low wall watching the activities in the yard. She looked up as he walked over and sat down beside her. "How are you feeling?"

He smiled. "Much better thank you and I've had time to think and make my decision final. I'm going to talk to Ryjel next but I wanted to talk to you first. Raven, it's a lot to ask you and I know what you've told me already but I have decided to go, will you come with me? I would fully understand if you don't want to come. I would actually prefer that you didn't come. But I can't stop you."

Raven looked hurt. "You mean you don't want me with you?"

Balen smiled. "I want you with me more than anything in the world but I also want something to fight for and something to come home to."

Raven smiled. "I will come with you but I will be careful. I've got a lot to lose now. None of us know how long we have got. To waste a day I could have spent with you would be more awful than I could possibly imagine. I know you feel the same way. If we want to be together I will move heaven and earth to make sure that we are. Whatever it costs me."

Balen looked serious. "Even if it costs your life?"

Raven smiled and drank a mouthful of coffee. "Even if it means drinking more of this awful dandelion coffee."

Balen laughed. "Now that is serious." He put his arm around her. "Well I guess I'd better go and tell Ryjel and

438

we can then tell the others. If we've set this place up right we should be able to leave without it falling apart. I know we'd like to think that we're indispensable but I doubt it. We have good people here. Well, here goes. We'll be going tomorrow morning.

Pack the bare essentials. You'll be wearing uniform at the HQ and that is provided." He stood up and walked across the yard to the house.

Balen went to the guest room where Ryjel and the others were meeting. It was neatly furnished with bunk beds and each had its own locker. Ryjel was in mid flow when Balen knocked and walked in. Ryjel looked up and smiled. "My Lord Balen, I trust that you are feeling well."

Balen gave an embarrassed cough. "I am feeling much better thank you. I have come to give you my decision."

Ryjel stood up and his men stood up with him. "You may speak in front of the men. Whichever is your decision we will of course support you and stand by you."

Balen smiled. "We will be coming with you. I would be honoured to accept the title of Archangel."

Ryjel smiled broadly. "That is indeed good news. We have been discussing how best we can present the news of Archangel's death. It is going to involve very careful planning. You said "we" I trust that you mean that Raven will be accompanying you?"

Balen smiled. "She will be."

Ryjel cast a sideways glance at his second in command who also smiled. "I am glad to hear it."

Balen noticed the glance and shifted his feet. "I trust that you will also ensure her safety."

Ryjel smiled thinly. "We will do everything in our power to deliver her to TX HQ safely. It is indeed a wonderful situation that she will be joining you there. We are ready to depart at any time so if you let us know when would be convenient for you we will make the appropriate arrangements."

Balen nodded. "I thank you. I will have one more night

here and we will leave in the morning. I trust that this will be acceptable to you."

Ryjel bowed slightly. "It would be acceptable. I will make the necessary arrangements."

That night Balen and Raven dined in the barn with everyone else. When the meal had ended and the plates had been cleared away he stood up and tapped a glass so that he got everyone's attention. He cleared his throat.

"As you know after the death of Archangel I am the next in the line of command. I have been offered the position of Archangel and I have accepted. I will be travelling to our headquarters to make the necessary arrangements.

This may not be a surprise to some of you but it will be to others. I have every confidence that you will be able to run this place most ably in our absence. Raven will be accompanying me, as will Frank.

I have left written instructions as to what needs to be done and I have also spoken to those who will be taking over both my responsibilities and Raven's while I am away. I must assure you that I intend this to be a temporary measure until a permanent solution to certain problems can be found."

The barn was silent, the only sound was the gentle occasional noise of an animal out in the other barn. Everyone looked at each other horrified.

Balen coughed. "I am unable to reveal every detail but my brother was about to undertake a major offensive that could make all the difference. I have to ensure that this does not fail in his absence. That is the only reason why I am going. As soon as this offensive is well on its way or if it succeeds quickly I will return. So you power hungry mongrels can stop eyeing up my office."

A nervous ripple of laughter made its way around the room but few managed a genuine smile. Balen put his hand on Raven's shoulder. "We are both greatly saddened to have to go. Some of you have known me for many years, others are just coming to know us now. I hope that in the future we get a chance to know you all a lot better. So all it remains for me to say is that I wish you luck and I hope that you will look after the place while we're away."

Balen sat down to thunderous applause. He looked at Raven who was looking sad. He smiled at her. "Shall we go and spend some time together before we have to go? I have one thing I have to do and then I'll be up."

Balen stood up. "Now if you'd like to enjoy the rest of the evening there are one or two things I need to deal with." He stood up as did Raven and they walked out.

Raven went straight upstairs. Balen had caught Frank's attention as he had left the barn and Frank had followed them.

Frank and Balen walked up to the field behind the barn. Frank was the first to break the silence. "Other than the obvious, what is the matter? Something is on your mind."

Balen looked up at the clear sky and the sparkling stars against the deep blue background. "Back in the day I would have been sitting down there with a piece of paper writing about stars. Now that I can see them so clearly I have no time to write about them."

Frank smiled. "That is often the way."

Balen stopped walking. "If you come with us you are going to die."

Frank's smile faded. "Well that was direct. What makes you think that?"

Balen turned to face him. "Because that is what is going to happen to us. They aren't taking me back to become Archangel. I'm no fool. They are taking me back so that I can stand trial for his death and if they can catch Raven as well then they will. I'm going to let them."

Frank looked horrified. "Why would you want to do that?"

Balen took a deep breath. "Because it is the only way this place is going to survive. If I don't then the new

Archangel won't stop until he has me executed. I know these people enough to know that they will defend me.

If they catch Raven she will be executed then as well. She will have to watch more friends die in the process. There has been too much bloodshed. I know that she would suffer all the more if I didn't take her with me. We are going to die Frank. I've seen the look on the Guard's faces, they aren't that good at covering it up. Perhaps I do deserve to die. I started this organisation after all. It was my stupid game that brought it all about."

Frank shook his head. "I beg to differ. It was Nemesis who started all this and it is Nemesis who deserves to die."

Balen kicked a stone. "But Nemesis is already dead and they need someone to blame so they are going to blame me. They have lost so many people and they can't get retribution for them. They can transfer that hurt onto me and unfortunately onto Raven. What I do ask is that if they are not planning to execute her immediately and are planning torture and a slow death and I can't get to her first I want you to kill her. Make it swift and make it painless.

You may stand a chance of getting away as you are only under my orders and they will probably want someone to come back here and report. I hope that will be the case but I can't guarantee anything. So it is not certain really, just probable that you will die."

Frank smiled. "I'm coming with you, whatever the risk and whatever you say."

Balen smiled back. "It is selfish of me but I'm glad of that. Tomorrow we will have to put on the best act of our lives. I want these people to honestly believe that we are going out there to try to make a difference. Leave them that at least for a little while. I have already mentioned my fears to Raven.

I want to have one more night with her if it is going to be my last on this earth. I want to spend it with her and I want to make her happy. I know what is coming and it is going to be hardest for her. I can't spare her it but I can do what I can to make it as easy as possible.

Will you promise me that you will kill her if it comes to it?"

Frank looked at the floor. "That is a hard promise to make me give you. Is there any way that you can think of that you can argue your way out of this?"

Balen took a deep breath and let it out slowly. "I doubt it. Archangel's men saw him cut down in cold blood in front of us."

Frank smiled. "But you didn't do the killing."

Balen shook his head. "You are one of my men, they will assume that you were acting under my orders and that I gave some sort of signal to you to kill him. Though why I would I don't know, he was my brother after all."

Frank looked thoughtful. "What does your law state, do you remember the exact wording?"

Balen thought for a moment. "If any person who is a member of Transition X takes the life of another member unlawfully then their life shall be forfeit. I have condemned Raven by making her my Life Partner. I never thought of it at the time. If I had not taken her as my life mate she would not have been a member. I cannot believe that I was that stupid."

Frank stared at the ground. "Would the child be spared? Would they spare her to have your child?"

Balen shook his head. "She is my life mate, my crimes are her crimes. Archangel died after I had conceived the child, the child will be deemed as guilty as we are."

Frank glared at Balen. "That is unreasonable."

Balen shook his head. "I know. I didn't think about it at the time but some of the laws my brother added in were extremely harsh. It didn't matter you see, it was just a game. None of this was supposed to happen."

Frank let out an ironic laugh. "I have a feeling that if Nemesis knew what circumstances had been unleashed he would be inclined to agree with you on that one. But you are both innocent."

Balen stared at Frank. "What do you mean?"

Frank shook his head. "Neither you nor Raven gave the order for any of those people to be killed. In fact there is no blood on your hands at all. I killed all of your men who came to the farm. Those that the farm boys shot at were only wounded, I finished them off. I was not ordered to do so. I didn't give Raven the chance to stop me. I also killed Archangel because he was going to have you killed. Neither of you either gave an order or carried out any of the killings. You are both innocent."

Balen shrugged. "Not in the eyes of the law, I doubt we can prove it. You are a person under my command now and you were under Raven's command when you eliminated my men. You might think of it as defence but the Agents at the HQ aren't going to see it that way. I know I'm going to die. I must go back now. You have a choice and I would strongly advise you not to come with us. I need to go back to my room and I must spend what little time I have left with my mate. I will hear your decision in the morning but I must bid you good night."

Frank put a hand on his arm. "You know this could all still work out."

Balen smiled. "It could, but at this moment I doubt it." He turned and ran back down the hill leaving Frank to look up at the stars.

## 21

The morning was overcast and grey. There was a slight drizzle in the air as Lord Balen, Frank and Raven climbed into the van. Just about everyone had turned out to see them go and it had taken them two hours to say goodbye to them. Instructions had been given, notes had been left and when they finally drove off with the members of Transition X both Balen and Raven were satisfied that they had covered anything that they could think of with those taking over those duties.

They drove through the morning and into the afternoon. Initially this was through the relatively unspoilt countryside but as they neared the cities the road became more broken up by craters and potholes. Villages that they passed were either highly defended or abandoned. Where they were defended they often had to take a detour to get around them.

There were few animals in the fields but the farms that they passed were all boarded and defended in a similar way to their farm had been and the Compound. Finally they came to their destination.

They drove over a hill and they could see their destination in the distance. It was a square stately home which stood resplendent in the middle of a walled estate and surrounded by thick mixed woodland. There was a stone gate house in the outer wall and both the gatehouse and the walls were still intact. A platform had been constructed around the top of the wall so that guards could patrol and they could see these people from a distance making their way around the walls at regular intervals.

Within the grounds there were areas set aside for camping. Neat military style tents had been erected in rows in the middle of the estate. There were animals there too. Areas had been hastily converted into animal compounds and a small farm on the estate was brimming with animals and bustling with activity.

As they approached the main gatehouse a couple of guards came out to open the large wooden gates and the van drove through.

They drove up the sweeping gravelled drive. Ash trees lined the route and the grass was a deep green. It was immaculately tended and small bushes and ornamental shrubs were laid out in beds around it. It was green as far as the woodland that circled the house.

The house itself had many windows. The main door was at the top of a flight of white stone stairs. A line of guards were waiting, standing to attention, assault rifles in hand. Balen tensed as they approached the house.

Raven too looked nervous. Balen took Raven's hand and squeezed it gently. She looked over at him nervously and bit her lip.

The van drew to a stop and the driver switched the engine off. Balen got out and helped Raven down. He took a deep breath and turned to face the guards. Frank got down from the seat behind the driver's one and he also turned to face the guards.

Ryjel had stepped down from the van on the other side and he slowly walked around it to stand in front of it. He took a long sweeping look down the line of guards and smiled. "Take them prisoner."

As a unit the men moved and pointed their rifles at the trio. Balen stepped in front of Raven and Frank moved in closer. Balen hissed. "Frank, do we stand any chance?"

Frank smiled ironically. "Not a hope. We have a choice, surrender or die.

At least if we surrender there is a chance they will listen

to the truth. You are going to have to trust me, both of you."

Balen put his hands up followed by Raven and finally Frank. A guard stepped forwards and searched them for weapons. When he had finally managed to remove the vast amount that Frank had secreted about his person he stepped back.

When he was sure they were no longer armed Ryjel walked around the van and stood just out of reach of the trio. "You don't think that I was seriously going to bring you back to take over after you murdered your own brother did you? You will both stand trial for what you have done. You Frank will stand witness to what has happened so that you can report back afterwards. Take them away. I want them put in separate cells. Take Frank as well, I want him in a cell until the trial and execution is over."

Raven managed a smile. "So it's going to be a fair trial then?"

Balen winced even before Ryjel moved to pistol whip Raven across the face with his revolver. She hit the floor and lay still for a moment. When she had recovered enough she got up onto all fours and Ryjel kicked her in the stomach. Balen stepped forwards to try to help her but one of the guards shouted. "Stand still or we will fire."

Raven fell back onto the ground clutching her stomach and screaming.

Ryjel laughed. "Murdering bitch! Get up."

Balen glared at the guard who had spoken to him, stepped forwards and grabbed her arm and hauled her up. He then pushed her behind him. She held onto him as she tried to get her breath back.

The guards stepped forwards and pushed them around the back of the house to a stable block which had been adapted to make prison cells. Ryjel followed them. "Put them far enough apart that they cannot communicate but close enough so that he can hear her scream. Cover the windows and leave them in the dark. I will issue my orders as to what you are to do to them later. They will be called to trial tomorrow. Tonight they are ours to do with as we wish."

Balen turned and put his arms around Raven. He kissed her. "I love you, don't you ever forget that." Two of the guards tore Raven from Lord Balen's grip.

As they finally had to let go Raven answered. "I love you too." They dragged her across the cobbles and threw her onto the floor.

They followed her in and lifted her up and chained her to the wall so that she hung about a foot off the ground. Ryjel walked over to Balen. "What you did to her will be minor considering what we are about to do to her now. Think on that while you spend your last night on earth."

Two more guards pushed Balen into a cell and chained him to the wall. He could just about reach the floor with his toes. They turned and marched out. The door was closed and he was left in the semi darkness. Then he heard movement and boards were put up at the window and hammered into place. He was then left in the absolute darkness.

He heard the guards leave. It was silent for what felt like hours before he heard a scuttling noise and a crunching sound. He could hear muffled voices in the distance but he couldn't make out what they said.

They took Frank to a store room and locked him in there. He had a chair and a table but there was no window. When they had gone he looked around for a way of escaping. He couldn't find one. The walls were thick.

The door was heavy oak and built to last. He tried his strength against it but it would not budge. He sat down, put his head in his hands and let all the fears and worries run though his mind, he couldn't stop them.

All that afternoon and night they were left in the dark. No food or drink was brought to them. Balen's mind was working overtime wondering what they were doing to

Raven. There had been a slight crack in the wood so he knew it had got dark. Hours later he heard voices and footsteps coming across the cobbles. Somewhere there was a wooden scraping noise followed by more muffled voices. Then he heard Raven scream. He tensed all his muscles and tried to pull free from the wall but he was tied too well with strong rope and the rings he was tied to were high above him. He didn't care, he struggled anyway. Hopelessly he fought the ropes for hours as Raven screamed. The sound cutting through him and he was unable to block it out. Then she fell silent and somehow he found that more terrifying.

He hung there all night, he could neither sleep nor rest and his mind kept showing him scenarios of what they had done to Raven.

In the morning two guards came for him. They opened the door and the bright morning sunshine cut into the pitch blackness. He shut his eyes and just listened as they crossed the room and cut him down. He opened his eyes again and they became accustomed to the light. He let them lead him. They took him out of the cell and he looked around. He could see them dragging Raven out of her cell. Her face and what he could see of her body that wasn't covered by her black boiler suit were covered in cuts and bruises and her hair was matted with mud, straw and dried blood. She fell helplessly onto the cobbles as they let her go. They grabbed her by her arms and dragged her across the cobbles and then onto the gravel towards the house.

She screamed in agony but they carried on. Ryjel was watching and laughed at the look of horror on Balen's face.

Frank was brought out to join them and he walked in front of the two armed guards and followed Raven into the house. Balen was taken in last.

They passed through what was a side entrance which led to a long corridor and then through a small room with a table in the middle of it. There were double doors at the end of this room which were open. The room beyond was stately. Tapestries hung on the walls and huge vaulted windows were made of stained glass at the top. In the centre of the room was a huge wooden dining table and seated around it were what looked like officials dressed in black suits.

Frank was taken to a high backed chair and handcuffed to it.

The twenty five chairs around the table were all filled with people Balen didn't recognise. Ryjel took his place at the top of the table facing them.

When he had made himself comfortable he looked down the table at the pair. Raven was trying to stand. Balen stepped to try to help her but a guard hit her with his pistol as he tried to prop her up. "You try and help her and we will hurt her more." Raven slumped to the ground and the guard hit her again. "Get up bitch."

Raven summoned all of her strength and got back up to her feet. She didn't look at Balen but he could see the blood from open cuts running down her face. She took a deep breath and held her head up defiantly.

Ryjel spoke in a slow and deliberate voice. "We are here to witness the trial of the Commander of X345 and his Life Mate Raven. Both are deemed to be members of Transition X and bound by our laws.

You have all read the reports of how our men were sent to the farm where Raven was in charge and none of them returned.

You have all read my report of how Lord Balen had High Commander Archangel, his own brother, assassinated while he was carrying out his duties and had given a lawful command for Lord Balen to be executed.

What say you? You only need to say guilty or not guilty. By law I have to remind you that the penalty for murder is death by whatever means is deemed suitable by the Head of the High Council for the day. I have such honour of being the High Council today. So what say you?" He was looking Balen in the eye as he spoke and smiled when he had finished speaking.

Frank coughed. "I believe that by your laws the defendants have the right for all the facts in the matter to be set on the table. This can only be done by an individual who has such information and was present at the events in question. I am such a person. I claim Right of Speech under Section 27, Subsection 2.11.45 of the Article of Law, Seventeenth Edition. That is page 469 if you would like to look it up."

The assembled jury looked at each other in amazement. A guard brought over one of the many assembled volumes of books in white covers and opened the book at the page in question. He looked down at the appropriate section. "Where the Defendant shall be deemed as being the perpetrator by want of having been the instigator of the action such Defendant should have the right to call the perpetrator of the said action to explain to the party of the second part the exact situation as defined by what he or she has seen and can prove to be true."

Ryjel laughed. "Well that is hardly going to be of any use now is it? Even if you testify that you shot those people and the two Defendants were innocent you can't prove it. Don't you think I anticipated this when you came along?" He looked around the jury who were also laughing. "I'm sorry Frank, nice try and I'm truly impressed as to how you managed to find that little gem but it won't do them any good. As I said, you have no proof."

Frank smiled. "Actually you are wrong."

Ryjel stopped laughing. "What do you mean? Go on produce some recording of the whole incident. I've checked you have nothing on you, no cameras and no playback devices. The jury must vote today you may not go and retrieve anything."

Ryjel was beginning to look a little nervous. He

shuffled his feet and looked around the assembled Council who had begun to mutter to each other.

Frank laughed. "I can play you back both incidents."

Ryjel looked at him with a very puzzled look and then laughed. "I would like to know how?"

Frank smiled. "By your law you are not permitted to intimidate a witness. Now that I count as such a witness I ask that my hands are freed and that I be made able to make my statement."

Ryjel looked a little worried. "You seem to know our laws remarkably well for a non-member."

Frank smiled coldly. "Yes I do, don't I? So free my hands. You can keep a couple of your armed guards with their weapons pointed at me. I really don't mind."

Ryjel nodded to a guard and he unlocked Frank's handcuffs. Frank stood up and rubbed his wrists. He walked into a clear space where everyone could see him. "Now, let me make my statement. I Frank was present on both occasions in question and I will testify that I was the perpetrator of all deaths that occurred both times. On both occasions I was acting without orders and under my own initiative. On the first occasion I purposely avoided allowing Raven any information about what I was about to do. On the second occasion I was in possession of prior information that the party of the third part Michael James Anthony Morgan, hereinafter called Archangel was not of a right mind. Considering previous reports from eminent psychiatrists and the likelihood that he was schizophrenic I deemed that Commander Balen was in danger of losing his life. As stated in your law in Book 2356 of the Collection of New Statutes, page 342, starting at line 6798. 'If any member of Transition X attempts or succeeds in taking a life of another member unlawfully his life shall be forfeit'.

At the point in question all present would have been able to justify that Archangel was not in his right mind and Commander Ryjel had been presented with hard written evidence of Archangel's mental instability by way of a report made by the psychiatrist handling his case. According to Law of Command, Book 56, Page 346 'Any individual of rank who is deemed to be mentally unstable or under the influence of another shall be deemed as not sanctioned to issue any command'. The command to have Lord Balen shot was therefore not legal as Archangel did not at that time have the authority to give the order. Therefore to order him shot was against your laws and his life was forfeit."

Ryjel looked like a stranded goldfish. He then thought of something. "But you are not a member of Transition X. It clearly says in our laws that a person who is not a member of Transition X may not be protected by our laws. Nice try and anyway you have no proof."

Frank turned to face the jury and so that Raven and Balen could see him as well. He took his right hand and dug his nails into his left arm. Blood dripped onto the polished wood floor as he dug his fingers in and pulled back the skin to reveal a metal endoskeleton. He looked up.

"I am Nemesis. By your laws I am not defined as "a person" so as I am not a person I am therefore protected by your laws. You asked for proof. I will give you proof." He reached up with his non bloody hand to his face and removed the cover to his eye. He turned to a blank wall. "If you would be so kind as to pull the curtains and I strongly suggest that you do what I say then we will begin."

The guards didn't wait for an order from Commander Ryjel. They pulled the curtain and returned to their positions.

Frank then projected a recorded image, firstly of his assault on Lord Balen's men and then a full recording of the events in the yard at the farm, including amplified sound where Lord Balen clearly stated "Don't kill him."

When he was finished he replaced his eye cover, flapped back the skin on his arm and casually bandaged it with a new bandage he pulled from his jacket pocket. "Sorry about the mess on the floor. I believe that I have complied with your laws and you will accept that these two lovely people are completely innocent of all crimes."

The jury spoke one by one saying "Not Guilty."

Frank smiled. "As Lord Balen is deemed to be not guilty and therefore there is no blemish on his record I trust that there is no objection to him taking up his position as Archangel."

Ryjel was spluttering and had fallen back into his seat. The head juror stood up. "You seem to know our laws almost better than we do but as Nemesis I suppose you would do. You are of course quite correct. Lord Balen, we would like to offer you the position as Archangel. Will you accept?"

Balen was stunned but he spoke clearly. "I accept. Now please get some help for my mate."

He caught Raven as she collapsed. He lowered her gently and knelt down beside her. She looked up at him, her face was covered in blood from her cuts. She choked slightly.

Action was fast and furious. A doctor was summoned and he treated her where she lay. He administered pain killers before putting her shoulders back into their sockets. Her screams echoed around the vast vaulted hall.

When that was done he looked up at Lord Balen. "I must take her away for a full examination."

Balen frowned. "She is pregnant, please make sure my baby is alright as well."

The doctor looked concerned. "I will do all I can but she has taken quite a beating. May I have your permission to take her away for further treatment Sir?"

Balen glared at the doctor. "You know that I have just accepted the position as Archangel. Should anything happen to her I will be holding you personally responsible. She has been judged innocent of the crimes she was accused of. She is my mate, as such she must be treated with the utmost care. The child is my heir, as such he or she should be given similar consideration."

The doctor smiled. "I will treat her well and I do understand that my life depends on it." He and his medics carried Raven carefully away.

Balen turned to the jury. "As you are here for a trial, shall we have one? Frank, what law do I quote for us to judge that bastard?"

The head juror stood up, turned to Commander Balen and spoke. "We do not need to see any more evidence, the Defendant known as Ryjel is guilty on all counts. He is a member of Transition X and sought to bring about the unlawful death of another member. His life is therefore forfeit. In these circumstances and considering the extreme mental and physical torture he has inflicted on your life mate it would be appropriate for you to sanction punishment prior to execution." The head juror looked to Balen for an answer. Ryjel looked horrified.

Balen stared directly at Ryjel. "Guards take him outside and shoot him."

The guards marched over to Ryjel and dragged him off. He didn't struggle or attempt any argument. The door was closed behind him and they heard a volley of gunfire from outside the window shortly afterwards.

Balen took his place at the head of the table. The head juror stood up. "If that will be all we will close the court."

Balen nodded. "That will be all."

The head juror then sat down and took out his notebook. "Now, I will make the necessary arrangements for your instatement as Archangel to be logged in our records. I must extend my condolences on the death of your brother and my good wishes for the swift recovery of your life mate. You will of course be afforded all the benefits that accompany the position and all rights and rank that go with it. Congratulations Lord Balen."

Balen smiled. "I thank you. Now, what of this offensive that my brother spoke to me about?"

The ex-juror smiled and bowed his head. "I am pleased that you have heard about that. It is indeed a plan that we very much hope you will still want to carry on with. We can arrange a briefing for you this afternoon as I am sure that you will want to freshen up and rest after your traumatic night.

We cannot apologise enough for Ryjel's actions. We can only state that he was acting on his own volition and did not carry the backing of the Council.

We were bound to follow his orders according to the Law as he was the last Life Partner of your brother."

Balen looked a little stunned. "I would like to see my new quarters and I would like to offer our hospitality to my friend, Frank or should I say Nemesis?"

Frank smiled. "I sort of like Frank. Please, call me Frank."

Balen was led up to his new quarters, his brother's room. He walked inside and closed the door. All around the room were mementos that he remembered from family holidays and bits and pieces of his past. There were photos everywhere. He started looking around the room which took him nearly an hour. There was a knock on the door. He looked up and commanded. "Enter."

The door opened and the doctor was standing there. He looked tired and there was blood on his white coat. "I have come to inform you that I have done my examination. Without x-ray or other scanning equipment it is difficult to tell what internal injuries she has sustained. Both shoulders had been dislocated as you already know where she had been hung up and beaten and I have put them back into place. She needs to be kept under constant supervision. It is too early to tell if she is going to lose the baby.

At the moment there are no signs of this happening. I want to give her every chance. I'm keeping her sedated. The cuts aren't deep, they won't scar. I can either keep her in the Hospital Wing or you can order her moved to more comfortable accommodation. We have no equipment that we can provide obviously so it will be a case of watching her and dealing with anything that may arise."

Balen frowned. "Was she harmed in any other way?"

The doctor looked confused. "I don't know what you mean Sir? She was hung by her wrists and severely beaten. Her injuries are consistent with that."

Balen scowled. "Don't be a fool man, I mean did they rape her?"

The doctor smiled. "There are no signs that she was harmed in that way."

Balen looked slightly relieved. "I want her moved up here immediately. I will watch over her, or Frank if I have other duties. You will make yourself available immediately should I summon you."

The doctor nodded seriously and left.

Balen looked down at the picture nearest to him. It was a picture of himself and his brother playing on the beach on holiday.

There was another knock on the door. Frank stood outside. His arm had been neatly re-bandaged and he looked as though he had had a shower. He was now dressed in a black boiler suit. "Can I come in? I think we have a few things to talk about. I saw the doctor leaving, how are Raven and the baby?"

Balen smiled. "Raven will be fine. You on the other hand, why didn't you tell me?"

Frank looked down. "I had originally intended to solve the world's environmental problems and then shut down. The more I processed the data the more I realised that I needed to assist, if only in the first few weeks.

So I opened a cloning facility and grew some accelerated growth clones in a vat. I took people who had already passed away and grew the clones to a suitable age. I downloaded the lives of those people and then took them on as my own. There was no need for the usual slow growing as I was not interested in cognitive development of the brain. I then had the body grafted onto a titanium endoskeleton and a bio microprocessor installed to facilitate movement and as a vessel in which to load my consciousness on shutdown. I took on various identities for each of these clones with all the memories of those people I was mimicking. I took the precaution of choosing people who had never had their deaths recorded and who had just "disappeared".

But I now understand why you have to live such a short time. I have experienced what I believe is very similar to a conscience. I believe that the longer you live the more this becomes an issue as it is impossible as a human not to make mistakes. I made a big mistake and I now am experiencing what you might call feelings about it. I would like to be considered to come along on any missions I can be useful on until my battery power runs down."

Balen put his hand on Frank's uninjured arm. "What you did back there was remarkable. I owe you our lives. What you did with shutting the power down, well I am not in a position to judge as I do not have the full information. It is a situation we have to deal with, as is the Lex Corporation. By the way, I have got to ask, why Nemesis?"

Frank smiled. "Father gave me the name. It was a friend's game. He had no idea back then that the little computer program he created would be a project he would work on and develop for the rest of his life. He thought it was, in his words, a neat toy."

Balen looked at Frank's bandaged arm. "Does that hurt?"

Frank smiled. "It hurt like hell. I have all the same nerve receptors as you do."

Balen rubbed his eyes. "You are Frank, my friend, nothing has changed. I'm going to call a meeting this afternoon so that I can be fully instated as Archangel. I will then begin working on the manifesto and rules that I helped to set up. There can't be any opposition to what I put forward.

Thankfully the authority of Archangel is beyond question. If I state that a rule is so, it will be so. But there are a lot of rules and I can't remember them, it was a long time ago. Will you work with me on this one? I could do with some help and a voice of reason to sound ideas off of.

Nobody without experience should ever try to write rules, especially four drunken students in a bedsit when one of them was clinically insane. Help me put that right Frank."

Frank smiled. "What are you going to do about the Lex Corporation?"

Balen smiled. "The first thing I'm going to do is find out exactly what I am dealing with. My brother was paranoid, what he claims to be true may not necessarily be the actual truth, just his perceived truth. I'm going to ask for documentation to be put on the table with hard evidence. We can then make our decisions from there. If there is an organisation to fight, then we will do what we can to fight them. If they are acting as reasonably as possible considering the situation they are faced with, then we will support them."

Frank nodded. "I had hoped that I could have kept surveillance over Raven."

Balen smiled. "Can you monitor her?"

Frank nodded. "I have the capability to run a medical surveillance unit if I run it from my own processor."

Balen smiled. "I'm having her moved up here. I don't want her out of my sight. Go to the doctor and arrange what equipment you need."

Later that afternoon Balen called a meeting of the Council while Frank watched over Raven in their private chambers. Balen stood at the head of the table and the Council members sat down both sides, alert, with pens held ready to take notes. Balen took a deep breath and addressed them.

"Council. In accordance with our Law I ask if I may assume the title and rights of Archangel being the next in line and entitled to the position. I confirm that there is no legal impediment which prohibits me from taking this position. Do I have your approval?"

The Council looked stunned. The member who had earlier acted as the head juror turned to Lord Balen. "It is not customary for us to be able to accept or deny anyone taking this position. It is already your right."

Balen smiled kindly. "I know but I want to give you the option. As Archangel that is my right. If you do not choose to accept me then you may freely choose another."

Each in turn raised their hand, stated their name and stated "I accept you as Archangel."

The Council member stood up. "I, Althane, Head of the High Council of the Transition, in accordance with our law and with the acceptance of all present declare that you are now Archangel."

Archangel smiled. "As you all know I am Gabriel Alexander Morgan. I was one of the original authors of the laws and one of the founders of the organisation. In accordance with my right as set out in the Law I may amend any law at any time. I choose to amend the law and to adapt the manifesto effective immediately."

There was a gasp around the room. Althane stood up. "This is unprecedented but it is acceptable by our laws. We accept that the rules will be changed."

Archangel smiled. "Then I ask that anyone who would submit their comments and suggestions should do so by the end of tomorrow."

There was a mumble around the room and Althane spoke again. "You are asking for our opinion on this?"

Archangel looked down. "I am. You have run the organisation. You know what works and what doesn't. We have a chance for change."

Althane looked down and Archangel could clearly see the relieved smile on the man's face. "Sir, may I ask what retribution you would like to take out on those who physically harmed your life mate? It is your right and your due."

Balen glared at him. "That is a situation I would like to take under advisement and I would like a full report so that I may decide what to do. Anyone who is guilty of a crime here will be brought to justice. Anyone who was merely following to the letter of an order will be dealt with fairly."

Althane smiled broadly. "If I may speak and this is completely out of turn I realise but we would like to welcome you to Transition X Headquarters and to express our heartfelt thanks that you are in a position to change the Laws as they stand." He looked around and everyone at the table nodded. "For too long we have been bound by these laws and I think I can speak for everyone at the table when I say that on occasion these have been laws that we do not agree with."

Balen looked around the faces. "Now I must turn my attention to Lex Corporation. You will all know by now that my brother, the former Archangel was suffering from an extremely fragile mental state. That may have affected his judgment on many things. I order you to bring all the facts and evidence about Lex Corporation to this table so that they may be considered by the whole Council. Once we have these facts then I am sure that we can come up with a solution to the problem."

Althane looked down. "We do not have access to such information. That was kept by Archangel. We merely undertook his bidding."

Balen stared at him in amazement. "I will make them available to you. This is a decision which will have a long term effect on every person in this organisation. I will of course make the final decision but I expect every man and woman here to know exactly what they are up against and why they are having to make sacrifices. We will convene again tomorrow.

Thank you gentlemen and ladies, you may now leave."

Balen returned to his room and after checking on Raven he began to look around for papers and documents. He turned to Frank. "Did my brother keep information on computer?"

Frank shook his head. "Your brother did not trust computers, nothing was committed to computer or I would have known about it."

Balen began to search the room and he finally found a pile of paper in the bottom of the wardrobe. There was a stack of paperwork about a foot high which comprised reports, photographs and other information about Lex Corporation and its dealings. He lifted it out and put it on the table. "Well, I think I've found what I was looking for. It is going to take a while to read this lot. I suppose you don't have advanced speed and speed reading do you?"

Frank smiled. "Of course."

Balen smiled back. "Well I want you to read and commit this lot to memory and number and catalogue each page so that nothing can go missing. I'd then like you to put together a summary for us less fortunate souls so that we can at least try to come up with an idea of whether Lex Corporation are helping or whether they are an organisation we should oppose."

Frank smiled. "I'm glad to be of assistance. Where shall I undertake this task?"

Balen looked around the room. It was large and stately, there was a door which led to the bathroom and a door that led to the bedroom. Raven was sleeping on a makeshift bed to his right. "I would like you to work here. Will you be able to maintain your surveillance over Raven while you are working?"

Frank looked over to the sleeping woman. "Of course I will. I will read and report back to you."

Balen smiled and walked to the window. He looked out over the green fields and the woodland in the distance. Men were marching in units and animals were grazing quietly on the lawn. He opened a window. The room was filled with the scent of grass and damp bushes as he went to sit in the large high back armchair next to Raven. He leant back into the chair and closed his eyes. "Well Frank, we'll have to see what tomorrow's meeting brings. I have a feeling this is only the beginning."

Frank looked up and smiled, his attention drawn to the bed where Raven lay. Balen looked down as Raven reached up her hand to take his. She looked tired but there was a confident serenity to her smile. "I think we will do just fine."

Balen took her hand and looked at Frank. "You know, somehow I think we will."

Frank looked at him in earnest. "So, do you have a plan?"

Balen walked over to a bookcase and looked along the books. "I'm guessing it has to be here somewhere. Yes, here it is. The book which started our first conversation all those years ago. Essays and New Atlantis by Francis Bacon. I wanted to use this as a template but my brother didn't like it. Now I think it is my turn. I think I'd better give it a read."

Printed in Great Britain
by Amazon

80942009R00264